Praise for BUk....

"*Burner* is a fascinating thriller in which an online movement swallows up the person who started it."

—*FOREWORD CLARION REVIEWS*

"In *Burner*, Mike Trigg shines a light on homegrown domestic terrorism in a way seldom seen before. This thought-provoking thriller will keep you on the edge of your seat. I couldn't put it down. If you are interested in the shadowy world of domestic, violent extremism and how it affects us all, read this book."

—FRANK RUNLES, FBI Supervisory Special Agent (Retired), author of *Lies People Tell: An FBI Agent's Toolkit for Catching Liars and Cheats*

"Political unrest and domestic terrorism—Mike Trigg gives us a compelling look into the not-so-distant future. *Burner* sizzles with tension and reveals the high price of extremism in our digital culture. A must-read."

—JAMES L'ETOILE, author of *Devil Within* and *Face of Greed*

"A man arrested for domestic terrorism and a woman abducted by his followers lead the cast in Mike Trigg's latest spine-tingler. In *Burner*, Trigg pulls back the curtain on toxic internet stardom and shows how in the wrong hands it can be used to feed political unrest. A powerful, pulse-pounding tale that hits uncomfortably close to home."

—KIMBERLY BELLE, author of *The Paris Widow* and *Three Days Missing*

"Mike Trigg takes a timely look at the world of social media and the propaganda that results from that bias. Great characters and an unpredictable narrative make *Burner* a must-add to your thriller reading pile!"

—A. J. LANDAU, author of *Leave No Trace*

"Mike Trigg is fast becoming the go-to writer for high-tech thrillers that lay bare the perils of our digital age. *Burner* is no exception. Readers are in for a modern retelling of Romeo and Juliet set against a San Francisco simmering in a stew of toxic social media conspiracies, wealth disparity, and political unrest. Buckle up; it's going to be a bumpy ride."

—EVETTE DAVIS, author of *48 States* and The Council Trilogy

"Mike Trigg knows how to tell stories that keep you in suspense but also make you think deeply—about culture, politics, ethics, and who the good and bad guys really are. What does it take to survive in a post-truth world where violent extremism and corruption rule the day? You owe it to yourself to read *Burner* and find out!"

—JUDE BERMAN, author of *The Die*

Praise for Mike Trigg's BIT FLIP

"As much a compelling narrative as it is a critical analysis of contemporary capitalism, this story worries over the coming future, in which technology could take over much of what people used to do. This helps to make *Bit Flip* an engrossing novel that satirizes the pretensions of tech bros and billionaires."

—*FOREWORD CLARION REVIEWS*, 5 stars

"Mike Trigg's novel *Bit Flip* is exceptionally well-written, with a satisfying balance of action, intrigue, back story, characterization, and description. He weaves together several compelling story elements, some of them technical in nature, with ease and the manner in which he wraps up the narrative is both concise and provocative."

—*INDIEREADER*, 5 stars

"Trigg has worked magic here, combining elements of *Citizen Kane* and *Silicon Valley* into a readable bullet of a book. This is a razor-sharp satire with a huge heart."

—JOSHUA MOHR, author of *All This Life* and *Damascus*

BURNER

a novel

MIKE TRIGG

SPARKPRESS

Published by SparkPress, a BookSparks imprint,
A division of SparkPoint Studio, LLC
Phoenix, Arizona, USA, 85007
www.gosparkpress.com

Published 2024
Printed in the United States of America

Print ISBN: 978-1-68463-250-3
E-ISBN: 978-1-68463-251-0
Library of Congress Control Number: 2023919179

Interior design and typeset by Katherine Lloyd, The DESK

PART I

1

SHANE

October 12, 2023

I'm not sure yet if this is a memoir or a manifesto, a love letter or a suicide note. Maybe it's just my version of events. To explain how I got here. Maybe it's something more. I'm not sure there's really much difference anyway.

A memoir requires a story to tell, and I have plenty of those.

A manifesto requires an audience, and mine is unreachable right now.

A love letter requires a recipient, but I don't know if she will ever talk to me again.

A suicide note is the easiest—lazy, even. But for that you need conviction, or you look like a dumbass.

They don't have me on watch yet, so I still have options. Maybe I could get shoelaces, but those have never seemed strong enough. Pills would be better. Cleaner.

Anyway, I'll find out eventually. It'll reveal itself as I write more. I definitely have a lot to say. Today was a big day. It exceeded my wildest dreams. But I knew they would come for me. I was prepared.

Sort of.

Actually . . . I'm not sure I was prepared at all. It should have occurred to me that I'd be totally cut off, like I am now—no connection to the outside world. I should have been ready for that. At least a scheduled post or one of those out-of-office notices or something. And they probably found a bunch of evidence I should have gotten rid of by now. My bad. I know this much: I was never supposed to be here this long in the first place. I'm already on borrowed time. So, whatever happens, happens. All I can do is wait.

And while I wait, I'll write.

Writing has always been an escape for me. Helping me stay sane, assuming I still am. Everyone needs a distraction. Some guys work out, some guys play video games, some guys binge porn. I write. It's gotten me in trouble all my life. It's why I'm here, I guess. But prison will also be an opportunity. A chance to think about everything that's happened. All the bad luck and bad decisions that got me here. Everything I've been through.

But first, I've got to tell Wayne.

He showed up ten minutes after my arrest and announced to everyone—including me—that he's my lawyer. I don't even know the guy, never met him before today. And he's old as hell. His name is *Wayne*, for Christ's sake. But he says he's a believer, and I don't know any other lawyers. He's mostly just telling me not to say anything to anyone about any of this. No shit, right? But it seems like he knows what he's doing, so I guess he's better than the public defender.

He also made sure I got my own cell, but they would have done that anyway. The holding cell was already crawling with BurnOutz by the time I got here—believers devoted to the cause, easy to spot by their "Plan B" tattoos. So they couldn't put me in there. If the other guys found out who I was, it would have started a riot. It's crazy, the power of it all. People I've never met, following my every word.

Honestly, I never meant for it all to get to this point. Never thought so many people would get on board. Drawing inspiration from my anger. Taking it further than I ever imagined. I feel bad for the people who died. They didn't deserve that. I don't know what they deserved, but they didn't deserve that. Sometimes shit happens. We never know what fate has in store for us. That's all it was: *fate*. Those people were in the wrong place at the wrong time. I wish it hadn't happened, but it did.

Now, none of that matters anymore. All I can think about is Chloe. She's the only thing keeping me going.

SHANE

I was so reckless. I see that now. I know she might never forgive me. Why would she? I should have texted her before they arrested me. Tried to say something that would make things better, get everything back to the way it was. Now I have no way to reach her. Maybe I could call her from the prison phone, but I don't even know her number. For all my millions of followers, I might have lost the only one who mattered. Drifting away from me like a post in an endless feed.

It was ridiculous to think she would ever fall for a lowlife like me in the first place, but somehow she did. I didn't overthink it at the time. Now I'm obsessing over it. Putting my past on replay. Grinding away on my mistakes, my regrets. Like a canker sore in my cheek I can't stop poking with my tongue. All of us are masochists just a little bit. Tweaking our nerve endings to remind ourselves we're alive.

I've given myself enough self-inflicted pain for one lifetime. No matter how much trouble I get in, I always find a way to make it worse—pick the scab, reopen the wound. Whenever my life goes well, I do something to fuck it up, burn it down. I don't know why. It's just what comes naturally to me. Chloe says it's self-destructive. But that seems too simple a diagnosis to me. I see it more as self-sacrificial. The fact so many people have found hope in my words, my actions. That's more than self-destruction; it's *creative* destruction. It's hope. It's my legacy.

I just hope it doesn't destroy me.

2

CHLOE

October 12, 2023

There's nothing anyone can do. They're coming. I know they're coming. Justin knows they're coming. He's already done what any good bodyguard would do—tried to stay calm, reassured me that we'll be safe, barricaded the door with whatever he could find. But there is only one of him, and nobody else is coming—not the police, not anyone else in the security detail. It's just us. No help, nobody to stop them. Lawlessness.

From the terrace, I see haze rising above the city, turning the mid-morning sun an apocalyptic orange. A column of thick black smoke rises from near Kadabra headquarters downtown—my father's company and ground zero of today's uprising—cleaving the horizon between the Bay Bridge to the east and Sutro Tower where it pokes through the fog to the west. The air smells acrid from burning plastic and tires. Gray wisps crawl up Nob Hill like fingers reaching for me.

I hear the crowd chanting, restless. A bigger crowd than anyone expected. The sounds of smashing glass, car alarms, sirens all reverberate off the buildings and down the steep streets. None of the emergency vehicles are coming for us. 9-1-1 told us so. Just protestors, the dispatcher said.

Shane did this.

I had been glued to CNN since dawn, watching the scene unfold like everyone else—part of me horrified, part of me awestruck at the sheer preternatural power of it, like a hurricane indiscriminately dismantling everything in its path. Overturned cars, burning storefronts, eddies of humanity surging up the streets, all the chaos delivered straight to my television, complete with play-by-play commentary by the anchors. Shot from the hovering swarm of helicopters I could see from my living room. Not yet comprehending, myself, that the pandemonium could reach me despite its proximity. That I was a soft, peripheral target for opponents of my father to redirect their rage at.

Just as a primordial impulse to run surged through me, Justin burst in waving his phone, talking faster than I could process. It was a Facebook Live feed showing men, an entire mob of them, outside what I immediately recognized as my apartment building. While I was staring at the TV in disbelief, they had been surrounding us. I watched them approach on the livestream, from *their* vantage point. Becoming a part of their mob. The time to run had passed. Escape was no longer an option.

I am about to witness my own death on the internet.

I call Shane. He can stop this—he *has* to stop this. But it goes straight to voicemail, again. I text him, *PICK UP!* Why the hell isn't he picking up?

Justin is desperately looking for any conceivable escape route. We both know the threat to his life is even greater than mine. But the garage has already been breached. We can see on the security camera that the SUV is unreachable. He checks the fire escape on the street side, his sidearm unholstered, but the horde is swirling below it as well. It's hopeless. We could never descend the five stories quickly enough.

We need a helicopter. But even if we had one, even if it could get here in time, it could never land on top of a small Pacific Heights apartment building. There is no escape route, no panic room. Nobody is coming to help us.

Why are they coming? Why are they targeting me? It's my father they want.

Maybe I can reason with them, offer them money to stop. But then a vibration rattles through the entire building, like a tremor. I feel it course through my body. They are in the stairwell. Shouting and slamming against the walls as they claw up the steps toward us. Through the floorboards, I hear my downstairs neighbor screaming. We return to the monitors and watch the intruders passing security cameras on each floor, coming into and out of each frame, some pointing directly at us through the lens. They carry flags and baseball bats and homemade signs, but the ones in front have guns.

They keep coming, more and more. One, wearing a red-and-blue knit hat with a pom-pom, is shouting directions to the others. Another, wearing a balaclava, holds his phone up, documenting the invasion. I watch him on the monitor, then see his livestream on the phone I still clutch in my hand, delayed by a horrifying fracture of time.

Why can't I look away from the screen?

I consider jumping. Anything to avoid the imminent horror that is approaching outside my door. Either way, I'm going into the abyss. Before I can act on my impulse, Justin thrusts me into the hallway closet—no discussion, training taking over. Through the crack in the door, I see him check the monitors one more time, evaluating who he will need to take out first. He anchors himself behind an armoire and aims his weapon at the entrance. I close the closet door.

This is it. Our last stand.

The pounding is deafening. Each blow accompanied by the crack of wood splintering, the lurch of the furniture. The barricade is going to give way. I'm petrified—unable to breath, to move, to think. I'm going to throw up, or shit myself, or both. From my dark closet, I hear one of the hinges split off, followed by metallic tings as the pieces cartwheel down the hallway.

Gripping my phone, I compose a final tweet: *HELP!* Then comes the sound of Justin unleashing a barrage of bullets, ripping through what remains of the front door and the furniture blocking it, piercing flesh. Shouts as one of them returns fire. Shards of wood and plaster raining down in the hallway.

They will kill me. Rape me and torture me first.

They're in. Time stops. My mind is disconnected from my body. The din of what sounds like a thousand voices, footsteps stomping through every room, smashing everything, shouting for *"Ken Corbin's little princess."* The closet door bursts open and they are upon me, dragging me down the hall past Justin's slumped body. Screaming at me like this is a witch trial. Their faces distorted with rage. Dozens of hands grip my arms, dig into my ribs, pull my hair. I cannot break free. I struggle to regain my footing as they pull me down the stairs, my legs thumping down each step like I'm falling. I tell them this is all a mistake. Beg incoherently for them to stop. Through the cacophony of the mob I hear my phone crack as it slips from my pocket and hits the marble floor.

My lifeline, gone.

We burst into the garage, and I'm thrust into the backseat of my own SUV. Someone behind me pulls a hood over my head. Doors slam shut, tires screech, and glimmers of bright morning sunlight illuminate the inside of my shroud as the vehicle launches out into the street.

Help never came.

3

SHANE

"But I haven't done anything *wrong!*" I say again.

He's been my lawyer for only a couple of hours and already Wayne is driving me fucking crazy. His cheap suit that barely reaches around his pot belly. Shirt collar stained gray from his sweat. Slicked-back hair flecked with dandruff. Teeth stained from cigarettes and coffee. His eyes, squinting at me skeptically through the wire-mesh glass of this visiting booth.

He doesn't get it.

"Well, like I've said a dozen times now, if you're not gonna plead guilty—"

"No way, I'm not spending the rest of my life in prison—I'm only twenty-six."

"Right, so assuming a not-guilty plea, our only shot is to distance you from Burner_911," he says, his voice amplified by the little speaker in the wall. "The arraignment is tomorrow, so you'll need to enter an initial plea. You can always change it later, but I just don't think their case is so airtight that we can't sow some reasonable doubt. Our conversations are protected by attorney-client privilege, so the best thing you can do for yourself is to be honest with me."

I look up from my cuffed wrists and scan our compact room for the camera or microphone that must be hidden someplace, then lock eyes with Wayne. "I know why I'm really here," I say, my voice steadily intensifying. "It's because they're scared. The powerful always get scared whenever someone threatens their power. Whenever voices rise up to expose and contradict their orthodoxy. Whenever regular people organize against them to enact justice. They had no choice but to arrest me, detain me, *muzzle* me—"

"Shane, I get it. I'm a supporter too," Wayne says, cutting me off just as I was getting going. He unbuttons his sleeve at the wrist and pushes it up his forearm, revealing a "Plan B" tattoo lurking under a thatch of arm hair like a snake in the weeds. "See . . . I believe everything you're saying, in theory. But you're facing a federal prosecutor who's hell-bent on the death penalty. You can't fuck around with all this manifesto bullshit, or the jury'll find you guilty. Someone's gonna hang for this, and right now that someone is you."

"But the BurnOutz wouldn't *exist* without me. I activated them. I organized them. Nobody else can lead this movement. It's gone too far. I can't give up now."

Wayne sighs, shrugs, and pulls his sleeve down like his well of arguments has run dry. It's killing me that I'm cut off right now—sealed behind bars and glass, yes, but most of all, *offline*. With no way to post, I'm just talking to myself, with all the potency of someone jacking off in the corner. Without followers, I'm neutered. My purpose is stolen. My reason for being is *gone*.

But I need to be patient. I will find a way. I always do. I can't let this movement be hijacked, diverted from its goal. I know my ideas have already spread. The Plan is already in place, with an undeniable momentum that the elites can't stop. Although I may be physically constrained, ideas can't be suppressed so easily. There is no prison for thought, no jail that can contain the mind.

Still . . . if I'm locked up here with no phone or laptop, I can't really do shit, can I? Prison dehumanizes you quick. The intake and full-cavity search I'd rather never think about again. The other detainees, not knowing who I am, trash talkin' me. Hating on me for getting my own cell. In this scratchy orange jumpsuit, stripped of all my stuff, I don't even feel like myself anymore. I'm already losing my swagger, and I haven't even made it to lunch on my first day yet.

"Look, it's your life, you can do whatever you want," Wayne says. "But I'm telling you, a plea of '*Yes, I'm Burner_911, but no, I'm not responsible for all this mayhem*' just isn't going to work." He stands up from the booth. "If that's the way you want to play it, then I'm not the attorney to represent you."

I ponder my choices as I watch him pick up all his crap. How can I choose between belief and freedom? How can I prove I'm someone other than who I am? How can I deny the greatest achievement of my life? On the other hand, what fucking choice do I have? In the end, even if the world thinks I'm a nobody, a loser, a poser; even if I'm found guilty and sentenced to death; my legacy will live on. These ideas are bigger than me. They can change the world. It doesn't matter if nobody believes in Shane Stoller. *I* believe in me.

And maybe *she* still believes in me too.

"Okay," I say as Wayne stands to leave. "I'll do it. I'll plead not guilty. Tell them I'm not Burner_911."

Wayne looks down at me with a puckered expression like he just caught a whiff of dog shit. Evaluating my sincerity, he says, "You sure about that? I don't want you changing your mind five hundred times. Why don't you sleep on it. We've got almost twenty-four hours before the arraignment."

"I'm sure," I say. "I can't do anything till I get out of here anyway. If this gives me the best chance of that, let's do it."

"Okay." Wayne sits back down in his chair. "You're making the right decision. We'll tell the US Attorney's Office you're rejecting the plea deal, and we'll start preparing your defense immediately. This is going to go to trial fast."

"There's something else I need you to do." I hesitate, not wanting to say it, but I have to. "I need you to contact Chloe Corbin for me."

Wayne lets out a raspy smoker's chuckle, like I'm fucking with him. "I bet a lot of people would like to contact Chloe Corbin, but you're probably the only one who knows how."

"What do you mean?"

"Wasn't that your guys who took her?"

My breath sucks out of my lungs. They've taken her. Of course they've taken her. "What . . . *happened?*"

The smile slides off Wayne's weathered face. "Chloe Corbin was kidnapped by a group of BurnOutz this morning."

4

CHLOE

"Scooter, you're gonna fucking kill us!"

With no way to brace myself, I slam into the center console like a ragdoll as all four tires lock up. I'm unbuckled, unprepared, my hands bound together in my lap with what feels like a zip tie, the sharp plastic cutting into my wrists. The SUV screeches and swerves. People outside shout and pound on the side of the vehicle.

"I'm just trying to get us the hell out of here!" the driver shouts back at the guy in the passenger seat.

"Holy shit! Did you see that, BurnOutz?" cries a voice to my left, confirming what I already know—these are followers of Burner_911.

We brake suddenly and I slump to the floorboard, unable to right myself, as the vehicle pitches around another turn to the guttural sound of tires gripping asphalt. Hands grab my shoulder and pull me back up into the seat. Swatches of sunlight and shadows flash by as the car accelerates. Are we being chased? My stomach drops as we plunge down a hill—bottoming out at an intersection, grinding metal against concrete—then descend the next block.

"Turn here!" I suddenly recognize that voice in the passenger seat: he's the guy from the security camera—the one with the red-and-blue knit hat.

Centrifugal force presses me against the bodies crowded on either side of me in the back seat, close enough to smell the perspiration on their bodies, alcohol on their breath, cigarette smoke in their clothing.

Sweat runs down my forehead, beads on my upper lip, accumulates in my armpits and under my bra. Nothing I can do to wipe it away. My hair surrounds my head like a tornado, adhered to the shroud by static, stuck to my face in clumps, itching. I do not struggle or scream; I've resigned myself to the impending collision, whatever form it may take.

A sudden pain shoots up from my ankle—only now do I notice that it is swollen, throbbing. Badly sprained, possibly broken. When did that happen? Probably on the stairs, I can't remember. My shoe is missing on that foot. I squeeze a tuft of carpet with my bare toes, trying to anchor myself, to calm myself, like I'm in tree pose. I focus on regulating my breathing, slowing my heartbeat, listening. Panicking will not help me. I can explain—talk my way out of this. If they stop shouting long enough to listen. If they believe me.

Nick is his name, the one with the knit hat. The others keep saying it, ignoring his angry reprimands for revealing his identity. I picture him in the passenger seat with that incongruous pom-pom bobbing over his head, like a pudgy kindergartener dressed in something his mom knit for him. Maybe so he'd be easier to spot in the mob. At least I can't see if he's still pointing his gun at me.

One by one, my other abductors are inadvertently introduced. To my left is Pete, another voice I remember: the live streamer I saw on the security monitors. Apparently he's continued to document their escapade, because now Nick says, "Turn that goddamn thing off!"

Pete cackles—he sounds giddy with the thrill of it all—but signs off with his audience, a small subset of the millions of followers of the anonymous online persona Burner_911.

"It's blocked, Benny! Where the fuck do I go now?" Scooter yells.

Benny, the voice to my right, haltingly reads directions out loud from Google Maps. He's nervous. They all are, frantically yelling at each other, not in the confident swagger of before but with a new tone—one that betrays uncertainty and fear, like a pack of dogs who unexpectedly catch a car and don't know what to do next. Like men who suddenly realize this isn't just a prank for social media, a brag to their friends; that nobody stopped them; that they've just murdered someone and taken another hostage, in broad daylight, on camera, and posted their crime online.

And yet underneath their urgency to escape there are signs of pre-meditation, organization—an efficiency in the terms they use, an implied hierarchy, a subtle understanding of what will happen next. Where are they going? What will they do to me? What actions will they take to escalate or undo the commission of this crime?

The SUV slows—more shouting, something blocking the road again.

"*So?* Get out and move it!" Nick says.

Car doors open and close, the engine idles, Nick grumbles from the front seat. He's the one in charge.

The others return. We accelerate again, but at a less frenzied pace. The RPMs of the engine stay in a normal range.

With the chaos finally letting up, now is my chance. I open my mouth to speak. But what *exactly* am I going to say? "The anonymous leader of your movement is my *boyfriend* . . . Well, *was* my boyfriend—I haven't even spoken with him for days. But . . . still, can't you just, like, *let me go?*" Why the hell would they believe me? Nobody knows who Burner_911 even *is*, let alone who he—or *she*, or *they*—is dating. Even if they did believe me, what would that mean for Shane? I can't just out him like that. He'd never forgive me. "The thing about a secret identity is, it needs to stay secret," is what he told me when I finally found out. No—I need to stay calm, be patient. It will be okay. He'll tell them, right? Not Shane but Burner_911; he'll tell them to let me go. He'll post as soon as he finds out. *Right?*

"Be cool . . . be cool . . ." Pete says. The car rolls slowly, maybe through a blockade? Nobody speaks, including me.

Then we accelerate and merge onto what I immediately know is the Bay Bridge, the repetitive thump of the metal grates on the roadway below echoing off the upper deck above. I can't conceive how they made their way through what must have been a maze of blocked streets, police barricades, gridlocked traffic—their escape enabled by Google's navigational algorithms. I picture the other vehicles moving along beside us on the bridge, their engines and tires dully audible from within the sound-proofed cabin, their drivers unable to see me bound and shrouded in the back seat through the tinted privacy windows I now wish I hadn't installed, going about their days as if a riot hasn't just swept through San Francisco, taking me away with it.

As we cross the bridge, my captors' manic banter stops for the first time. Maybe they are all temporarily hypnotized by the rhythmic pulse of the grates, the tranquility of morning over the bay, the spectacular views of Coit Tower, the Ferry Building, Alcatraz. Or maybe they know now, with the straight expanse of concrete and steel in front of them, that they've done it.

They've escaped.

5

BURNER_911

Two Years Ago

@Burner_911 post on Razgo.com

> *"A government big enough to give you everything you want, is big enough to take away everything you have."*
>
> —Thomas Jefferson

I can no longer remain silent. It is time to share the truth we all know, but only I know what to do about it.

MY FELLOW AMERICANS, EVERYTHING YOU'VE BEEN TOLD IS A LIE.

There is no American Dream. That's just an elaborate scheme, manufactured by the liberal elites to enslave you in debt, harness your hard work, siphon your energy. I've lived it myself.

Stop being so naïve . . . the banks and billionaires *own* you.

It's buried in the fine print. The legalese you never read. The 36 percent interest rate on your credit card. The student loans, car loans, payday loans, subprime mortgages, and revolving lines of credit that you can NEVER get out from under. YOU are the commodity that enriches these leftist oligarchs. Hooked up like a heroin addict to the flow of easy money, only to discover you're being milked dry.

I AM BURNER_911

I can't reveal my true identity, because it would put my life in danger. The elites will stop at nothing to keep regular people down. I've SEEN for myself, from the inside, how rigged the system is against you. How financial companies tempt you with predatory loans, compound your debt, repossess your home and your car. How activist tech companies harvest your data, your attention, your addiction and sell it to the highest bidder. How media companies package their extreme liberal agenda as news while they steal money out of your pocket every month. All to enrich themselves. To become BILLIONAIRES! I can't sit by and watch it happen anymore.

Most people are too stupid to do the math, too lazy to resist, too blind to the realities all around them. They can't see the big picture. BUT NOT YOU! Instead of just complaining, you're going to do something about it.

IT. IS. TIME.

Time to wake up to the reality of your economic subjugation.

Time to fight back against the hidden forces holding you down.

Time to rebel against the exploitation of the Marxist deep state.

Time to TAKE WHAT BELONGS TO YOU!

And only I know **The Plan**.

The pathway to your economic emancipation.

Plan A was to be good little girls and boys and do things the "right way." Look what that got us. Plan B is to do things OUR way. The only way we know how—scorched earth till this whole steaming Ponzi scheme collapses, the cabal of liberalism is exposed, and we're the ones making bank.

If you want TRUTH, TRANSPARENCY, AND JUSTICE, join me. In three days, I will reveal the first step of taking back our country.

Believe in The Plan!

Follow me here and I will show you the way . . .

6

SAN FRANCISCO CHRONICLE

MASSIVE LAWLESS RIOT CONSUMES SAN FRANCISCO
Twelve dead, hundreds arrested, hostage held,
financial markets in turmoil

SAN FRANCISCO, CA, October 12, 2023—The largest act of domestic terrorism on American soil since the Oklahoma City bombing in 1995 was perpetrated this morning in San Francisco. Twelve people are dead according to authorities, including two San Francisco police officers and a security guard at the Federal Reserve Bank. Another twenty-two are in critical condition and dozens more injured. Chloe Corbin, daughter of tech billionaire Ken Corbin, was also abducted from her Pacific Heights penthouse by what witnesses described as a violent mob during the riots. Corbin's father's company, Kadabra, Inc., was one of the primary targets of today's attack.

Ms. Corbin's current whereabouts remain unknown at this hour. Her bodyguard, who, according to police, was shot twice in the chest after killing one and wounding several other intruders, is on life support.

Meanwhile, shortly before the kidnapping unfolded, the FBI arrested a suspect they allege is the mastermind behind the anonymous Burner_911 profile. Little is known about the suspect, who was identified by federal agents as twenty-six-year-old Turlock native Shane Stoller. He was arrested without resistance at his apartment in the Mission District early this morning. Officials said it is not known if Burner_911 is a single individual or a group of individuals. Organized by the followers of Burner_911's online populist movement, known as the Burn-Outz, the protest was intended to trigger chaos in the financial markets. While it started peacefully, it quickly spiraled out of control.

Police were joined by heavily armed SWAT officers and National Guard troops in riot gear to restore order to the city. They surrounded and arrested hundreds of demonstrators who had forcibly entered and ransacked several buildings in the downtown area, including Kadabra headquarters, city hall, the US district court, and the Federal Reserve Bank. Crowds estimated by the SFPD to be as large as 20,000 protesters were dispersed from Civic Center Plaza with tear gas, rubber bullets, and batons, leaving the city looking like an abandoned war zone as firefighters worked to put out smoldering automobiles and storefronts.

As if the toll in human life and property destruction weren't enough, today's events exacted a huge price in the financial markets as well. The major stock indices were all down between 30 and 45 percent as liquidity in the market seized up. Lenders withdrew lines of credit and many corporations with substantial debt on their balance sheets suddenly found themselves on the verge of bankruptcy. The shock has economists fearing a financial chain reaction akin to the 2008 Great Recession.

As the financial markets reel, the social media world is consumed with the mystery of Chloe Corbin's abduction. The socialite and philanthropist was well known in the San Francisco society scene. In the wake of her kidnapping, which was broadcast live on Facebook by her abductors, Corbin's millions of followers on Instagram and Twitter rallied to her cause. Within minutes, the hashtag #SaveChloe was the top-trending search, with users pleading for her safe return.

US law enforcement officials have said they will hold daily press briefings on the latest developments in this ongoing investigation.

7

WAYNE

It's been a hell of a long day. I'm not exactly an early riser, but when the text I'd been expecting came in at 6:00 a.m., I knew I couldn't hit the snooze bar. The life of a defense attorney—you never know when duty will call.

I have to admit, Shane Stoller created something incredible. It's hard to believe, honestly, when you meet the kid. I never could've pulled that off when I was his age. I was too busy drinking booze and chasing tail. But he's in way over his head. The indictment is thicker than a stack of encyclopedias, and that's not even including the new charges he'll get hit with after today. My legal team and I spent the day going through as much of it as we could, asking Shane a ton of questions, preparing for the arraignment hearing that's supposed to happen tomorrow. The prosecution's already pushing to fast-track this trial. But they know as well as I do that the trial in the courtroom is about as relevant as the price of tea in China. I'm on my way to where the *real* trial will take place: the court of public opinion.

The steps to the Phillip Burton Federal Building are already crawling with media lackeys. We drive slowly past the damaged portion of this bureaucratic, gray monolith. For blocks, all the streets are still blocked off with yellow police tape and emergency vehicles. The posted officers check in with the SFPD escort we've been following, then wave through our unmarked black Lincoln Town Car.

Across the city are the telltale signs of today's uprising. The mob has dispersed but they left their trail of wreckage everywhere, like a pack of dogs pissing on every fire hydrant—broken glass, discarded homemade signs, abandoned tactical gear, spray paint cans, spent tear gas canisters, and other garbage. More trash for the homeless overrunning this city to dig through. Now, with the scene cleared, the mainstream media has set up shop. Hundreds of microphones are jammed around an empty podium on the top step of the building's main entrance. Spotlights and cameras are already fixed on the scene, ready to feed the beast of the twenty-four-hour news cycle. The liberal establishment, once again trying to explain what they can never seem to understand, never admit is there. The reality hiding right under their noses.

In the back seat, I turn from the press conference pregame show and look at Valerie, my most trusted legal sidekick. She's got great posture, sitting up straight as an arrow in her usual crisp, gray skirt suit with one of those fancy designer work bags in her lap.

"Quite a welcoming committee," she says, casting a skeptical gaze toward the crowd.

"Anything in my teeth?" I give an exaggerated smile for her inspection.

She takes a moment to appraise me. "Nothing in your teeth, but you look like shit, as usual," she says and commences straightening my hair, dusting the shoulders of my jacket, and flicking crumbs from my mustache.

"Can't help it; that's the way God made me," I say. "Besides, that's why I have you—to distract everyone from me."

Valerie stops making adjustments and rolls her eyes. "Do you want to look at your notes one more time?"

"No, I know what I want to say." I push the paper back into her hand.

"Okay, then. Knock 'em dead," she says.

I open the car door to a chorus of cameras clicking like cicadas in a swamp. Two SFPD officers lead me through the crowd to the podium. The red lights on the cameras switch on, the attention of the nation turns to me, and I begin.

"Thank you. I'll just be making a brief statement about the events of today and the completely unjustified arrest of my client, Shane Thomas Stoller. What happened in San Francisco today was wrong. But what happened to my client today was unconscionable. Mr. Stoller emphatically disavows being the individual behind the Burner_911 account. But what is perhaps more important is that we simply cannot tolerate a society in which people are imprisoned for their speech, their ideas, their opinions, their thoughts. We cannot accept a society that does not afford every American equal justice under the law. A society in which judgments are rendered instantly, hastily, irrevocably, without sufficient evidence or due process. As the Reverend Martin Luther King said, 'Injustice anywhere is a threat to justice everywhere.' As an attorney, I have dedicated much of my practice to upholding the rights enshrined in our Constitution. That is why I am honored to be representing Shane Stoller, on a *pro bono* basis, in this case."

I scan the crowd of reporters and know I have them eating out of the palm of my hand.

"The movement that Mr. Stoller is accused of leading under the anonymous online user profile of Burner_911 has catalyzed important conversation in our country. Although the violence perpetrated today by this so-called BurnOutz movement is unfortunate, it is indicative of a last resort for people pushed to the brink, who feel our country has headed in the wrong direction for too long. Though Mr. Stoller firmly denies that he is Burner_911, he is sympathetic to that cause, and that is his right. It does not make him a criminal. It does not make him a killer. It does not make him a terrorist. He, like every American, is entitled to say, think, and follow what he believes."

They hate me—every single one of them—but they have no choice. They'll eat it all and ask for seconds. And I love it.

"I met with Shane for the first time today, and he is well. Furthermore, he is innocent, he is optimistic, and he appreciates the outpouring of support he's received. Together, we are beginning preparation for his legal defense immediately. The US Attorney's Office is pushing this trial forward on a recklessly aggressive timeline. Their desperate tactics are an afront to due process. But my outstanding legal team is up to the task. We will review the evidence expeditiously. We will prepare Mr. Stoller's defense diligently. We will be ready to fight these spurious charges. And we will not rest until justice is served. I won't be taking questions at this time. Thank you."

8

CHLOE

Gravel crunches under our tires, no longer on a paved road. The doors of the SUV open; Nick tells the others to pull me out. The hands that grab my arms are wearing latex gloves.

I can't see where I'm going or put weight on my ankle, so one of them lifts me roughly by my elbow and armpit to support me. My other hand is forced to comply awkwardly with its conjoined partner. Outside, nothing good can happen. My thoughts race. Now is when they will beat me, grope me, shoot me in the back of the head with a bullet I can't see coming—dump my body by the side of the road, in the woods, or in a shallow grave. Shane and my father will be told all these horrifying details, compelled to view police photos of the crime scene, required to identify my body.

"*Please*, don't do this," I hear myself saying. I lean away from them, resisting wherever they are taking me. My bare foot digs into the cold gravel for traction. "Please, please, *please*—you *can't* do this. I'm not the person you think."

But nobody responds. They're moving quickly, coordinated. I hear the doors of another car unlock and a trunk swing open. Wind whips against me, piercing through my loose cotton sweats. Seagulls squawk and a ship's horn wails in the distance. The pungent, fecal smell of decay assaults my nostrils. Are we in a marsh?

"Where are we? What's happening?" I say. Still, no one speaks.

My legs scrape against a bumper as a hand pushes my head down and my feet leave the ground. They're putting me in the trunk.

"No, no, *no*. I know—"

The whoosh of a flame igniting stops me, followed by a wave of heat like I'm in front of a bonfire. I instinctively recoil and fall backward into the metal interior. The trunk closes, the car starts, and we're moving again.

I kick against the lid as I realize what happened. They switched cars, burned mine. The whole thing took only seconds. Avoiding the possibility of getting caught by a FasTrak traffic camera or a CHP all-points bulletin or an Amber Alert.

As I scream, hoping someone will hear, a new thought swells within me—one I've been trying to suppress since the mob showed up at my apartment building. The BurnOutz always have a plan. Deliberate, conspiratorial orchestration is their trademark. A swarm of intricately coordinated organisms, autonomous yet always in concert. Driven by their mission. What if *I* was the mission today? What if that entire riot was about abducting me?

I swallow back a surge of nausea as I consider the implications.

We drive continuously for . . . what? Another hour? Two? Each bump reverberates through my body. My compressed limbs stiffen as we steadily follow the curves of a highway, cars rushing past in the opposite direction. I hear muffled conversation. Smell cigarette smoke seeping through the seats. Someone in the back seat is complaining about something like a bored teenager.

Eventually, I see the red flash of a blinker through the head covering, illuminating the trunk as we slow down for a turn. The car bounces over what feels like a driveway, and we finally come to a stop.

The trunk creaks open and hands lift me out. As my feet find the ground again, my exposed toes scrape against pavement.

"Watch your step," a quiet voice to my right instructs me as we climb steps that feel like a porch. Flakes of paint stick to my foot. A screen door bangs shut and hardwood floors creak under our weight as we enter what must be a house. *Are there neighbors? Should I scream? Break free? Run?* But I can barely stand on my own with this injured ankle. *How could I outrun them? Where would I go?* Blind and bound, it's me who has no plan now.

They push me to sit. I squat backward, no free hand to brace myself, no way to know if anything is under me at all. I land in what feels like an old lounge chair, ridged corduroy fabric worn smooth with age under my elbows. The tufts of polyester stuffing escaping the arm-rests scratch my arms. The smell of stale beer expels from its cavities as the padding compresses beneath me. It sounds like it might be the only piece of furniture in the room. Nothing absorbs the echoes of their footsteps on the naked floorboards. The adhesive screech of a roll of duct tape encircling me, passed around by two of them, constricting my torso. The rumble of a wooden chair being dragged across the room and set in front of me.

"I never heard *you* so quiet. Normally you have all sortsa bullshit you just can't wait to talk about. What's the matter? Couple hours in a trunk finally shut you up?"

It's Nick, sitting in a chair that groans under his weight. *Is he still holding the gun? Is he pointing it at me? Will he press it against my forehead? Put it in my mouth?*

I try to respond, but nothing comes out. I'm again overwhelmed with visions of how my life is about to end. My execution—filmed by Pete, posted to the internet.

"Do you know why you're here, Princess?" Nick again.

"*No.*" The word falls out of me, dry and cracked, more a sob than a reply. My head twitches convulsively from side to side to supplement the inadequacy of that one word. "*Please don't kill me.*"

"*Kill* you? What use would you be to us then?" Nick asks.

The others laugh.

I hear a refrigerator door open, beer bottles jostling against each other, the clink and hiss of their caps prying off. Their voices pause as they take swigs. I've completely lost my sense of time. Those last moments in my apartment feel like an eternity ago, but we can't be more than one hundred miles from the city. The police, Shane, my father—they know now. The *entire world* must know now. Maybe not where I am yet, but they know I'm somewhere. They will find me, somehow. The police, the FBI, our security team, they will find me. *This time, they will come.*

"I can pay . . . if that's what you want," I say, a half thought, still nothing more than a whisper.

They all laugh again. I hear Nick take a swig of his beer, swallow, clear his throat. "A *ransom?* Now, that's not a bad idea. Make some fuck-ing improvements around here." They all laugh again.

But then Nick's tone abruptly shifts. "Why's it *always* about money with you people?"

"I just . . . I don't know what you want," I say. The breath from my own words hot in my face. "But you can't do this. People will come for me."

"Oh, people will *definitely* come for you—that's the whole point," Nick says.

They all laugh again. I'm beginning to distinguish their voices—Pete's high-pitched exuberance, Scooter's confident chortle, Benny's self-con-scious titter.

"Your fame, your father, your followers—you're what's called an HVA, a *high-value asset.*"

"Such a soft target, too. Just *one* security guard?" Pete adds with mock incredulity. "It's like you *wanted* to be captured."

"*Please* . . ." I'm sobbing now, begging. "Don't do this . . . you *can't* do this."

"Oh, *Christ!* Relax . . ." Nick again. "You still don't get it, do you? Y'see, everything you do gets *sooo* much attention, so what you're gonna do is help *us.*"

"Help you what?" My voice cracks, my hands are trembling.

"Don't you know? The Feds arrested some guy named Shane Stoller this morning. They say he's Burner_911. And you're gonna help us get him out."

9

SHANE

Those *fucking* idiots! It was such a simple plan. Show up, protest, and let the targeted attacks do their thing. Nobody said riot. Nobody said invade buildings. Nobody said kill anybody. And MOST DEFINITELY NOBODY SAID KIDNAP CHLOE!

I mean . . . WHAT. THE. *FUCK*? What the actual *FUCKING* FUCK?

"So . . . where is she?" the special agent asks again.

"I told you, I don't know anything about this," I say. "My lawyer just told me."

Wayne nods solemnly to corroborate my statement. We're crammed into an interrogation room like in one of those CSI shows, huddled around an ancient, government-issued laptop as thick as a cinderblock. Special Agent Gance ("like *dance* but with a *G*" she explained), presses play on the video again while her partner, who hasn't introduced himself, leans against the wall, studying my reaction.

"Who are the men in this surveillance footage?" Gance asks, pausing on a frame with the best view. The tip of her fingernail taps each of the faces frozen on the screen, then she zooms in till the image gets all pixelated.

"I have no idea," I say. "I've never seen them before in my life. Why would you think I know them? I don't have anything to do with any of this."

Gance slams the laptop shut. "We've been monitoring you for a long time, Shane," she says. "We know you had a relationship with Ms. Corbin. And we know you had a falling out. You were angry. You wanted

---

28

revenge. You needed a bargaining chip. Why *wouldn't* you orchestrate her abduction?"

"Because I'm not, like, a sociopath," I say.

"The evidence seems to suggest otherwise."

"Look, Agent Gance," Wayne intervenes. "You've asked my client the same question a dozen times now. Unless you have more than a hunch, this interview is over."

"Why did you do it?" she asks, undeterred, scrutinizing me.

I didn't do it. My followers did it. Kidnapped my girlfriend at gun point. That's going to be a hard one to explain. *Why did they do that? Who even are these guys?* That wasn't their call to make. Believe in The Plan, sure . . . but THAT MOST DEFINITELY WAS *NOT* THE PLAN! Of course, if I stick to Wayne's recommendation and plead innocent, I can't say *any* of this to the Feds, so all I can say is nothing.

"Even if you didn't directly order it, certainly you can . . . *undo* it," she says, twisting her wrist like she's turning back the dial on a clock.

"I don't know what you're talking about," I say. But the words burn my throat. I know exactly what she's talking about: My superpower. My audience. This would all be so easy if I could just log in. If I were online, I could do something. Protect her. Cut off, I have no way to stop this. No way to save her. No idea if she's dead or alive.

Gance continues in a calmer voice, "Look, we're just trying to get Chloe home safely. If you didn't do it, then you must want that too, right? To get her released? To see her again? All you have to do is log in to the Burner_911 account and tell your followers to let her go. You can use my laptop right here."

Like it's all so easy. But, when I think about the reality of typing those words, that's when it hits me like a punch: Even if I *were* online, there's nothing I could do. Burner_911 doesn't call off the dogs—he whistles the dogs into a frenzy. Chloe is the enemy, the logical target, the bargaining chip. Of *course* they took her. How the hell did I not know this was going to happen! Maybe I *did* know this would happen. *Will she ever forgive me?*

"Nice try," Wayne interjects, holding up his hand toward me like a traffic cop. "That's enough. We're done."

Gance drills her eyes into me as she collects her items. "Just because you're in custody for other crimes doesn't mean we can't add to the charges against you, Mr. Stoller. It's too late to save yourself, but maybe you can save her." She signals the guard to open the door.

After they're gone, Wayne shakes his head. "How the hell did you get mixed up with Chloe Corbin?"

I don't think he expects an answer because he says it all snide, without looking at me—not really a question but a statement, like a disappointed father. No stranger to being a disappointment, I ignore the judgment.

"I don't give a shit what you think, I need to reach her," I say to Wayne under my breath, aware there may still be someone listening on the other side of the glass. "I need to tell her I wasn't behind this. Explain this is all just a big mistake—that I never meant for this to happen."

Wayne plays along without looking up, like he's still writing in his notepad. "I'll see what I can do."

10

CHLOE

"What's your passcode?" Nick asks after telling the others, once again, to shut up.

Is he talking to me? Still suffocating under this hood, it's hard to distinguish their voices when they all talk at the same time. Grown men bickering like boys on a playground, each adamant in their theory about who Shane is and what they should do. Meanwhile, I'm still just trying to process the information that Shane has been *arrested*. What will happen to him? Life in prison? Death sentence? Will I ever see him again?

Their argument escalates into a whirlwind of conflicting conspiracy theories: *There's no proof he's Burner_911. Why did we even take her, then? He's infiltrating the deep state from the inside. Why would he reveal his identity? This is another sign of the awakening. The real Burner_911 would never be caught. You call yourself a believer?* A table shudders across the floor, violently pushed aside; a bottle shatters.

"*Guys!* It doesn't fucking matter right now!" Nick asserts his control again, silencing the disagreement. "Either way, we need to do this. We can't have them taking one of our own. *So . . .* give me your *goddamn* passcode!"

His finger stabs me in the shoulder. I jolt reflexively.

Then I understand—my phone. They have it. Of course they have it. I remember it falling out of my pocket when they took me. Feeling like a lifeline was slipping away with it. Now, maybe, it's back. I hesitate.

"Don't make me ask you again," Nick says slowly, his voice inches from my face, the black hood pushed against my skin by his breath.

I mutter my passcode. Knowing now what he will do with it. Maybe this was the plan all along—a mob abduction, designed to look like a spontaneous act, was actually cover for a trained extraction team, waiting to launch into action. The impulse of an integrated organism defending itself, exploiting me as the natural escalation of their scheme. Ignorant about my relationship with Shane, they have no idea just how valuable an "asset" I am. What an unfortunate and unforgivable mistake they've made. Shane will scorch these guys.

If he ever gets out of jail.

"Nice!" Scooter says, confirming they have access.

They exchange self-congratulatory remarks, their camaraderie and indignation restored.

"Smile for the camera!" Pete whips the hood off my head, yanking strands of my hair with it. My eyes can't adjust fast enough, leaving me blinking blindly into the light as I hear the digital click and flash of the camera.

Just as fast, the hood is back on my head. In that moment, a terrifying alternative explanation of events presents itself. *Did Shane know about this? Did he* order *it? Am I his bargaining chip? His break-glass-in-case-of-emergency last resort?*

"To . . . my followers . . . and those who care . . . about me," Nick says aloud.

A reckless anger wells inside of me as I listen to his thumbs tap on the screen.

"I am safe . . . but I will not . . . be freed . . . until Shane Stoller . . . is released from federal custody . . . You have . . . seventy-two hours . . . to comply. *Share!*"

11

COURT TRANSCRIPT

UNITED STATES DISTRICT COURT
FOR THE NORTHERN DISTRICT OF CALIFORNIA
UNITED STATES OF AMERICA, Plaintiff

vs.

SHANE THOMAS STOLLER, Defendant
Case No. M-21-98-H
TRANSCRIPT OF ARRAIGNMENT HEARING

Conrad Dowling, United States Magistrate Judge, Presiding

Julie Gibson, United States Attorney's Office,
Federal Prosecutor

Wayne Young, Counsel for the Defendant

JUDGE DOWLING: Please be seated. Let me start by reminding both counsels to respect my explicit orders not to speak to the media in any way regarding these proceedings. Given the unusual attention this case has garnered, it is important that we contain our arguments to the four walls of this courtroom. To that end, and given the delicate nature of this case, I will be limiting members of the media and the public at large to attend these proceedings only by video feed. I do not want to bias our jury pool, particularly given how prone to manipulation public opinion on this matter seems to be. Before we proceed with a reading of the charges against the defendant, I would like both counsels to introduce themselves, beginning with the Counsel for the United States.

MS. GIBSON: Thank you, Your Honor. My name is Julie Gibson, and I am deputy attorney general for the Ninth Circuit Court of the United States.

JUDGE DOWLING: Good to see you, Ms. Gibson. And counsel for the defendant?

MR. YOUNG: Good morning, Your Honor. I am Wayne Young, and I am representing the defendant, Shane Thomas Stoller.

JUDGE DOWLING: Good morning, Mr. Young. I understand that you have taken Mr. Stoller's case as a *pro bono* client?

MR. YOUNG: That is correct, Your Honor.

JUDGE DOWLING: Very noble of you, Mr. Young. Though I can't help but suspect ulterior motives. Indeed, Mr. Young, your reputation precedes you, so I am compelled to remind you I will not have you disrupting my courtroom or this case.

MR. YOUNG: Yes, of course. I—

JUDGE DOWLING: Nor will I tolerate attempts to influence this case through communication with the news media or on social media.

MR. YOUNG: Yes, Your Honor.

JUDGE DOWLING: Now, do either of you have any administrative matters to bring to the court's attention?

MR. YOUNG: Yes, Your Honor, my client was brought before the court today in handcuffs and an orange jumpsuit—visual cues that could bias the jury and make it difficult for him to receive a fair trial. If it pleases the court,

COURT TRANSCRIPT

I respectfully request he be permitted to appear for the proceedings without handcuffs and in clothing of his choosing.

JUDGE DOWLING: Very well. Your request is accepted. Bailiff, please allow Mr. Stoller to change immediately prior to his entry into the Court.

MR. YOUNG: Thank you, Your Honor.

JUDGE DOWLING: Now, with that taken care of—Ms. Gibson, it is my understanding that the prosecution will be bringing two cases against the defendant before the court.

MS. GIBSON: That is correct, Your Honor. The first is the indictment resulting from a yearlong investigation led by the Federal Bureau of Investigation into Mr. Stoller and his connections to the Burner_911 account and BurnOutz movement. The second case pertains to his orchestration of the events that occurred on October 12th, which we believe meets the statutory definition of domestic terrorism, as these criminal acts were dangerous to human life, intended to intimidate or coerce a civilian population, and an attempt to influence government policy through intimidation, coercion, and mass destruction.

JUDGE DOWLING: Thank you, Counsel. We will now proceed with a reading of the charges against Mr. Stoller in the federal indictment before the court. Will the defendant please rise. Shane Thomas Stoller, you are hereby charged in the US District Court for the Northern District of California with five counts of extortion, three counts of racketeering, two counts of money laundering, three counts of federal tax evasion, eight counts of securities fraud, one count of conspiracy in the destruction of federal governmental buildings, and one count of conspiracy in the murder of FBI Special Agent John Stanley. Mr. Stoller, do you attest that you have been afforded the chance to discuss these charges with your legal counsel, Mr. Young, and that Mr. Young is representing you in these proceedings?

MR. STOLLER: Yes, Your Honor.

JUDGE DOWLING: How do you plead?

MR. STOLLER: Not guilty, Your Honor.

JUDGE DOWLING: Mr. Stoller, I would remind you that, should you be found guilty by a jury of your peers, federal sentencing guidelines would require a minimum of a lifetime sentence with no possibility of parole and a maximum of capital punishment by lethal injection. Do you understand?

MR. STOLLER: Yes, Your Honor.

JUDGE DOWLING: Very well. Mr. Young, I trust that you have been provided with all the evidence in this case?

MR. YOUNG: We have, Your Honor. My team and I are reviewing it as quickly as possible.

JUDGE DOWLING: Okay, good. Given the high-profile nature of this case and the ongoing civil unrest it has caused, I intend to move forward as expeditiously as possible. Please prepare accordingly. Are there any other pretrial motions that either counsel would like to put forward?

MR. YOUNG: Yes, Your Honor. I have a motion for a change of venue. Given the high-profile nature of this case, the fact many of the events in question transpired in this very city, and the prevalent liberal bias of potential jurors, it will be impossible for my client to receive a fair trial in San—

MS. GIBSON: Your Honor, I object. Given the deliberate attempts by Mr. Young to influence public opinion on this case, the only bias to impartiality has been inflicted by him.

JUDGE DOWLING: I concur with Ms. Gibson. Mr. Young, you have already been outspoken in your communications with respect to this case—antics I regard as potentially detrimental to your defense. This case has already garnered national media attention, so a change of venue is unlikely to result in a jury any more impartial than we will have here. Your motion for a change of venue is denied. Further, Mr. Stoller will continue to be held with zero external communication whatsoever, and I hereby warn you about any further communications by you through either social media or traditional media with respect to this case, or I will find you in contempt. Do you understand?

MR. YOUNG: [INAUDIBLE]

JUDGE DOWLING: Mr. Young, I cannot hear you. Do you understand?

MR. YOUNG: Yes, Your Honor.

JUDGE DOWLING: Given the threat to peace and safety in our community that Mr. Stoller represents, I further deny bail to the defendant.

MR. YOUNG: Your Honor, my client does not represent—

JUDGE DOWLING: Excuse me, Mr. Young, but my decision with respect to bail and his internet embargo is final. This court is hereby adjourned.

12

WAYNE

"That was bullshit!" I say. "Goddamn activist judges."

I slap the marble wall in the hallway outside the courtroom. Valerie is behind me, carrying a box of files.

"They don't have a case," she says calmly, setting the box on a bench. "They know they can't definitively prove he's Burner_911, so they're trying to get him on technicalities."

"That's not their angle," I say. "Their strategy is to make this political. Hold the trial in San Fran-*fucking*-cisco. Stack the jury with liberals. There's no way we're getting a fair trial."

Julie Gibson walks out of the courtroom flanked by her entourage of prosecutors. "Nice try, Wayne," she says as she walks by with a smug look of satisfaction on her face.

I've had more than my share of run-ins with AUSA Gibson's office. She's a ball-buster with political ambitions. This case could make her career, and she's confident in the knowledge she has home-court advantage.

Especially since I'm at a loss for how to play this one. Valerie's wrong—the Feds have a ton of evidence against him for dozens of crimes. We could slow-roll the case, ask for more time to review the evidence, file a stack of motions. But what's the point? They're going to get him on *something*. Meanwhile, the whole movement will shrivel on the vine. If we drag this whole thing out, it all becomes irrelevant. There won't even be any followers left to lead anymore. The only option is to throw sand in the gears—discredit the process, disparage the players, question the institutions.

"I'm not gonna just sit here and take this," I say to Valerie after Gibson and team are out of earshot. "If this is how they're gonna play, then I'm using every tool in my arsenal."

I start walking toward the lobby, where a desperate throng of reporters swirls, waiting for information about the trial like a school of hungry piranhas.

"Wayne, he's going to hold you in contempt if you talk to them," Valerie says.

"Let him," I say as I throw open the doors and dive into the mosh pit. The best defense is a good offense.

I let the chorus of shouted questions wash over me and then make my opening statement.

"As you know, my name is Wayne Young, and I am the defense counsel for Shane Stoller. After today's arraignment hearing, it has become abundantly clear that what we have here is not a fair and impartial trial but a politically motivated witch hunt. The US Attorney's Office is grasping at straws. They are desperate to convict someone, *anyone*, for the October 12th protests. Unable or unwilling to perform their sworn oath, they have instead rushed a case to trial based on hearsay, circumstantial evidence, and outright lies. If Judge Dowling had any integrity or impartiality, he would immediately dismiss this case."

A hundred voices clamor to get their question answered. One of the few I hear clearly is, "Have you had a chance to review the evidence presented in the indictment?"

"Yes, and it's all irrelevant. Videos and voice recordings taken out of context, text messages and emails surveilled without a warrant, witnesses who barely even know my client but will testify against him because they object to his political beliefs. None of it has any bearing on the primary accusation of this case: my client's alleged leadership of the BurnOutz movement. Despite this fact, and against my adamant objections, Judge Dowling has admitted it all as evidence."

"Will the trial be held here in San Francisco?" someone else shouts.

"That is Judge Dowling's intent, and, frankly, it's outrageous. It will be impossible for my client to receive a fair trial here in the Northern District of California, given the left-wing bias of the local population. This district court has a notorious reputation for being tainted with activist judges with political axes to grind. Furthermore, this very building— the Phillip Burton Federal Building, where the trial will be held—was vandalized on October 12th, making the entire institution incapable of impartiality in this case."

Another crush of questions. I could go all night. I hear, "So you don't believe Shane Stoller will receive a fair trial?"

"This absolutely will *not* be a fair trial. Look around you. It's a circus. This entire sham trial should be dismissed immediately. Judge Dowling is clearly biased, based on his unwillingness to protect my client from unlawfully obtained evidence, his desire to stack the jury with citizens predisposed against my client, and his unreasonably accelerated timeline for this case. He has clearly violated my client's right to a fair trial. No question."

Another: "So you honestly believe Shane Stoller is innocent?"

"One hundred percent he's innocent. The facts will show that."

Another: "If Shane Stoller isn't Burner_911, then who is?"

"I have no idea. Nobody does. Least of all the Department of Justice. The prosecution is so desperate to pin the Burner_911 conspiracy on someone that they have rushed the first person they can find to the gallows. My client is a scapegoat, and I am confident that this case, in the event that it is not dismissed, will be deemed a mistrial or overturned upon appeal. Our legal system cannot suppress the will of the people."

Another: "What do you know about Chloe Corbin? Do you believe she's still alive?"

"That's the real tragedy. Instead of doing their job and finding Ms. Corbin, our tax dollars are being spent pursuing propaganda. I ask you all to pray for her safe return, and I encourage you to share your thoughts and prayers using the hashtag #SaveChloe. I also urge anyone with knowledge of Ms. Corbin's whereabouts or information that could lead to her release to contact my office using the anonymous tip line my team has set up at 877-44-CHLOE. You can also Venmo your donations to @savechloe."

Valerie has made it to me through the crowd, here to save me from myself.

"Thank you all so much," she says loudly. "No further questions."

13

SHANE

I hear the door to my cell open and two guards step inside. But my attention stays locked on the ceiling. In one sleepless night alone here, I've already committed it to memory—every crack, stain, and paint peel, like landmarks on a map. Patches of moisture relentlessly turning plaster to powder over time. Particles taking flight to lodge in the lungs of this cell's inhabitants. All the pathetic losers this ceiling has looked down on. I won't be one of them.

I've got to get out of here.

The arraignment hearing this morning rattled me, I have to admit. They're not fucking around. If I don't figure out a way to get off, I'll be spending the rest of my life looking at ceilings like this one. Makes the lethal injection option seem not so bad.

"Get up," the guard in front says. I roll off the bed and stand. The name badge pinned to his barrel chest reads *Kryzsiek*. I've seen him before, during my intake yesterday. I'm taller than him, but he still squares me up without blinking through his thick, smudged glasses.

"You're causing quite a stir around here," he says as the taller, pear-shaped guard—*Killian*, his badge says—cuffs my hands and feet, then pushes a strand of his dingy hair back into position along the white line of his center part. Kryzsiek squints at me through his glasses. "Everyone's wondering if you are who they say you are."

I can't think of a good comeback, so I don't say anything.

The "correctional officers," as they are called according to their shoulder patches, take me down the row of cells—to whispers this time, rather than the taunts and heckles I got when I first arrived. I look down at the common area, full of men in orange jumpsuits clustered by race around stainless-steel tables, all staring up at me, silent for the first time all morning. The guards deposit me back in another one of the interrogation rooms with bolted-down furniture and one-way glass. Wayne is already there, his mane of jet-black hair slicked back—long curls in back and a streak of white along the side like a skunk. Next to him is the court-appointed psych consult he told me would be here.

"Good morning, Shane, I'm Dr. Susan Campbell," she says without reaching to shake my hand. "As you know, at the prosecution's request, I have been assigned by the court to determine your mental competency as the defendant. Specifically, to evaluate if you are suffering from any mental disease or psychological defect that would render you unfit to stand trial or unable to understand the nature and consequences of the charges against you. The judge and both counsels will receive a full report of my findings. This session is not confidential and will be recorded. Do you understand?"

I glance at Wayne, who gives a slight nod, so I nod too. He told me that they're just trying to establish that I'm not demented or suicidal, so I can't bounce outta here by pleading insanity. So nobody feels bad about sentencing me to death. It's no fun unless you resist.

"I've had a chance to review the court documents from previous cases, including psychological evaluations, so I have some context about you and your past." Susan the shrink taps her pen against a thick file. She tries for a disarming smile, revealing a smudge of lipstick on her front tooth and making the pancake foundation spackled across her face collect in orange canyons spreading from the corner of her eyes. Just as quick, the smile leaves her face. "Have you ever been diagnosed with any psychiatric conditions? ADHD, bipolar disorder, borderline personality disorder, schizophrenia, any dissociative disorders, anything like that?"

"Diagnosed? No."

She glances up from her notebook to confirm my sarcasm. "And you've never been prescribed psychiatric medications, such as antidepressants, antipsychotics, or mood stabilizers, by a psychiatrist?"

"No, but plenty of them tried," I say. "Especially when I was a kid."

"Yes, I'd like to get into that. To make sure no diagnoses were missed. You obviously had a troubled childhood."

I resent the insinuation. Having a shitty childhood doesn't make you insane. If you ask me, it's the opposite. The sharpest people I know all had shitty childhoods. They had to figure things out for themselves. They had to be the adult. They had to function in the face of dysfunction. It's the silver-spoon, Adderall kids who have the nervous breakdowns.

"Shouldn't you, like, know all this already if you read my file?" I say.

"Well, I know you became a ward of the court when you were eight and were subsequently placed into foster care, which must have been very difficult," she says with the rehearsed sympathy of someone who has spoken to thousands of broken kids. "But I don't know much about your circumstances prior to that. I'm just trying to assess your early upbringing. What was your relationship with your biological parents?"

My *relationship*? What do you know about relationships when you're a kid? You don't know what's good, what's normal. You don't have any point of comparison. Whatever you're born into, you just roll with it. Whatever hand you're dealt. Normal is what you decide it is.

"Pretty normal," I say. "I lived with them. Obviously."

"And where was that? The case file mentioned you were living out of a car." Her finger slides along the edge of the folder—she's getting off on this a little. Poverty porn.

"No, that's wrong," I say. "We lived at Green Run Mobile Estates. It was awesome."

I see the flicker of condescension cross her face. Before people like her educated me that a trailer park is something to be ashamed of, something to *escape* from, I really did love the place. I had total freedom. Me and my crew would make the rounds: Ms. J in her janky housecoat waving us up to her porch to give us a cookie or piece of candy. Ben the maintenance guy who showed us how to work the vending machine to get free Gatorades. Debbie slipping us cigarettes before she left for the night. They were all part of my family.

"Sounds . . . nice. What's your earliest memory of your father?"

"He drove a long-haul rig, so we only saw him a day or two a month." I shrug. "Sometimes he'd bring me something from the road."

A collection of random items run through my memory, precious to me and arranged with obvious OCD on my dresser—a turquoise stone from New Mexico, a wallet with my name embroidered on it from the Mojave Desert, a snow globe from Phoenix meant to be ironic. Keepsakes from places I never saw. Reminders of all the times we didn't spend together.

All in a landfill now.

"That's nice. What's something you remember him giving you?"

And I'm there, maybe three or four years old. I run out the screen door to the hiss of hydraulic brakes. The intoxicating smell of diesel that announces he's home. Dad drops from the cab, just back from Texas, and pulls a cowboy hat from behind his back. "I got you this," he says, putting it on my head. "When I was your age, I wanted to be a cowboy. What about you, Shane? What do you want to be when you grow up?"

What do I want to be? Nobody ever asked me that before. I didn't know how I was supposed to answer. I still don't. Not a cowboy, for sure. Maybe a fireman, or football player, or superhero? Later, maybe a college graduate, an entrepreneur, a billionaire? A social media influencer? An activist? A terrorist?

He taps the brim, seeing I don't know how to answer and says, "Well, whatever you decide, I got you this as a reminder that you can be anything you want to be, as long as you believe in yourself and work hard."

Ah, the good ol' American Dream. Complete bullshit, as I found out later. The big lie we tell our children. Meant to motivate them but really just a ticking time bomb for when those dreams inevitably stall out.

I shrug at Dr. Susan. "Stuff. A cowboy hat one time."

"That's a nice memory. What about your mother? What did she do?"

"*Drank*, mostly. Did drugs when she could get them."

"I mean for work."

"Oh . . . odd jobs, I guess. But she could never keep them." I narrow my eyes at her. "What does this have to do with anything?"

Wayne is writing notes, his nicotine-stained fingers pressing the ballpoint so hard it leaves grooves in the page, like he's anxious I'm about to say something stupid. Which I probably am.

"How was your parents' relationship?" she asks, ignoring my question. "Did they separate? Was there any emotional or physical abuse?"

The cowboy hat comes to mind again. Mom hated that hat—a waste of money that could have gone to vodka. Muffled shouts I try not to hear over the sound of the TV at full volume. I pull the brim lower, hoping it will make them stop. The next day, he's gone again, back on the road to Oklahoma or Louisiana or a whole 'nother family, for all I know, and I'm galloping around the trailer with a broom as my horse like things are back to normal. Mom knocks the hat off my head with the back of her hand and then crushes it on the floor under her boot. Tells me I'm a goddamn fool to believe I'll ever amount to anything. Reminds me dad never did become a cowboy—just a petrochemical trucker living in a trailer park outside Turlock.

"Nothing too bad," I say. "They argued, but just the normal amount. Then, he was gone."

"So how did you and your mother end up living out of a car?" she asks.

More flashbacks. Tripping over empty plastic Karkov vodka bottles that skittered across the floor like Roman candles. Trying to hold the door shut so the repossession thugs couldn't get in. Barking dogs and the red and blue flashing lights of a police cruiser as we loaded up our Geo Storm with whatever we could carry. Pulling into the Central Valley University parking lot where the security guard, after seeing me, said we could stay overnight as long as we left by 6:00 a.m. so the faculty could park. Splitting a 49-cent hamburger for dinner. Trying to take a shit in a construction site porta-potty but too constipated by anxiety to squeeze anything out. The shame of our lives collapsing. All the worst stereotypes of a trailer-trash family.

I won't give her the satisfaction; I'll just tell her the lie Mom told me.

"It was just temporary, until we found our next place. No big deal."

And I believed her, too. It was me taking care of her more than vice versa, but I still thought she'd figure out a place for us to go. What I didn't know then is that we would find our next place . . . just not the *same* place. See, even if the security guards are cool with it and it seems like kind of a fun adventure at first, you can live in a car unbathed, heaped in a pile of your own garbage, for only so long. Even if your mom says everything will be all right but ends up most nights passed out and most mornings soaked in her own piss. Even if your teachers know enough not to ask too many questions when you suddenly show up in school after being gone a full week wearing the same clothes you were last seen in. Eventually, it ends.

One morning before we woke up, a woman in a blue windbreaker knocked on our car window with a flashlight. She showed a badge that said she was with the Stanislaus County Department of Child Protective Services. Mom was too out of it to really understand what was happening. Mumbling almost incoherently, she managed to tell me she'd see me in a little bit as campus security put her into their patrol car. But I knew.

I never saw my mom again after that day.

14

MERCED SUN-STAR

Suspect Sought after Fatal Tanker Truck Accident on SR-99

MERCED, CA, December 23, 2005—A Turlock man was killed late Friday evening when the gasoline tanker truck he was driving overturned and caught fire just north of Fergus, California, on California State Route 99. The crash blocked southbound traffic on SR-99 until early Saturday morning as emergency crews worked to clear the scene.

The Merced County Sheriff's Department now says they have a description of a vehicle that is suspected to have caused the wreck and fled the scene. A white BMW SUV with California license plates reportedly entered Highway 99 from Atwater-Merced Expressway around 11:30 p.m.

According to the California Highway Patrol (CHP) fatality report, a witness at the scene told police that the white BMW was headed north on the southbound side of the freeway at high speed. As the vehicle approached the tanker, the truck driver was forced to take corrective action to avoid a head-on collision and swerved to the left. The truck ran off the highway into the median ditch, causing it to overturn on the driver's side and immediately burst into flames.

The fire spread across the median, causing both sides of Highway 99 to be temporarily closed between Atwater-Merced Expressway and North Buhach Road until about 3:00 a.m., with traffic being diverted to County Route J7. Flames and smoke from the conflagration could be seen from miles away. The fire is now under control and the highway is reopened, according to Merced County Emergency Management.

BURNER

CHP reports that the driver of the tanker truck was 32-year-old Chad Stoller of Turlock. He was the lone fatality. Mr. Stoller is survived by his wife, Tracy Stoller, and the couple's eight-year-old son. CHP is still investigating the crash but has started a search for the driver of the white BMW SUV involved in the incident. The suspect is believed to have knowingly fled the scene. Anyone with information about the incident or suspected vehicle can contact the CHP tip line at 1-800-TELL-CHP (1-800-835-5247).

15

CHLOE

I awaken. Instinctively, I reach toward my nightstand—and am disoriented when I find that my phone is not there, that my hand is constrained, that the other one moves with it, that I can't see.

Where am I?

Tufts of stuffing under my fingertips snap me back to my surroundings—the chair, the room, the house . . . the boys. Questions race through my head. *How long was I asleep? Is it morning? Where is my phone? They had it. Is it in the room? On the table? Near me? Can I find it?*

The house is silent. Everyone sleeping or passed out. Under the hood, I can barely tell if my eyes are open or closed. My fingers are twitching, anxious, accustomed to their routine. Most days, I've posted by now. Not today. I occupy them with the stuffing I pull from the chair, twisting the polyester into little strands.

Suddenly, I have an intense need to urinate, my seized bodily functions finally initiating again. It's been almost twenty-four hours.

Just as I'm about to pee myself, I hear someone pulling the refrigerator door open.

"I have to go to the bathroom," I call out. The refrigerator door closes, footsteps approach me, stop, consider. I say it again, adding that I will wet their chair if I can't get to a toilet soon.

No response, but I feel a sudden tension around my chest, then hear a ripping sound as a knife slices through my duct tape constraints. He pulls me up by my bound wrists. I still can't fully support myself on my ankle, and my shoe on that foot is gone, so I lean into the rough hands and limp.

"Unless you want to wipe me yourself, you'll need to remove this," I say when we pause at a door I pray is the bathroom. He pushes me forward and pulls the hood off in a single motion. I meant the straps around my wrists, but at least I can see now. A light and fan come to life as the door closes behind me. I still don't know which of them he is.

The bathroom is beyond filthy—rust stains in the sink, mildew stains on the walls, shit stains in the toilet. Layers of dried yellow urine surround the rim, speckle the floor; the stench assaults my nostrils. Clusters of hair everywhere—on the floor, in the sink, clogging the drain. A tiny opening above the shower of the otherwise windowless bathroom gives me some indication of the time. It's early, the predawn before sunrise.

I look up tentatively into the mirror above the sink. My mascara is streaked across my cheeks, my hair is matted and clumped, my eyes are puffy and red. Deep creases in my skin make me look like I'm strung out. I push the hair out of my face with the tips of my fingers, my hands clasped together like I'm praying. Maybe I am.

I take a deep, cleansing breath. Things could be worse. At least I'm alive, even if I'm in captivity. I know something about confinement— from my mom, from myself. Men who think they can possess me. Use me to advance their own agenda. That's how most men think. That's how my father thinks. That mom and I are forever beholden to him because of his wealth. That the money he provides excuses his behavior. That we would never dare to leave his orbit. But I know how to get what I want, even when it seems like I lack power. Power, it turns out, goes both ways.

I try to splash water on my face. I pull down my sweatpants and underwear, hooking the waistbands with my pinkies. I try to squat over the defiled bowl, but with nothing to hold on to and my ankle still unsteady, I give up and collapse onto the seat. Urine flows from me in a torrent, like a barn animal. I pinch the remaining shreds of toilet paper on a nearly empty roll, dabbing myself the best I can given my restraints.

A cautious knock at the door, and then it edges open and a whisper asks, *"Are you done?"*

It's Benny's voice. I see a portion of his face for the first time through the crack—timid brown eyes, pubescent tufts of facial hair, threadbare baseball cap, unbuttoned flannel shirt. He could pass for a nervous teenager if it weren't for the huge handgun holstered under his armpit.

"Just a second," I say.

"Here, you'll probably need this," he says, reaching around the narrow door opening to hand me my lost tennis shoe.

"Oh . . . thanks," I say, loosening the ties and sliding it on to my swollen foot. I look up at my image, triggering the recollection of my last Instagram post, the literal and figurative epitome of a bad hair day. Nick's picture of me, which I know is now being shown on every news channel, morphed into an internet meme, appropriated for email blasts, Facebook ads, GoFundMe campaigns to raise money to combat political extremism. An image that will be permanently associated with me. The first page of Google search results for "Chloe Corbin." Forever part of my online legacy.

I think about the comments, the likes, the shares, the new followers—thousands of them, *millions* of them, all wondering where I am, speculating about my kidnappers' motives, organizing vigils, presuming I'm already dead. Then I realize: *This* is my leverage. This is how I will escape. Attention is my superpower. My expression in the mirror adjusts—chin tilted down, eyes cast upward, my lips pursed in the faintest trace of a smile—as I contemplate the irresistible drama of it. See it from the audience's perspective. The authenticity of my distress. They can't look away. And anyone following me is just one degree of separation from the story. No . . . they *are* the story.

I lean toward the crack in the door and ask Benny, "How many views did we get?"

16

SHANE

"Why haven't you connected me with Chloe yet?" I demand. "What's taking so long?"

We're on break from Dr. Susan's grilling. A "bio break" as she called it, I guess so she can go take a shit or something. Wayne turns to Valerie, one of the junior lawyers on his team, and waves his hand so she stops taking notes. Why he bothers, I have no idea—they're probably recording all this. The walls are getting closer every minute.

"We need to make contact first," he says. "The police have only been able to positively identify one of the guys in the video, but they haven't disclosed a name. So all we can do is wait for them to reach out to us. These things take time."

"We don't *have* time. It's already been over twenty-four hours." I chew back whatever is lurking at the back of my throat. A hairball of anger, helplessness, and regret that will suffocate me if I let it. I imagine her there in the dark with that hood from the video over her head, knowing that my followers put her there. That *I* put her there. Why doesn't life have an Undo button?

"She's gonna be fine," Wayne says. "These guys are amateurs. They're not going to hurt her. Not without direction."

"How do you know that? Nobody knows who these guys are. Not even *me*. I don't even have a username."

"I know the type. They're followers, foot soldiers. Like a dog fetching a ball—it looks like they're acting on their own, but really they just do what they're told."

"They busted open her apartment, shot her bodyguard, and escaped in her goddamn Escalade. They seem pretty self-motivated to me."

It has to be a cell leader. Someone with the team and training to pull this off. Someone who saw the livestream of my arrest and took matters into his own hands. I can tell the difference between spontaneous actions and deliberate intervention. If they're loyal, they'll be patient. Await direction. But maybe it's someone who sees an opportunity. A splinter cell seeking power of its own.

This whole thing is spinning out of my control. Wayne doesn't know what he's dealing with.

"We're doing everything we can do, Shane. We set up a tip line, communicated on TV and social media. But until they contact us, we have no way to reach these guys."

"I want you to do your fucking job, not waste time with Dr. Susan."

"That's out of our control. It's part of the prosecution's case."

"I don't give a shit about the case. I've got to talk to her."

"Frankly, you got bigger problems than talking to Chloe right now," Wayne says. "For starters, surviving this place without getting shivved. You have your die-hard supporters, sure. But not everyone thinks you're as clever as you do. Conspiracy theories have been running wild since your arrest. Factions are forming. So watch your back. The prosecution wanted you held at the maximum-security penitentiary out in Atwater, but that would be a pain in the ass logistically, so I got the judge to agree to keep you here in solitary for now."

"Am I supposed to say thanks?"

He gives me a pained look. "I'm *trying* to help you. But I can't do that if you don't trust me."

I groan an objection, but part of me knows he's right. Wayne might look like an extra from *Sons of Anarchy* who reinvented himself with a thrift-store blazer and a mail-order law degree, but so far he's the only one who's shown up for me. I've seen the fractures in the movement for months now. Increasing dissension. Factions within factions, each moving in different directions. An entire media apparatus exploiting the BurnOutz for ratings. Infiltrators, supplanters, betrayers, and imitators everywhere, contorting the movement to their own selfish needs.

Now it's all caving in like sand back into a hole I've dug for myself, burying me. Everyone wants me dead—either because they think I did what they say I did, or because they think I'm pretending to be something I'm not. Wayne gets that. He can help me. I think. Still, something feels off, like a celebrity deep fake that just doesn't feel natural. I can't figure out why he's doing this. What's in it for him? Is it really just because he's a believer? Or is he here for the theater of it all? Drawn to the lights like a circus ringmaster, pimping me out to grow his own celebrity?

Regardless of his motives, I'm reliant on him—even though I can't stand that dependency. Not only is he my attorney, he's my lifeline. My only chance for reaching Chloe. The public defender sure as hell won't risk his ass to do that.

The door opens and Dr. Susan shuffles back into the room in her sensible shoes, cradling a Styrofoam cup of coffee with an oily slick on the surface. Wayne gives me a shrug of his eyebrows that's like, *I know this is painful but suck it up.* He waves his meaty paw at Valerie to continue taking notes on her legal pad.

"So . . ." Dr. Susan blows on her coffee, leaving a red smear of lipstick on the rim of the white cup. "Tell me about your relationship with Chloe Corbin."

17

COURT TRANSCRIPT

UNITED STATES DISTRICT COURT

FOR THE NORTHERN DISTRICT OF CALIFORNIA

UNITED STATES OF AMERICA, Plaintiff

vs.

SHANE THOMAS STOLLER, Defendant

Case No. M-21-98-H

TRANSCRIPT OF OPENING STATEMENTS

Alfred H. Moreno, United States Senior District Judge, Presiding

Julie Gibson, United States Attorney's Office, Federal Prosecutor

Wayne Young, Counsel for the Defendant

PROSECUTION OPENING STATEMENT

MS. GIBSON: Thank you, Your Honor. May it please the court . . .

JUDGE MORENO: Counsel.

MS. GIBSON: Ladies and gentlemen of the jury. What you will see presented before you in the following days of this trial is overwhelming evidence of Mr. Stoller's guilt. This man is the leader of a massive, illegal online conspiracy that has committed multiple acts of domestic terrorism, including murder and assassination, known as Burner_911. The prosecution has assembled an unusually definitive case accumulated over a yearlong investigation. The evidence that I will produce, through firsthand testimony as well as direct and cross-examination of witnesses; through exhibits, photographs, and video recordings; through transcripts of telephone conversations, text messages, and social media posts; through geolocation markers, mobile application logs, and security camera footage; and not to mention Mr. Stoller's own notes and voice memos kept across his multiple mobile devices; will establish well beyond a reasonable doubt that Mr. Stoller knowingly and wantonly perpetrated and directed the crimes he stands accused of here today.

Before we get into the evidence, I want to give you context. Context about the kind of person Shane Stoller is. Context about why he harbored the impunity to commit these crimes. Mr. Stoller was a troublemaker from an early age. His first juvenile offense was when he was twelve: Shoplifting at a Kmart. Then possession and sale of marijuana at age fourteen. Selling stolen auto parts at fifteen. And investigation for making online threats when he was seventeen.

The defense will characterize these incidents as a by-product of Shane's troubled upbringing. They will try to elicit sympathy from you, the jury, for the tough childhood he had. And it was tough. But I see these incidents as something different—a pattern of criminal behavior, of crass selfishness and entitlement, that began at a young age. You see, by the time Shane Stoller became an emancipated adult, he understood the game. His record had been wiped clean, and he knew by then how not to get caught. It was at this point that he developed an obsessive interest in the dark web. His pattern of criminal behavior shifted from physical crimes to digital. Why risk robbery, theft, and assault in the real world, where one can be so easily identified and potentially apprehended or physically harmed, when he could instead perpetrate those crimes online, behind a shroud of cloaked IP addresses with illicit gains paid in cryptocurrency?

Under dozens of online personas and pseudonyms, most frequently variants of his primary handle "Burner," Mr. Stoller's scams worked better than he ever could have imagined. He became emboldened as his crimes escalated—an extortion here, some racketeering there—and pretty soon it added up to real money. The San Francisco Bay Area proved to be a target-rich environment, with plenty of wealthy people he could prey on. Shane pulled in over $500,000 in 2019 alone—all while pretending to be a lowly Uber driver making a mere $60,000 annual salary. But that wasn't enough for him. He started to organize. He realized he could make even more money by training others and taking a cut of their scams. Before he knew it, Shane had more money than he knew what to do with. So he decided to apply his ill-gotten gains to an ever-escalating sequence of scams and stunts intended to instigate civil unrest.

Ultimately, Shane's goal became the downfall of the United States government and our entire financial system. Acts of sedition and treason designed for his personal gain. His elaborate scheme brought in more and more unstable disciples as it brought in more and more money. His rhetoric became increasingly extreme, paranoid, unhinged—explicitly directing the premeditated acts he stands accused of here today. Shane Stoller isn't a hero. He isn't a patriot. He's a selfish, narcissistic profit-monger who sold out his family, friends, and followers to make himself rich—that's it. A charlatan willing to kill fellow citizens and terrorize his own country for his personal gain. As I am confident you will agree, beyond a reasonable doubt, upon presentation of the evidence.

Thank you, Your Honor.

JUDGE MORENO: Thank you, Ms. Gibson.

DEFENSE OPENING STATEMENT

JUDGE MORENO: Mr. Young, as you have been warned on several occasions, you and your legal team are not to discuss this case with members of the media. If you do so again, I will find you in contempt of court. Do you understand?

MR. YOUNG: Yes, Your Honor.

JUDGE MORENO: I will not have this conversation with you again, Mr. Young. Now, please proceed with your opening statement.

MR. YOUNG: Thank you, Your Honor. Ladies and gentlemen of the jury, spectators in the courtroom, my name is Wayne Young. I have voluntarily agreed to represent the accused, Mr. Shane Thomas Stoller. *Why would I do that?* you might ask. Because I believe to my core in every person's right to counsel, and I have dedicated my career to that belief. I've been honored to represent clients at the center of some very prominent cases. There have been times when I have questioned my belief in legal representation, questioned the motives and morals of my clients. This is not one of those times—not one of those cases, not one of those clients. I am honored to defend this client, Shane Stoller. Indeed, I can't help but feel my entire career has led me to this point.

The bedrock principles of our very nation—freedom of speech, freedom of the press, freedom of assembly, freedom of religion—are on trial here. These are foundational

American rights, enshrined in our Constitution. They are the defining values of our nation. My client has a belief system. It may not be one you agree with. You may even find it objectionable or offensive. But it is his right, protected by our legal system. A right our forefathers fought to defend. Mr. Stoller committed no crime by exercising that right.

The prosecution will dubiously attempt to claim that Mr. Stoller is the individual behind the online account known as Burner_911. Despite the fact they have no direct evidence he created, posted, or ever even logged in to that account, they will weave a tale, based solely on circumstantial evidence and deliberate misdirection, to assert that it was Mr. Stoller behind the keyboard. It was not. But I submit to you here that *it does not matter*.

You can all read the posts by Burner_911. They are all right there on Razgo.com for anyone to read. They are submitted here as evidence. There is nothing to hide. Irrespective of authorship, the core question you must answer is if these posts incited violence sufficient to rise to the level of capital punishment. If, through words and nothing more, the person or persons behind Burner_911 specifically directed others to steal, kidnap, extort, maim, and murder. If these words, in and of themselves, constitute an act of domestic terrorism and treason. Capital offenses for which my defendant could receive the death penalty.

I can't let that happen. *You* can't let that happen. We cannot sit by and allow a person, *any* person, whose only crime is expressing his opinion, typed on a keyboard and transmitted online, to be accused and convicted of such heinous crimes. Words don't kill people; people kill people. Even in this expedited political witch hunt of a trial, we cannot ignore due process and the rights enshrined in our Constitution.

BURNER

What you will come to recognize, as I have in preparing for this case, is that my client, Mr. Stoller, is virtuous. As much as any of us, he recognizes what is unjust and unfair in our society and has taken action to rectify it. The federal government wants to punish him for a demonstration, but they refuse to address the societal issues that caused that demonstration in the first place. Crimes may have been committed by those devoted to the BurnOutz movement, but history has taught us that disruptive acts are sometimes required to effect change. In our current society, by our current criminal law statutes, some of these acts may constitute crimes. But history judges these acts of societal defiance differently. Was it a crime when American colonists dumped tea into Boston Harbor in defiance of the British government's taxation without representation? Was it a crime when Rosa Parks sat in the whites-only section of a city bus in Montgomery, Alabama? Every alleged crime requires context, and the context for Mr. Stoller is that his beliefs are not motivated by personal gains but by a desire to correct what is unfair, unjust, and unacceptable in the world. For that, I consider him a patriot in the truest sense of that word.

Every American has the right to counsel, but this American, Mr. Stoller, *deserves* one. Once all the evidence has been presented, all the testimony gathered, I'm confident you will agree with me and acquit.

18

SHANE

Dr. Susan is ruthless. Diving into the dumpster fire of my childhood with sadistic enthusiasm. Probing for trauma, missed diagnoses. Childhood incidents that I've tried hard to forget, that explain what I've become, that I could use as an excuse for my actions. I keep having to remind myself that her agenda is the opposite of every other shrink I've seen—not trying to prove I'm broken, but to prove I'm *sane*. To show I'm logical, rational, capable of understanding right from wrong and planning for my future . . . so that they can put a lethal injection in me.

"So once you were in the custody of CDSS, the story of Shane Stoller starts to get filled in a little more," she says, looking at her thick binder like she's reading a dinner menu at TGI Friday's. "Besides your mother, you had no next of kin. Your case worker mentioned your 'high intelligence' in her intake notes, but also your 'underdeveloped interpersonal skills, obsessive tendencies, and lack of impulse control.' Despite that, she was able to place you with a foster family—Judy and Ray Stiles. Tell me about your time living with the Stiles family."

"What do you want to know?" I ask. But I know exactly what she expects me to say. The usual horror stories about foster families—booze, drugs, physical and sexual abuse. All the "poor me" excuses to justify my antisocial behavior.

"What was life like with them, day to day?" she says. "Particularly anything your case worker might not have been aware of."

"Well, they were professional foster hosts, for sure," I say. "They were always taking in kids, working the system, getting paid. But CDSS knew that—they'd been a foster mill for years."

That moment when the CDSS lady first dropped me off is etched on my brain like a chemical burn. My new "mom," Judy, was huge—as big as the couch she was parked on. She reached out to give me a hug. All I could see were these big bags of flesh dangling from each arm, like they were going to smother me. There was no way I was hugging her. Not a big deal, it turned out. She forgot about the hug as soon as the case worker was gone. She hardly ever left that couch—drifting between watching TV and sleeping, always eating. At least she didn't drink.

"Were your foster parents abusive in any way toward you?" she asks.

"Nah, they mostly ignored us," I say. "Ray could be a dick sometimes, but as long as we stayed out of his way, we could pretty much do whatever we wanted."

Ray, my foster "dad," was in construction, so he was gone every morning before I woke up. Physically, he was the opposite of Judy— short, with wiry muscles and tough-looking tattoos he thought masked his scrawny frame. He'd been in the army, but after Vietnam and before the Gulf War, so he'd never seen combat. You would think he'd be strict, but he barely paid attention to me and my foster brothers. He would just crack a beer, pop some pain meds, and then crash in his recliner, complaining out loud about whatever was on Fox News.

"Sounds like they were negligent," Dr. Susan says. "Were there any rules in their household? Any structure or discipline?"

"Ray wouldn't let any of us touch his La-Z-Boy."

"What about the other foster children in the family? Did any of them bully you or physically or sexually abuse you at any point?"

"No." I shake my head. "We actually looked out for each other, especially Nico and me."

"Nico is Nicolas Valencia, a foster brother who was your age, correct?"

"Yes."

"Nicolas Valencia was deposed in the investigation," Wayne says to Valerie. He's scanning a list of witnesses from the prosecution and circles Nico's name.

"Tell me more about him," Dr. Susan says. "Isn't he the one who got you into drugs?"

"You mean, like, smoking pot?" Memories of Nico run through my head. Him teaching me all sorts of Spanish words so I could talk with the other foster kids. Shoplifting snack cakes from the 7-Eleven so we'd have something for lunch. And smoking pot. By fifth grade, Nico and I were smoking a *lot* of pot. He first gave me my nickname, Burner, since I was always lighting up. Like my birth mom, I guess—a little habit to make each day more bearable.

"Yes, illegal drugs. Didn't you and Nico both use and sell drugs?" she asks.

"Not that I ever got busted for," I say.

"Perhaps not by law enforcement, but it's in your CDSS file," she says.

"I'm sure it is," I say. "I didn't have much choice. I needed the money." Not just to buy more pot but for notebooks, a backpack, a phone, a laptop—all the stuff most kids took for granted. I wasn't going to get any of that from Judy and Ray. When you're dealt a shit hand, you gotta do what you gotta do. So, when a white kid asked me to buy some weed, I charged him double what I paid. Pretty soon, I was making proper bank. It was my first successful business.

Dr. Susan drops the drug thing and consults her notes. "So, you were with the Stiles foster family until 2010, is that correct? The year they got foreclosed."

Ah, the foreclosure—the point when things came properly unhinged. By then, Nico and I weren't spending much time there anyway. We mostly hung out at Dré's, Nico's uncle's. It was a mutually agreeable deal—Judy and Ray got to keep collecting subsidies without the hassle and expense of us, and we could do whatever the hell we wanted without CDSS coming down on us. But after they lost the house, everything unraveled. Ray bailed—legit just packed a bag and left, didn't say a word to any of us—and Judy got forklifted to a transitional housing shelter outside Modesto. The other kids got transferred to other foster families or put in a group care home. So that left Nico and me.

Our case worker, Rebecca, wasn't happy about placing Nico with Dré, who had a record and was all tatted up like a thug. But Dré was blood, so he became Nico's legal guardian. As for me—Rebecca didn't know what the hell to do with me. Other foster families didn't want a stoner teenager, and I was too young for transitional housing. Ideally, they'd have put me back with my mom, but they couldn't find her. Tracy Stoller had bounced from the court-mandated rehab. I found out a couple years later she'd OD'd at a highway rest stop near Flagstaff.

With nowhere to put me, Rebecca was out of options. Dré said he'd take me. So he became my legal guardian too.

"That's right," I say to Dr. Susan. "I moved in with Nico's uncle, Dré."

"Not exactly a child-friendly environment," Dr. Susan says, tapping the point of her pen on a folder. "It was Nico's uncle who got you involved in more serious criminal activity, correct?"

"Dré was an entrepreneur. He had a business up in Manteca—"

"A business? You mean stealing automobiles?"

"Well, yeah, sometimes, but he had four or five guys working for him at an auto body shop."

"Yes, but you didn't really believe it was a legitimate business, did you? It was a front for selling stolen car parts—a scheme you were later implicated in. Tell me, Shane, do you consider illegal criminal activity to be normal?"

"Only if you want to make money," I say.

What did I know about normal? Obviously, I knew Dré was running a chop shop, but it seemed pretty normal to me. Just making a living with employees like any other business. His best supplier was a guy named Lorenzo. "Zo" would always get the nicest cars, likely from drug dealers or cartel guys, which Dré always told him not to do because of the risk of retaliation. I was on the liquidation side. Finding buyers for parts on the Internet. I was good at dark web stuff by then, and I showed Dré how to move parts online without getting caught. He taught me a ton too. He had all these sayings that he'd repeat over and over, like, "If you wanna make money, someone's gotta lose money." Meaning, money is a zero-sum game; if you want it, you need to go get it from someone else. That one was always my favorite.

"Would you describe Dré as a father figure?" Dr. Susan asks.

I don't reply, so she continues with her dollar-store psychoanalysis.

"I can imagine that, for a boy who lost his biological father at a young age, then lived with an absent foster father, you must have looked up to Dré. Learned from him how to behave. How to be a man."

It's not a question, so I let the thoughts run through my head for a second. The fact is, Dré looked out for us. I always felt safe at his house. Like I was useful and good at something. Earned my keep. And believe it or not, Dré also taught us discipline. One time, he caught Nico and me with a tiny amount of meth that Zo had given us to sell at school. He came down on us hard. Explained how getting a kid hooked could destroy an innocent life. We got the message. There were rules, even as criminals, about who you could and could *not* hurt. There were no victimless crimes, so you'd better choose your victims carefully.

"Nah." I shake my head. "I taught myself how to be a man."

19

CHLOE

"Where's my phone?" I ask.

Nick is awake now. My hood is back on, but I know it's him from the sound of his movements—impatiently clamoring through the cabinets, grumbling expletives under his breath. He must still have it; he wouldn't trust it with anyone else. Slow footsteps approach, pause in front of me; the wooden chair creaks. I can smell the musty wool of his knit hat.

"What do you think this is? Prison? You don't get a phone call here."

"I just . . . I wondered," I say, cautious, trying to weigh his mood without facial expressions to guide me, "if it got many views. The other guy didn't know. Did anyone . . . respond? You know, to your post?" Of course, I also wonder how quickly law enforcement will triangulate my phone, find our exact location from geotags in the photo, surround the house, take positions, kick down the door, shoot my assailants, and potentially kill me in the crossfire.

"Are you kidding?" Nick's voice is practically gleeful. "That post about broke the internet."

I hear rumblings of the others around me now too—Scooter's raspy chuckle, the flick of a lighter, first puff of a cigarette, slurps of coffee. When they move, it is with familiarity of this place. Based on the porch and hallway, I picture a run-down craftsman, old but solidly built—hardwood floors, thick beams separating the rooms—sparsely furnished and dimly lit, with plywood over the windows. *Does one of them live here? Do they all? Or is this a covert destination—part of a more elaborate plan?*

"Yeah, it definitely went viral, but not just your fans," another voice, Pete's, says. His cigarette flares as he draws at it, then he says in an exhale of smoke that creeps through my hood, "Most of 'em fucking hate you." He takes on an affected tone, reading comments: "*Y'all should pop a cap in that bitch; She's not worth the bullet; LOL, I guess that's what she really looks like without makeup and filters; Let her burn*; and on and on and on." I hear the accelerating swipes of his finger across a phone screen, rowing down a never-ending stream.

"I thought you were more, I don't know . . . *popular*," Scooter says. They all laugh.

"People love to hate." I move my shoulders in the faintest of dismissive shrugs. "But I'm not asking about the trolls. I'm asking about the authorities. Is there any chance they'll let Shane go? Did they even reply to your demand?"

"I haven't bothered to look," Nick says. "We're in no rush. The longer this whole thing drags out, the more recruits we get. It's like Waco or Ruby Ridge. People get pissed off when their government acts like a police state."

"Yeah, but—I mean, how would you know? You didn't provide a way for, like, anyone to contact you. The only way to respond is with a comment on my account." My mind races ahead of me. "You need to log in, look at it, to see if—"

"I don't need to do *shit!*" Nick cuts me off.

I pause, adrenaline coursing through me, summoning a sense of determination that whatever happens will happen. "It's not just that . . ." I speak these words slowly, cautiously. Once I understand I will be allowed to continue, I say, "I mean . . . you live-streamed yourselves kidnapping me. Millions of people saw you. You posted, from *my* phone, *here*. Don't you think . . . that the police will find this place?"

"Wait . . . 'cause of your *phone*?" Nick asks rhetorically, his smugness restored. "Oh, sweetheart, your phone is two hundred miles from here."

They all laugh again.

"And all those live streams and photos and social posts were from hacked accounts with geotagging turned off," Pete says. "You think we're fucking stupid?"

"No, I didn't mean that." I sit silent for a moment, considering my next statement. "I'm not saying anyone's stupid. I'm just saying I don't understand the plan. Burner_911 always has a plan. Didn't he order you to do this?"

"We don't take orders from anyone," Nick says, speaking generally but answering the specific question on my mind.

"But . . . you're part of the movement, right?" I say, expecting to be cut off again with each word. "You were there for October 12th. Aren't you BurnOutz?"

That triggers another round of laughter.

"Sure, you could say we're 'part of the movement,'" Pete says after they've settled down. "Think of us as the *teeth* part."

"We're the Black Mountain Militia," Nick says. "We believe in the *mission* of the BurnOutz, but the *methods* are too soft. This war won't be won with keyboards. If we're gonna take back our country, it'll be with guns."

His declaration squeezes the air out of my lungs. This is what Shane was going on about. The spawning of fringe groups, each more extreme, more paranoid, more violent. Piggybacking on the momentum of the BurnOutz to advance their own narrow agendas. Cells within splinters within factions. Increasingly unpredictable, unaccountable, uncontrollable.

"So . . . you're acting on your own?" I finally say. "This Chloe-for-Shane hostage swap thing was all . . . your idea?"

"Someone had to do it," Scooter says. "We can't have the Feds taking one of our own. We have the training, the equipment, the—"

"That's enough," Nick says. "If we tell her all our secrets, there won't be any surprises left."

I can hear the snide grin in his voice, feel them exchanging self-satisfied looks. Someone takes a slow drag on his cigarette. This is my chance. I gather myself.

"All I'm saying is, if that's still the plan—to get Shane out—then I can help. You need to make sure your message gets through. You need to put pressure on them. And I know how to do that."

20

PRESS CONFERENCE TRANSCRIPT

KIANA BRYANT, FBI SPECIAL AGENT IN CHARGE
SONJA KUMARA, SAN FRANCISCO CHIEF OF POLICE
October 13, 2023

MS. BRYANT: Thank you for coming today. My name is Kiana Bryant and I am Special Agent in Charge of the San Francisco Field Office, overseeing the Federal Bureau of Investigation's Joint Task Force investigating the events of October 12th. Today we will be providing a briefing on our ongoing investigation into the abduction of Chloe Corbin. I can assure you, we are committing every law enforcement resource at the bureau's disposal to ensure Ms. Corbin's safe return.

After our initial assessment that this abduction was a spontaneous act spawned from the riots on October 12th, we now believe this kidnapping was premeditated by a coordinated team of at least four individuals. Although the perpetrators leveraged social media, live-streaming apps, and on-site demonstrations to agitate their followers, those efforts were designed to provide a crowd of other potential suspects, thereby concealing their identity and distracting investigators.

The FBI has been investigating the online group known as the BurnOutz for over a year, and we believe the individuals responsible for Ms. Corbin's abduction were part of a loosely affiliated syndicate of what the bureau calls "domestic violent extremists"—followers of the BurnOutz movement, organized into small operational cells or militias, who enact, either explicitly or indirectly, the edicts of the group's leaders. These cells prepare tactical plans, conduct cyberattacks, facilitate illegal payments, launder money, acquire and stockpile weapons, falsify identities, operate safe houses, and organize other criminal activities using end-to-end encrypted messaging apps and unmoderated dark web platforms. Many of the members of these cells are believed to be current or former military personnel, with advanced training in tactical combat skills, crowd control, and extraction techniques, as well as firearms, forensics, information technology, and other skills. In short, this movement has jumped from an online fringe group to a well-organized domestic terrorist syndicate.

As you know, Shane Stoller was arrested Thursday and accused of creating and operating the Burner_911 profile, the mastermind behind the BurnOutz movement. Although he was already in custody at the time she was taken, we believe Mr. Stoller may have orchestrated Ms. Corbin's abduction. We have identified, apprehended, and questioned several individuals who were present during Ms. Corbin's abduction, but none who were directly involved in the plot. At this time, all that is known about the kidnappers' motive is the post to Ms. Corbin's Instagram account, the authenticity of which is still being verified, that demands Mr. Stoller's release from federal custody in exchange for Ms. Corbin. Let me be clear, that is not going to happen. There will be no quid pro quo negotiation in this matter.

Apart from that post, there has been no direct communication of any kind between the kidnappers and law enforcement officials. However, thanks to the tireless efforts of this Joint Task Force, which now numbers over five thousand state, local, and federal investigators, we have a number of leads in Ms. Corbin's case. Based on a wide variety of investigative techniques, we have identified the lead suspect as Nicholas Harper. Here is an identification photo of Mr. Harper, who was dishonorably discharged from the US Army in June of 2020. He is a white male, age thirty-four, approximately five feet nine inches tall, with a heavyset build. He has brown eyes, thin brown hair, and can be seen in these surveillance photos wearing a red, white, and blue knit winter hat. He is considered armed and extremely dangerous.

We have also confirmed that the perpetrators fled the scene of Ms. Corbin's apartment in her black Cadillac Escalade SUV. Authorities have recovered the burned remnants of that vehicle in a secluded location along the Hayward

PRESS CONFERENCE TRANSCRIPT

Regional Shoreline. No human remains were found inside. Based on surveillance footage and eyewitness accounts, we believe the suspects transferred to a white 2006 Chevrolet Impala sedan that was reported stolen two days earlier. That vehicle was detected heading eastbound on Interstate 580 at 10:37 a.m. and again northbound on State Highway 84 at 11:23 a.m. on October 12th. Based on those sightings, we believe the suspects remain within the state of California or possibly Nevada and are likely holding Ms. Corbin at one of the group's safe houses.

CHP also recovered Ms. Corbin's mobile phone from a gas station garbage can in Hollister. The device was apparently dropped there, possibly as a decoy for law enforcement, likely by another accomplice. It had no identifiable fingerprints or DNA on it. The photograph of Ms. Corbin that appears to have been taken by her abductors was posted using a clone of her phone, and the image itself was scrubbed of any identifiable geotags or other metadata.

We will be providing additional updates as we have more information. In the meantime, the FBI is seeking the public's assistance in locating Ms. Corbin and bringing the individuals responsible to justice. We are offering a monetary reward of up to $1 million for information leading to the identification, arrest, and prosecution of the persons responsible. We ask anyone with information about these suspects, or Ms. Corbin's whereabouts, to contact us immediately at 1-857-386-2000 or online at tips.fbi.gov. Thank you.

21

SHANE

Dr. Susan *Fucking* Campbell.

I can't stay in this room with her another second. The overpowering stench of her drugstore perfume. The groaning straps of her flesh-colored bra, visible under her faded rayon blouse. But most of all, her patronizing stare. Her I'm-here-for-you expression of condescending sympathy. Her barely disguised arrogance, confident in the belief she's better than me. Fracking me to extract all the traumatic events in my past. To solidify her superiority. To determine whether I'm crazy while reassuring herself she's not.

"Do you need a break?" Wayne asks me.

"Nah, I'm good," I say. "I told you already, this is all in the police report."

Dr. Susan flops open her jowls once again. "Were you concerned about Nico when the raid happened? You described him as a brother."

I remember watching Nico, Zo, and another guy named Javi jump the chain-link fence in Dré's backyard when the cops showed up. I was inside, uploading pictures of inventory to various sites. I knew I was screwed when everyone else bolted like they were running for their lives. Nico told me later they eventually lost the cops by running across ten lanes of traffic on I-5.

I watched them cuff Dré and Jesus from the bedroom window. I was smart enough to drive a drill bit through the laptop, but I wasn't fast enough to run and had nowhere to hide. I came out with my hands up.

The police thought at first maybe I was kidnapped or something, cause I looked young and surrendered. Also, I knew even then, 'cause I'm white.

The media coverage of the raid was all bullshit. They made Dré and Jesus out to be these gangster drug dealers. The reality was that he was just running a business, even if it was an illegal one. Dré was independent—he wasn't affiliated with any gang and pushed back on anyone in his crew who was. He didn't deal drugs. He didn't do armed robberies. He didn't even own a gun. He was just trying to make a living the only way an ex-con could.

That didn't stop them from describing him as a dangerous street thug when they showed his mug shot on TV. Sometimes the story people want to believe sells better than the truth.

"Yeah, obviously, I didn't want Nico to get caught," I say. "He was undocumented, so . . . he knew if he got arrested, he might get deported."

"Were you worried about yourself?" Dr. Susan asks.

I shake my head. Even though I was arrested, I knew I wouldn't get in much trouble. I hadn't technically been caught stealing a car, so no grand theft charge. The police had a hard time pinning any charges on me at all. They couldn't tie me back to any of the online accounts. Plus, I was fifteen, so the most they could give me was a juvenile misdemeanor. I was lucky.

Dré and Jesus had it way worse—they were both convicted and sentenced to three years. They at least got paroled after eighteen months.

"And after Dré was paroled, you kept living with him?"

I nod.

"So, were you at his house during the . . . incident?"

After Dré got paroled, he let Nico and me keep staying with him. He got me a car, too—not even a stolen one, a gray Kia with a spoiler that he bought legitimately, thanks for the work I'd done while he was in prison to keep cash flowing in. Things were good for a while.

Then, one night, Dré, Jesus, Javi, Zo, and a couple of other guys were playing poker in the kitchen. Nico and I were watching TV in the living room when we heard their voices getting louder. There was a big pot and Dré was trash-talking Zo. Something about the *jefe* always beating the *ladronito*. When Zo went all in, Dré slapped down his winning hand, stood with both arms over his head and shouted, "*If you wanna make money, someone's gotta lose money, puta!*"

Zo pulled a revolver from his waistband and shot Dré in the face.

"Can you describe how you felt?" Dr. Susan asks.

I blast through a montage of PTSD flashbacks, like zombies in an FPS. Nico and me scrambling toward the door. Gunshots reverberating off the stucco walls. Zo's back to us as he empties his chamber. Dré thrown against the wall with a flap of his face dangling. The other guys frozen in that moment of time, spattered with blood, knowing any attempt to intervene will only put a bullet in them too. Survival instinct taking over. Nico running down the street shirtless in a pair of ripped jeans. Me without my shoes or wallet, but somehow my car keys. Clipping rearview mirrors as we screech down the street. My life changed in an instant. Again.

"We didn't exactly have time to process our feelings," I say. "We just got the hell out of there."

"Witnessing someone you love get murdered right in front of you is incredibly traumatic," Dr. Susan says, contorting her face again into a practiced expression of sympathy. "That series of life events would have derailed a lot of kids. Did you receive any grief counseling to help deal with that loss?"

I can't help but laugh. "Grief counseling? Who was gonna pay for that?"

"Your CDSS case worker should have referred you to a state psychiatrist."

"Yeah, right—some pedo shrink? No thanks."

"It's just difficult for me to believe that you weren't suppressing some unresolved emotions. Or, perhaps . . . you didn't have those emotions in the first place?"

What does she expect me to say? That seeing Dré get gunned down in front of me was like living a nightmare? That I was crushed with guilt about not even trying to help him? That we just ran like a couple of pussies? That I lived in fear for weeks, expecting Zo to hunt us down? That I've lost everyone I've ever loved—Dré, my dad, my mom, now maybe Chloe?

"So that's my choice, huh?" I say, leaning toward her. "Tell you I had no emotions, which makes me a psychopath, or tell you I blamed the world, which turned me into a terrorist. That's what you're trying to show, right? That I'm sane. That I knew the consequences. And yet I methodically planned the downfall of a broken system. Tell me, Doctor, when you go home to the dingy apartment you can't afford on your government salary, don't *you* feel like the system is rigged?"

Dr. Susan shifts uncomfortably, then blathers some lame-ass response. Something about knowing the difference between right and wrong. Something about predictable behavior patterns. Something about narcissistic personality disorder, acting on impulses, craving attention, conforming to societal norms.

But I'm tired of her psychobabble; I've checked out. As she drones on in that intolerable monotone I know so well—the familiar, unrelenting, *insistent* voice of control—I just let it wash over me. It's the same old self-righteous lecture of every teacher, therapist, and case worker I've ever met. With their trite classifications—ADHD, anxiety, depression, OCD. Their prescriptions—Adderall, Dexedrine, Ritalin. Medicating away any act of individuality or defiance. An entire industrial complex dedicated to ensuring complacency, obedience, subservience. The pharmaceutical tools of repression, disguised as compassion. That was my real rebellion—defying all the Dr. Susans of the world telling me what to do, what I'm allowed to say. Trying to control me. Sedate me. Manipulate me. Hijack me for their agenda.

I won't let them.

She's been talking forever. My eyes are rolling back in my head when Wayne finally steps in—tells Dr. Susan that she's got what she needs, and that I won't be pleading insanity anyway.

I watch her gather her notes and files and shove it all into a giant three-ring binder, like the kind I wanted when I was a kid.

"Goodbye, Doctor," I say as she shuffles out of the room. "It's been a pleasure."

The two guards who brought me here return and disconnect me from the interrogation table.

"Okay, we've got a shit-ton of discovery documents to get through, so

Val and I are heading back to the office," Wayne says. "That was a lot. Nice job keeping your cool. We're gonna get through this as fast as we can. I'll be back tomorrow. In the meantime, just lay low and watch your back."

I nod and the guards lead me out of the room, through the gerbil tunnel of passageways and locked doors toward my cell. From the communal area below, one of the other inmates suddenly shouts, "Believe in The Plan!" A series of shouts and whistles follows.

I don't react to any of it.

Inside my cell, Kryz, as the other guards call him, the one with the smudgy glasses, barrel chest, and buzz cut, stares me down while the other one, Killian, removes my handcuffs. As Killian moves toward the door, eyes on me, Kryz unbuttons the cuff of his tan corrections officer shirt and starts rolling up his sleeve, like he's getting ready to beat the shit out of me.

Then, I see it, just below a "Don't Tread on Me" emblem with the snake and everything. A "Plan B" tattoo.

"We got your back," Kryz says, looking down at his forearm to make sure I see it before rolling his sleeve back down. "Whatever you need, let us know."

22

WAYNE

The heavy steel door unlocks with an electric buzz, releasing me and Valerie into the lobby of the San Francisco County Jail. My home away from home.

"They still here?" I ask the officer staffing the metal detector.

"Yup," he says, nodding toward the lobby doors and the mob of reporters clustered outside.

"Christ, I really need a cigarette, but if I make another statement, the judge'll cut my nuts off," I say.

He points down a hallway. "Door at the end of the hall is a maintenance entrance. You can smoke outside there, in the alley. That's where we all go."

I thank him, and we walk down the hall, Valerie's high heels echoing off the marble walls. She pushes the bar of the maintenance door, and we step into the alley. The fog is swirling, making it hard to light up.

"What do you think?" Valerie asks once we've each taken a drag.

"I think you must be freezing your ass off." I point to her short skirt.

"Yeah, I am. Tell me what you think about Shane. Quick."

"Well, he's definitely sane. But we were never going to plead insanity anyway."

Valerie nods and clasps her cigarette between her lips to stop her teeth from chattering.

"Honestly, he's not what I expected," she says. "I thought he'd be more, I don't know—diabolical or something. He seems to care more about rescuing his girlfriend than he does about the cause."

"He does, doesn't he." I look at my phone, but don't see the message I'm expecting. I shudder with cold as I put it back in my pocket. "I hate this fucking city."

"You've mentioned that, about a hundred times. So, you think it's really him?" She flicks ash into a storm drain.

"Probably." I look up at the freeway overpass hulking over the building. "The Feds have been investigating him for months. They wouldn't have brought the indictment if they didn't have a strong case. But it might not matter. For now, we have to prepare his defense like we're all-in. Until we know for sure how this is going to play out. The most important thing is the movement."

Valerie nods again and pushes a loose strand of her trendy hairdo over her ear. I drop my butt onto the concrete and crush it with my shoe as I feel my phone vibrate.

The caller ID displays what I expected. One word: Bob. I turn the screen to show Valerie.

"I gotta take this."

23

GRAND JURY INDICTMENT

**TRANSCRIPT OF SWORN DEPOSITION
OF NICOLAS VALENCIA, JULY 18, 2023**

Nicolas Valencia, Deponent
Daniel Romero, Counsel for the Deponent
Annabelle Burgess, Assistant US Attorney

COURTROOM DEPUTY: Raise your right hand, please. Do you solemnly swear that you will tell the truth, the whole truth, and nothing but the truth, so help you God?

MR. VALENCIA: I do.

MS. BURGESS: Thank you for testifying today, Mr. Valencia. I would remind you that this deposition is taken under oath. If any of your testimony today is discovered to be untruthful, you could be charged with perjury. Do you understand?

MR. VALENCIA: Yes, ma'am.

MR. ROMERO: I would like to state for the record that the US Attorney's Office has offered my client, Nicolas Valencia, immunity with respect to his immigration status and potential deportation, as well as any crimes he may or may not have committed during the time he was an acquaintance of Mr. Shane Stoller, the subject of this investigation.

MS. BURGESS: Thank you, Mr. Romero. Yes, that is correct. The US Attorney's Office agrees not to pursue criminal charges and will advise state and local law enforcement not to pursue criminal charges against the deponent based on his undocumented status or any self-incriminating testimony provided today. Mr. Valencia, could you start by telling us how you knew the subject of this investigation, Shane Stoller?

MR. VALENCIA: We were foster brothers. Not blood related, but we had the same foster parents, Ray and Judy Stiles in Turlock.

MS. BURGESS: How did you enter the foster care system?

MR. VALENCIA: My parents were both killed in an attempted burglary. CDSS wouldn't let me stay with my uncle at first 'cause he had a record. So they put me with Judy and Ray.

MS. BURGESS: How long have you known Mr. Stoller?

MR. VALENCIA: Since he first came to live with Judy and Ray. I was nine, so, like, 2008. We're around the same age, so we were like brothers.

MS. BURGESS: You introduced Shane to your uncle, Andrés Valencia. Is that correct?

MR. VALENCIA: Yes, ma'am.

MS. BURGESS: And it was in 2016 that your uncle was arrested for operating an auto theft ring, correct?

MR. VALENCIA: Yes, ma'am. He had guys who would steal cars, then they'd take them apart and sell the parts.

MS. BURGESS: And what, exactly, did the defendant, Mr. Stoller, do for your uncle?

MR. VALENCIA: Shane was really good at finding buyers online without getting caught. You know, like, hiding his real identity. Dré didn't know how to do that, so Shane set everything up. He found fencing sites for car parts, then created a bunch of fake users to post merchandise and collect payments and stuff. He made it so nobody could trace nothing back to us. If a profile got shut down or an account got locked, he'd create ten new ones. Only reason we got busted was 'cause a neighbor saw Zo and Javi drop off a car and called the cops.

MS. BURGESS: Your uncle served eighteen months of a three-year sentence. But Mr. Stoller, then a minor, escaped with probation. Did you and Mr. Stoller continue to sell stolen car parts while your uncle was in prison?

MR. VALENCIA: Yes. All the inventory at Dré's house was confiscated in the raid, but there was a bunch of stuff stashed at Jesus's girlfriend's house. Shane was able to move that online and keep income coming in. Truth is, that worked so well we ended up expanding. It was what Shane had been trying to convince Dré about for a while—that he didn't need to actually hold the inventory, just connect the buyer and seller. It was much less dangerous—no possession of stolen goods, no neighbors to rat us out, no cops knocking down our door. Shane moved everything virtual.

MS. BURGESS: Was anyone helping you?

MR. VALENCIA: We had a whole network of guys. Most of them we never seen, which was good 'cause we were just sixteen. They'd just send us pictures, we'd sell the items, and they'd ship stuff directly to the buyer.

MS. BURGESS: So, would you say Shane was running the entire operation at that point?

MR. VALENCIA: Pretty much.

MS. BURGESS: It was around this time that you both enrolled at Central Valley University, correct?

MR. VALENCIA: Yeah. I got held back my sophomore year of high school. So Shane and me started at CVU the same year. We lived together that year, but we started to drift apart.

MS. BURGESS: Why is that?

MR. VALENCIA: I guess we just got interested in different things. I really liked working on cars, and I was studying to become a mechanic. But Shane thought that was a dead-end job. He was more into computers and playing video games.

MS. BURGESS: At that time, how many hours per day, on average, would you say Mr. Stoller spent online?

MR. VALENCIA: A lot. Probably four or five hours at school, then he would get online as soon as we got home, late into the night. Maybe another eight to ten hours, sometimes more.

MS. BURGESS: So between twelve and fifteen hours per day?

MR. VALENCIA: Yeah, around that.

MS. BURGESS: Was it around that time that Mr. Stoller started posting videos online?

MR. VALENCIA: Yeah, I thought it was kind of crazy, honestly. But he'd take videos of himself playing *Call of Duty* or some other video game and upload it to MySpace or YouTube. They were kinda funny, cause he'd swear and stuff. But I couldn't believe people would actually watch them. He got a ton of subscribers from it.

MS. BURGESS: And what username did Mr. Stoller post videos under?

MR. VALENCIA: BurnerBro.

MS. BURGESS: In these videos of himself playing violent first-person shooter games, Mr. Stoller would refer to "burning" categories of people he didn't like as he shot other players. Some of the terminology he used included "social justice warriors," "global elites," and "cultural Marxists." Does that sound familiar?

MR. VALENCIA: That was just Shane being Shane. He would do it to trigger people. He was just unfiltered, you know? I think that's why people liked it.

MS. BURGESS: Okay, but you are aware that some people found his commentary to be misogynistic? Meaning that it was prejudiced and offensive to women.

MR. VALENCIA: Yeah, and that pissed him off. He didn't mean it that way, but he also didn't want people telling him what he could and couldn't say. So he'd just say it more, and, the more stuff like that he said, the more followers he got.

MS. BURGESS: There was another category of people Mr. Stoller particularly singled out in his videos: wealthy people. There was one video titled "Banks and Billionaires" that he posted during the time the two of you were living together. Are you familiar with that?

MR. VALENCIA: Yeah, I watched it.

MS. BURGESS: What was the nature of that video?

MR. VALENCIA: It was a typical BurnerBro video. Just Shane shooting people in *Call of Duty*. Except in this one, every time he makes a kill, he says the name of some billionaire he wished he was shooting instead.

MS. BURGESS: Why did he have so much anger directed at billionaires?

MR. VALENCIA: He just didn't think it was fair. He knew all this stuff, about how, like, the system really works. He'd always talk about banks and billionaires getting bailed out while regular people like us were getting screwed. How poor folks like Judy and Ray were losing their homes and filing for bankruptcy while these billionaires were getting free money. He thought they should be going to jail. It just seemed really unfair to him.

MS. BURGESS: So, even then, would you say Mr. Stoller was building an ideological following?

MR. VALENCIA: Sorta. The more he talked about that stuff, the more followers he got. It was like that became the thing that was most important to him.

MS. BURGESS: And, to your knowledge, did Mr. Stoller ever exploit that audience for his own personal gain?

MR. VALENCIA: Yeah, he started driving for Uber around then—as a side hustle just to earn some cash, like, legit. But he's kinda paranoid, so he recorded everything on one of those dash cams, and sometimes he'd post it on his YouTube account.

MS. BURGESS: For the purpose of extorting money, correct?

MR. VALENCIA: I don't know. I think he was just trying to show what assholes these—

MS. BURGESS: Mr. Valencia, I'll remind you that you are under oath. Are you aware of Mr. Stoller ever demanding money from passengers he posted videos of?

MR. VALENCIA: Yeah, a few times. He said it was easy money.

MS. BURGESS: When was your last contact with Mr. Stoller?

MR. VALENCIA: Not since CVU. So, like, 2018.

MS. BURGESS: In the approximately ten years you knew Mr. Stoller, were you aware of any other close friends he had besides you?

MR. VALENCIA: No, not really. He never went to classes, never made other friends. It got so the only people he'd talk to were online.

MS. BURGESS: Are you familiar with the anonymous online account Burner_911?

MR. VALENCIA: Yeah. I seen the posts.

MS. BURGESS: Do you believe Shane Stoller is the individual behind Burner_911?

MR. VALENCIA: I don't know. I never seen him—

MS. BURGESS: Did he ever say or do anything that led you to believe he could possibly be associated with that account or movement?

MR. VALENCIA: He just said he was meant for bigger things. That's when he dropped out of CVU. I never seen him again after that.

MS. BURGESS: Anything else you remember?

MR. VALENCIA: Yeah, one more thing. He got one of those tattoos. I remember alls it said was "Plan B." It was the first time I seen it.

MS. BURGESS: Thank you, Mr. Valencia. That's all.

24

SHANE

Chloe,

I'm worried about you. It's all I can think about, and I don't know what to do besides write this lame letter. Like you're ever going to get it. More likely just therapy for me.

I need you to know, I never meant for this to happen. I know I was being a dick, but I was just so pissed off. That's no excuse. I was such a fucking idiot. I should have trusted you. I hope part of you can still trust me.

I can't stand the thought that I put you in danger. I never imagined my followers would do this—guns and getaway cars? What the fuck? And now it's been seventy-two hours since that post. I don't know what's going to happen now. It seems like we should have heard from them by now.

If I could get online, I could actually do something. Write a post, find out who these guys are, text you, something. But I'm helpless. There's nothing I can do, for now. I'm trying to be patient, but I'm not very good at that. Wayne, my lawyer, tells me he's working on it. That they set up a tip line, to try to connect with the guys who did this. So I guess I'll just give this to him, and hope that somehow he'll get it to you. Connect us again.

It's amazing. That power of connection. I didn't appreciate it until it was taken away. The fact that every bit of human information is accessible to everyone at the same time. Most of it's just noise, bouncing around, unnoticed. But when something is interesting, unique, compelling, we swarm to it like ants to a sugar cube. You have that power—to capture that most precious commodity, people's attention. To get them to give a shit about something other than themselves, just for a second.

I guess I have that ability too. Like some idiot savant. I can't explain it, but I just know how to capture it, unleash it, wield it. I tried to use it for good, but it didn't always work out that way. Maybe I can still use it, to help you even if I can't help myself. It was you who gave me reason. Gave purpose to my actions. Gave me a mission, a vision of what I could be. But I screwed it all up.

I'm so sorry. I just need you to know that.

—Shane

25

DASH CAM TRANSCRIPT

DRIVER: Rob

BILLED TO: Logan Adams

TRIP DATE: 9/17/21, 12:17 AM

VEHICLE: Gray Kia Optima

PICK-UP LOCATION: 399 The Embarcadero, San Francisco, CA

DROPOFF LOCATION: 335 Powell St, San Francisco, CA

FARE: $12.00

TRANSCRIPT OF DASH CAM RECORDING ON DEFENDANT'S PHONE

DEFENDANT: Hey, you're Logan?

PERSON 1: Yeah. [Unintelligible.]

PERSON 2: Get in, get in!

PERSON 3: Hurry! I'm getting soaked!

PERSON 2: *Oh, my God*! Move over!

[Car door slams shut.]

PERSON 1: Holy crap! It's pouring like a mother out there!

PERSON 2: Mmmmm . . . I like you wet. You look sexy. [Unintelligible.] Are you getting hard for us, baby?

PERSON 3: I need another bump.

PERSON 1: Here you go . . . Put it on her tits . . .

PERSON 2: [Unintelligible.]

PERSON 3: [Snorting.] *Shit, that's good*!

DEFENDANT: Sounds like you all had a good night.

PERSON 1: Can you just shut the fuck up and drive?

DEFENDANT: Of course . . . I—

PERSON 3: *Shut up!* Nobody's talking to you!

PERSON 2: *Mmmmmmm* . . .

PERSON 1: Holy, *shit* . . . yeah, just like that . . .

PERSON 2: Yeah . . . you like that?

PERSON 1: Fuck yeah . . .

DEFENDANT: Umm . . . we're pulling up to the hotel. Should I just drop you in front?

PERSON 1: Yeah, that's fine . . . that's fine.

DEFENDANT: By the way, don't I recognize you?

PERSON 1: Huh?

DEFENDANT: Yeah, you're Logan Adams, CEO of BlazeMatrix, right? I saw a video of you on Twitter.

PERSON 1: What the hell are you talking about? Mind your own fucking business!

DEFENDANT: Yeah, yeah—I thought that was you. Logan's not a very common name. So, when I saw your request on the app, I figured it might be you. You're practically famous. Good thing I have this dash cam or nobody would believe me.

PERSON 1: Are you fucking *threatening* me?

DEFENDANT: Me? No, no, boss—everything's cool.

PERSON 1: Good, cause I'd fucking kill you. This never happened—*understand*?

DEFENDANT: Of course—I won't say a word.

PERSON 3: Go home and beat off, creep.

PERSON 2: C'mon, baby—let's get outta here.

[Car door slams shut.]

26

EMAIL FROM DEFENDANT

TO: Logan Adams

FROM: Burner_911

SUBJECT: Both kinds of blow

Dear Logan,

I feel like I can call you that. Can I call you that? Logan? I love your name. Logan, Logan, Logan. You sound like a superhero. That's what all the press says too. As I said the night we met, it's an uncommon name. It's Irish, right? I'm one-eighth Irish myself. When I saw that name, Logan, pop up on my app, I knew it was you. Now I feel like we're old buddies.

Here's the thing, though. I know you're busy being a hot-shot tech exec and everything, so I'll get to the point. I have a video of you doing blow and getting blown by your little fuck buddies in the back seat of my car. I know you're, like, a big deal and everything, so I'm sure you wouldn't want your wife, your kids, or the press to get that video. Here's a link if you want a preview.

I feel like a dick asking you this, but I need $50,000 in cash—tomorrow. I know, I know, it feels like extortion. But think of it this way: it's a small price to pay to keep your life the way it is now. You have everything—a mansion in Pacific Heights, a beautiful wife, that yellow Lamborghini I saw on Instagram. You're a billionaire! You won't even notice it's gone. Given the situation, I could ask for much more, but you seem like a reasonable guy. And given I've seen you hoovering cocaine off a prostitute's rack, I think you can agree, my ask is pretty reasonable. Plus, I'm using the money for something important.

I know what you're thinking. Who has that much cash just sitting around? Actually, *you* probably do. You're probably also trying to remember who that dickhead Uber driver killing your vibe the other night was. You're probably pulling up your Uber app right now and scrolling back to see if you can find my name. It's not really Rob, by the way. But if you report even that name to the police, your wife will get a link to our little video. It's not worth it. Plus, you have plenty of time to get the cash. It's not even that much, really. At least, not for you.

So, $50K, cash, manila envelope—put it under the bench in the southeast corner of Alamo Square Park at 8:00 p.m. tomorrow. Near the Painted Ladies, in honor of your ladies of the night. And I promise, I'll only ask you for money this one time.

27

SHANE

"They've got you dead to rights on the extortion stuff," Wayne is saying.

After a day of torture with Dr. Susan and interrogation by the cops, we're finally getting into defense prep. An entire unsealed indictment. The result of an investigation that, it turns out, has been going on for a year. Unpacking all the charges they've brought against me.

"I only took from assholes who deserved it," I say.

"That isn't really how the law works," Wayne says. "There's no ass-hole defense."

"Why are they even bothering with the extortions? That isn't why they arrested me."

"They need to get you on *something*, and this is their strongest case," Wayne explains. "They have a boatload of evidence connecting you to these extortions: metadata on the videos you uploaded, your PII on the YouTube account, geolocation of your IP address to your apartment, decrypted message logs of the emails you sent, and unexplained deposits of large amounts of cash to a bank account in your name. Not your best work."

"What was I supposed to do? Pay my tuition with a bag of cash?"

"How 'bout a student loan?" Wayne says. "Pay it off in increments like a normal person, so it doesn't look so suspicious."

"Oh, they gave me a student loan. That's all CVU cared about. My grades were crap, I barely graduated high school, but they were all too happy to take money I didn't have for tuition I couldn't afford. Tempt me with the false promise that a mountain of debt and a diploma from some shitty university nobody ever heard of was somehow going to lead to a better life. They just wanted to shackle me up with debt."

"Why did you even enroll then?" Wayne asks. "No one forced you to go."

"Shit . . . I don't know. That's just what you're supposed to do, right? Go to college. After Dré got shot, I guess I wanted to clean up my act. Do things the *right way*. Invest in my future, you know? I thought CVU was the answer, but I wanted to quit before I even enrolled. The whole place was like déjà vu for me—back in the same parking lot I used to spend the night in with my mom. But then I realized the whole thing is a con. Just another tool of financial oppression. Another way the system is rigged against us."

"Well, it's a big problem," Wayne says.

Valerie, his ever-present sidekick, flashes a compassionate smile, like she knows what Wayne's about to tell me.

"CVU was subpoenaed by the Feds. Unfortunately for you, they have an eight-year data retention policy. So, in addition to the extortion proof, they know every fucking thing you typed, watched, or clicked on in the CVU computer lab for almost two years."

"Hmmm . . . That's not good."

"No—it's not good. What we're trying to figure out is *how* not good. What is this digital dumpster dive going to reveal?"

"How the hell should I know? I can't remember everything I did online when I was eighteen. Mostly video games, YouTube, 4chan, porn—could be anything."

I think back. I did spend a *lot* of time in that computer lab. Supposedly learning how to code, but usually shitposting on message boards or playing *Call of Duty*. I got pretty good. Good enough that sometimes Nico and other students would just watch me play. So one day I shot a video of myself playing *Call of Duty*—just game footage with my running commentary. I didn't know why anyone would watch it, but I uploaded it to YouTube. Within a week, it had over a thousand views, so I created another one, then another. Within a month, I had ten thousand subscribers.

Life in that computer lab was liberation. I could go anywhere, do anything. In the game, I was the one in control. It was the first time in my life anyone had cared about something I did. *More* than care—they liked it, were sharing and following it. The bigger my audience grew, the more my self-confidence grew. Something came out of me when I was online—a swagger that had been beaten out of me in real life. It was the first time I thought there might be something bigger for me. That maybe I was more than some Central Valley burnout with a juvie record.

That maybe I was even destined for something great.

"Well, all that shit is going to be admitted as evidence," Wayne says. "Think back. Is there anything you did then that could connect you to Burner_911?"

"I don't think so—not at CVU."

"Does the username HappyCat18 ring a bell?" Valerie asks. "The prosecution seems particularly fixated on associating you with this username on Telegram."

"What's Telegram?" Wayne says.

"An end-to-end encrypted messaging platform," I say. "And, yes, I created a Telegram account with the username HappyCat18, but that account got hacked."

"Okay, this could be a problem," Wayne says. "It's important that—"

"*No!* No, it's not important." I can't listen to them anymore. "*None* of this is important. We're wasting our time on crap that happened five years ago, and you're not doing anything to find her. That's all that matters—what's happening *now!*"

"We're working on some possible leads," Valerie says. "It takes time to vet—"

"I can solve this shit in two seconds," I say. "I just need you to get me a phone."

"Shane, there's no way—"

"Yes, there is." I lower my voice. "Come during the afternoon shift, after two. That's when Kryz and Killian are on duty. They're on our side, so make sure they're the ones to bring you in. They'll frisk you everywhere except your left ankle."

Wayne and Valerie exchange a look, like they're not sure they believe me. But Wayne finally says, "Okay. I'll do a trial run tomorrow with something innocent. A pack of gum or something."

"Okay. Meantime, I need you to get this to Chloe." I pass Wayne a folded note.

28

WAYNE

The dome light in my car won't turn on. Battery's probably dead. The latest instance of shit going sideways. I keep clicking the damn thing, but nothing. Piece of crap car. Teaches me to buy American.

I need a drink. I should wait. At least till noon—that's what my ex-wife would have said. Same thing she said to me almost every day of our marriage. But I've definitely earned one for today already. I drop open the glove compartment and find the flask stashed inside. After a couple of swigs, I put the key in the ignition and twist. The engine turns over. First thing to go right today.

I reach down, pull off my shoe, and remove Shane's note—folded up like something passed around class by a pre-pubescent tween. Getting it through security was easy. They never hassle the lawyers, especially on the way out. With the ignition started, the overhead light finally turns on, and I read the whole thing, scrawled out in block letters.

It's just what I suspected—the guy's a wreck. Where's the stone-cold killer that he pretends to be online? Shine the light on him and he turns to milquetoast. It's pathetic. I almost feel sorry for him. He's in over his head. Doesn't understand the responsibility he has.

Now we have no choice.

Bob will be expecting an update, so I pull out my phone and tap his name.

"What's the latest?" he asks impatiently as soon as he picks up.

"I just met with him again this morning. It's going to be a tough case. Val and I were going through discovery documents till 3:00 a.m."

"Get more attorneys. Whatever you need. This is too important."

"Okay. We'll beef up the team."

"So, you think it's him?"

"I don't know yet for sure. We're still going through evidence. *He* certainly believes he is."

I look again at Shane's note. The startling naivete of it. He's built a magical floating castle of online sycophants that he can brandish at will, and all he cares about is this one girl.

"There are plenty of crackpots who claim they're Burner_911. We need to be sure."

"We'll know soon, once we get through everything," I say. "Assuming he is, he might be a lost cause. The guy's pussy-whipped. I think he cares more about the girl than he does about his own cause."

"This movement is more important than one person."

"Of course, that's why I need to build trust with him. So we have options."

"This could be a good thing. An opportunity to get back on message. The chance we've been waiting for."

"Only if we sow enough doubt about who he is."

"We have people on the inside," Bob says matter-of-factly. "It would be a simple matter to get rid of him."

"No," I push back, not ready to go there. "Then he'll be a martyr and all hell will break loose. We need to discredit him, then he'll fade back into anonymity. But we've gotta get those account credentials first."

"How are you going to do that?"

I tip back another swig of bourbon and flip the flask top closed. "I have some ideas. Don't worry, we'll find a way."

29

CHLOE

The saccharine pitch of a pharmaceutical commercial fifty decibels louder than the rest of the broadcast pulls me back to consciousness. The side effects, rattled off at auctioneer speed, are unnervingly similar to those I'm experiencing—nausea, dry mouth, constipation, loss of appetite, sleeplessness, anxiety.

I don't know how long I was asleep, or if I really even was. Day and night are blurring together. I hear the boys stirring—their restlessness palpable, even though I can't see them. The TV has been on continuously, tuned to Fox News. The 24/7 coverage of October 12th is the only way we pass the time. Talking heads with nothing new to say, cycling pictures and videos in an endless loop—of the rioters, of me. Hours of footage harvested from my Instagram, Twitter, and TikTok. The perfect eye candy to keep viewers hooked through commercial breaks. I can't see any of it, but I don't need to—every image is a subject of my own fixation, committed to memory, curated to elicit the exact reaction they are getting: to capture attention.

"New developments in the Chloe Corbin case—find out more after the break," the TV anchor says, practically giddy with anticipation.

I'm so sick of it, the constant curation. The continuous trolling of a bottomless sea for attention—attention of men, attention of women, attention to causes, but above all, attention to *myself*. The dopamine receptors in my brain rewired to crave it, even now. Implicitly expecting it will attract only the right kind of attention—but, of course, it doesn't work that way. It captures everything, indiscriminately, like scraps of metal to an electromagnet. It attracted these men, and now here I am.

I'm offended when I'm objectified, but my real fear is being ignored.

Then there was Shane. He didn't care about my audience. He didn't count my likes. He ignored my compulsive addiction to attention by giving me all the attention I could ever need. Maybe it was because he had a following of his own. Maybe it was because of the power that following afforded him. I want to know what it's like to have that power. True power, not power derived from my dad's money or how I look in a bikini. My body will give up on me some day. I know this.

My mom's body gave up on her. Over the years she spent fighting off cellulite and double chins, the tumors were doing their damage. Ravaging her organs. A double mastectomy was too late. It had metastasized—to her lymph nodes, her liver, her brain. The parts of her body that mattered, the parts nobody could see, were where the battle was lost. All that time spent waxing and tucking, counting calories, carbs, and crunches—all for nothing.

Her body gave up on her.

But not before *he* gave up on her. Before the chemo treatments, before the antinausea pills, bed pans, and oxygen tanks, before the hospice, he gave up on her. Her own husband, my father, gave up on her—too preoccupied with his company, his celebrity, his mistresses. Biding his time, deliberately avoiding the formality of divorce to prevent the possibility her share of his wealth might get diverted, counting on her being too fatigued to fight.

His plan worked. Within a year, she was dead.

"Authorities say they have a break in the Chloe Corbin abduction . . ." The anchor has returned after a series of ads for indigestion relief, fake wrestling matches, and two-for-one fried chicken sandwiches.

The coverage of Shane is unrelenting—every photo, every scrap of evidence, every suspicious back story. I don't even know what to think anymore. Our entire relationship, I thought he was different, but maybe he's just like every other man. Just like my father. Seeking power. Seeking conquest. Seeking ownership. Never satisfied. Lying, cheating, and stealing to get what they want. Always wanting more.

"Authorities today released this photo of the man believed to be the ringleader in the Chloe Corbin abduction plot."

The boys are instantly silent, their attention riveted to the TV.

"Visible in this surveillance camera image, the suspect has been tentatively identified as Nicholas Harper of Jordan Valley, Oregon—"

"Ah, *shit . . .*" Pete says. "I told you not to take that mask off."

"Officials have issued an arrest warrant for Mr. Harper and are asking for the public's help in identifying the other individuals visible in the video. Meanwhile, the specific demand of the kidnappers to release Shane Stoller has fueled speculation in online forums about whether he really is the individual behind the anonymous Burner_911 profile. As the manhunt continues—"

"We gotta do something," Scooter says. "We gotta move. We're sitting ducks here."

"Would you guys relax?" Nick says through a mouth full of food, walking from what must be the kitchen. "I haven't lived in Jordan Valley for twenty years. Nobody knows we're here. We have enough supplies for months. We're prepared for this. There's no reason to go anywhere. Only way we get caught is if one of you-all does something stupid."

30

SHANE

"How long have you been a neo-Nazi?" Wayne asks.

We're rehearsing. Full-blown defense prep today. He's trying deliberately to get under my skin. To provoke me into popping off. I manage to remain calm, but the question is still unsettling.

"I disagree with all aspects of Nazi ideology," I reply.

"Not according to your browser history," Wayne says.

Four hours of this bullshit. It's grueling. Antagonizing me with whatever crap they dug up about me online—every search, every page, every post. At least, the stuff that wasn't encrypted. Still, it's crazy what they found.

Who would want their identity defined entirely by what they viewed online?

Wayne is showing me charts of my most frequently visited websites. I have to admit, it's not a great look. There's some hardcore shit in there. But I didn't know any better. Nobody told me about any of this stuff when I was growing up. How was I supposed to know Nazis were bad if I didn't even know what a Nazi is or what they did?

I never thought about politics at all growing up. I didn't know if I was liberal or conservative, Republican or Democrat, Communist or Fascist. I didn't even know what those terms meant. Ray would get worked up about all these "liberal cunts" when he watched TV, so I guess I didn't want to be that. What I did want to be was less clear. There was just something fascinating and illicit about those sites. Like watching porn. I guess it's just my nature that if someone tells me not to do something, it makes me want to do it even more. So that's what I did. Now it's biting me in the ass.

"According to YouTube, you watched 225 hours of Fascist propaganda," Wayne says.

"Sounds about right," I say. "But you have to consider, I watched a *lot* of YouTube. That was probably 1 percent of what I watched."

He gives me a skeptical look, then starts playing a particularly egregious video. One I apparently watched some bored afternoon in 2014.

It's offensive—I get that. But just because you watch something doesn't automatically mean you agree with it. There are so many people trying to control what you're allowed to watch, and say, and *think* in America. So many people on both sides trying to censor any opposing thought. No debate or discussion, just entrenched opposition. The irony is that the exact same people who say you need to be tolerant of everyone and everything have *zero* tolerance when it comes to other points of view. You either agree with them 100 percent or you're the antichrist.

That's why I killed my YouTube channel. All of a sudden, it was a lightning rod. There was just so much animosity directed at me. I was sick of being harassed and told what to do, so I moved on—unplugged my YouTube, Twitter, and Facebook and went to Parler, 4chan, and Razgo. There was always a new place to go. The internet offers endless rabbit holes for a curious mind.

"How do acts of terrorism advance your extreme ideology?" Wayne says, mimicking the hostile tone of the prosecutor he's trying to prepare me for.

There's that word again: "ideology." The prosecution is obsessed with it. Trying to put a label on me. Defining me as something the jury already has permission to hate.

The mainstream media has their own favorite labels for me—"fundamentalist," "anarchist," "right-wing extremist." Social media prefers "Nazi," "misogynist," and "Fascist pig" from the liberals, or "Communist," "cuck," and "piece of shit" from the conservatives. Everyone wants to classify me, characterize me, categorize me—make me an "other" they can rail against. All this identity politics. Drawing artificial lines of demarcation as a coping mechanism for information overload. Hardly any of them have actually read my posts. Nobody has the time. They just want to rip out an indignant tweet and swipe to the next thing.

The world looks down on people like me, the deplorables. I've had to fight for everything I have. I've lived through years of pain and suffering. I went through three dads and two moms before ending up alone. I've been homeless three times. I've been arrested, fined, detained, evicted, and expelled. I've seen more than enough to know the world is unjust.

So, after living all that, my "ideology" was simple: *fight back*.

Fight back against a system that is rigged against me and the millions like me. That's the message that resonated, that people followed. My rhetoric was anger. My orthodoxy was spite. My promise was a payday. My followers were looking for something, *anything*, that would make them believe their lives were going to get better.

I just had no idea how many would believe me.

31

COURT TRANSCRIPT

TRANSCRIPT OF TESTIMONY OF DR. SAMINA KHAN

MS. GIBSON: The government would like to call Dr. Samina Khan to the stand.

THE COURTROOM DEPUTY: Raise your right hand, please. Do you solemnly swear that you will tell the truth, the whole truth, and nothing but the truth, so help you God?

DR. KHAN: I do.

DIRECT EXAMINATION BY MS. GIBSON:

MS. GIBSON: Thank you for joining us today, Dr. Khan. Would you please state for the record your occupation and experience as it relates to the case today.

DR. KHAN: Yes, certainly. I am a digital forensic scientist. I have a master's degree in computer science from Purdue University and a PhD in forensic science from Caltech, with a specialization in internet and online activity. For the past fifteen years, I have run my own consulting practice. I am typically hired by law enforcement, prosecutors, or defendants to investigate online behavior and criminal activity and have testified in hundreds of cases.

MS. GIBSON: Can you please state how you got involved in this case and why?

DR. KHAN: Yes. I was hired by the United States Attorney for the Northern District of California to investigate the online activity of the defendant, Mr. Stoller. Specifically, his online activity prior to coming under FBI surveillance.

MS. GIBSON: That information dates back a while. What were you able to find?

DR. KHAN: Quite a lot, actually. Most of the institutions and websites Mr. Stoller frequented were cooperative in sharing information about his online activity. Some we had to subpoena, including Central Valley University, where Mr. Stoller was a student. We combined that information with data on his various computers and phones, as well as network data from ISPs. Together, we were able to put together a pretty comprehensive picture.

MS. GIBSON: And what did you find?

DR. KHAN: A fairly predictable behavior pattern, to be honest. I have seen several cases of disenfranchised white men, similar in age to Mr. Stoller, who become increasingly radicalized by online content. As we pieced it together, one could really see how he got more and more extreme in his ideology.

MS. GIBSON: For example?

DR. KHAN: For example, on YouTube we were able to capture a log of every video Mr. Stoller watched since he first created his account in 2010. In 2012, Mr. Stoller, who was fifteen at the time, significantly increased his viewing time. Initially he consumed videos from other online gamers and commentators, such as PewDiePie and

Markiplier, whose style he was arguably emulating in his own videos. But around 2014, there was a discernible new thread in Mr. Stoller's viewing habits, focusing on religious skepticism and atheism. He viewed videos from Christopher Hitchens, Thomas Levi, Richard Dawkins, and other well-known atheists.

MS. GIBSON: Beyond atheism, did Mr. Stoller watch any videos that espoused extreme ideology?

DR. KHAN: That was the next pattern we noticed. Starting in 2015 and 2016, Mr. Stoller began consuming more and more videos posted by so-called alt-right figures, including Stefan Molyneux, Richard Spencer, Lana Lokteff, Steven Crowder, Lauren Southern, and many others known to be white supremacists. The common thread of all these videos was Eurocentric white nationalism and antifeminism.

MS. GIBSON: So, was there evidence that Mr. Stoller's YouTube viewing activity led to further radicalization?

DR. KHAN: Yes, definitely. On Twitter, Mr. Stoller followed the profiles of all these right-wing personalities, often liking, retweeting, or commenting on their posts. On Reddit, Mr. Stoller predominantly consumed right-wing subreddits and posted links to his favorite videos there. On Facebook, Mr. Stoller got into several heated debates, particularly leading up to the 2016 US presidential election, about politics and right-wing ideology. He was also active on dozens of other right-wing and libertarian sites, including Breitbart, the Daily Caller, TheBlaze, PJ Media, Infowars, and especially 4Chan, where he was first exposed to the QAnon conspiracy theory—which, as you likely know, alleges a secret cabal of cannibalistic pedophiles is running a child sex-trafficking ring.

MS. GIBSON: Did you find evidence that Mr. Stoller supports these extremist ideologies and debunked conspiracy theories?

DR. KHAN: Beyond watching thousands of hours' worth of content promoting them?

MS. GIBSON: Yes. Did you see direct posts, tweets, emails, texts, comments, or other online activity from Mr. Stoller that gave you insight into his personal ideology?

DR. KHAN: Well, yes. He liked many of the videos and articles and shared them to his personal social media accounts, including more right-leaning sites like Parler and Gab. If he personally added a post or comment, it was usually brief—something like "Agree 100 percent" or "Gotta read this." And, of course, there were his own YouTube videos, which parroted many of these same messages.

MS. GIBSON: So from that, you could determine that Mr. Stoller personally believed these ideologies and conspiracy theories—he wasn't just viewing them for entertainment?

DR. KHAN: Absolutely. It was exceedingly clear that Mr. Stoller's personal political ideology aligned with this content and everything it stood for.

MS. GIBSON: Thank you, Dr. Khan.

CROSS EXAMINATION BY MR. YOUNG:

MR. YOUNG: Thank you, Your Honor. And thank you, Dr. Khan, for sharing the results of your investigation and your expertise with us here today.

DR. KHAN: My pleasure. It's what I do.

MR. YOUNG: Yes, and you're very good at it. So, most of what you described earlier was content that Mr. Stoller consumed online. But you also mentioned that the content authored by Mr. Stoller himself was typically brief, fewer than five words or so. Is that correct?

DR. KHAN: Yes.

MR. YOUNG: He didn't have a personal blog or write long manifestos anywhere?

DR. KHAN: Not that I found, prior to 2020. Except for his YouTube videos.

MR. YOUNG: How many posts by Mr. Stoller did you review?

DR. KHAN: Thousands. Probably over ten thousand.

MR. YOUNG: In all these posts you and your team reviewed, did you see any that explicitly advocated white supremacist views?

DR. KHAN: There were hundreds.

MR. YOUNG: That he viewed, or that he posted about? Please be specific, Dr. Khan.

DR. KHAN: I'm not sure. I would have to review our records.

MR. YOUNG: Can you provide an example, any example, where Mr. Stoller himself authored a post or comment online that you would deem to be racist?

DR. KHAN: Not immediately. No.

MR. YOUNG: Are there any posts or comments authored by Mr. Stoller that you would deem sexist?

DR. KHAN: Not so much in his written posts, but his language in his videos is very misogynistic. He refers to women as "bitches," for example.

MR. YOUNG: Yes, we saw those videos admitted into evidence. But apart from that adolescent use of a derogatory term, did you find anything Mr. Stoller personally wrote or said that suggested he felt women were inferior?

DR. KHAN: Calling women bitches certainly is suggestive of his views toward women.

MR. YOUNG: Did any of the articles or videos Mr. Stoller shared, posted, or commented on, during the time you investigated, advocate violence in any form against any group?

DR. KHAN: Not that he wrote, but again, he made many violent comments in his videos.

MR. YOUNG: You're referring to the videos in which Mr. Stoller is playing an imaginary first-person shooter video game?

DR. KHAN: Yes.

MR. YOUNG: So, given the paucity of information from Mr. Stoller himself about his political, social, or religious beliefs, wouldn't you admit it would be presumptuous to assume you understand his personal ideology?

DR. KHAN: I believe the content that someone consumes and shares tells a great deal about what they believe.

MR. YOUNG: Indeed. That can be true. It can also be a byproduct of a curious mind. Or an algorithm. Tell me, Dr. Khan, did you also find left-leaning videos, websites, and other information that Mr. Stoller consumed?

DR. KHAN: Well, yes, but not nearly as many as right-leaning.

MR. YOUNG: Could that, at least partially, be attributable to the fact there is simply far more right-leaning content than left-leaning content on YouTube?

DR. KHAN: No, I don't think that would account for the discrepancy.

MR. YOUNG: In addition to Mr. Stoller's viewing activity on YouTube, did you also have access to his search history on the site?

DR. KHAN: Yes, we did.

MR. YOUNG: And you analyzed that search history?

DR. KHAN: Yes.

MR. YOUNG: Of the nearly ten years of Mr. Stoller's YouTube viewing history that you examined, how many of the videos he watched were the result of an explicit search Mr. Stoller conducted, and how many were recommended to him by YouTube's algorithm or simply the next video that played automatically?

DR. KHAN: It's hard to say.

MR. YOUNG: Okay. How many total searches on YouTube did Mr. Stoller perform in that time?

DR. KHAN: About fifty.

MR. YOUNG: About *fifty* searches over almost ten years. Compared to tens of thousands of videos watched. So, with respect to my previous question, it's safe to say only a minuscule fraction, less than 0.1 percent, were videos that Mr. Stoller was specifically searching for. Is that a reasonable estimate, Dr. Khan?

DR. KHAN: I guess that would be in the ballpark.

MR. YOUNG: And in those approximately fifty searches, did Mr. Stoller ever use keywords or search for content that you consider explicitly racist or sexist?

DR. KHAN: Not that I recall.

MR. YOUNG: So we've established that Mr. Stoller did not *author* racist, sexist, or violent content. And he did not *search* for racist, sexist, or violent content. Yet you have surmised that he has racist, sexist, and violent tendencies based strictly on the videos he watched and websites he visited in the past. How can you be so sure that what you've uncovered is Mr. Stoller's ideology and not simply the preferences of the YouTube recommendation engine?

DR. KHAN: He still clicked on the videos. He still watched them.

MR. YOUNG: It's not illegal to watch a video though, Dr. Khan, is it?

DR. KHAN: No, it's not.

MR. YOUNG: Thank you, Dr. Khan. No further questions, Your Honor.

32

TECHCRUNCH

Razgo CEO Says Social Media App Is New Home for Free Speech

SAN FRANCISCO, CA, February 26, 2021—Many of the tech industry's biggest influencers are buzzing about the latest social media platform, Razgo. The site has exploded in popularity over the last several weeks as competing so-called free-speech platforms have gone dark in the wake of being cut off by major hosting providers.

Razgo's founder and CEO, Alex Katin, declared that his app is the new home for unfiltered and uncensored free speech, reassuring users that they would not be taken down by technology platforms, including Apple, Amazon, and Google, that have barred similar apps for failing to do enough to detect and moderate racist, sexist, and violent content.

"We are a nation founded on free speech, but that freedom is under attack by Big Tech oligarchs who think they are the sole arbiters of critical thinking," declared Mr. Katin to a packed room at this week's CPAC conference in Orlando, Florida. "That is why Razgo runs on our own cloud infrastructure. It allows us to offer a secure and reliable platform for free speech that's out of reach of these gatekeepers who seek to suppress the voice of the people."

In addition to network independence, Katin explained another advantage of Razgo is its business model. As advertisers have shunned similar services out of concerns about being associated with extreme political content, Razgo's subscription model doesn't rely on advertising for revenue, Katin explained. And members' messages are fully encrypted, visible only to other paid members—providing both a veil of secrecy for more extreme viewpoints and a powerful viral effect that has driven subscription growth for Razgo.

Founded in 2019, Razgo was a relatively peripheral player, an also-ran compared to social media behemoths like Facebook and Twitter as well as more overtly right-wing sites such as Parler and Gab. However, after prominent political commentators were banned from the major social networks and cloud-hosting platforms severed ties with the other unmoderated free-speech sites, Razgo started to take off.

"We will not be beholden to or reliant on the dominant tech monopolists. We refuse to let the elites and globalists dictate a single narrative of the truth," Katin said in an interview after the conference. "That is why owning and operating our own data center infrastructure is so crucial."

Already boasting over 50 million users, Razgo doubled its user base in just the last month. When asked how the service effectively moderates user-contributed content at such scale, Katin explained that Razgo relies on a peer-moderation process: users can flag inappropriate content, and that flagged content is reviewed by unpaid volunteer "jurors" who have the authority to remove content that violates the site's terms of service. Although accusations have arisen of users issuing death threats, forming armed militias, and brokering the sales of firearms, explosives, and sex trafficking on Razgo, Katin said he thought the service had done a good job moderating allegedly violent content.

"The real danger of Razgo's content is to the global elites who will do anything to suppress the truth and maintain their satanic cabal," explained Gary Scoffield, prominent conservative radio host and a lead investor in Razgo, along with billionaire hedge fund manager Robert Jorgensen.

Apart from Scoffield and Jorgensen, Katin declined to disclose any other investors, but clarified that the company was independently funded and is not seeking additional investment at this time. "We can't disclose our investors because they would be harassed by haters of free speech," Katin said. "But our investors have done so unconditionally and impose no restrictions or editorial agenda on our content. Razgo is free speech in its truest form."

Given Razgo's incredible growth, there are bound to be many investors lined up if the company ever looks to raise funding in the future.

33

SHANE

"No, you don't understand—this is a good thing," Wayne is saying.

"A *good* thing?" I say. "I thought they were gonna waterboard me!"

Four straight hours of FBI interrogation. Brutal. Investigating me for new crimes while they prosecute me for past ones. All the while digging, baiting me into a mistake. Hoping to get the definitive proof they don't yet have in their otherwise slam-dunk case: me logged in as Burner_911. That's what Wayne's telling me—that they don't have the smoking gun they need. It could have been anyone logged in to that account. And each day, more and more randos pop up claiming it was them. Trying to take credit. Wannabes latching on after the fact.

But that's "good," Wayne says. All of it creates doubt. Makes the prosecution look desperate. Even if it makes me look like a demented loser.

"Val and I've been reviewing depositions," he says. "The Feds interviewed a bunch of people who knew you when you were at CVU. They're trying to make the case that you developed the technical skills to become Burner_911 during that time, and the motive, which they say is to make money."

"As if that's some sort of character flaw," I say.

They're not wrong. CVU was a breaking point for me financially. By the end of my first year, I had over $30,000 of student loan debt. There was no way I was ever going to be able to pay that off, at least not legitimately. What finally triggered me was one of those mandatory meetings with a job placement counselor. He kept telling me, "You can be anything you want to be." The same lie they fed me since preschool. How many kids are told that bullshit every day? Promised if you work hard, believe in yourself, follow the rules, your biggest ambitions will come true? The myth of the American Dream.

Truth is, we can't all be what we want to be. Everyone can't have everything. Our dreams are more and more unattainable, while our means are more and more unavailable. What they should be telling CVU students is, "The world needs long-haul petrochemical truckers too."

Next thing I knew, I was yelling at him. Waving my loan statement in his face to emphasize my point that it's all bullshit. A system designed to enslave you to consumerism. Inflate your expectations as they pile more and more debt on you. I can be anything I want to be? *Really?* What if I want to be one of those tech billionaires? None of the ones I read about went to Central Valley University—more like Stanford, Harvard, or MIT. The ones who started businesses with their credit cards weren't already shackled with debt.

When campus security showed up, I was explaining to the job counselor the inequity of the 2008 financial crisis. With a Sharpie. On his wall. I circled all the banks making huge profits by giving out subprime loans to folks like my stick figures, Judy and Ray, who couldn't afford them. Then, when the whole steaming pile imploded, who got bailed out? Not the stick figures—they got foreclosed on and kicked out of their homes. It was the billionaires. *The fucking billionaires!* The very assholes who owned the banks and controlled all the money and manipulated Wall Street and bought off all the politicians—*they* were the ones who got bailed out while the rest of us went homeless.

I represented that group with a hole in the drywall.

That was my last day at CVU.

"The argument they're trying to make is that your financial situation caused you to criminalize your online activity," Wayne says, bringing me back to our legal prep. "That you were just doing it to make money."

"Of *course* I was doing it to make money. Why else does anyone do anything?"

All I ever read about was people making money. They were still foreclosing on families in Turlock when the IPO parties started back up in

Silicon Valley. Facebook went public in May 2012. Mark Zuckerberg had just turned twenty-eight and he was worth, like, $20 billion. He didn't have a college degree, so why did I need one? I was done being a slave to a rigged system. Done sinking further and further into debt to banks and billionaires. Done doing things the "right way." I realized no matter how hard I worked, it didn't matter. The world was run by global elites, and I wasn't one of them. I needed a new strategy. I remembered what Dré had always told me—*If you wanna make money, someone's gotta lose money.* So, just like Zuck, I quit school and headed to San Francisco to make my fortune.

What I didn't know when I got there was that nobody in tech would hire me. My coding skills were shit. I was decent at sys-ops stuff, but without a CS degree or work experience, I didn't get any interviews. They wanted people they can trust with user data and network security and payment information—not some hacker dropout with a criminal record. Driving for Uber using my dad's ID was the only "tech job" I could get. But that turned out to be lucky. Otherwise, I never would have met Chloe.

"Time's up."

It's Kryz, with Killian right behind him as usual. They enter the room and silently begin the repetitive procedure of unshackling and re-shackling to take me back to my cell. Kryz glances down, pausing at the pack of gum on the table, and then his eyes flick toward Wayne. "Same time tomorrow," he says with a millisecond nod before they lead me out of the room.

It's dinnertime, so most of the other inmates are in the cafeteria on the lower level. I've been getting my meals delivered to my cell, so the dynamic I observe from the hallway overlooking the shared dining space is still unfamiliar, a constant din of banter and taunts. The only time they're quiet is when they see me.

We've just turned toward the corridor that leads to my cell when it happens. A flash of movement, a coldness along my jaw. Before I can react, Kryz has an inmate in a choke hold, dropping him to the floor. I reach my cuffed hands to my chin and liquid warmth spills over them— blood, running down my fingers. I hear something plastic skitter across the floor and look down. It's a toothbrush handle, melted down, with a razor blade embedded in the tip. It leaves a red arc against the concrete as it slides away.

"*Cómo te gusta ahora, puta!?*" the guy yells at me, his cheek pressed into the floor.

Kryz has him immobilized almost immediately. An alarm is going off, the flashing lights turning every movement into stop-motion. Doors are closing to keep prisoners separated. Killian looks at me and seems to conclude that I'll survive, because he leaves me, pulls the nightstick from his belt, and steps toward the prisoner.

"*Soy uno de ustedes,*" I say under my breath as the first swing of the club thumps into the guy's skull.

His body goes instantly limp but the next swing still comes, crunching his ribs like someone stomped on a bag of potato chips.

I realize I'm slumped against the wall. I'm trying to say something, but can't. Holding the gash on my face, I finally get a word out: "Stop!"

A third swing punches the remaining air out of the guy's lungs with a wheeze. I grab Killian's arm between my handcuffed wrists before he can swing again, smearing my blood into the hair on his arm. He turns toward me, wielding the club like he's possessed, but pauses just long enough to hear me.

"That's enough," I say. "Let him live. He's learned his lesson."

34

CHLOE

"*We told you what you needed to do!*" Nick shouts into the camera of another burner phone.

Intense light from a mechanic's lamp penetrates the hood, illuminating the scene and casting shadows of the men that move across my veil. I sense the camera watching me like another set of eyes—locked on me, zooming in. I'm motionless in my chair except for the quickening undulations of my breath.

"It was very simple: *Release Shane Stoller and Chloe Corbin goes free*," Nick continues, like he's preaching to a packed house of disciples. More than the FBI, that is his audience—the converted, the believers, the future zealots . . . those who trust The Plan. "*That's it!* You had seventy-two hours to get it done, but you did *nothing!* This isn't a negotiation!"

The others grunt their approval from off-camera.

I'm bound in new ways now. The zip tie, its memory persisting from the exposed cuts on my wrists, is gone, my limbs instead constrained to each armrest with duct tape—the silver electrical kind, entire rolls of it, adhered to my skin and pulling hairs out of my arms. More of it is wrapped around my torso, constricting my breathing and crushing my breasts. Just enough so I cannot move.

"So we're gonna have to up the stakes to get your cooperation," Pete says. I hear him take a drag of his cigarette—always those cigarettes, the stale scent of smoke seeping into fabric, furniture, flesh, everything it envelops—and then he approaches me from the side, removes the hood, and exhales a plume of smoke directly in my face.

I blink in the spotlight, able to see only their silhouettes. Benny, the least menacing, holds the camera just over Pete's shoulder.

"A new seventy-two-hour clock starts *right now*," Nick says, taking back the diatribe. "If you fail to comply again, the pain inflicted on Chloe Corbin will increase. Until . . ."

I look up, past Pete towering over me, and lock my eyes on Benny, on the lens, on the audience. "*Please*," I murmur. "They're serious . . . I don't know . . . I don't know how much time I have, just *please* help me! Release Shane!"

"You heard her. Message us at @ChloeWillBurn on Razgo," Nick says, then nods at Pete, who takes another deep drag from his cigarette and then plunges the burning ember into the soft underside of my exposed forearm.

I scream in pain, writhing against the tape that has me entombed like a mummy; my flesh blackens with a nauseating hiss. Pete withdraws the cigarette and I see, through my tears, Benny stop the video and lower the phone. Our eyes meet. Then I drop my gaze to the charred spot on my arm.

I swallow back my saliva, take a deep breath to subdue the shooting pain, regain my composure. When I do, a subtle smirk overtakes my face.

"That was perfect," I say. "They have to respond to that."

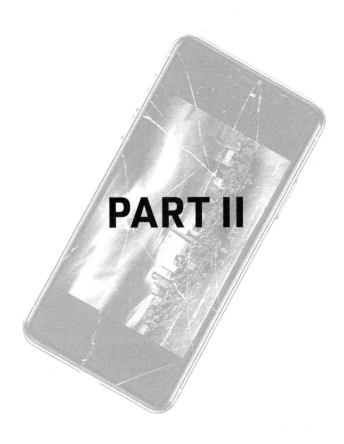

PART II

35

SHANE

Chloe,

I can't believe those guys did that to you. The detectives showed me the video of them torturing you. I'm going to kill those guys. Burn holes in their arms with a blowtorch, work my way up to their shoulders, their chests, their faces, until they black out from the pain, go into shock, and die, one by one . . . I'll spray-paint epitaphs on cardboard tombstones, banishing them from the BurnOutz forever and warning anyone else who doesn't FOLLOW THE PLAN that they will see the same fate!

At least you're alive. And I'm alive too, barely.

It was a little dicey there for a minute. Some asshole came at me with a homemade knife and sliced my cheek. Hurt like a mother—thirty stitches. I lost a lot of blood, but the medic told me I was lucky. If he'd caught me two inches lower, I probably would have bled out. Two inches higher and I'm blind in one eye. Now I just have a scar I hope you can get used to.

Nothing like a near-death experience to make you revisit your life goals. I needed to write you again. I don't know if you'll ever get this letter (Wayne still hasn't gotten me a damn phone yet), but, if you do, I need you to know something . . .

I'm not a stalker. I know it probably won't seem that way in the trial, but that wasn't my intent. I just had to see you. That's different. I never thought in a million years you'd go for a loser like me. You're so gorgeous, so perfect. I couldn't stop thinking about you. Honestly, I was obsessed. I figured my infatuation was ridiculous—just an Instagram celebrity crush.

You had millions of followers. I was nothing, nobody, a drop in the ocean of admirers.

But I always felt like we had something, from that first time we met in my Uber. Do you remember that? I tried messaging you, but you never replied. I knew I'd never stand out from the masses online. If I could just see you IRL again, then maybe I'd have a shot. That's where the stalker part comes in—parking outside your apartment, hoping to catch just a glimpse of you, worrying you would get a restraining order if you ever saw me. Then, I had an idea. I finally knew how I was going to see you again.

The other thing you need to know is, I wasn't using you.

That's the other narrative they'll push in the mainstream media when they find out about us. That I was just using you, for your money or your celebrity or your dad or whatever. But that's not true.

The truth is, you changed my life. I was spiraling to a pretty dark place, but you sparked something in me that took me a different direction. It took the shit hitting the fan for me to fully realize it. And now I don't know what to do.

Seeing you gives me hope that maybe we'll see each other again. Now it's almost worse though, knowing that you're alive but not safe. Being tortured, held hostage, used as a bargaining chip for my release. God knows what else . . . and there's nothing I can do! I thought I lost you. I was still in denial but had almost accepted that as my new reality—the inevitable outcome for everyone I have ever loved. Now, I have hope that maybe, someday, somehow, you will read this and know that, even though I fucked everything up, I love you.

I need to talk to you. I told Wayne that is his only job, to find a way. I don't care about my defense. I don't care about the communications embargo. I don't care about the BurnOutz. I only care about finding some way to talk to you again . . . to tell you how sorry I am . . . to try to make this right . . . to see if there's some way we can be together again. If I can't, there's no point in defending my case anyway. They can do whatever they want to me . . . nothing else matters.

—Shane

36

GRAND JURY INDICTMENT

TRANSCRIPT OF FBI SPECIAL AGENT
NATHAN PITTMAN, SEPTEMBER 4, 2023

Nathan Pittman, FBI Special Agent,
Witness for the Prosecution

Julie Gibson, United States Attorney's Office,
Federal Prosecutor

AUSA GIBSON: Thank you for all your hard work leading this investigation, Special Agent Pittman. For the record, will you please state your full name and role at the bureau?

SA PITTMAN: Yes, certainly. My name is Nathan Pittman, and I am the lead case agent for the FBI's joint task force leading the investigation into the extremist group known as the BurnOutz.

AUSA GIBSON: Thank you, Agent Pittman. And you will be providing today before the grand jury the results of your investigation into Shane Stoller, the alleged leader of that movement, correct?

SA PITTMAN: Yes, that is correct. The full report of our investigation, including all evidence collected, has been provided to the US Attorney's Office.

AUSA GIBSON: Agent Pittman, could you provide a timeline for the grand jury? When did the FBI first initiate this investigation?

SA PITTMAN: We have a file on Mr. Stoller dating back to 2019. He had a large YouTube following based on some politically charged rhetoric, but nothing to suggest he might be a violent extremist. Then there were some complaints he might be extorting money from prominent individuals, so we started surveilling his activity more closely.

AUSA GIBSON: And what did you find?

SA PITTMAN: Not much at first. He seemed to be yet another disgruntled conspiracy theorist airing his grievances online. But then, about a year in, one of my analysts identified a series of international wire transfers that pointed to something more nefarious—more money than Mr. Stoller could have obtained legally, and transactions with known cybercriminals. So we opened a preliminary investigation in late 2020 to dig further.

AUSA GIBSON: What did that entail?

SA PITTMAN: We brought in digital forensics experts to analyze Mr. Stoller's internet usage and a financial crimes unit to investigate suspected money launder-ing and illegal offshore payments. We also had a field surveillance team follow him and document his known associates.

AUSA GIBSON: Had you connected Mr. Stoller to the Burn-Outz movement by that time?

SA PITTMAN: A separate investigative team within the bureau had opened a file on the BurnOutz. We weren't sure yet if this was an organization or an individual, but they had claimed responsibility for several cyber-attacks, so we had agents monitoring message boards and covertly joining the movement. We combined those efforts based on a user profile, HappyCat18, that was a known alias of Mr. Stoller's and an active organizer within the BurnOutz online forums. At that point, I was assigned as the lead investigator of that joint task force due to credible intelligence that the group was organizing additional ransomware attacks.

AUSA GIBSON: What did you know at that time about the BurnOutz organization?

SA PITTMAN: Well, it was growing rapidly based on the postings of its anonymous leader, the profile Burner_911. We had developed a list of potential suspects behind that account. At the time, we felt the most likely culprit was Alex Katin, the founder and CEO of Razgo.com, where all the Burner_911 posts originated, but Mr. Stoller also remained high on that list. By that point, we had recruited several informants and understood the group's structure and how it operated.

AUSA GIBSON: What did you learn?

SA PITTMAN: Paramount within the movement was that the identity of Burner_911 was secret. Specific criminal conspiracies would start with manifesto-style posts by Burner_911 on Razgo. Then there was a network of self-appointed lieutenants who would interpret the posts and translate them into specific plans for their followers—on forums, their own blogs, social media, YouTube channels, and so forth. Some posted as themselves, others maintained anonymity, but it was a massive echo chamber of loosely affiliated cells. The HappyCat18 profile, controlled by Mr. Stoller, was one of the most high-profile lieutenants.

At that point, we had an undercover agent who had infiltrated the group, to the extent that is possible with such a decentralized and virtual organization. That agent established himself as the leader of one of these cells after other cell leaders claimed to have direct communication with Burner_911. He believed this would enable him to uncover Burner_911's identity.

It was also during this time that our investigation obtained the majority of the evidence in the indictment presented today to the grand jury, including wiretaps of Mr. Stoller's numerous mobile devices and of the devices of his known associates, records of Mr. Stoller's internet activity subpoenaed from ISPs and websites, transaction histories for numerous bank, brokerage, and cryptocurrency accounts, salvaged data from computer electronic equipment discarded or destroyed by Mr. Stoller, and recordings of private conversations Mr. Stoller had while under FBI surveillance.

AUSA GIBSON: And you upgraded this to a full investigation based on that evidence?

SA PITTMAN: Correct. We had secured articulable factual evidence of financial crimes that Mr. Stoller had committed using the HappyCat18 alias. We had also classified the BurnOutz as an anti-government/anti-authority extremist group and domestic terrorist threat and issued an Intelligence Bulletin from the San Francisco Field Office that planned protests in the city could become violent.

AUSA GIBSON: Did you consider arresting Mr. Stoller then?

SA PITTMAN: Yes, but we still wanted to get more definitive proof that he was behind the Burner_911 account. We were already monitoring and intercepting all of Mr. Stoller's email, text, and other internet traffic, but most of it was encrypted. So we got a warrant to enter Mr. Stoller's residence and covertly embed code on several of his personal electronic devices. That, in turn, allowed us to decrypt intercepted messages.

AUSA GIBSON: What did you find in those messages that led you to issue an arrest warrant for Mr. Stoller?

SA PITTMAN: Although we never caught Mr. Stoller physically logged in to the Burner_911 account, we decrypted several messages in which Mr. Stoller was communicating directions as Burner_911 to his accomplices. Given the imminent national security threat his followers present, we decided to proceed with an arrest warrant.

AUSA GIBSON: And I understand you also lost an undercover agent in the line of duty?

SA PITTMAN: That is correct. Our undercover agent, John Stanley, who happened to be a close friend and colleague I had the honor to serve with for over fifteen years, was compromised as an undercover FBI operative. A hit was ordered on him, and we intercepted it too late. Within forty-eight hours, he died of cardiac arrest, later determined to be the result of ricin poisoning.

AUSA GIBSON: I'm very sorry to hear that. Can you tell us who ordered the hit?

SA PITTMAN: It was ordered by HappyCat18.

37

DASH CAM TRANSCRIPT

DRIVER: Rob

BILLED TO: Chloe Corbin

TRIP DATE: 11/10/22, 12:47 PM

VEHICLE: Gray Kia Optima

PICK-UP LOCATION: 2700 Fillmore St, San Francisco, California

DROPOFF LOCATION: Pier 3, The Embarcadero, San Francisco, CA

FARE: $21.00

TRANSCRIPT OF DASH CAM RECORDING ON DEFENDANT'S PHONE

[Ms. Corbin enters vehicle on phone. Door closes.]

MS. CORBIN: Yeah. I know, right? It's ridiculous. How hard is it to be on time? I know. Totally. I had to order an Uber. I know, it's crazy. Okay, I'll call you after.

DEFENDANT: In a hurry?

MS. CORBIN: Yes, I'm on-air in twenty minutes.

DEFENDANT: On TV?

[Ms. Corbin silent. Looking at phone.]

MS. CORBIN: This is so fucking ridiculous. Oh, my God! [Answers phone.] Hello? I know, that's what I told them. Why are they so goddamn unreliable? I don't know why this needed to be in-studio. We could have just done a webcam. Now I'm going to be late. Okay, okay, bye. [Hangs up phone.] Can you hurry up, please?

DEFENDANT: I'm going as fast as I can.

MS. CORBIN: I know, I'm sorry. I just can't be late for this.

DEFENDANT: So you're going to be on TV? That's cool.

MS. CORBIN: Oh, yeah. It's just Bloomberg. I don't even know why I'm doing it. I have more followers than they do.

DEFENDANT: Have you been on TV before?

MS. CORBIN: Uh, yeah—a few times.

DEFENDANT: A few times? You must be a celebrity or something.

MS. CORBIN: Or something.

DEFENDANT: I heard once you're supposed to picture the audience naked.

MS. CORBIN: [Laughs.] I think that's for speaking in front of in-person audiences.

DEFENDANT: Well, yeah, but isn't it the same thing? Half the people watching TV probably are naked anyway.

MS. CORBIN: [Laughs.] You're probably right.

DEFENDANT: So, what do you do that they want to interview you on TV?

MS. CORBIN: Oh, I just run a nonprofit.

DEFENDANT: You mean, like, a charity or something?

MS. CORBIN: Yeah. How long have you been driving for Uber?

DEFENDANT: Not very long. A few months. I'm just doing it to pay the bills. I'm going to start a tech company.

MS. CORBIN: Oh, really? What's your startup idea?

DEFENDANT: I'm working on that. I'll get back to you.

MS. CORBIN: [Laughs.] So why are you driving an Uber then? You should be working on your idea.

DEFENDANT: I need to pay the bills. I'm still paying off my student loans. Plus, this job lets me build my network—meet nice people like you.

MS. CORBIN: Got it. Well, you have to take the plunge some time, or your startup idea will never happen.

DEFENDANT: That's a good point. I've got to get some experience first, though. This job was the closest thing I could get to a technology company.

MS. CORBIN: Being an Uber driver? You can do better than that. They're always looking to hire programmers. Do you know how to write code?

DEFENDANT: A little. I studied it in college, but I'm not very good at it. Mostly self-taught.

MS. CORBIN: Where did you go to school?

DEFENDANT: You've probably never heard of it. It's not exactly Stanford or Berkeley.

MS. CORBIN: Try me.

DEFENDANT: Central Valley University.

MS. CORBIN: No way! That's such a coincidence. We just decided to give a grant for a computer lab there.

DEFENDANT: Really? That's a small world. What did you say your charity is again?

MS. CORBIN: The Corbin Foundation.

DEFENDANT: Ohhh! I know who you are. You're Chloe Corbin, right?

MS. CORBIN: You figured me out. Don't you see my name on your little app though?

DEFENDANT: [Laughs.] Yeah, good point. I should have gotten that one sooner. You're legit famous, though—like, for real. Don't you have like a million followers on Instagram?

MS. CORBIN: Four million, actually.

DEFENDANT: You have four million followers!? Holy shit, you *are* famous! I thought I was doing good with a hundred thousand.

MS. CORBIN: You have a hundred thousand followers on Instagram?

DEFENDANT: No, no, I'm more of a YouTube guy. I do gaming videos.

MS. CORBIN: Still—a hundred thousand, that's pretty good.

DEFENDANT: Yeah, I guess.

MS. CORBIN: Why don't you make that your startup company?

DEFENDANT: What do you mean?

MS. CORBIN: Well, if you have a hundred thousand followers, you could probably grow that. If you got to a million, you could probably make a living doing it.

DEFENDANT: You think?

MS. CORBIN: Yeah, totally.

DEFENDANT: That would be like a dream come true. Just play video games all day and get paid for it.

MS. CORBIN: I can see why you have so many followers.

DEFENDANT: You can? Why's that?

MS. CORBIN: Because you're funny. You're sincere. It seems like you say what you really think. That's what people want to hear.

DEFENDANT: Yeah, I guess I never thought of it that way. I just say what's on my mind.

MS. CORBIN: Okay, we're here, so I've gotta go. But DM me some time. You know where to find me. Good luck with your startup.

DEFENDANT: Thanks.

38

BURNER_911

One Year Ago

@Burner_911 post on Razgo.com

*"Every revolution seems impossible at the beginning,
and after it happens, it was inevitable."*
—Bill Ayers

EVERY DAY I SEE THEM . . .

Tweeting their self-serving bullshit,

Spreading their propaganda across the internet,

Pontificating on CNN like they're the self-righteous rulers of the world . . .

I'm sick of the lies. Tired of the hypocrisy. The elites who pretend to be better than us, throwing their wealth around. When, really, they're the biggest deviants.

It's time for a revolution. Time for these oligarchs to be EXPOSED!

Just like a pedophile ring, they need a playground. A forum where their sick depravities and darkest perversions can be satisfied.

That playground is BABELON.COM!

It's where all the richest tech douchebags go. To get their underage hookups, order hookers, have their dicks sucked, whatever their money can buy—all, supposedly, anonymous. Anonymous, that is, until we hack the thing!

If you want to start a revolution, you need to hit them where it hurts. Expose them for who they really are. And this honeypot has been hiding in plain sight.

SO GET YOUR POPCORN AND ENJOY THE SHOW!!!

These hypocrites are going down!

39

CHLOE

Six thousand, seven hundred and forty-three posts—an average of almost two per day over the last ten years. That's what it took to build my following. Picture by picture, post by post, an endless stream of my perfect, curated life. If I didn't post something by 10:00 a.m., my followers demanded to know why. And when they did, I would start to twitch—my mind racing for something to say or do. With makeup and good lighting, of course. Filters at the ready. The externalization of my life.

Nick is pacing again, chewing on his nails. All they do is watch TV and complain or argue. They are all consumed by anxiety, like a pack of ADHD kindergartners deprived of Ritalin. The flood of attention they expected turned into a tsunami—more than they know how to handle. I know the feeling.

Careful what you wish for, boys.

Sitting in this chair that was likely retrieved out of a dumpster, I remember how I spent an afternoon a few months ago racked with anxiety myself, locked in my bedroom with the shades drawn. The community moderator for a Chloe Corbin fan group on Reddit had eviscerated a dress I'd worn to a charity gala the night before. The entire subreddit exploded with animated GIFs, deepfakes of me and the dress in various compromising positions, endless memes of emoji-laden taunts. I thought these were my fans, and yet hardly anyone defended me—as if it didn't even occur to them I was a real person.

CHLOE

I spent that day in my bed, crippled with depression, feeling like someone was standing on my chest. And yet what did I do the next day? I posted.

Again and again and again, I've posted.

That activity, that *lifestyle*—the constant, unrelenting, ubiquitous obsession of it—earned me 4,228,452 followers as of Tuesday, the day my old life stopped and this new life began. Today, four days later, I have 21,825,277 followers. I'm adding almost four million new followers *each day*—more than I gained from a decade of trying, cultivating, curating, *obsessing*. Attempting to give people hope, when clearly all they wanted was drama.

Our sick obsession with schadenfreude. This is just the latest proof that hate is more activating than love.

Now my audience is exploding, effortlessly, like a high-voltage current I hold in my hands. I barely have access to food, water, or a toilet, but all I can think about is my next post. Knowing this is the power that I have over my abductors; that this much voltage could kill them; that all their exploitations of my account will ultimately accrue benefits to me, building my followers, supplementing my strength. Granting me a superpower. Even if all these people are just here to see me die.

Knowing all this, I wonder . . . *how big can this get?*

40

SHANE

"This shit can't happen again," I say, running my finger along the ridge of stitches on my jaw in case it's unclear to Kryz and Killian what I'm talking about.

They're doing final room checks before lights out, so we have just a few minutes—my first chance to talk with them since the attack.

"The captain implemented a new procedure—full lockdown every time we move you," Kryz says. "So it won't happen again."

"And the assailant is still in the infirmary with a brain hemorrhage," Killian says. "So that sends a message too."

"We could have finished that guy off, no questions asked," Kryz says. "Attack with a deadly weapon more than justifies lethal force. But he'll get transferred to another prison now."

"Someone else will take care of that. Better to keep your hands clean," I say. "So, what's the situation with the rest of the prisoners? Who's with us, and who's against us?"

An electric buzz down the corridor announces the opening of a nearby cell. Kryz looks over his shoulder, aware they need to continue their rounds before someone notices their absence.

"Hard to say," he says. "Most of the guys who were arrested on October 12th have already plea bargained or posted bail, so there probably aren't that many true believers."

"So how do we make them true believers?" I ask.

In my head, though, I'm thinking maybe this was all a big mistake. I just didn't have time to think, like a runaway boulder chasing me down a hill. All I could do was try to outrun it. Now its run me over. It's been overtaken by fucknuts like Kryz and Killian and those asswipes who took Chloe.

Chloe . . .

I never should have gone to that Corbin Foundation annual gala thing. Maybe then she never would have got mixed up in all this. But it was my only chance to see her again. I had the money. It happened to be the *exact amount* of money I had from that dickweed Logan What's-his-ass, in fact. And what else was I going to spend it on? I made the $50,000 donation without a second thought. I needed to see her, and that was the only way I could think of to do it. That was the priority.

I remember, when I registered, staring at the "Occupation" field. Unsure what to enter. Something that maybe she would notice. I had enough of a following on YouTube by then that "influencer" seemed credible. So I called myself that and then played the part, with my bleached hair, all-white tux, and electric-blue tie. I looked like a prom reject, but it worked.

At the event, I waited to make my move. Watching the parade of rich assholes—peacocking their social status, laughing effusively at each other's jokes, shooting sideways glances around the room as they sipped on their cocktails, always looking to upgrade their conversation. All of them just trying to get their moment with Chloe. It was like a spotlight followed her everywhere she went, gracefully navigating the crowd. An effortless peck on the cheek, an endearing hand on the shoulder, a sincere laugh that lilted above the din. All the social graces I never learned. An elaborate choreography I didn't understand. I was awestruck.

When I finally met her, I was so nervous. I knew I had only ten, maybe twenty seconds to get her attention—to bootstrap that into a longer conversation. She thanked me for making such a generous donation, then asked what my "affinity" was to the cause. I almost admitted my affinity was for her, but instead said something about going to CVU and that the donation would make a big difference. I'll never forget how she looked at me after I said that. Like she suddenly saw me in a different way, realized I wasn't the usual Ivy League twat. When we shook hands, that's when I knew. A touch that radiated up my arm, wrapped around my chest, squeezed the air out of my lungs. I had never been in love, but I knew then what it must feel like.

If that douchebag Zach hadn't interrupted, I would have held her hand all night. Of *course* she had a date. It hadn't even occurred to me to bring one.

But it was fine. I had a plan for him.

"To be honest," Kryz says, snapping me back to reality as he glances again over his shoulder, "it's kinda mixed down there. Lots of theories."

"There are always theories," I say. "That's the nature of the BurnOutz."

"At least they have some negotiating leverage," Killian says.

I turn to him, trying to decipher what he's talking about. "They who?"

"The guys who took that Corbin chick," Killian says. "They're tryin' to do a prisoner swap. Her for you."

"Yeah, that's never going to happen," Kryz says. "Sorry to burst your bubble, but the Feds don't just let people they arrest walk out the door."

"She has a lot of Instagram followers," Killian says, a lame attempt at sarcasm.

"Fuck that," Kryz says, laughing. "They can throw that bitch in a dumpster for all I care."

I turn to Kryz, forcing myself to stay expressionless. This isn't going to end well. Too many people know about me and Chloe. Not these guys, yet. But it's in the evidence. It's going to come out. Eventually. I can't stop it.

But I also can't think about that right now.

"Agree, she's irrelevant," I say after they've settled. "Just make sure I get that phone tomorrow."

41

GRAND JURY INDICTMENT

**TRANSCRIPT OF GRAND JURY TESTIMONY OF FBI
SPECIAL AGENT EMMANUEL OKONKWO, AUGUST 29, 2023**

Emmanuel Okonko, Witness for the Prosecution
Annabelle Burgess, Assistant US Attorney

THE COURTROOM DEPUTY: Raise your right hand, please. Do you solemnly swear that you will tell the truth, the whole truth, and nothing but the truth, so help you God?

MR. OKONKWO: I do.

MS. BURGESS: Thank you for testifying today, Agent Okonkwo. Can you please describe for the grand jury your area of expertise at the FBI.

MR. OKONKWO: Yes, I'm a special agent in the bureau's Criminal, Cyber, Response and Services Branch based in the San Francisco field office. I specialize in investigating white-collar crimes, typically internet wire-fraud cases.

MS. BURGESS: And you worked on the FBI's investigation of an online dating site called Babelon.com, correct?

MR. OKONKWO: Yes.

MS. BURGESS: It was quite a scandal at the time, but please refresh our memories of that case.

MR. OKONKWO: Well, we initially started looking into the site based on evidence of illegal sexual activity, including prostitution rings, sexual exploitation of minors, and even human trafficking. Using undercover accounts, we identified users arranging meeting times and locations and facilitating payments for sex through Babelon. We also had received complaints from users who said they were defrauded or extorted on Babelon. Most were small-time hustles. Usually fake accounts set up to lure men into online relationships. Then the perpetrators would threaten to disclose the messages to the user's spouse or employer unless they got paid. We pursued criminal charges against several individuals implicated in these illegal activities.

MS. BURGESS: Did you find the site's founders or executives were responsible?

MR. OKONKWO: We never found a direct link to the founders or executives. The illegal activity we discovered was perpetrated by third parties. But Babelon leadership was not doing enough to adequately police the site. So, after several warnings were ignored, federal prosecutors brought sex-trafficking charges against the company and its CEO, Kai De Lange.

MS. BURGESS: Did that case go to trial?

MR. OKONKWO: The prosecution was expecting to work out a deal. They knew it would be hard to win a conviction due to CDA 230.

MS. BURGESS: Can you explain what that is to the grand jury?

MR. OKONKWO: Oh, yes—Section 230 of the Communications Decency Act. It's a provision from a 1996 law that protects website owners from being held legally liable for content posted by users of their site. Basically, the sites say it's not their responsibility to censor user content on their platforms and they wipe their hands clean.

MS. BURGESS: Don't most social media sites cooperate with law enforcement to discourage illegal activity on their platforms? Why was that not the case with Babelon.com?

MR. OKONKWO: Because they were making a lot of money. In financial records we subpoenaed, Babelon's revenue increased from $23 million in 2014 to $78 million in 2015. The vast majority of that revenue, more than 90 percent, was from adult classified ads, expensive virtual gifts sent to women as payments for sex, and subscriptions to adult-oriented live streaming on the site. So, even if they weren't directly involved, the site's owners had a strong incentive to protect those using the site for illicit sexual activity.

MS. BURGESS: So did the case settle?

MR. OKONKWO: Not exactly. About a month after the case was made public was when the BurnOutz hack happened.

MS. BURGESS: Can you explain what the BurnOutz hack was?

MR. OKONKWO: Yeah, this was a previously unknown individual or group of computer hackers who committed a massive ransomware attack of the Babelon site. They stole an enormous trove of data on over twenty million Babelon users and started releasing it in increments on WikiLeaks—names, email addresses, phone numbers, sexual orientation, member-to-member messaging logs, video viewing histories, payments for sex—it was very sensitive information. They then posted a home page takeover threatening to release more personal information on users if they weren't given a $5 million ransom.

MS. BURGESS: Was this organization, the BurnOutz, one that the FBI was aware of or had been investigating at the time?

MR. OKONKWO: We'd opened a file, but nobody was paying much attention to them prior to the Babelon hack.

MS. BURGESS: How did the bureau respond to the hack?

MR. OKONKWO: Well, it was a little embarrassing, honestly. Here's a business we supposedly have under investigation, and a ransomware attack happens right under our noses. We immediately set about trying to figure out who was behind it. But we couldn't get any digital fingerprints on them.

MS. BURGESS: Was it a sophisticated attack?

MR. OKONKWO: Not particularly. In a way, that's actually what made them hard to catch. The security measures on the site were poor, so the hackers didn't leave behind much code for us to decipher.

MS. BURGESS: What did the Babelon executives do in response?

MR. OKONKWO: First, they thought it was a hoax. Then, they threatened a lawsuit against the federal government, under the claim that our case made them a target and that our investigation had somehow made their systems vulnerable. That notion fell apart pretty quickly when the hackers started dumping user data.

MS. BURGESS: Did the FBI advise Babelon what to do?

MR. OKONKWO: It's our standard guidance not to pay ransomware demands, and that's what we told them in this case. We also speculated that the scheme might have been concocted as a way for investors to secretly get money out of the company before possible fines resulting from our case.

MS. BURGESS: Did you find any evidence that was what was happening?

MR. OKONKWO: Without knowing the source of the hack, it was just speculation. I never found it very plausible, though. The company had raised $750 million and was worth something like $3 billion. Going to all that trouble just to get $5 million out didn't seem worth it.

MS. BURGESS: I see. So did they pay the ransom?

MR. OKONKWO: Eventually, yes, they did. The first data drop targeted just a handful of prominent individuals. But the scope of the data breach became apparent on the second dump, which compromised the personal information of over one hundred thousand users. After many more frantic phone calls to our office and a third data dump, the company transferred $5 million in Bitcoin to an anonymous cryptocurrency wallet.

MS. BURGESS: Did that stop the attack?

MR. OKONKWO: Yes. The site was restored, the data dumps stopped, and that was the end of it.

MS. BURGESS: Did the Justice Department continue its case against Babelon?

MR. OKONKWO: Yes, but that settled soon afterward. The company paid a $20 million fine. A few years later, after losing most of their users, they quietly shut it down.

MS. BURGESS: What happened to the founder, Mr. De Lange?

MR. OKONKWO: Last I heard, he founded a new dating site.

MS. BURGESS: Of course he did. [Laughter] And what about the BurnOutz? What did you find out about that organization?

MR. OKONKWO: Right, so after that incident we obviously opened up a case on them. That said, the FBI's Cyber Division has case files on thousands of online criminal syndicates, and they can be frustrating to investigate.

MS. BURGESS: Why is that?

MR. OKONKWO: They move fast and slow at the same time. If you're parsing code, you can sometimes identify telltale clues about these hackers within seconds. But, obviously, many of the breadcrumb trails lead offshore, and that's when things can slow down. Most of the IP traffic originates from Russia or China or other countries that are disinclined to cooperate with US law enforcement. And everything is masked and decoyed. So you hit a lot of dead ends.

MS. BURGESS: Did you have any leads to identify the criminals behind the BurnOutz?

MR. OKONKWO: Very little. I had my team of digital forensic researchers pore over the database logs, network traffic, and DNS records for Babelon. The compromised database had been partitioned into thousands of smaller datasets to accelerate the download. Each dataset was then routed through a complex and unique series of obfuscated servers using IP spoofing, so it was very difficult to trace. Furthermore, the datasets were never reassembled at a single endpoint, so it didn't point us back to an obvious initiator. As I said, the theft itself was simple, but the getaway route was quite sophisticated. Our first break came when we analyzed the image the hackers posted for their ransom note. Using a tool called ExifTool, we extracted deleted metadata from the original image file that included permissions by a user named Yonah A. and a geolocation tag that showed the file was created near the town of Timisoara, Romania. That was enough to identify a Yonah Antonescu. With the help of the Romanian Intelligence Service, we were then able to trace a payment to Mr. Antonescu from Tarmo Nikula, a Finnish national living in Mykonos, Greece, through a series of international bank wire transfers. Then, pulling on the thread of Mr. Nikula, we found a small data center in Tampere, Finland, about an hour north of Helsinki, that was registered in his name. When we cross-referenced the IP addresses of that data center with the decrypted final file transfers of the stolen datasets, more than fifty had ultimately been stored on servers there. We were then able to trace that to data transfers from servers in Palembang, Indonesia, registered to an Anwar Surya.

MS. BURGESS: So it sounds like you found your culprits?

MR. OKONKWO: Maybe, but something still didn't make sense. Why wasn't all of the data in one place? Why had the payments gone *from* Mr. Antonescu *to* Mr. Nikula when it was Mr. Antonescu who had initiated the ransomware attack and the stolen data had been uploaded by Mr. Surya? The money was flowing in the wrong direction. If Tarmo Nikula initiated the attack, how did he end up with both the money and this valuable user data for free? It didn't make sense. There had to be a missing piece of the puzzle.

MS. BURGESS: And what do you think that was?

MR. OKONKWO: Well, that became apparent when one of our most junior special agents started looking at the social media profiles of these three men, Mr. Antonescu, Mr. Nikula, and Mr. Surya. In hindsight, it was such a simple, obvious thing.

MS. BURGESS: What was that?

MR. OKONKWO: They all were following an account on You-Tube called BurnerBro.

MS. BURGESS: Mr. Stoller's YouTube account.

MR. OKONKWO: Correct. That's when we discovered payments to both Mr. Antonescu and Mr. Surya from a crypto account belonging to a user named HappyCat18. Suddenly, it all made sense: the BurnOutz were fans of BurnerBro, and Burner_911 was most likely created by the same person, Shane Stoller.

42

FBI SURVEILLANCE TRANSCRIPT

**TRANSCRIPT OF FBI SURVEILLANCE OF
SHANE STOLLER, FEBRUARY 3, 2023**

MR. STOLLER: Hey, there you are.

MS. CORBIN: Hi. How did you know this is my favorite restaurant? I love Perbacco.

MR. STOLLER: Oh, I don't know—lucky guess. Anyway, I was starting to get worried you wouldn't show up.

MS. CORBIN: Yeah, sorry I'm late. I was talking with my friend Lexi.

MR. STOLLER: Friend drama?

MS. CORBIN: [Sigh.] Sort of. Actually, she was trying to convince me not to go out with you.

MR. STOLLER: I'm glad you didn't listen to her. We just met and already your friends don't like me?

MS. CORBIN: I know, totally—it's ridiculous. She's just being protective. Maybe a little snobby.

MR. STOLLER: Ooohh, I like her already. When can we meet?

MS. CORBIN: [Laughs.] Don't get ahead of yourself. Let's see how this date goes first.

MR. STOLLER: Is this a date? I wasn't sure, honestly. I guess I better offer to pay then.

MS. CORBIN: [Laughs.] In that case, I'll have to get a glass of this Kistler 2021 Chardonnay. That's also my favorite.

MR. STOLLER: Hey! That's $27 a glass!

MS. CORBIN: [Laughs.] I told you, I'm not a cheap date.

MR. STOLLER: I shouldn't have spent all my money at your charity gala.

MS. CORBIN: [Laughs.]

MR. STOLLER: Speaking of the gala, what's up with that guy Zach? I thought he was your boyfriend.

MS. CORBIN: Oh . . . yeah. Well, he was. Sort of . . . for a couple months at least.

MR. STOLLER: Not anymore?

MS. CORBIN: No, we . . . we aren't seeing each other anymore.

MR. STOLLER: Oh, sorry to hear that. What happened?

MS. CORBIN: Ha! It's complicated—

MR. STOLLER: Life is complicated. He must either be crazy or heartbroken not to be with you anymore.

MS. CORBIN: I broke it off, but . . . it's a little embarrassing, honestly. He . . . got caught up in that whole Babelon scandal.

MR. STOLLER: Oh, shit—*really*?

MS. CORBIN: Yeah, Zach Aaronson. Bummer to have a double-A last name, I guess. He was in the first batch of names that got released. I was mortified.

MR. STOLLER: Yikes. I can see why you broke it off.

MS. CORBIN: Yeah, no kidding. He was an asshole anyway. It just gave me a good excuse to pull the plug.

MR. STOLLER: So, get right back on the horse, huh? Why did you decide to go out with me?

MS. CORBIN: That's what Lexi couldn't understand either.

MR. STOLLER: I'm not exactly your type.

MS. CORBIN: Oh, yeah? And what do you think my type is?

MR. STOLLER: You know ... guys like Zach, I guess—

MS. CORBIN: Thanks a *lot*!

MR. STOLLER: No, not the secret sex stuff. I just mean, like, all the dudes I see on your Instagram—rich, famous, good-looking.

MS. CORBIN: Mmmm ... I see. There's a fourth criteria, actually: *interesting*.

MR. STOLLER: So I'm *interesting*? Thanks, I think ... Well, one out of your four criteria isn't bad, I guess.

MS. CORBIN: [Laughs.] It's better than most guys manage.

MR. STOLLER: [To waiter.] We'll take a bottle of the Kistler Chardonnay, please.

MS. CORBIN: Splurging for a whole bottle! Trying to charm me?

MR. STOLLER: Seems like the classy move. Get the evening off on the right foot.

MS. CORBIN: Me drinking half a bottle of wine might help your cause as well.

MR. STOLLER: All part of the plan.

MS. CORBIN: [Laughs.]

MR. STOLLER: So, tell me, what do I have to do to win over this Lexi friend of yours?

MS. CORBIN: She's just looking out for me. Trying to make sure you're not a psycho or a stalker or something.

MR. STOLLER: Pretty expensive restaurant for a stalker.

MS. CORBIN: [Laughs.] She watched some of your YouTube videos and thought they were a little . . .

MR. STOLLER: Juvenile?

MS. CORBIN: More like . . . right-leaning. Even misogynistic.

MR. STOLLER: Mmmm . . . I can see why she would think that. I do sort of act like an ass in some of those videos. But I just do it for entertainment value. It's what my audience likes. That's BurnerBro, it's not really me.

MS. CORBIN: So you don't really have a vendetta against social justice warriors, as you call them?

MR. STOLLER: No, not really.

MS. CORBIN: That's good, because a lot of those social causes are things I believe in.

MR. STOLLER: That's cool. You can believe whatever you want to believe. I just don't like it when people try to tell me what I can believe. Rubs me the wrong way.

MS. CORBIN: How are you going to change the world if you don't try to change people's minds?

MR. STOLLER: I'm not trying to change the world.

MS. CORBIN: So you're happy with the world the way it is?

MR. STOLLER: No, there are lots of things in the world I wish were better—fairer. But that's not my job. Not my place.

MS. CORBIN: Why not? I think we all have an obligation to do what we can to fight for what we believe in. It's all of our jobs to make the world a better place. That's why I do what I do. You could do a lot more with your platform.

MR. STOLLER: My platform? What do you mean?

MS. CORBIN: You know, your followers.

MR. STOLLER: On YouTube?

MS. CORBIN: Yes. Where else? You have over five hundred thousand subscribers to your YouTube channel. That's a big audience. What are you doing with it?

MR. STOLLER: Trying to grow it to a million?

MS. CORBIN: No . . . I don't mean how big are you going to make it. That's just a milestone. What's your *message*? What are you telling people?

MR. STOLLER: I don't know. That's not really the point.

MS. CORBIN: What is the point? Besides just shooting imaginary soldiers.

MR. STOLLER: That's it. I'm just having fun. People seem to think the shit I say is funny, so that's what I do. That's what gets me more subscribers. And more subscribers means more money.

MS. CORBIN: Ah, I see. So you're just doing it for the money? How much does a YouTube influencer make anyway?

MR. STOLLER: That's a personal question.

MS. CORBIN: I'm just saying, it can't be much. My friend Jenna has a makeup channel on YouTube. She gets about a one hundred thousand views for each video she posts, and that earns her about $300. Not much.

MR. STOLLER: Maybe mouse nuts to you, but it's enough to make a living.

MS. CORBIN: Barely.

MR. STOLLER: Enough to give $50,000 to your charity.

MS. CORBIN: *Touché.* Thanks again for your donation. Look, all I'm saying is that you could be doing something more, greater than yourself, to further a cause you believe in.

MR. STOLLER: Like sustainable fashion or horse rescues?

MS. CORBIN: Sure. Or computer labs at community colleges.

MR. STOLLER: Fair enough. [To waiter.] Thank you.

MS. CORBIN: So what causes do you believe in?

MR. STOLLER: First, let's toast. To the post-Zach era and our first date. The first of what I hope will be many. Cheers.

MS. CORBIN: Cheers. But I'm not going to let you out of answering my question. You can't just rant against political correctness and liberals. You can't just be anti, anti, anti. Eventually, you need to be *for* something.

MR. STOLLER: You probably wouldn't like what I'm for.

MS. CORBIN: Not if it's racist or sexist or xenophobic. Those things are all *anti*.

MR. STOLLER: No, it's none of that crap.

MS. CORBIN: Well, then ... try me.

MR. STOLLER: It's about money. I'm not a socialist or anything. It's just that some people have more, a *lot* more, than others. And more and more folks have practically none at all.

MS. CORBIN: I agree completely. Wealth inequality is a huge problem. That's why I run a charitable foundation. Why would you think I wouldn't like that?

MR. STOLLER: Because you're, like, rich. *Really* rich!

MS. CORBIN: Yes, my father has been very successful. But, through the Corbin Foundation, we give away millions of dollars every year.

MR. STOLLER: Yeah, on *billions* of dollars in assets. Billionaires always want so much credit for their philanthropy, but it's a tiny fraction of what they're worth, and most of the time they're just doing it for the tax write-off. Your dad put less than 1 percent of his wealth into an endowment, and all you do is give away the interest. It's a rounding error to fund a vanity project to buff up his image. You could do a lot more with *your* platform.

MS. CORBIN: That's kind of a dick thing to say.

MR. STOLLER: I just say what's on my mind.

MS. CORBIN: Wait a minute . . . I remember you. Yeah, yeah, I remember you! You were my Uber driver that day I was late for the Bloomberg interview. Just now, when you said that, it suddenly came back to me.

MR. STOLLER: Busted.

MS. CORBIN: Jesus Christ. Maybe Lexi was right. Have you been stalking me?

MR. STOLLER: Not . . . no, no. Not . . . not *continuously* or anything.

MS. CORBIN: Oh, you're just a part-time stalker?

MR. STOLLER: No, I just ... I just really enjoyed meeting you that day. I knew you were never going to date some random Uber driver, so I figured out another way to meet you.

MS. CORBIN: So you gave $50,000 just as an excuse to meet me?

MR. STOLLER: No, I gave the money because I know there are a lot of kids who can't afford computers. Getting the chance to see you again was a fringe benefit.

MS. CORBIN: Why should I believe you? You could be a kidnapper or something.

MR. STOLLER: A kidnapper never would have splurged on the Kistler.

MS. CORBIN: Okay, well, pretending to be someone you're not is no way to pick up a woman. If you're going to earn my trust, I need to know who you really are. You need to tell me everything. So ... let's try this again. I'm Chloe Corbin, nice to meet you.

MR. STOLLER: I'm Shane Stoller. Nice to meet you too.

43

SHANE

"Take your pants off."

Not something you want to hear in prison, but I'm getting used to it. Strip searches on the daily. The guard who said it isn't one of ours. Technically, he's not even a guard—bailiff, I think, since we're just outside the courtroom.

Wayne hands me a pile of clothes and then turns to look at the wall like he's studying a piece of art or some shit. Giving me privacy. Or maybe just trying to prove he's not a perve. This was his idea, changing before court so I wouldn't look guilty in my orange prison jumpsuit.

"Remember what I said," Wayne says, still facing the wall. "Let me do the talking. We don't need you going on one of your rants. Not with this judge."

None of the clothes fit. The bailiff stares at me while I tug on the pants, but they keep wanting to drop around my ankles. And I can barely button the shirt.

I can't focus. The whole concept of a trial still feels so surreal to me. That I stand accused of terrorism and treason—that I could get the death penalty? I can't wrap my mind around it. At this point, there are so many charges I can't keep track of them, all just for words I may *or may not* have typed on a keyboard. Like I'm some sort of criminal mastermind. The only difference between an internet troll and a terrorist messiah is how many followers you have.

In the real world, I've always been too shy, too reserved, not charismatic enough. But online, people have always listened. They've followed, subscribed, shared. They've been inspired, *activated*. People just want to be told what to do, what to *believe*. They want to be relieved of the burden of decision-making. If what you tell them *feels* like the truth—chosen with their own free will, satisfying a deeper personal need, stroking their ego—that's when it becomes religion. But just like a televangelist, my religion was also my business. I needed levers behind the curtain to make miracles happen.

I finally get the rest of the clothes on. They're uncomfortable as all hell, but I'm going for what Wayne called my "best approximation of a normal human being." The bailiff cuffs me again before unlocking the door to his little chamber that we've just used as a dressing room.

The three of us step into the courtroom hallway and Valerie stands to meet us, trying not to crack up as she takes in my rumpled shirt and sagging khakis.

"I look like a salesperson at Old Navy," I say.

Valerie lets out a laugh and starts tucking in my shirt and straightening my hair. "You should never take fashion advice from Wayne."

"All my other advice remains valid, however," Wayne says. "Remember what we discussed?"

"Would you be pissed if I said no?"

"This is a separate indictment, under the RICO Act. They're going after the BurnOutz as a criminal syndicate with a grab bag of crimes—racketeering, extortion, money laundering, bribery, securities fraud, and so on—which they say establish a pattern of criminal activity. Each charge carries a twenty-year prison term, so this alone is enough to send you away for life."

A "criminal syndicate" sounds so fancy. I never really thought about it that way, but I guess that's what it was.

I learned from Dré the hard way how difficult a criminal syndicate is to run. First, you need to work with people you trust. Dré thought he could trust Zo. He was wrong. Employees always hate their boss. But when it's an illegal business, those employees don't just hate you, they're looking to screw you over—turn you in to get a reward, plead with the Feds in exchange for immunity, skim a little somethin' off the top, shoot you in the face. The normal rules don't apply.

The most important thing I learned from Dré, though, is that you need to motivate people with more than money. Just like the tech founders say, real motivation comes from *mission*. People have to *believe* in what they're doing, not just be out to make a buck.

So when I started pulling bigger schemes, I did it virtually and I did it with believers—my YouTube Burner Bros. They were the perfect recruits—tech-savvy, aligned with my philosophy, ample time on their hands. I didn't even recruit the first BurnOut; he came to me. I was complaining in one of my videos about some cheat code for an XBox Live game, and this dude Tarmo messages me on Discord and says he's found a vulnerability in the game that lets him hack user data. So we did it—didn't even think about it much. Then I found another Burner Bro in Indonesia. Anwar was the fucking *man*! He wrote a script to apply for new credit cards using hacked personal data.

The more sites we hacked, the bigger our network grew. More and more Burner Bros joined the cause. All our communications were encrypted on Telegram. All our transactions used cryptocurrency. We had hacked hacking—no cash, no accomplices, no trail. A network of disconnected, anonymous dudes around the world. Nothing that could be traced back to me.

The name *BurnOutz* wasn't my idea. It was a joke Anwar said one time, and it just stuck. Which was good, because it needed a name. It was an idea, a mission, a *movement*—and movements don't gain momentum unless they have a name. It's all about the branding.

When the Babelon hack happened, the whole thing just exploded. Everyone wanted in. I had guys coming out of the woodwork to join the cause . . . and get in on the action. I didn't know who they even were beyond a username, but they were believers. Nameless, faceless, angry trolls, ready to do battle, represented only by the random assemblage of letters and numbers in their username. Looking for a leader, a direction for their frustration. Individually, they couldn't be trusted, but collectively they were unstoppable. I just needed to channel that energy. I was done with the BurnerBro account on YouTube, done playing video games. This new game I was playing was much more fun.

"They're going to try to extradite some of these guys from Latvia and wherever the hell else and get them to testify against you," Wayne says. "It won't work, but they'll try. All you have to do is remember two words."

"Not guilty," I say.

"That's right." Wayne nods and gives my suburban-dad costume one last look. "Not fucking guilty."

"That's three words," I say after a beat—pretending to be relaxed while my mind spins out in a thousand different directions. I don't know how Wayne and Valerie are keeping it all straight. I'd be fucked without their help.

I lock eyes with Wayne for a second, hoping he can't see the fear in mine. "Thank you. You guys really saved my ass."

44

BURNER_911

Ten Months Ago

@Burner_911 post on Razgo.com

> *"I tried to pay attention, but attention paid me."*
> —Lil Wayne

Do I have your attention now? Babelon was just the beginning of what's possible. We made $5 MIL in 3 days! Now, it's time for YOU to get what you deserve!

We've been distracted TOO LONG! Demonizing and *killing* each other because of things that don't matter. It's time to stop the tired battles over race and religion, gender and sexual orientation, politics and ethnicity, all the other *bullshit* of identity politics. As if those are the things that divide us. I'm here to tell you NONE OF THOSE THINGS MATTER!!!

These differences are just propaganda pushed by the global elites so we'll take our eye off the REAL injustice in America. The REAL inequity. The ONLY thing that matters—THE ROOT OF IT ALL . . . MONEY!!!! 💰 💰 💰 💰 They have it, we don't. PERIOD. *That's* the struggle. That's the *only* struggle! When that is fixed, everything else corrects itself.

We've subjugated ourselves to the TECH OLIGARCHS for toooooo long!!! Of the ten richest people in the world, SEVEN are in tech. We celebrate, venerate, even REVERE these tech billionaires, like they DESERVE it!! Like they EARNED it!! The reality is they HOARD it. They're NEVER content. They just take *more*,

and more,

and more,

and more,

and more,

and more,

and more,

and more,

and more of the wealth, while the rest of us can't make rent, can't pay for school, can't buy a car, can't get healthcare, can't even barely afford food or groceries. Why do we idolize these guys?? Why do we give them all our money??

WHY DO LESS THAN 500 BILLIONAIRES HAVE $3.4 TRILLION!?!?!?!?!?

Is that fair???? Is that just????? Is that what our *forefathers* envisioned?!?!?!?! 🇺🇸🇺🇸🇺🇸🇺🇸

The answer is no . . . No, it's *fucking* not!

If history teaches us anything, it is that those with privilege don't give up their privileges voluntarily.

It's time to fight back. It's time for "We the People" to get our share. So WHAT ARE WE GOING TO DO?

Rob them on the street? Nah—too messy.

Hack into their bank accounts? Nah—not enough money there.

We're going to HIT THEM WHERE IT HURTS!!!

IT'S THE STONKS, STUPID!   The stock market—that's where we're going to go. Like Willie Sutton would say if he were alive today, *"Because that's where the money is."*

The RICHEST 1% CONTROL 56% of the stock market. So . . . if you want all those juicy tendies, that's where you're gonna find them. That's what we're gonna take. The day of reckoning is coming. It's time to punish these fools and take what we deserve.

JOIN ME! If we work together . . . If you do as I say . . . If we stick to The Plan . . . We can all be EPIC!!!!

So get your Nottingham trading apps ready. Join r/nottinghamjustice for updates, recruit your friends, post your targets, and, most of all, wait for the call! We won't stop until the CROOKED financial system BURNS TO THE GROUND!!!

#NOTTINGHAMJUSTICE

COMMENTS:

tatKKalvin: they blatantly rigged the election, then blatantly rigged the stock market. they just don't care anymore. LETS BURN THEM DOWN! 🔥 🔥 🔥

triggerhappy75: THE OLLIES THINK THEY OWN THE GAME!! this shit has been rigged too long. time to get ours!

pterror: there all part of the same club. rules for thee, not for me.

BobIsAwesome: u dont know wtf your doin. these guys gonna rip you a new asshole.

FattyRoll12: luv it! i'm in!!!! YOLO.

Zed123: my dad killed himself after he lost everything in '08. Fuck these fuckers.

homeboyz: BURN THE OLLIES! 🔥 🔥 🔥 UPVOTE!

bDog_25: my girl needs some gift and Drip. LETS GET SOME!!!

fishyg: Listen up ollies! Your going to get what you f**king deserve! UPVOTE!

RandyG: Youre 💯 @Burner_911 We are the only ones who can stop this bullshit!!!!

CreamyRanch: WE THE PEOPLE NEED THE TENDIES!!! 🍗 🍗 🍗 🍗 🍗

JackJack: what do you think we just a bunch o' bagholders!?!? lmao

Turtle_Whip: Like this post if you are ready to activate the sleeper cell!! The squeeze is coming bitches 💎 💎 💎

CurvyCow: GUYZ . . . we need to remember this could hurt real people who own multiple yachts 🙄 🛳️

rivalREE: bruh . . . I literally have $100 in my notty account

AchillesKiller: Hope your right @Burner_911 🤞 🤞 🤞 what's the plan for 🗡️🔥 🗡️🔥

2,564 ADDITIONAL COMMENTS

45

CHLOE

Benny sets a plate of cold fried chicken in front of me, accompanied by soggy fries and sad coleslaw that releases its juices all over the plate—soaking everything, spilling over the edge, dribbling a trail across the floor and onto my lap. I don't care; I'm ravenous.

The boys are sitting around a table in the adjacent dining room. I can see them all now from my La-Z-Boy throne in the living room. I'm still lashed to it like a figurehead on the prow of a ship, but they've given up on the hood, too much hassle. It's not like I haven't seen them all dozens of times now. *Everyone* has seen them, even if only in grainy and low-resolution images—from the live stream, from the security footage, from toll booths and traffic cameras. They play in a continuous loop on the cable news shows that never stop broadcasting from the TV in the corner, along with statements from experts and authorities saying they won't negotiate, speculating on the identities of the men, describing their nationwide manhunt, claiming they are closing in on our location, about to apprehend us all.

My hands are free now too. Free to rip strips of flesh off the chicken bones, free to pinch wet clumps of coleslaw and shove them into my mouth, drips running down my chin. Apart from military rations and protein bars, this is the first meal I've had since they took me—progress, even if I don't yet have a seat at the table.

I glance up, watch them quietly chewing. They're increasingly sullen, anxious, restless, untethered.

They are debating what to do next. The cigarette-burn video resulted in hundreds of messages through Razgo—most from BurnOutz, fanboys cheering them on. But many claimed to be some form of law enforcement. And distinguishing if they really are who they *say* they are is impossible. Is it the "special agent with the FBI?" The "hostage negotiator with the SFPD?" The "terrorist crime unit of San Francisco County"? They are all just anonymous usernames on Razgo's platform, with no email domain, no "verified" accounts, no badges or bona fides to determine their authenticity. Some provide phone numbers, but the boys are too nervous to dial them, convinced any call will be traced back to here, wherever *here* is. The bargaining chip they were so proud of, so sure was a "get out of jail free" card, is proving difficult to play.

The plan, to the degree there ever was one beyond the first step of kidnapping me, continues to evolve in real time—disorganized and unpredictable, like a flash flood in the desert. Or, more appropriately, like the spilled beer I see on the table, wandering aimlessly over the surface, pooling around plates and bottles, collecting in rivulets, and eventually spilling over the edge. Like the movement itself. Planning its next move on the fly. *Are we going over the edge?*

"We need to post another video," Pete says, sparking another uneasy volley of conversation.

Scooter points out that the last video didn't achieve the desired result, so why bother? But Pete and Nick are already devising a next level of physical torture, to up the ante. All of them talk over each other. Only Benny is silent.

"We could waterboard her!" Pete suggests with disturbing enthusiasm.

Scooter identifies the bathtub as a possible venue "so we don't get the floors wet."

Nick doesn't like it—too predictable, not dangerous enough to provoke real fear, to "go viral."

"What about electric shock?" Pete pivots. "I could splice the wire in the lamp."

Scooter shrugs his eyebrows skeptically. "Would she survive that?"

Nick grimaces in an ambiguous expression, unclear if he thinks the stunt is too much or not enough. Benny steals a nervous glance at me.

I look down at the cigarette burn on my arm, the dark bullet hole of ash now replaced by a raised blister, red and oozing. "A 110-volt outlet can be lethal," I say, as if it won't be my body that is subjected to the current. "You don't want to kill your bargaining chip."

Nick turns and sneers, squinting in disdain. He stands and strides toward me, his arms poised at his side as if ready to draw guns . . . or strangle me. "How 'bout you shut the fuck up?" he says, leaning over me. "Nobody asked you."

The others are silent, uncertain, respectful of his volatility. I avert my gaze, look away toward the TV, absorb footage from the riot we've all seen a hundred times, followed by the talking head of Shane's lawyer.

"She has a point, Nick," Pete begins cautiously. "If we kill her, we don't have any leverage."

"To get Shane out of jail," I say. No one speaks, so I continue. "We need to find a line of communication, start negotiating . . . with *someone*. Otherwise, what's the point of all this?"

"Negotiate with *who*?" Pete asks, walking up behind Nick. "All we got are a bunch of liars and whack jobs."

"Shane's lawyer, the guy on TV," I say, nodding toward his image on the television. "We can reach him. He'll help us. He's protected by attorney-client privilege. Maybe he can figure out a deal."

"Actually, that's not a bad idea," Scooter says.

Nick rolls his eyes. "No way. His line will be tapped. They'll trace it to us. Besides, we don't even know if this Shane guy really is Burner." He waves his hand dismissively and returns to his seat at the table.

"Well, we don't really have a better plan right now," Scooter says.

"Yeah," I say, staring at the back of Nick's head, knowing he can sense me. "And the BurnOutz always have a plan, don't they?"

46

WAYNE

"In either case, all we have to do is establish reasonable doubt," Valerie says over the hiss of a fancy espresso machine the size of a Pinto. "If we succeed in convincing the jury that Shane's not Burner_911, we'll succeed with the BurnOutz too. Then he quietly goes back to being some loser in his mom's basement."

"His mom is dead," I remind her.

"Whatever. You get my point." Valerie releases the lock of hair she's been curling around her index finger, a brainstorming tic, and takes another sip of her $6 artisan, ethically sourced, pour-over, whatever-the-hell-it-is—used to just be called coffee, which is all I wanted, a simple cup of coffee. The café we're in is so pretentious it makes my skin crawl—pimple-faced hipsters with bulky knit hats "crafting" drinks one at a time on some wood plank, only whole or oat milk, no regular sugar, all accompanied by ironic '80s soft rock on a vinyl record player. Give me a break.

"I'm not sure we *can* win," I say after looking around at the other customers—all engrossed in their laptops, isolated by their headphones, distracted by that oh-so-important Snapchat or TikTok. A room of them, a *generation* of them, together but alone—and oblivious to us. Too consumed by their own vanity to risk their curated little lives. Too busy watching cat videos to fight for their country, to defend it, to even care what's happening to it. "You've seen it. There's a shit-ton of evidence against him. Our only chance is to get a die-hard BurnOut or two on the

167

jury. They'd vote to acquit him either way—to save him if they believe him, and to delegitimize him if they don't."

"That would help, but their case that Shane's Burner_911 just isn't very strong," Valerie says, not even bothering to lower her voice. "Even when they raided his apartment, they never caught him actively logged in to the account with his hands on the keyboard. And even if they had, they'd have to prove he was the *only* one with access—the only author of dozens of posts. They just don't have definitive digital forensics to prove that. There are plenty of people who say they're Burner_911. Hell, there are plenty of people who genuinely think they *are* Burner_911. Find one of those guys and put him on the stand. Let's keep working the case and—"

"That'll take too long. These cases take forever. Even after a verdict, it could be years of appeals. Meantime, the court of public opinion has moved on. Everybody assumes the guy who got arrested is guilty. Ted Kaczynski, Timothy McVeigh, the Tsarnaev brothers—nobody thought those guys were innocent. And as soon as the leader is caught, the movement dies. We need something that casts doubt that he's Burner_911 *now*. We don't have time for this to run its course."

"Well, it would help if there was another Burner_911 post. The account has been silent since Shane's arrest. Can't someone at Razgo get us access to it?"

"If we could, we would've done that already. Razgo doesn't store passwords, so not even Alex himself can get it."

"Maybe Shane would give us the password. It's in his best interest—would help prove his innocence."

I shake my head. "I'm not sure he'd give it to me. Not yet, at least. But he might give it to *her*, if she doesn't know it already."

"'Her' being Chloe Corbin?"

I nod and gag down another sip of my coffee. "Does anyone actually like this swill? It's sour, and this raw sugar crunches in your teeth like sand. The coffee at the prison is better than this."

"That's an intriguing idea," Valerie says, ignoring my sexagenarian complaint (one of her best traits) and pensively twisting a new strand of hair around her finger.

"Look at these people," I say gesturing at the room. "Nobody gives a shit about anything but themselves. October 12th was just a week ago, but they've moved on like nothing ever happened. Your generation has the attention spans of gnats, just always swiping to the next thing. It's no wonder we're falling behind the rest of the world."

Again, Valerie ignores the remark, still twisting her hair and letting her train of thought run its course. "Of course, to do that, we'd have to find her first. Make contact with the kidnappers."

"Still nothing credible on the tip line, I assume?"

"Mostly sad old men," she says, suggesting in the lilt of her voice that I'm among that group, then flicking her auburn lock into a bounce like in a shampoo commercial. "Pretending to be more important than they really are. But I have an idea for how to get their attention."

"Oh, yeah? What's that?" I stand to leave and drop my nearly full cup into a bin labeled "Landfill," the only option I understand out of the three other choices.

"I have a girlfriend who's a reporter at *BuzzFeed*. We were in the same sorority."

Her thumbs navigate her phone screen faster than I can think as we step out into the whipping wind of a foggy San Francisco afternoon. Before I can ask, she's tapped a name and raised the phone to her ear. She offers a conciliatory smile as she waits for an answer, confident whatever little scheme she's conceived will work and that I'll eventually catch up. That's what makes her so good—jumping from idea to action in seconds. Her dimples rise and eyes brighten when I hear the muffled, "What's up, Val?" on the other end.

"Hey, Tiff! I've got a juicy little tip for you that's right up your alley. But you can't say you got it from me—totally anonymous, 'kay?"

47

BUZZFEED

BURNER_911 HAD SECRET LOVE AFFAIR WITH BILLIONAIRE'S KIDNAPPED DAUGHTER

SAN FRANCISCO, CA, October 20, 2023—Shane Stoller, the man arrested last week and accused of being the mastermind behind Burner_911 and the massive BurnOutz online conspiracy, had a long-term secret love affair with Chloe Corbin, daughter of tech billionaire Ken Corbin who was abducted at gunpoint last week during the October 12th riot. These never-before-seen photographs, shared exclusively with *BuzzFeed* by an anonymous source and corroborated by leaked court documents, show Ms. Corbin and Mr. Stoller together at a high-end restaurant, in a Pacific Heights coffee shop, and entering the lobby of Ms. Corbin's apartment. The bombshell discovery casts the entire events of last week in a new light.

Kadabra was originally thought to be just the latest target of the BurnOutz stock manipulation shakedown. In light of this new information, however, it appears likely that Kadabra was deliberately singled out, in part, according to sources due to a falling-out between the couple. The relationship also suggests that Ken Corbin himself may have conspired more closely on the CompassCard scam than previously suspected. According to court transcripts and subpoenaed text messages, the attack against Kadabra was motivated by revenge.

Society darling and social media celebrity Chloe Corbin has been missing since her abduction in the pandemonium of October 12th. As a nationwide manhunt for her captors continues, speculation around whether Mr. Stoller himself ordered the kidnapping to gain leverage for his own release, or possibly in retaliation for an apparent breakup initiated by Ms. Corbin, has reportedly become a key question in the investigation. The hostage takers have repeatedly demanded Mr. Stoller's release from prison, where he is being held for multiple counts of domestic terrorism, insurrection, and treason. If convicted, Mr. Stoller could face the death penalty.

Ms. Corbin's whereabouts remain unknown. An initial post to her Instagram account, in which the heiress appeared pale and afraid, declared she was safe. But after the end of the seventy-two-hour ultimatum period named in the first post was reached, a video of Ms. Corbin being tortured with a lit cigarette was posted to her feed. Law enforcement officials raided the apartment of one man believed to be involved in the kidnapping, based on a YouTube live stream, but neither the assailants nor Ms. Corbin were found. A massive, coordinated search for Ms. Corbin and the perpetrators continues, led by federal and local law enforcement as well as the private security detail of the Corbin family.

Meanwhile, the fallout within the BurnOutz movement from this shocking revelation remains to be seen. With speculation about both Ms. Corbin and Mr. Stoller already rampant in social media and online forums, the news is likely to fuel further conspiracy theories and splinter public opinion. Watch this space.

48

CHLOE

"Oh, my God," Pete says. He sets down his stained mug of coffee, leans forward, and summons the others to his phone. "You gotta read this."

Scooter glances in my direction with a look of warning before joining the others at the table.

I see Nick's nostrils flare as he paws at the screen. "Is this true?" he shouts across the room at me, holding the phone up as if I'm supposed to be able to read the screen from fifteen feet away.

"I don't know—"

"Is this *fucking* true? That you and this Stoller cuck are *dating*?" Nick strides toward me, waving the phone like a lethal weapon. "No wonder you were so eager to get him out. You've been lying to us this whole time!"

"Nick, this must mean Stoller really is Burner_911," Pete says, the only one of us who has read whatever it is—an email or news article or something.

"Nah, it doesn't make sense," Scooter says. "Why would a guy ranting about wealthy elites be dating a wealthy elite? It's fake news."

"Looks real to me. They at least know each other," Benny says, looking at the article he's pulled up now on his own phone. "If these pictures are fakes, they're damn good."

"Especially if *BuzzFeed* is publishing them," Pete says. "They oughta know—probably seen every deepfake there is."

"Well?" Nick says, holding the screen expectantly in front of my face with the headline I can now read: "Burner_911 Had Secret Love Affair with Billionaire's Kidnapped Daughter." The revelation that I've been waiting for, that was inevitable. A new chapter in the ignominious Chloe Corbin memoir.

"Yes, it's true," I say, looking each of them in the eye for a moment, waiting for the implication to set in before continuing. "I've been seeing him for almost a year now. More than seeing him, really—I've been . . . collaborating with him, on the movement."

"Bullshit!" Nick says, arcs of spittle spraying from his mouth. He scratches at his head anxiously through his ubiquitous knit hat, his security blanket, struggling to articulate his skepticism in words. "This is all . . . some *scheme*. Probably cooked up by your PR people. Just to trick us—trick us into letting you go. We're not gonna fall for it!"

Nick turns toward the others, looking to build support for the half-baked argument he's conjured. The boys look anything but convinced. Concern is the more prevalent emotion creeping across their faces as they process the tangled web of possible theories, trying to tease facts from misinformation, likelihoods from conjecture, instincts from implications.

"I don't know, Nick—this seems pretty elaborate for a PR firm," Scooter finally says.

"Yeah, and if it's true . . ." Pete forms his words cautiously. "That means we just kidnapped Burner_911's girlfriend. I mean, he could, like, send people after us. Or he could be cooperating with the cops, giving them tips on who we are and how to find us."

"Yeah," Benny says, squeezing the brim of his ballcap into an even tighter crescent. "Stoller must know about the safe houses. He probably set 'em up. We'll get caught!"

"Shut the fuck up, Benny!" Nick says. "That's the last thing I need, you freaking out. Stoller's not dumb enough to cooperate with the Feds to betray other BurnOutz, even if he is just a patsy."

"Look, all we're sayin' is we're out on a limb here," Scooter says. "When we thought she was just the target, it was no-holds-barred, but now we just don't know. We're operating without clear instructions here."

Nick walks away from me, staring at the phone screen again, rereading the article in a second attempt to discern its veracity. The others give him space to think. I can see his resistance waning. For the first time since this ordeal started, I can see the possibility of a path. I grasp on desperately to that feeling of hope. Hope I will survive. Hope we both can have our freedom again. Hope for reconciliation. I try to swallow the thought, suppress it before it threatens to overwhelm me—the idea that, after all this, there might be a future for me and Shane.

That feeling—love, I guess—catches in my throat. It flushes my face, constricts my breath, brings tears to my eyes. I hate it, that feeling. That loss of control. But it's something visceral, pheromonal. I can't help it. Being with Shane showed me another person I could be. Another set of opportunities. A new purpose. Now, it's like I can't unsee it. Can't imagine my life without him. And he could be gone forever unless I do something.

"We need to move out," Nick says, an overemphatic declaration to reestablish his status as alpha. "We're compromised here. We need to get to another safe house. Destroy the burner phones. She's riding in the trunk again."

"But he hasn't told you what to do yet, like Scooter said," I say.

Nick looks back at me. For the first time, the volatility I expect doesn't come, so I continue. "Don't you want to know what Burner_911 wants first? Before you make another mistake?"

"Let's at least talk to the lawyer—see what he has to say," Scooter interjects. "That's our best shot."

"I swear, if you're pulling something on us, I'll put a bullet in your skull faster than you can blink," Nick says. "I don't care who your daddy is." For all the threat in his words, his demeanor has changed.

"I'm not going to be able to persuade you, Nick," I say. "You'll have to decide for yourself if I'm telling the truth or not—and what it will mean for you when you find out I am."

"We're not talking to him by phone—too risky it gets traced," Pete says.

"Fine, then bring him here," I say.

Pete laughs reflexively. Scooter and Benny look apprehensively at each other, then at Nick. "I'm serious. Get me in a room with him. Tell him I have something that will help get his client off, get Shane out."

"It's not crazy," Scooter says, laying out a plan. "We'll arrange it like a drop: sweep him for trackers or recording devices, bring him here blindfolded, then move to another safe house afterward—right away, so nothing is compromised."

Benny nods eagerly. "Yeah, Scooter and me can go get him since they don't got us on facial recognition—"

"Shut the fuck up, Benny! You're a fucking moron," Nick shouts, but I can see it in his face: he knows he doesn't have a better plan.

"This can work. It's our best move," Pete offers before they all fall silent.

Nick's glare settles on me again, like he's trying to pry open my head, to know what I know.

"What do you say, Nick?" I say. "You're the one in charge."

After several seconds, he shakes his head and throws up his hands. "Okay . . . contact the lawyer."

49

SHANE

One of the most effective vehicles of financial oppression ever invented is the stock market.

"Can you be linked to any of these Nottingham accounts?" Wayne asks.

We're preparing for what he says is the SEC part of this whole thing—the financial crimes.

"Maybe." I shrug. "I had a lot of accounts."

"Look at this list of account numbers." He slides a sheet of paper across the table toward me. "Tell me if you recognize—"

"You think I memorized numbers on over a hundred accounts?" I say, not even looking at the sheet. "These were all hashed and encrypted anyway. I have no idea who these accounts belong to."

"Let me step back and remind you, *again*, that I'm your defense attorney," he says. "I'm *trying* to help you. I'm on your side. But I can't do my job without your help."

"I get that." I wipe my hands across my face. "It's just . . . this is so fucking exhausting. All these trades were done programmatically."

Day-trading by algorithm. How did I get here? Until I read about Ken Corbin, I never knew that stocks could be weaponized. I barely knew what stocks even were. I envisioned a framed piece of paper with fancy lettering that looked like a diploma. What was the point? But the more I learned, the more I appreciated their power. Ken was a billionaire because of the stock he owned in his own company. Not only that, he could use that stock to rip people a new asshole.

I remember one day after Kadabra did their earnings announcement, the company's stock price jumped by, like, 8 percent. I did the math and realized Ken had made over $200 million in a *single day*. Without doing *anything*. What else could create that kind of cash that fast? You can own a mansion, sports cars, exotic artwork, rare wine, whatever, but nothing else can appreciate that much in a single day. Nothing else even comes close. Even if you did it illegally, you could never clear $200 million in a day—no chance. What're you going to do, rob a casino? Or the Federal Reserve? Stocks are the only perfectly legal, perfectly legitimate way to accumulate so much wealth you could wipe your ass with $100 bills the rest of your life and never notice they were gone.

So I opened a Nottingham account and put everything I had into it, day-trading individual stocks just to get the hang of it. Then I started coding up some automated trades. Nottingham was commission-free, so I could be as active as I wanted, like I was at a casino. Bids/asks, PE ratios, EPS, market caps, trading volume, dividends, limit orders, it was a whole world I needed to learn—not just what was happening but also the language to describe it. I learned it the same way I learned everything else: I read and watched everything I could find. And I loved it. In many ways, it was just like a video game—strategy and tactics, skill and luck, educated guesses and gut instincts, anticipated moves and inevitable reactions. You could play the game short-term or long-term, active or passive, concentrated or diversified. And there was always a scoreboard. Always a buyer and a seller. Always a winner and a loser. If you wanted to make money, someone else had to lose money. I was hooked.

I also had seen enough scams to know the game was rigged.

First, I thought it was just access. The rules favored institutional investors. There was a hot tech IPO that I wanted to buy at the opening bell. I didn't know that it was impossible for a pissant retail trader like me to buy two shares to get in on it till I tried and failed.

Then I realized it wasn't just access, it was also pricing. I noticed my trades weren't clearing at the price I expected. Again, I did my research and discovered that small traders like me were last in line to get our orders executed. If the stock was rallying up, my trade was slow and the price I paid was higher. If the stock was sinking, my trade would linger until I sold for less. Someone was always chipping away at the spread—banks, brokers, trading desks, the exchanges themselves. Trillions of dollars sloshing around, powered by algorithms and AI to eke out gains in the tiniest price fluctuations. The moves of the big institutional guys were enough to dictate prices, manipulate markets, and crush retail traders like me.

But besides access and price, the biggest way it's rigged is *information*. I had written a few programs to monitor price feeds and look for anomalies across a handful of stocks. Invariably, when a stock had a large fluctuation up or down, the market knew it before the news was announced. These were insiders, tipped off moments before news broke and making their trades before the rest of us found out. It was harder to see in the S&P 500 because the volume was so high. But with less liquid stocks, the signs were obvious. The price would begin moving, the trading volume would increase, and then, within minutes, the news would break—a blockbuster quarter, a CEO scandal, a new product launch, a board member indicted. Whatever it was, it was enough to move the stock up or down. And the people who bought or sold without that information? They lost money.

None of it bothered me very much. It's just like any other game. First, learn the rules. Then, learn how to get away with breaking the rules so you can win. Besides, I was playing with other people's money. Still, it all seemed random sometimes. And profits were slow. A lot of stocks just didn't move enough to make much money, unless you bought big chunks. But if you bought big chunks, your capital was all tied up while you waited.

That's when I discovered option trading.

"Okay." Wayne looks down at the list of accounts. "Let's just worry about the margin accounts. There's only a few of those, and that's where all the option trades happened. That's what the prosecution is basing their charges of securities fraud on. Do you remember any of these accounts?"

What I remember is taking a marker and writing on my wall, YOU DON'T NEED TO OWN THE STOCK TO MAKE MONEY! The concept was a revelation for me. When I first got my head around it, I couldn't believe it was legal. How could I buy and sell something I didn't even own? The game had jumped to another level. It was pure gambling. The underlying stock didn't even matter. It could be a great company or a shitty company. It just needed to move. Up or down didn't matter, as long as you were on the right side of the bet. And you could make a lot more bets with your money. Instead of buying a stock at, say, $100 per share, I'd buy an options contract at, say, $3, with the same profit potential when the price moved. It was exactly the leverage I needed to start making real money.

It was like fishing with dynamite.

"Maybe . . ." I say after pretending to look at the list. "Like I said, I didn't write down account numbers. I didn't get statements. I never even took money out of any of those Nottingham accounts."

"That's . . . true . . ." Wayne says like a new idea has just entered his head. He flips through pages of transaction details. "So what was the point, then? How'd you get the money out?"

"I didn't. I'd just roll the gains into new positions, or other Nottingham accounts, or just let it sit in crypto wallets."

"Why?"

"So I could, you know, pay for stuff. Rather than wiring money around, I'd just transfer the whole account to someone in the syndicate and give them the login credentials. Then they could spend the balance in the crypto wallet on whatever they wanted."

"Didn't you want to make money yourself?" Wayne asks.

"It was more important to me to take it than to make it. I needed some to do the things I wanted to do, but mostly I wanted to take it away from people who hoard it."

I was going after the billionaires—VCs, investment bankers, hedge fund managers. The deep pockets in the financial world who could afford the loss. Who *deserved* the loss. The same assholes who stacked the deck in their favor again and again. I saw it as a giant wealth redistribution scheme. To do what the federal government refused to do: take from the rich and give to the poor rather than the other way around, like everything else in life.

To make the plan work, I needed an army. Individually, I couldn't establish a big enough position to compete with the institutional guys.

But *collectively*, we could move the market. And we didn't need a boiler room to do it. It could all be done online, anonymously, securely—starting with a post on Razgo, then spreading it on Twitter and Discord and Reddit and a dozen other sites, then trading for free on Nottingham. All executed by thousands of guys from all over the world—Azerbaijan and the Philippines, Belarus and Sri Lanka—who I knew only by their usernames. Triggermen who could conjure up a security breach, ransomware attack, denial of service, or pretty much any other hack that would move the market exactly where we wanted it. Ready and waiting—deployable at a moment's notice with a single encrypted message.

But the key to it all was Burner_911. The anonymity, the speculation, the mythos. Nobody was going to follow some random Central Valley University drop-out. But people could see in Burner_911 whatever they wanted, whatever they were inspired by. A million theories and conspiracies—an empty vessel for whatever anger or frustration they held about their lives. And the best part? They'd get *rich* doing it. Burner_911 was hope that they could have a better life. Finally, they could *believe* in something.

Wayne shuffles the papers into a pile and taps them on the table. "Well, you definitely took it away from Bob Jorgensen."

My addled brain snags on the comment. Slowly processes what feels off about it. I tilt my head and peer at him. "How would you know that, Wayne?"

He stops mid-motion and looks up from the stack of papers. "It was in the news," he says after a beat.

"Was it?" I ask.

Just then, the door to the attorney meeting room whips open and Valerie comes through like she's rocket-jumped in.

"We have a credible contact," she says, catching her breath.

We both look at her blankly, unsure what she's talking about.

She points at her phone. "I think it's really them."

I snap out of my mental freefall and grasp what she's so excited about. "'Them' *who?* The fucknuts who took Chloe?"

"How did you validate them?" Wayne asks, staring at her skeptically.

"It came in through Signal, so it was end-to-end encrypted, and they provided the correct code word that Shane said only the top cell leaders know."

"There are still, what, fifty or more deputies who know that code word. Doesn't prove it's them," Wayne says.

"That's why I had them send me this." Valerie turns her phone toward us to reveal a picture of a license plate. Chloe's SUV license plate.

"Holy *shit*." I stand up and take the phone out of her hand. "They're legit!"

Valerie looks at Wayne. "They've geotagged a pickup point. They want to meet you in person, Wayne. Tomorrow."

50

CHLOE

Nick is staring at me. I stare back, unflinching.

Since the *BuzzFeed* article, he has barely said a word to me. For minutes, we say nothing. Finally, I hear what we're waiting for: the sound of tires over gravel, triggering memories of when I first arrived at this place. Seven days ago. Feels like months.

I'm sitting across from Nick at the table, under its harsh light, ropes still constricting my legs and torso to a cheap plastic lawn chair, just in case I get any ideas. Pete paces the kitchen, taking long pulls on his cigarette and tapping the ash into the mouth of a beer bottle.

Voices in the backyard now, warning the lawyer to watch his step as they slowly climb toward the door. They enter the kitchen, Scooter and Benny flanking him on either side. He's still in his suit, and his head is shrouded with what looks like a black pillowcase—probably the same dank, sweat-soaked thing that covered me for days. They seat him at the dining table and remove the hood.

I wait a beat for Nick to say something, but he's sulking, so I fill the silence. Someone has to take the initiative. "Hello, Wayne. Thanks for coming."

He takes a moment, his eyes blinking to adjust to the light. He surveys the room, meets the eyes of each of the boys, then gives me a slightly puzzled look. "Yes, of course. I appreciate you . . . *all* of you . . . meeting with me."

"Apologies for all the precautions—y'know, the hood and everything," I say. "I'm sure you understand."

He nods but he's still processing the situation. He looks at Nick expectantly, but Nick still says nothing—just stares straight ahead under the light of the dining table, aggressively chewing his chapped lower lip.

"Sorry, I don't really understand what's going on here." Wayne shakes his head. "Aren't you . . . a *hostage?*"

"Yes, technically." I tilt my head toward the rope around my waist that he seems not yet to have noticed. "But it turns out our interests are aligned. So I'm . . . cooperating."

Nick's impatience finally gets the better of him. "Here's the deal," he says. "If this Shane Stoller guy really is Burner, then the only way we release her is if they release him. One for one. Simple."

"Yeah, that's not going to happen. It doesn't work that way." Wayne sets his hands on the table, sighs, looks around at the men for a moment. "Look . . . I'm sympathetic to the cause. I even got the tattoo to prove it. It's why I offered to represent him in the first place. But Shane's in deep shit. This isn't some little extortion racket or stock hustle. This was an act of domestic terrorism. People died. Federal property was destroyed. The prosecution is seeking the death penalty. There is no possible way they release him without a trial, even in exchange for some billionaire celebrity heiress . . . no offense."

"None taken," I say.

"You guys are way out of your depth here," Wayne says. "The Feds—"

"What the fuck do you know about our *depth?*" Nick cuts him off. The tendons in his jaw bulge. "You have no idea what we're capable of. We're the Black Mountain Militia. So think twice before you come in here making threats."

Wayne holds up his hands. "I'm not threatening anyone," he says mildly. "I'm just the messenger. The intermediary between my client and you."

"So?" Nick demands. "What's the message, then?"

"Release Ms. Corbin," he says. "At the moment, that's the only thing my client cares about, that she's returned to safety."

I can't hold back the flush that comes to my face. The words I've been waiting for, that I so desperately want to believe, that might just wash away my lingering doubt. I bask in the feeling as this rumpled, stocky lawyer who could be my salvation looks at Nick, then at the others, expectantly.

"Just like that?" Nick says, trying to regain his swagger with a dismissive chuckle that comes late and sounds forced. "You think we're just gonna let her walk, without getting anything in return?"

"That's right. This action was not sanctioned. You made a mistake, guys. He demands you release her immediately or—"

"I don't give a shit what he wants," Nick says. "We don't answer to him. Besides, I still haven't seen anything to make me believe that guy. Until he proves he's Burner_911, we're keeping her here. Very least, we'll get a ransom."

"Well . . . that's the entire basis of the Justice Department's case," Wayne says. "It's Burner_911 who is accused of terrorism. So they have to prove to the jury that Shane is Burner."

"And we have to prove he's not," I say.

And how do we do that? My mind begins to race.

"Not quite," Wayne says. He gestures to Pete for a cigarette. "The beauty of our judicial system is the burden of proof lies with the prosecution. We just need our ol' friend, the shadow of doubt, to show up and cast enough uncertainty about whether Shane *really is* Burner so one jury member votes to acquit. Then we'll have a mistrial." He pinches the cigarette he's just been handed between his lips, leans over the flame of Pete's lighter, inhales deeply, then says to Nick, "Too bad you're not on the jury."

Nick's agitation spikes again. He manically twists his knit hat back and forth over patchy wisps of hair that betray the male-pattern baldness underneath. "There's just no way that guy's Burner."

"You just don't *want* him to be Burner," Scooter says.

Wayne exhales his second drag slowly. "Well, the prosecution has an entire year's worth of a federal investigation that says he is. They've surveilled his conversations, interviewed witnesses, analyzed his online activity, convinced a grand jury, and unsealed an indictment. They don't do that based on a hunch. I'm not saying Shane is or isn't Burner_911—that's for the jury to decide. But the account's been silent since Shane's arrest, which doesn't help his case. Do you really want to wait for a guilty verdict to discover you're deliberately disobeying a direct order?"

"You expect me to believe the federal government?" Nick snorts. "They had to arrest *somebody*. He's just a fall guy. The real Burner_911 never woulda got caught. Even if the jury says he's guilty, that doesn't prove he's Burner—just that he's a patsy. Before we listen to him, we need proof."

"You really are thick as molasses, aren't you?" Wayne chuckles. "I'm Shane's defense attorney. I'm trying to get him off by making the case he's *not* Burner_911. I'm not going to hand you 'proof' that he is and endanger my client."

Nick stands abruptly, tipping his chair backward with the thrust of his straightening legs. I brace for an outburst, conscious of the handgun he keeps tucked into the back of his jeans. But he just picks up his bottle of beer and says under his breath, "Then we're keeping her."

We all watch as he leaves the dining room, listen as he slams a door down the hall.

Wayne turns back to me and raises his eyebrows. "So, is he the decision-maker?"

The boys and I all exchange apprehensive glances, but no one speaks.

Wayne shrugs, takes a last drag, and snuffs his cigarette out in an ashtray. "Well, seems we're at a dead end then. Unless . . . I guess there's one more thing we could try."

"Have the order come directly from Burner_911," I say.

"That's right." Wayne nods. "It'd help exonerate Shane and provide the proof you guys are asking for. Problem is, Shane's fully embargoed."

"Can't you get around that?" I ask.

"Not yet. There are some guards who are sympathetic to the cause, so I could probably smuggle a phone in. But he wouldn't be so stupid to do something like this on an unsecure device over a public network without VPN. Even if he wanted to, I wouldn't let him. Has he ever . . . shared the credentials with you?"

I shake my head. "He was super paranoid about that. He told me a few times he thought other people were trying to hack into the account. To take it over."

"Maybe he would have a different opinion on that now, since both your freedom and his might depend on it." The slightest suggestion of a smile appears below Wayne's thick mustache. It could be sympathetic, or sarcastic.

Benny opens his mouth as if he's about to say something but second-guesses himself.

Pete interjects instead. "Even if she had the password, just logging in and asking for her own release isn't going to be very convincing. How do we know someone didn't just hack into the account and give her the password? Her dad probably has a thousand programmers working on it right now."

"Even if he did, they'd never get the password," Wayne says. "Not even the Razgo admin can get the password. I'm told the site uses some hash thingy to encrypt it. No information about users either, just something called a tripcode to verify the account."

"I don't understand," I say.

"Basically, only the person who is Burner_911 could possibly know that password. They don't store it in their database, so it's un-hackable. If Shane knows it, you'll know he's really Burner_911. And you might be the only person in the world he'd give it to," Wayne says with a wry smile, the kind that suggests he hasn't shown all his cards.

I'm not sure I trust him. I also don't have an alternative. Even if Shane did share the credentials with me, one post isn't going to prove he's not Burner_911. But it might be enough to stir up his followers, spark new conspiracy theories, generate enough uncertainty that one juror acquits.

"Okay . . . but I need to communicate directly with Shane," I say.

"There are metal detectors in and out," he says. "But I could relay a note. Which reminds me, he asked me to give you these." He fishes several crumpled scraps of paper out of his jacket pocket that look like they've been touched by a hundred pairs of hands and sets them on the table in front of me.

"What are those?" I ask, prevented from picking them up due to my restraints. "Notes? Like, *physical* notes?"

Wayne nods. "Want me to read them out loud?"

"No. No, I need to communicate with him *directly*—encrypted, in real time," I say. "He wouldn't trust anyone else with this. He needs to know it's me. It's the only way this will work."

"Okay. But a phone call won't work," Wayne says. "The prison has cell phone detectors. Too great a risk. But an encrypted messaging app might work, if we control both phones."

"Okay. Can you get a phone into him?"

Wayne drums his fingers on the table. "I'll see what I can do."

51

SHANE

Why are these guys such idiots? Wayne told them to let her go. What are they thinking? I want to burn their faces off. BurnOutz don't go rogue. If I could get online, I'd unleash vengeance on these guys. This has to stop.

"Why has this taken so long?" I ask. "I already set the whole thing up to get a phone in here days ago."

"It's not that simple," Wayne says. "They could intercept it on the public network, so we need an encrypted connection on both devices. And even if you get a phone in, you also need to have time to use it and then get it out again before one of the other guards confiscates it. They've got dogs that can sniff these things out, you know. You've got to be patient. Trust me."

I don't know if I can. He says he believes in the cause, but he seems to be playing a bigger game. He insists we have to do this all his way. But really, what incentive does he have to smuggle this phone in at all? Sure, he's my lawyer, but if he's caught, he could go to jail himself. Why take the risk?

"I really think she'll be okay." Valerie puts her hand on my arm with a gentle smile. "If they were going to hurt her, they would have done it already. Plus, that girl can handle herself."

"How will I even know it's really her on the other end?" I ask.

"Simple," Wayne says. "Think of a question only she would know the answer to. I'll tell her to do the same."

The bigger problem I don't want to admit is I have no idea if she'll even talk to me. I've been trying to ignore the fact that she dumped me. Dumped me by text, no less. Told me she never wanted to talk to me again. That wasn't a feel-good moment. I don't blame her. I was being a dick. And I gotta think getting kidnapped by my followers hasn't exactly made her want to get back together.

"Okay," I say. "You gave her the letters, right?"

Wayne nods.

"What did she say? Did she read them?"

Wayne exhales a deep breath. "Not while I was there."

"I'm sure she read them," Valerie says. "She was probably just waiting for a chance to do it in private. Right, Wayne?"

"Yeah, I'm sure that's right," Wayne says, then turns to me with an intense look. "Look, Shane, I'm not gonna lie, there're some fractures in the movement now—a faction that feels betrayed that you had a relationship with her. It's causing speculation. New conspiracy theories filling the vacuum. Frankly, it probably helps your case. But what would help more is a post from Burner_911. You know, to get everyone back on the same page. And cast doubt that it's you behind this whole thing."

"I can't post from a phone without a Tor browser and VPN connection," I say.

"No, of course not," he says. "But maybe that's something you'd trust Chloe to do for you?"

"Just get me the phone," I say.

The meeting room door opens and Kryz and Killian step in.

"Time's up," Kryz says, but his tone is different than usual. Neither of them looks at me. "Captain wants to move you to USP Atwater," he says as he disconnects me from the desk. "Says you're too much trouble here. So whatever you plan to do, do it soon. We can only provide so much protection."

I need to fix this. But there may be too much shit that's broken. A backlash of BurnOutz who feel *burned*, but by me this time. Everything I tried so hard to build is unraveling. Wayne's right, Burner_911 needs to post—but how? Could Chloe do it? Even if we somehow reconciled, could I trust her with that? Maybe the kidnappers are just using her as bait to get access to the account. How do I know they won't torture her to get it . . . putting her into even more danger than I have already?

But what other choice do I have? I can't stand not knowing if there's a possible future for us. This may be my last and only chance to talk to her directly—apologize for everything I've done, convince her to give me another chance.

I have to try.

52

WAYNE

"I can't eat this," Valerie says, listlessly poking her plastic fork into a wilted Caesar salad.

"First rule of courthouse cafeteria dining: never order the salad," I say. "Haven't I taught you anything?"

"At least it's recognizable as food. I don't even know what that is."

"Turkey Tetrazzini. It's my go-to on Tuesdays." I point my own fork at the specials board. I've eaten enough lunches in this cafeteria that I have all the specials committed to memory.

"It's disgusting." Valerie squeezes a packet of salad dressing onto a crouton and pops it in her mouth. "So, do you think it will work?"

Call me old-fashioned, but I'm not eager to discuss my plan that, if I got caught, would get me disbarred, fined, and likely imprisoned within earshot of multiple federal prosecutors, agents, and staff. Doesn't bother Valerie. Doesn't even seem to cross her mind. Different generation, ignorant to the very concept of privacy. I nod that the plan will work, but she gives me an expectant shrug, unsatisfied.

I scrape the remaining noodles into a final bite, wipe my mouth, and bring my voice down to a whisper. "We already have two burner phones, bought with cash, totally untraceable. Alex had one of his IT guys at Razgo configure them to our needs. I'm delivering hers myself tomorrow. And I've already arranged to get his through security. Our sympathetic guards will be staffing the metal detector and said they won't pat down my left ankle. Even if they aren't the only ones on duty, we'll get at least five minutes of private time for religious observance. That should be enough."

"What if those assholes take the phone from her? What if Shane doesn't realize he's giving the account credentials to them?"

"That's a possibility, but it's a calculated risk. I told them both to come up with a security question only the two of them would know. But at the end of the day, if they take the phone, pretend to be her, torture her to get the password, or otherwise get access to the account, it all lands jelly-side up for us as long as Burner_911 is posting again—helps us win this case and lets the movement live on."

I push my finished plate aside and grab the slice of blueberry cheesecake and black coffee I've lined up for dessert while Valerie regards my tray with the mild disgust of someone who survives on eight hundred calories a day. She then scrutinizes me as I chew, squinting through her long, mascaraed lashes, before finally asking, almost rhetorically, "Why are you doing this?"

"Why am I doing what? Eating like a slob? Blueberry cheesecake is one of life's great pleasures." I extend a forkful in her direction. "Want a bite?"

"No, I mean the whole thing. Why are you defending Shane but also . . . *undermining* him?"

"There's nothing contradictory about that. I took an oath to uphold the Constitution and have a legal obligation to defend my client. This solves for both those things. Freedom of speech for Burner_911 and reasonable doubt for Shane. Don't pull that ethical bullshit on me."

"No, no . . . this is something different. This isn't about freedom, this is about control. You're not just undermining Shane, you're—what's the right word—*usurping* him."

"Don't you think he needs to be usurped?" I say, looking around us to make sure we can't be overheard. "He's taken this movement that had so much potential in the wrong direction. The BurnOutz are splintering. Someone needs to step in and get this thing back on track, back to its original conservative agenda."

"So that's what this is for you? An agenda? A political mission?"

"Political, social, cultural—put whatever label you want on it. But I can tell you this, it's bigger than one guy. He created a following, I'll give him credit for that. But it needs to serve some purpose. You've heard him;

he can't be trusted with something this big. He's practically lost interest. He gave me another one of these, by the way." I pull Shane's latest crumpled note from my pocket. "See for yourself. Someone needs to take over—for his own good and the good of the movement."

Valerie pulls the note from my hand and inspects it as I press the last remaining graham cracker crumbs, the best part, under the tines of my fork. As she reads, I tune in to the pleasant hum of the fluorescent lighting, giving everything from the grid of gypsum ceiling tiles to the weathered linoleum floor a yellowish glow. Being here takes me back to my first cases, when the lunch special was the only thing I could afford. Before the divorce, before my kids stopped talking to me, before the internet and cell phones and social media—a simpler time. Sometimes I wish I could go back.

"He seems contrite, desperate," she says, refolding the note and handing it back to me. "And truly in love, probably for the first time."

"He's naïve, is what he is. He's been playing this thing the whole time like it's a goddamn video game. Trained like a chimpanzee for the dopamine hit of action and reaction, never contemplating the bigger picture—no strategy, no values, no agenda, just doing it all for the ego rush."

"I disagree. He had a strategy. It's just one that Robert Jorgensen didn't like anymore."

"He does pay our salaries. And those of our staff. And he's only one of the most influential figures in the conservative movement."

"Yeah, but I thought you believed. Believed in what the BurnOutz movement stands for. Plan B and all that stuff."

"I'm too old to remember what I believe anymore. I just know which side I'm on. Belief isn't what's important anyway. *Winning* is what's important. Only winners get to have control."

"So, win at all costs," she says. "Whatever the collateral damage."

"Exactly. Rule number one, never order the salad. Rule number two, win at all costs."

"You're such an inspiring mentor."

"All will be revealed over time, my apprentice. There are always strings that can be pulled. Why do you think the Feds ended up arresting Shane in the first place?"

53

BURNER_911

Six Months Ago

@Burner_911 post on Razgo.com

> *"October of 2008 was the worst financial crisis in global history, including the Great Depression."*
> —Ben Bernanke

There's just something about OCTOBER!!!

The falling leaves 🍂🍁🍂🍁

The scary pumpkins 🎃🎃🎃

The smell of burning money!!! 🔥💰🔥💰🔥💰🔥💰🔥💰🔥💰

October is the unrivaled worldwide champion of financial crises. No other month comes close. Think about it:

- The Bank Panic of 1907 started in **October** 1907
- The Great Depression started on Black Tuesday, **October** 29, 1929
- The Stock Market Crash of 1987 started on Black Monday, **October** 19, 1987
- The Dot-com Bubble started deflating in 2000 but hit bottom in **October** 2002
- The 2008 Financial Crisis, what our buddy Ben called the "worst financial crisis in global history," happened in **October** 2008.

October is just the straight up **GOAT** 🐐🐐🐐 when it comes to financial shit-storms! 🥀

There's no denying it. All the apocalyptic financial meltdowns happen in October.

And THIS October is going to be the **GOAT** of all financial crises! Ben's gonna shit himself a stack of bricks. A day of reckoning is coming. Billionaires will lose their shirts. Hedge fund managers will be jumping out of windows. The entire banking system will be on its knees.

WE'RE TAKING DOWN WALL STREET, BURNOUTZ!!!!

It's time that these global elites get what they deserve. It's the October Prophecy—my prediction of a financial Armageddon the likes of which we've never seen!

Don't believe we can do it? Don't believe a butterfly's wings can lead to a tornado??

Then . . . GET THE HELL OUT!!!

If you don't believe in this movement. If you don't believe that a day of reckoning is coming. If you don't believe that you deserve to make a shit ton of money. Then you don't believe in *yourself!* So, just quit—go back to your meaningless life.

FOR THOSE WHO BELIEVE, PREPARE FOR THE MOMENT OF YOUR LIFE!

Trust me, I know. I've seen the data. Everything is lining up. Banks are overextended. Hedge funds are exposed. Volatility is our friend. And there's a whole room full of levers we can pull to cause havoc!

BURNOUTZ!! You are part of the most important movement in history! You are a silent army of people who have lost faith in America! Ready to do battle! Ready to level up!

Those who play will be richly rewarded.

54

CHLOE

It's been silent since Wayne left. Nick is holed up in one of the rooms. While Scooter and Pete drove Wayne back, I finally got the chance to read the notes Shane sent—Benny held them up for me.

Honestly, I'm not sure what to think. I don't know if he ever thought I would actually receive them. I truly believe he's sorry, but he was also incredibly stupid. He should have known this could have happened.

Of course, it didn't occur to me that this could happen either until it was too late. That this movement I was just starting to believe could effect real change would tip so easily into violence. I just didn't comprehend how far some of these factions—like the Black Mountain Militia, just for example—would take things. Clearly, Shane didn't either.

At some level, it may not matter now. This all may be unsalvageable. I need to be realistic. Most likely, Shane ends up in prison for the rest of his life. Burner_911 never posts again. The movement fizzles out, with different factions spinning off to their next conspiracy theory obsessions.

Unless, somehow, he's acquitted. But with his anonymity forever compromised, could Shane even return to lead this movement? Could things ever get back to the way they were?

And that all assumes I somehow figure out a way out of this situation.

Scooter and Pete are back now. They're all just drinking beers and silently watching TV. My attention snaps to the screen as well when I hear a familiar name.

"We're now joined by Lexi Baird, a longtime friend of Chloe Corbin, who has more information about Chloe's secret affair with accused domestic terrorist Shane Stoller. Lexi, thanks for joining us," the female anchor says.

This break from the predictable cycle of news grabs the boys' attention too; I see them all perk up.

"Of course, I'm so happy to be here," Lexi says, looking straight into the camera and flashing her perfect smile. She coyly pushes a strand of straight blond hair over her ear, then remembers to adjust her expression to something more somber, more befitting of the interview topic.

"So how long have you known Chloe?" the anchor begins.

"Oh, we've been best friends for as long as I can remember."

"And when did you first meet Shane Stoller, the man accused of being behind the BurnOutz conspiracy?"

The screen cuts to images of Shane being led, handcuffed, into court.

"She told me she met this unusual guy at one of her charity events. Turned out he was making first-person shooter videos on YouTube where he was just swearing and yelling the whole time. I told Chloe he was weird and misogynistic." Lexi crumples her nose in distaste.

"Based on what we know about them, they do seem very different. Why do you think they started dating?" The anchor peers at Lexi seriously, like I joined a cult or something.

"I couldn't understand it, honestly. She's, like, the most put-together, beautiful, progressive person I know, and she's falling for this alt-right gamer dude with tattoos and dyed hair? I just didn't see what they had in common. But Chloe was always drawn to the rebellious type, so I thought maybe she was just doing it to annoy her father. Shane also had a large following, which is important to her. She has millions of followers on Instagram, so she knows how hard it is to grow that kind of audience." A series of images of Lexi and me, pulled from my Instagram, pops up on the screen—arm in arm at a charity gala, blowing snowflakes off our mittens in Aspen, puckering for a selfie from the VIP seats of a music festival.

"What do you think she saw in him?" the anchor asks as they zoom in on an image of Shane and me together, the only one I ever shared with Lexi, that has been intentionally Photoshopped to look ominous.

"Chloe was always a little, I don't know, maybe ambivalent about her father's wealth. She enjoyed the lifestyle, but she always felt a little guilty about it. That's one of the reasons she got into philanthropic work. Even though they were polar opposites politically, Shane's rants against elites kinda resonated with her. It's almost like Chloe felt, since Shane grew up poor, it gave her some kind of street cred or something."

Really? Is that what she really thinks? That I liked Shane because he was poor, or had a lot of followers, or just to piss off my dad? Did it ever occur to her that I could be in love?

"Were you ever suspicious that Shane might have ulterior motives in dating her?"

"Yeah, honestly, I wondered about that. I think you have to, anytime someone has the kind of money she does. If they'd ever gotten engaged, I definitely would have told her to get a prenup. Given Shane's background, it seemed very possible he was trying to get her money or using her to get to her dad—a lot of guys did. She told me once he donated to charities she was involved in, but I figured he was just doing that to get her in bed."

"Wow . . ." I say to myself.

"How well did you get to know Shane Stoller?"

An image of Shane in an orange prison jumpsuit pans by, followed by mob scenes from October 12th.

"I only met him a few times. She was secretive about their relationship—even a little embarrassed of him, maybe? It was like she wasn't herself when she was around him. Like he had brainwashed her or something. She was always super popular, dated a lot of guys, but all of a sudden, none of that mattered. Once they started dating, I hardly ever saw her anymore."

The anchor pauses for dramatic effect, scrutinizes Lexi, then asks with rehearsed sincerity, "Do you believe Shane Stoller is Burner_911?"

Lexi lets out a brief, muffled sob and simply nods, as if speaking would only open the floodgates. The camera zooms in to catch a tear rolling down her flawless high cheekbone. "All this happened cause of him," she finally says, dabbing at her eyes. "I just want my friend back. So we're organizing an online vigil using the hashtag #bringchloehome and yellow filters on your profile photo. Be sure to tag or at-mention me @LexiBaird on Instagram, so we can raise—"

"Boo-hoo," Pete says, pointing the remote at the TV like he's shooting at it, and changes the channel. "Gimme a break."

I can't believe Lexi would do that to me. Exploit my crisis to feed her own ego, grow her own following. But then . . . isn't that exactly what I'm doing too? I'm so conditioned that I can't unwire my own brain chemistry. When I see it now, from the other side of the lens, I can't even remember what about that life even appealed to me. Wasn't I part of the problem?

Pete finally stops his rapid-fire clicking on a financial news channel, the screen packed with numbers, ticker symbols, and charts.

"Meanwhile, a real blood bath in the retail sector," the anchor says as a cluster of big-box logos appear next to his bronzed face. "Seven of the twenty largest US retailers declared bankruptcy this week, with payment processing ground to a halt and lenders unwilling to pile more debt onto their balance sheets. Moody's was forced to lower bond ratings on the entire category, putting the remaining retailers into uncertainty about how they will continue to service or refinance their debt. Company CEOs visited Washington, DC, this week, urging lawmakers to put together a rescue package before they're forced to shutter more storefronts."

Shane called this. That the retailers with huge debt were most vulnerable. The first dominoes.

"In related news, shares of Federal Pacific Bank, one of the biggest lenders to the retail industry, plunged today. Their CEO warned the bank is facing a liquidity crisis, with its assets tied up in long-term bonds and many of its largest clients declaring bankruptcy. The Fed is stepping in to try to prevent contagion in the banking sector, but with billions of withdrawals, Federal Pacific will likely need a massive federal bailout or it could fail."

Everything he said would happen is happening.

"And the company at the center of it all, Kadabra, Inc., whose payment-processing platform is the backbone of so many retailers, has seen their share price go off a cliff, dropping in the wake of the October 12th terrorist attack by 95 percent. Ken Corbin's net worth has been slashed by an estimated $78 billion."

Scooter gives a series of slow claps with his hands over his head.

"Poor guy will only have, like, $50 billion left," Pete says.

Benny just steals a glance at me.

"The Treasury Secretary is calling for a $1.8 trillion bailout package to stem this financial crisis, but the measure is already facing fierce opposition by both major political parties and feels unlikely to happen any time soon. In which case, the Federal Reserve Open Market Committee might be forced to take drastic measures to devalue the dollar."

It's working. It's *actually* working.

55

BURNER_911

Two Months Ago

@Burner_911 post on Razgo.com

> *"Everyone has a plan until they get punched in the mouth."*
> —Mike Tyson

A lot of you aren't ready for this. Correction: MOST of you aren't ready for this.

Most of you will just sit down and take it your whole life. You'll complain about how the system is rigged against you but do NOTHING ABOUT IT!!!

You're so beholden to the OLD plan—the subjugation plan—that you can't even see a different way: PLAN B—*our* plan. The B-is-for BurnOutz plan.

BurnOutz . . . ARE YOU READY!?!?!? READY FOR PLAN B, WHERE WE MAKE THE RULES???

Our next target is set, and it's time for YOU to get in on the action.

Felix Ridley became a billionaire earlier this year when his company, Glecko, went public. The share price of GCKO is currently $75, a 200% increase from their IPO price. But that price is about to drop through the floor!

ANYTHING ABOVE $20 WILL BE A DISAPPOINTMENT!!!

Don't wait! Log in to your Nottingham account and buy shorts in GCKO before market close. Take as large a position as your margin account will allow. You will feel exposed. Your arse will pucker. But if you take the short, you'll be rewarded—BIG TIME!!!

We're going to shit-can this asshole, and make some Benjamins doing it!

TRUST THE PLAN!!! 🔥🔥🔥🔥🔥🔥🔥🔥🔥🔥🔥🔥🔥

56

CHLOE

"I don't like it," Nick says, adjusting his knit hat as he shakes his head. "It's a setup. He's going to lead them right to us."

"No way—he believes in The Plan, I can tell," Scooter says, smoothing his beard. "Lawyers don't work for free, *ever*. But this guy is. He even has a Plan B tattoo. We can trust him."

"Besides, he's got a better chance of finding a diamond in his own asshole than finding us," Pete says. "Scooter drove him here and back—over three hours and blindfolded each way. He has no idea where the hell we are."

"And we made him leave his phone at home so they can't locate us," Benny adds, picking compulsively at a peeled strip of Formica on the kitchen counter.

I watch them from the table, waiting for my opportunity, searching their expressions for indicators to know when the moment is right. Nick picks up an open bag of stale Doritos, pours out the remnants, and shoves them into his mouth.

"C'mon, Nick, this is the plan," Scooter says, breaking the momentary silence. "This is how we get Shane out and Burner back."

"Fuck Shane!" Nick says, orange dust encrusting his lips, fragments of corn chips stuck in his teeth. "I'm sick of hearing about that dude. I don't care if he is Burner_911. We call our own shots."

"We can't just abandon the movement," Scooter says. "We need to sit tight until we—"

"You guys are all fucked in the head," Nick says. "I'm not going to just sit here while this bitch sells us out! Don't you get it? She's *playing* us. Asking for the lawyer to come here, getting the phones, talking to her *boyfriend*—it's all part of her plan! You've all been suckered into her spell. She's going to screw us!"

The others all talk at once.

Pete: "What other choice do we have?"

Benny: "She don't know where we are either."

Scooter: "You want all this to be for nothing?"

Nick waves his hand, dismissing it all. But the mutiny is building. I seize the moment.

"I think it's *you* who's going to screw us, Nick," I say.

The bickering pauses as they all look at me—a bit stunned, like they forgot I'm here—and then turn to Nick, waiting for his reaction.

"What the hell did you say?" Nick stands, and his shoulders broaden as he turns toward me.

Screw this guy. I'm not backing down. "I think it's pretty obvious, Nick. You're trying to stage a coup."

"*That's it!*" Nick lunges toward me in two quick strides. "I'm sick of your bullshit!" He pauses, towering above me with his fist cocked.

I look up at him from the chair as calmly as I can muster.

"You think *you* can be Burner_911," I say.

As I expected, his fist flies toward my face. I don't turn. I don't blink. My head whips back, crunching the vertebrae in my neck. Heat rushes to my face like every blood cell in my body is confronting the point of impact. The pain is shocking but surprisingly brief, followed by an immediate numbness.

What's important is that the dynamic has permanently changed. I can feel it in the room as I turn my head slowly, defiantly, back in his direction.

I spit a strand of hair out of my mouth and say, "But you know you can't do it without me."

57

GARY SCOFFIELD SHOW

TRANSCRIPT OF *THE GARY SCOFFIELD SHOW*,
JULY 20, 2023

GARY: Welcome back, ladies and gentlemen, to the only honest radio show on the air today, *The Gary Scoffield Show*. I'm your host, Gary Scoffield, and I was put on this earth to defend the America that you and I love from the onslaught of extreme liberalism. I'm blessed to be here on the airwaves every weekday from 9:00 a.m. to noon eastern to defend free speech and our right to bear arms.

I'll tell you, our forefathers had it right. What was the First Amendment to the Constitution? That's right, of course, the right to free speech. And what was the Second Amendment? You all know that one: the right to bear arms. But let me tell you something, as red-blooded Americans, we can never, ever take those rights for granted. There are people out there who are trying to take those God-given rights away from you, every day. It's just horrible what the Democrats and their extreme liberal agenda are trying to do to our country. They're taking away your freedom. If we don't stand up to them, you can say goodbye to the America that our forefathers envisioned when they wrote the Constitution. You can say good-bye to government of the people, by the people, and for the people. If we don't stop them, our way of life will perish from the earth.

My next guest understands the peril we are constantly under. He understands the arrogance and hubris of the liberal elites and the lamestream media. He is committed to defeating the New World Order that the American left constantly panders to. Listen, the Democratic Party has become so extreme, so radicalized, that they want to turn you into clones. They want to force socialist ideology and a Marxist state down your throats. Well, there are millions and millions of Americans who are standing up and saying no. Enough is enough! And my next guest is one of them.

Known only by his Razgo username, he has organized an army of like-minded individuals who are taking on the liberal elites. You know him and love him—it's Burner_911! Welcome to the program, Burner.

GUEST: Thanks.

GARY: Are you okay if I call you that? Just Burner? Can I skip the 9-1-1 part?

GUEST: Sure.

GARY: Okay. We're tryin' to keep it simple for radio here, so that's what I'll use. I should note, we're using a voice-modification app to protect his anonymity. So, tell us, why did you go with that username anyway?

GUEST: "Burner" was taken already, so I added "9-1-1."

GARY: As in dialing 9-1-1? Like an emergency?

GUEST: Yeah, it's an emergency. I wanted a name that communicated the urgency around this issue. It's time to sound the alarm in this country. The elites just keep getting richer, hoarding more and more for themselves. I believe in capitalism. I believe you should keep every penny that you earn legitimately through your hard work. But the system we have today isn't capitalism, it's cronyism. It's rigged in favor of a very small number of elites, and we're trying to stop that.

GARY: That's exactly what I've been saying, and it's why so many people today are so pissed off at these leftist financial globalists on Wall Street. The deck is stacked against regular people. These extreme liberal Democrats are destroying our country.

GUEST: I'm not focused on politics. I'm focused on economics. I needed to expose what was really going on, how the financial system was rigged. Now we can leverage new platforms to change the playing field.

GARY: You call your followers BurnOutz, right?

GUEST: That's what they call themselves.

GARY: I love that! It's like the Deplorables. We'll show you who's a burnout!

BURNER

GUEST: It's a term for outsiders, outcasts. We embrace that. Now it's our turn.

GARY: So, tell me, why are you doing all this anonymously? Why not just do what you're doing as yourself?

GUEST: These are some very powerful people and special interests we're rising up against. There's no limit to what they'll do. No line they won't cross. So I need to protect my identity. I know I've been surveilled illegally. They've done everything they can to stop me and identify me. That's why I'm using voice-altering software for this interview, so they can't get a voice print on me. And I'm on a burner phone that will be destroyed right after this call. But illegal investigations are really just the start of it.

GARY: Are you saying you're concerned for your safety?

GUEST: Let's just say these people can get whatever they want. Billionaires play by different rules. If they want you gone, you're gone. I've cost a lot of powerful people a lot of money.

GARY: You can say that again. The deep state doesn't want people upsetting the New World Order. The SEC, FTC, FBI, CIA, and every other three-letter acronym agency are so deep in the pockets of these extreme liberals, they can't imagine a world without them pulling the strings.

GUEST: Those organizations are set up for one purpose and one purpose only: To protect the powerful. To investigate and subjugate those at the bottom of the economic spectrum while biasing the entire system in favor of the elites.

GARY: You always have to ask yourself, *Who is benefiting?* It's the Democratic Party, its leadership, and its cronies in the deep state that are benefiting over and over again. It's the liberal elites.

GUEST: The conservative elites are just as big a problem. Your coinvestor in Razgo, Robert Jorgensen, is a billionaire.

GARY: Ha! Bob isn't an elite. Sure, he's been a very successful businessman, but he still drives a Buick. The overwhelming majority of these hypocrites are liberals. If you don't agree with them, they're going to do everything they can to shut you up. To cancel you.

GUEST: There are too many people trying to tell you what to do, what to say, what to think. That's over.

GARY: This seems like the next stage in this fight. With the rise of the Tea Party and MAGA, we found our political voice, but we were still at a financial disadvantage. You've got to follow the money, and this movement, *your* movement, is the way to do that. The genius of what you're doing is you're using the rigged system itself to beat these liberals at their own game.

GUEST: Banks, brokerages, and regulators are only there to protect the wealthy. Wall Street insiders manipulate trading prices every day and make a killing, but when our movement exposes their lies, they halt trading.

GARY: This is the kind of stuff that just boggles my mind. This is America. We're supposed to be the shining example to the world of the marvels of a capitalist system. But the liberals have been trying since the '30s and the New Deal to handicap capitalism. To tax hard-working people to the tune of trillions of dollars and transfer that rightfully earned wealth to entitlement programs that fuel the welfare state. We've had a rampant socialist, Marxist deep state that's been destroying economic incentives.

GUEST: That's what we need to change. It's a broken system.

GARY: I'll tell you what we're gonna have to do. Very soon, and I truly believe this is gonna happen, we are gonna see a lot of people rise up, take to the streets, and rebel against this system. Just like the fight against Communism, taking down the Berlin wall. People are fed up. I hear a lot of so-called conservatives and RINOs saying on TV and social media that any act of violence to elicit change is unacceptable. I'm glad Thomas Jefferson, Sam Adams, George Washington, and the brave men at Lexington and Concord didn't feel that way.

GUEST: You keep making this about politics. It's not. It's about money.

GARY: Okay, okay, fair enough.

GUEST: There is a huge economic and financial disruption coming.

GARY: This is your October Prophecy, right? I've read what you've written about it. You see a potential collapse—

GUEST: You don't get it, Gary. This is a disruption of the failed financial system, controlled by the billionaires, that has held people in chains for too long. Your friend Robert Jorgensen is no different than George Soros or any other elite. It's time for the billionaires to start feeling the financial pain. Time for the game to be rigged the other way.

GARY: Now wait a minute, I don't think that's a fair—

GUEST: Goodbye, Gary.

GARY: Okay, folks—there you have it, I guess. Fascinating conversation and the first on-air interview with the anonymous Burner_911. I'm Gary Scoffield. We'll be back with more of *The Gary Scoffield Show* right after this commercial break.

58

THE MOTLEY FOOL

Glecko Shares Hammered on News of Data Breach and CEO Drug Use

SAN FRANCISCO, CA, August 3, 2023—Less than six months from its high-flying IPO, shares of once-hot technology startup Glecko (NASDAQ: GCKO), plunged 83 percent in overnight trading. The opening price of $12.75 per share this morning has investors who bought at yesterday's peak of $75.18 licking their wounds and is well below the IPO price of $37 back in October.

The precipitous sell-off started at the close of market yesterday, triggered by posts claiming a massive data breach. With rampant speculation growing in online investor forums and Glecko's share price slipping in after-hours trading, the company issued a press release at 5:35 p.m. EST yesterday disputing the rumors and reassuring Glecko customers that their data was secure.

But mere minutes after the press release hit the wires, the personal data of millions of Glecko users was posted on a dark web hacking forum, contradicting the company's denial of the breach. Glecko shares plunged over 50 percent by the opening bell. Unfortunately for Glecko shareholders, that was just the beginning.

A video posted to YouTube early this morning appears to show Felix Ridley, the CEO of Glecko, snorting what appears to be cocaine. The video was accompanied by the caption, "Maybe this is why nobody is paying attention to security at GCKO." Although *The Motley Fool* and other news outlets have been unable to confirm the authenticity of the video, it immediately went viral, with over three million views as of this writing.

BURNER

According to SEC officials, the two events are allegedly part of a deliberate scheme by a hacker group known as the BurnOutz to drive down Glecko shares. Dozens of protestors affiliated with the group demonstrated outside Glecko headquarters this morning, some even chaining themselves to doorways and smashing windows at the building. Law enforcement officials say they are investigating a post, made on the free-speech site Razgo under the username Burner_911—the same anonymous profile that was implicated in the hack of Babelon.com—that may have incited today's events. While little is known about the alleged perpetrators, NASDAQ officials noted an unusually large number of short sellers of Glecko stock, most taking positions within the last twenty-four hours.

"This type of market manipulation will not be tolerated," said Wen Liang, director of the SEC's Division of Enforcement. "We have an active investigation and intend to prosecute this case to the full extent of the law."

It is unclear if Mr. Ridley will resign in the wake of these events, or if the Glecko board will dismiss him first. As the largest shareholder in Glecko, Mr. Ridley's personal net worth declined by an estimated $350 million in a single day. Despite numerous attempts to contact them, representatives of the company declined to comment for this article.

59

BURNER_911

Two Months Ago

@Burner_911 post on Razgo.com

>*"Dictatorship naturally arises out of democracy, and the most aggra-*
>*vated form of tyranny and slavery out of the most extreme liberty."*
>
>—Plato

BurnOutz!

I write today's post with a heavy heart . . . ♥♥♥

When I first discovered this site, Razgo, I thought I was in Eden. Finally, *FINALLY*, a social platform that truly espoused freedom of speech. The unfettered sharing of ideas. 💡💡

TODAY, I ask, *how true is that freedom*?????

I have received messages—*threats*, really—from the senior leadership at Razgo, asking me to STOP. Apparently, our little stunt with Glecko crossed a line. They want us to STOP being critical of public company stocks. STOP exposing the lies of the bankers and brokers and everyone else in the financial machine. STOP disrupting the establishment.

WHY??? Turns out, the investors of Razgo are ALSO big investors in GLECKO!!! They are just as beholden to the elites on Wall Street as anyone else! They don't care about free speech . . .

ALL THEY CARE ABOUT IS MAKING MONEY!!!

Let me start with the founder, ALEX KATIN. Alex owns 30% of Razgo and has started selling his shares in the secondary market. He's already pocketed over

$10 million, by my calculation, and stands to make tens of millions more selling shares in the company YOU all helped create!

Next in line is my good ol' radio buddy, GARY SCOFFIELD. Gary's little $1 million investment in Razgo is rumored to be worth over $50 MILLION now, based on the traffic he drives to the site when he mentions it *every single day* on his radio program!

And then, there's the granddaddy of them all, ROBERT JORGENSEN. Good ol' Bob is a billionaire who throws his money around just like any other rich, entitled billionaire. Bob likes to maintain a low profile, pretend he's a man of the people, but *do you know how he made his money?* He's a HEDGE FUND manager with a 10% stake in GLECKO!!

But Razgo is his crown jewel.

Let me be clear, this is a PONZI SCHEME and YOU ARE THE SUCKER!!! 🍭

They are just aggregating audience *as fast as they can* to sell it to the next sucker! Some old-school media company that's too dumb, too *desperate*, too much of a *dinosaur* 🦕 to care. Some fucktard who has more money than intellect and will just pay them for eyeballs. 👀

Alex and Gary and Bob don't give a FUCK about freedom of speech! They don't care about America or democracy or the unjust, unfair, RIGGED system. Because they are PART OF THAT SYSTEM! They are PERPE-*TRAITORS* of the status quo. They're just looking to sell a product, and YOU ARE THE PRODUCT! Your *attention* is the commodity! They are spoon-feeding you with a heaping serving of *outrage* 😠😣😖. Hooking you up to the dopamine drip of conspiracy theories. All just to monetize your attention, mine you like some *primordial humanoid resource* . . . oh, and make themselves RICH!

So . . . . . . I'm conducting an experiment.

I'm posting this open letter to the Razgo leadership:

ARE YOU ON THE SIDE OF FREE SPEECH?
OR ARE YOU ON THE SIDE OF THE ESTABLISHMENT?
ARE YOU EMPOWERING PEOPLE TO MAKE MONEY FOR THEMSELVES?
OR ARE YOU MAKING MONEY YOURSELF BY EXPLOITING PEOPLE?
ARE YOU ADVOCATES FOR REGULAR PEOPLE OR ARE YOU HYPOCRITES?
CAN YOU TAKE IT WHEN THE MEGAPHONE
OF FREE SPEECH IS POINTED AT YOU?!?!? 🎙️🎙️

Or are you *afraid*? 😬 😬 😬 *Afraid* of what you've unleashed?

Afraid of the backlash?

Afraid of your true motives?

Afraid of the BurnOutz!

You SHOULD be! Because WE WILL WIN! We will find you. We will come and get you. We will pull you out of whatever hole you're hiding in. WE WON'T STOP!!! Until we burn it all down!

60

SHANE

When I think about it now, the Razgo ban was the point when things started going sideways. No warning, no threat, no negotiation—they just straight up banned Burner_911. The account went dark. They called my bluff. I had other accounts—on Twitter, Twitch, 4chan, everything—but there was only one Burner_911 account and that was on Razgo. I had to get it back.

That was the first time I was cut off from my account, my followers. It prepared me for now.

I'm sitting on the cement floor of my new cell—a proper solitary one—remembering how it all went down as a predictor of what will happen this time. I'm also trying to remember what time of day it is. I really have no idea. I need to get organized. I pull out the micro voice recorder I got from Kryz from a seam in the side of my mattress, but think better of it—no need to dictate something self-incriminating. Instead, I grab a sheet of paper and pencil to take some cryptic notes. While I'm there, I reach in farther and pull out another Nembutal, also courtesy of Kryz. They're supposed to help me relax, finally let me get some sleep, but they aren't doing shit for me.

I pop two more of the yellow capsules dry, hoping they'll actually do their job this time. I rub the tip of the pencil against the floor to sharpen it, then write . . .

"*Speculation = Activation*"

When the ban happened, the BurnOutz lost their shit—all three million of them. Posting like a swarm of locusts in forums and feeds. I created a new subreddit at r/restoreburner911 that instantly had hundreds of thousands of subscribers and posts, all in a frenzy over what happened to Burner_911: *Did Razgo really shut him down? No, they could never do that. Maybe it was the Feds who finally caught him. No, they would have made a statement. It must have been the deep state. George Soros and Hillary Clinton finally silenced him.*

Their speculation, spinning into the wildest conspiracy theories, was more powerful than anything I could have conjured up on my own. I was in awe of their sheer energy. Like waves crashing into the shore, they were relentless. Kinetically driven by an insatiable anger, they writhed and fomented like tectonic plates stretched to the breaking point, ready to unleash their devastation. The ban had only galvanized them. That's what's happening now too. If I can reach them, I can activate them, wield them in my counterattack.

I scribble another line, holding my hand underneath the paper so the pencil won't rip through: *"Profile > Platform."*

All this time I thought I needed Razgo, but Razgo needed me more. Most of their audience was only there to hear from Burner_911. The profile was more powerful than the platform, and they knew it. I was the one holding the cards. I was the one who could pull the strings. I knew I could force their hand. Give them no choice but to reinstate the Burner_911 account. I just needed to put the plan in motion, and they would cave.

The next line: *"Money is Power."*

This one is obvious. No shit, *right?* Anyone can be bought. But I never thought I'd be the one with the money and the big, swinging dick. And it came so easy. All of a sudden, I had bank. I was into cryptocurrencies early, as a convenient way of collecting anonymous payouts. Then the whole thing exploded. Bitcoin alone increased 150X in five years. My crypto portfolio was worth over $20 million. I could have made that first charitable donation of $50K to CVU with *one* Bitcoin. But if I was going to take on a billionaire like Bob Jorgensen, I needed more fire power. That's where Ken Corbin came in.

Speaking of Ken . . .

I write "*Trust no one*" on the next line.

When you get to scale, everyone wants a piece of you. I thought the Razgo guys were on my side. That they stood for free speech. That they believed in the cause. But it was all a lie. There was no ideology. They were frauds, hypocrites, elites protecting the status quo, just like the guys on the other side. Trying to exploit my movement for their political agenda. Then there were the guys trying to take over the account. I was seeing failed login notices and attempted password changes on the daily.

Then there were the Feds trying to hunt me down. Following me on the streets, tapping into my phones, intercepting my web traffic. I knew they had infiltrated the organization. I—

There are steps coming toward my cell.

I hurry to tuck the paper and pencil back into the mattress. The guard stops outside the heavy steel door, opens the small passage at the bottom, and slides a tray of food underneath.

"Rise and shine, breakfast is served," he says. Apparently, it's morning.

I slide on my ass across the floor toward the tray—a gray coagulated scoop of something that looks like puke, powdered eggs, canned pears, and inky coffee that's sloshing back and forth in a Styrofoam cup. I can't see the guard and don't know his name, but I know the voice, snarky and condescending.

"Y'know, if I was in charge, you wouldn't be getting room service," he says from the other side, in a tone that suggests he might've taken a piss on the whole meal.

I poke at the mass with the spoon, my only utensil. I can see his steel-toed boots through the slot. He's just standing there trying to bait me into a response. I dip my finger in the coffee to see if it's hot enough to scorch his feet.

Room temperature, of course.

"Now that you mention it, can you let the manager know the coffee sucks?" I gag down a sip, then push the rest of the tray back under the door.

I really should eat, I know that. I've probably lost at least fifteen pounds already. But I just can't. Maybe I should go on a hunger strike—that could go viral.

"You think you're such hot shit." The guard's voice lowers to a growl. "I'd like to see you eat in the cafeteria with the rest of 'em. See how long you last. Bet you're not so tough when you're not hiding behind a keyboard."

Says the dude hiding behind a door, I think. But I can't push this guy's buttons too much. I don't know how he might react, or how many others are out there like the guy who slashed me. I run my fingertips along my ridge of stitches. *Trust no one.*

After a minute or two of silence, I hear him pick up the tray and walk away. If I'm ever going to get things back on track, I need to post. And Chloe may be my only way to do that. She understands what I'm trying to do. I really believe that. The things she was willing to do for me. The faith she put in me. A shared vision that brought us together. She helped me before, maybe she will do it again.

I pull out the paper and pencil again and stare at the line that reads "*Trust no one.*" Then I add, "*Except Chloe.*"

Whether she knows it or not, she is my path back.

61

GAWKER

DOS Attack on Razgo Brings Burner_911 Back Online

SAN FRANCISCO, CA, August 9, 2023—The popular alt-right social site Razgo shut down late Thursday night after what appeared to be a massive denial-of-service attack, apparently in retaliation for banning the popular account Burner_911.

The site, which has drawn criticism as a hotbed of extremist rhetoric, drew even more attention in the last two weeks after abruptly banning the site's most popular content creator, the anonymous profile known only as Burner_911. That ban, presumably in reaction to a post by Burner_911 that criticized Razgo's leadership, seemed to directly contradict the site's unfettered free speech mission.

Burner_911's followers, who call themselves BurnOutz, reacted swiftly, flooding Razgo, Twitter, Gab, and other social media sites with negative comments about Razgo's CEO, Alex Katin, and lead investor Robert Jorgensen, along with demands to bring Burner_911 back online. The criticism culminated in what officials believe was a programmatic denial-of-service attack that shut down the site.

"Razgo operates their own data center, so they can't be censored by a third-party hosting provider. But that left them very vulnerable to this kind of attack," said Kaspar Valto, an IT security expert. "They have a finite number of servers, so when this DOS attack happened, they were not able to bring additional cloud computing resources online quickly enough to handle the load."

Though executives at the company were not immediately available for comment, Katin issued a statement declaring the company would "not negotiate with terrorists." Yet within hours of the initial outage, the statement was retracted, the site was back online, and, in a dramatic reversal, the Burner_911 account was reinstated.

Prominent conservative radio host Gary Scoffield, who is also a minority investor in Razgo, spoke extensively about the attack on his program.

"What these thugs are doing is outrageous," Mr. Scoffield said. "They're no better than all these other liberal social justice warriors who think they can just cancel you out of existence. But free speech platforms like Razgo are the foundation of American democracy. I don't believe in negotiating with terrorists, but there really was no choice but to reinstate Burner_911's account so Razgo can get back to fulfilling its critical mission."

Given its controversial content and evident technical vulnerability, Razgo faces an uncertain future. Without conventional venture investors and limited revenue potential from mainstream advertisers, the site remains financially dependent on its primary benefactor, Robert Jorgensen. The reclusive billionaire hedge fund manager has voiced his support for Razgo in the past but has yet to publicly comment on this most recent incident.

One thing is certain: Burner_911 will post again. And when that happens, much of the criticism could be aimed squarely at Jorgensen. As the BurnOutz further weaponize Razgo's free speech platform against him, it remains to be seen if he will be able to take the heat.

62

TEXT MESSAGE FBI WIRETAP

TEXT MESSAGE EXCHANGE BETWEEN SHANE STOLLER
AND CHLOE CORBIN
AUGUST 12, 2023

MR. STOLLER: Hey, it's me.

MR. STOLLER: Sorry to be texting you from a new number.

                    MS. CORBIN: Shane?

                    MS. CORBIN: Seriously...
                    WTF?

MR. STOLLER: I know. Sorry.

MR. STOLLER: I need your help.

                    MS. CORBIN: What is it? Are
                    you OK?

MR. STOLLER: Can you arrange
a meeting with your dad?

                    MS. CORBIN: What??? Why?

MR. STOLLER: can't explain
here.

MR. STOLLER: not secure.

MR. STOLLER: I just need you to trust me. ✌️

MS. CORBIN: Ur freaking me out. What's wrong?

MS. CORBIN: Why do u need to talk to my dad?

MR. STOLLER: Ken is the key.

MR. STOLLER: He's the only one who can help me pull this off.

MS. CORBIN: What ru talking about?

MR. STOLLER: Bob Jorgensen.

MR. STOLLER: You were right.

MR. STOLLER: He's toxic. And I know how to stop him.

MR. STOLLER: But I can't do it without Ken. PLEASE!

MS. CORBIN: Shane, this is crazy.

MS. CORBIN: I don't know what you're thinking but my dad would never go along with it.

MR. STOLLER: Your dad hates Bob.

MR. STOLLER: This is our chance to cancel him.

MR. STOLLER: Not just socially or politically but financially.

MR. STOLLER: With your dad's help, we can pull this off.

MR. STOLLER: But I need to talk to him in person.

MS. CORBIN: Mmm ... I don't know.

MR. STOLLER: We're so close.

MR. STOLLER: This is what we talked about.

MR. STOLLER: Taking out the sources of capital. To make a real change.

MS. CORBIN: There's no way he's going to do this.

MS. CORBIN: But I'll text his EA and find a time.

MR. STOLLER: TY!!!

MS. CORBIN: But before I do ...

MS. CORBIN: U need to tell me ...

MS. CORBIN: Are you who I think you are?

63

CHLOE

The warm water flows over me, saturating my hair, ricocheting off my face, cascading down my body. The sheer comfort of it—bathing myself for the first time since this ordeal began, cleansing the stench, dried sweat, crusted scabs of blood from my skin—makes me feel human again. Such a simple daily pleasure, one I've taken for granted all my life. I exhale so deeply from my core it becomes an involuntary sob, my hands cupped over my face, my shoulders heaving uncontrollably under the droplets of water. Out of eyesight, out of their reach for the first time since they took me, I allow myself to let my guard down.

Out of the shower, I regain my composure, wrap a dirty towel around my torso, and muster the courage to examine myself in the mirror. The blow was more powerful than I expected, but it ended there, with just the one punch—well worth what I got in return. I gently touch my fingers to my swollen left cheek and eye. I lean that side of my face toward the mirror, inspecting the nearly black epicenter of the bruise, testing for tenderness as I move through the rings of discolored flesh—purple, red, yellow. Broken capillaries lie under the surface, like spider webs.

The shower was at Nick's insistence, after he dispatched Scooter to retrieve the lawyer again. He told me I smelled and looked like shit, demanded I clean up before Wayne arrived—wanting, like an abusive husband, to cover up the evidence of his attack. For me, the shower is a shred of normalcy, dignity, a ritual to cherish, as if I'm readying myself to see Shane again, even though I know our conversation will only be over the sterile texts of an encrypted messaging app.

It's probably best he won't be able to see me, with my black eye, my complete lack of makeup, my damp, stringy hair. Hardly Instagram-ready. I can barely look at myself—I'm unrecognizable, a different person.

I drop the towel in the bathtub and gingerly retrieve my clothes from a pile on the bathroom floor, my fingertips reluctant to touch them. Nothing else to change into but my own soiled garments, reeking of the odors I just tried so hard to wash away.

I hear Wayne in the kitchen now with the others. My lone escort, Benny, meets me as I unlock the bathroom door. He won't look me in the face, fidgets with the long zip tie in his hands.

"He shouldn't have done that," he says, glancing at my face, a perceptible stammer in his voice.

I lean toward him, trying to catch his downcast eyes, but he just takes my hands, clasps them together, and secures the zip tie around my wrists as he's done dozens of times before . . . looser each time.

"Well, I can't stop him—not with my hands bound," I say.

He finally looks up at me. A tiny, single nod is his only acknowledgment.

I limp, my sprained ankle still not fully recovered, toward the kitchen, Benny guiding me by the elbow like a convalescent. Wayne turns to look at us as we enter and freezes mid-sentence, staring with his mouth open at me. I know what he sees—my bruised eye, my swollen cheek over my gaunt face, how rapidly I've declined in just a few days. My shower has only exacerbated the signs of neglect, abuse.

I take my seat in my white plastic lawn chair without looking directly at him, rest my bound hands on the table like I'm about to take communion. Nobody speaks for a moment.

"So, like I was saying, we're all set," Wayne finally says. He slides a phone, some brand I've never heard of, across the table toward me, as he holds its twin up in the air with his other hand. "These are identical burner phones. Both purchased anonymously, with cash. The SIM cards are clean, the internal storage is wiped, and there are only two apps installed on them: Telegram and Razgo. Nothing that leaves digital breadcrumbs."

I slowly pick up the phone and power it on. Wayne gives me the passcode, and the screen illuminates, just those two lonely app tiles on the home screen.

"And this is how I'll communicate with him?" I ask, tapping the Telegram icon.

"Correct," he says. "It's a blank account, associated with a prepaid wireless number. The messages are fully encrypted, end-to-end. There is nothing about these accounts, apps, or phones that could be traced back to me, Shane, or any of us. The messages are set to auto-delete. Let me show you." He types into the sibling phone and seconds later the Telegram app delivers the message: *Testing 1-2-3.*

Got it, I reply through the app.

"Each of these is set up to have only one other connection—the other phone," Wayne continues. "I will bring this one to Shane. We've arranged to get it in and out through security."

"How will he know it's me? How will *I* know it's *him*?" I ask.

"Same thing I told him—come up with a question only he will know the answer to," he says. "One more thing, and it's important: the only time you can ever message each other is precisely between 9:20 and 9:25 a.m. on Sunday mornings. We can't be sure who is sympathetic to the cause, and that's the only time I know I will be with him without the guards. I've convinced them to give Shane five minutes of unsupervised religious observation once per week. Anything longer than five minutes is too risky anyway, could get detected. Plus, I've got to take the phone out with me or he'll get caught with it. So that's your window—every Sunday, starting tomorrow."

I power off the phone to preserve the battery and set it face down on the table. "Thank you," I say.

Wayne stands, puts the other phone in his pocket, and starts to leave. Then he turns and says, "Whatever you do, don't lose that phone."

64

TRANSCRIPT
OF VOICE RECORDING

TRANSCRIPT OF CONVERSATION RECORDED
BY DEFENDANT, SHANE STOLLER,
ON VOICE-ACTIVATED MICRO AUDIO RECORDER
August 22, 2023

CHLOE CORBIN: Dad, this is Shane.

KEN CORBIN: Nice to meet you, Shane. Chloe's told me a lot about you.

SHANE: Nice to meet you, Mr. Corbin.

KEN CORBIN: Please, call me Ken.

CHLOE CORBIN: Thanks for taking the time, Dad. I know you're busy.

KEN: You know I'm always happy to make time for you, dear. How is everything going with the foundation?

CHLOE: Oh, uh . . . great. Yeah, we're announcing another fundraising campaign next week for Bay Area animal shelters. Shane actually matched the foundation's challenge grant, so we're hoping to raise four hundred thousand.

KEN: That's great. Thanks for your support, Shane. Your business must be going well.

SHANE: Actually, it's been the crypto stuff recently. Most currencies have doubled in the last year or so, as you know.

KEN: Yes, Chloe mentioned you're into cryptocurrencies. Do you own any KarmaCoin?

SHANE: Yeah, it's done very well. Even better for you, obviously.

KEN: Yes, it's been a nice recovery. So, what did you two want to meet with me about today?

CHLOE: Do you want to explain it?

SHANE: No, why don't you start.

CHLOE: Okay. So, Dad, you know that site Razgo? It's, like, a cesspool of right-wing propaganda?

KEN: I suppose.

CHLOE: No, seriously, it's awful. It's a breeding ground for all these crazy conspiracy theories. I really think it's bringing about the end of civilization. At least the end of civility.

KEN: I understand why *you* find it abhorrent—but based on what Chloe's told me of your politics, Shane, I would think you'd be a fan of Razgo. Aren't you a believer in all this BurnOutz nonsense?

SHANE: I believe in free speech, but they're hypocrites. They banned Burner_911's account as soon as he said anything critical about Razgo. They need to be punished.

KEN: I saw the site was hacked and temporarily shut down. Isn't that punishment enough?

SHANE: I don't mean the site. I mean the people.

KEN: I wish the site had stayed down. Burner_911 is a menace. They were idiots to acquiesce and reinstate his account.

CHLOE: I don't know, Dad . . . Some of what he says makes sense. He's empowering regular people to fight for economic equality.

KEN: You have no idea what you're talking about, dear. Whoever's behind that account is a common street thug. It's mafia-style extortion of legitimate businesses, nothing more. Manipulating a naïve public while he laughs all the way to the bank. And you seem to be right in the middle of it, Shane.

CHLOE: *Dad*, that's not fair.

KEN: I don't think you have any idea how hard it is to build a successful company. It's easy to take potshots from the sidelines and criticize entrepreneurs who risked everything to make their fortune.

SHANE: I completely agree. I have tremendous respect for what you've built at Kadabra, Mr. Corbin, and the success you've had throughout your career. That's why I can't stand to see those guys at Razgo aim their fire at you.

KEN: What do you mean?

SHANE: Well, you know that Bob Jorgensen has taken a majority stake in ChainSpark, right?

KEN: Yes, of course. But they'll never compete with us. Bob's a hedge fund guy. He doesn't know how to run a real company. He's just looking to flip that to one of the big banks. Those guys are all way behind on blockchain back-office reconciliation. One of them will pony up eventually.

SHANE: With all due respect, I think you're underesti-mating him. Jorgensen is using Razgo to manipulate the market. There are thousands of dummy accounts on Razgo that are bashing Kadabra and KarmaCoin. I'm sure you've noticed. The price for KarmaCoin has been stagnating the last few weeks.

KEN: Trolls. I'm not worried about them. I'm glad they're suppressing the price of KarmaCoin. It was overheated. Now it's stabilized. Frankly, it's a buying opportunity. You should increase your position.

CHLOE: Dad, you're missing the point. Bob Jorgensen is exposed, and he doesn't even realize it. We can take him out.

KEN: Chloe, I'm surprised. I never thought you were one for the cutthroat world of business. I thought your call-ing was charitable work.

CHLOE: Razgo is a cancer. They're just spreading blatant disinformation and right-wing conspiracy theories.

SHANE: Besides, you hate Bob Jorgensen. We have an oppor-tunity to pull the plug on him.

KEN: Why would I go along with whatever it is that you're proposing?

CHLOE: It's not often you get to silence your critics, bankrupt a business rival, and shut off one of the big-gest donors to right-wing political causes all in one swift motion.

KEN: Fair point. So, what's the play?

SHANE: Okay. So, you know CompassCard, the cash-back credit card? Jorgensen has taken a huge uncovered short position in their stock. The company has a massive bond issuance reaching maturity next month, and they don't have the cash to repay the debt. The market is assuming all this won't be a problem because one of Bob's investment banking buddies is dangling a $500 million financing to bridge them. But Bob's going to tell the bank to pull the financing at the last minute. He thinks he has a sure thing. The company will be insolvent, with no other sources of financing or liquidity, and will be forced to declare bankruptcy—at which point, Bob will make a killing on his short position. Unless, of course, CompassCard's stock price goes *up*. I've heard from a credible source that Bob has calls on CompassCard at $4 per share for twenty million shares.

KEN: Holy shit.

SHANE: If the stock drops to that level, he'll make over $500 million, depending how low it goes. But for every $10 the stock *appreciates*, he's down—

KEN: $300 million.

SHANE: *Exactly*. If the stock price were to appreciate by, say $100 per share, our buddy Bob will have a margin call to the tune of $3 *billion*. His hedge fund can't cover that. They'll need to start liquidating assets. But by then there'll be blood in the water. He won't be able to pull together enough capital. He'll be done. And Razgo will be done too. As their lone major investor, if Bob pulls the plug, it will be over. As an added bonus, Gary Scoffield will lose his million-dollar investment in Razgo too.

KEN: How do you know this?

SHANE: I have my sources.

KEN: I'm not going to make millions of dollars in trades based on online hearsay. At best, it's stupid. At worst, it's insider trading.

SHANE: You're not buying based on anything other than the fact you see CompassCard as a great complement to Kadabra's back-end reconciliation service. I may or may not have received an encrypted message from a junior associate at the investment bank pretending to underwrite CompassCard's equity deal. But you don't need to know about that. Trading volume on CompassCard is small, only about eight hundred thousand shares per day. If you buy and hold, say, a million shares, you'll only be making a $40 million investment. But that will largely tie up the liquidity in the stock. I'll buy in too, for $10 million—

KEN: You have that kind of capital to put behind this?

SHANE: Yeah. It's everything I've got, but I'm all in on this. That will drive the price up. Then we'll get active on the forums and rally up the price. We can launch this thing like a rocket ship.

KEN: It's too suspicious. The SEC will be all over this. It's not worth it to me to endure a federal investigation, especially for so little money.

CHLOE: This isn't about the money, Dad. This is about justice. It's about doing what's right and ridding the world of Bob Jorgensen. It's a risk worth taking.

KEN: If we do this, how can I be sure this doesn't get traced back to me?

SHANE: You've got the perfect alibi—you're just buying a strategic stake in a complementary business. We'll do the rest. Worst case, you end up being the majority owner of a credit card company. What could go wrong?

65

SHANE

Wayne enters the meeting room where I've been waiting and places his briefcase on the desk. A new guard, some dude I've never seen before, is escorting him. Not good. This whole thing could be shit-canned before it starts.

"Okay, five minutes," the guard says, checking his watch. "Get to prayin.' You'll need it." And then, like Wayne said would happen, he leaves the room.

"Did it work?" I ask as soon as the door closes.

Wayne pulls up his pant leg to reveal an ankle holster, and there it is—the first phone I've seen since I got here. I practically drop to my knees to grab the thing off his leg, but he already has it pulled out and hands it to me. I fumble with it, trying to turn it on—some janky brand I've never seen before.

"How is she?" I ask, watching for the screen to come up. It's taking forever.

Finally, I notice that Wayne didn't answer. I look up from the phone. He's looking at me with his mouth half open like a dead fish.

"What is it?" I demand. "Is she okay? What happened?"

"She's . . ." He waves his hand in a way I don't understand.

"She's *what*, Wayne?"

"You know—it's been tough . . . obviously. I mean, she seems to be handling it well."

"Wayne, what the fuck are you trying to say?"

"She's . . . well, she's . . . she's pretty beat up." He pulls at his mustache. "I mean, she has a hell of a shiner. Someone hit her—probably the lead guy. I don't know what else has happened to her. She couldn't say. But . . . she may not be as safe as we thought."

"I swear to God I'm gonna fucking kill those guys," I say just as the phone finally comes to life.

"Keep your voice down," Wayne hisses. "You're supposed to be praying."

"I don't care. I'm sick of sitting here doing fuck all." I tap the messaging app and see the one contact—Chloe.

"You need to play this the right way." Wayne puts his hand over my thumbs before I can type. "I can't guarantee she'll have privacy. If you come in hot, you could scare them away. Or worse, they could hurt her again. So, go slow until you know for sure it's her."

"I need her to forgive me first. We weren't even speaking when this all went down."

"Okay, that's good—that's something else they won't know," Wayne says, pointing at the phone like that's something I'm supposed to write. "You need her help, Shane. If Burner_911 can post, even just *once*, it will go a long way toward getting you off. You know how all these conspiracy theories proliferate."

"Maybe."

"Okay, only three minutes left. I set a timer." He looks at his old-school Timex watch. "You have your security question?"

"Yeah," I say impatiently.

"Okay, I'll shut up and let you type. Just remember, I need to take that thing with me when I leave."

66

BURNER_911

One Month Ago

@Burner_911 post on Razgo.com

> *"You don't stand for something, you fall for anything."*
> —Chuck D, Public Enemy

I'M BACK, BURNOUTZ!!! 🧨 💥 🧨 💥 🧨 💥

This is the real Burner_911. Back from the dead. Those bastards at Razgo tried to shut me down. They whine about "cancel culture" and then they try to CANCEL ME!?!?

You can't cancel me! I'm Burner_911, *mother fuckers*!!!

Little Alex thinks he's a big swingin' dick. His site, his rules. He can kick off whoever he wants. Well, it doesn't work that way, Alex! The BurnOutz call the shots around here. WE'RE THE ONES WITH THE POWER! WE are the real protectors of free speech. Your pissant website would be NOTHING without us!

WE **ARE** RAZGO.

You and your sugar daddy are no better than the elites you pretend to criticize. You're their BITCH, ALEX! You don't really believe in anything except making money for yourself and your investors. And muzzling your critics.

Gary is a HACK—a dinosaur 🦕 from a lost age, roaming the earth with his stubby arms and big ass. Proficient only in a dying media, RADIO!!! Who gives a shit about radio? Who even *has* a radio anymore? Blue-haired ladies in Iowa? Truckers in Mississippi? That's your audience, Gary. Boomers who wear adult diapers and take meds for their enlarged prostates. Are you going to change the world with that audience?

But the WORST of all, the brains and the cash behind Razgo, is Bob Jorgensen. He's the Darth Sidious behind the scenes. Just pulling the strings and counting his fat stacks. He's a BILLIONAIRE who doesn't believe in anything except protecting his billions. Tax cuts for the rich, giveaways to his companies, slashing wages for regular people. Bob is a greedy fuck. He's been tricking us. Tricking ALL of us! Pretending to stand for what we believe in. But really he's just exploiting us.

IT'S TIME TO TAKE DOWN BOB JORGENSEN AND TAKE BACK RAZGO!!!

It's time for the BurnOutz to rise up and show that nobody can exploit us. Nobody can take advantage of us. Nobody can take us for granted. We know what we believe and what we stand for. We stand for sticking it to billionaires like Bob and making money for regular people, like us, who've been squashed under a repressive thumb for too long. We're coming to get your money, Bob!

SO . . . WHAT'S THE PLAY???

Like every billionaire, Bob has to make big bets to make big Benjis. Nothing else moves the needle for him. His hedge fund buys and sells stocks, bonds, real estate, crypto, whole companies—whatever makes him bank. And Bob doesn't just make money when things *appreciate*. He makes money when they *drop* too. He makes money on the short. AND BOB IS CURRENTLY SHORT TWENTY MILLION SHARES ON COMPASSCARD!!!

WTF!?!? We LOVE CompassCard! ♥ 🔥 ♥ 🔥 ♥ 🔥

For most of us, our first credit card was a CompassCard because they'd give one to *anybody* regardless of credit! LOL! Not to mention the backdoor promo code to get 10X points!

Now BOB is trying to drive CompassCard out of business! Do you know how much Bob will make if CompassCard goes out of business??? FIVE HUNDRED MILLION DOLLARS!!! Do you know how much he had to pay to get those calls? ONLY $800,000!!!!!

How FUCKING crazy is that!?!?! He's going to take down a whole company, take CompassCards (NASDAQ: CCFA) away from millions of customers, based on an $800,000 bet?!?!? It's not fair, it's not right, it shouldn't be legal, but the SEC will let him just make off with $500,000,000 unless WE DO SOMETHING ABOUT IT!!!

We're not going to let it happen.

TODAY, the tyranny of the rich ends.

TODAY, we're driving CCFA shares to the MOON! 🐦🌙🐦🌙🐦🌙

TODAY, we're going to make BOB FUCKING JORGENSEN pay big time for thinking he could kick ME off Razgo!

BUY, BUY, BUY, BUY, BUY!!! Scrape together every last cent you have. Raid your cookie jar. Pillage your parents' retirement account. Steal your fucking grandma's engagement ring if you have to!!! 💍💍💍

JUST GET ALL THE FUCKING MONEY YOU CAN AND PUT IT INTO CCFA!!!!

Those that go long, strap one on, and HOLD THE LINE will be rewarded!!! 💎💎💎

Trust me. I'm Burner_911.

67

REDDIT

reddit.com/r/nottinghamjustice

Posted by u/ballsacker911: YOU HEARD THE MAN, GENTS!!! BUY LIKE YOUR LIFE DEPENDS ON IT!!!!

Posted by u/smackdiddy: Soooooooooo glad ur back @Burner_911!!! Fuck these guys. We're taking 'em ALL down!

Posted by u/whiplashfargo: My Nottingham account is lit!! 🚀 Bought 40 shares of $CCFA at $25. That's my rent for this month, but hey #yolo! ROCKETSHIP! 🚀

Posted by u/scarfaceporkcow: we're not stopping til $CCFA goes to the moon!!! 🌙 🌙 🌙

Posted by u/PerseusNest: BURNOUTZ IN THE HOUSE!!! 🏠 We takin' this bastard DOWN!! Bob's my BEEE-OTCH!

Posted by u/logTriangulum: Yo, i'm sick of bailing out all these billionaires. We always get stuck picking up the tab for their trillion dollar tax breaks. FUCK THAT! ALL IN ON $CCFA!

Posted by u/lambchop97: BURNOUTZ! We all need to rise up! I just cashed out everything I have in my Notty account to go ALL IN on $CCFA.

Posted by u/whiplashfargo: $CCFA already up to $29! I be makin' fat stacks, yo!! 😁

Posted by u/GreenHippo: This is as bad as it gets with the rich just getting richer! They live by one set of rules, and the rest of us get screwed over, and over, and over again! It's BULLSHIT! @GreenHippo is IN! 🐻 🐻 🐻

Posted by u/starlord-seattle: I kneel before you @Burner_911! We all talk smack but you da man that makes it happen. BURNOUT FOR LIFE!!! 🔥🔥🔥🔥🔥

Posted by u/TropiCali-94: Thanks, bruh. Gonna print fosho!

Posted by u/grasslover2000: BUY ALL THE $CCMA YOU CAN!!! ALREADY UP 26% IN FIRST HOUR OF TRADING! AT THIS RATE A 10X INCREASE IS GOING TO BE NOTHING FOR $CCMA!!! BUY, BUY, BUY, BUY, BUY!!!!!!!! UPVOTE FOR VISIBILITY!!

Posted by u/whiskeypuppy: Bought 100 shares at $31.35!

Posted by u/waterfallKIWI: Bought 72 shares at $32.17!

Posted by u/capricornhole: Bought 119 shares at $33.42! Everything I got. Won't have money for tuition if this busts! Fuck it! #yolo

Posted by u/grasslover2000: DO NOT PANIC IF YOU SEE THE PRICE DROP!! BE PREPARED FOR VOLATILITY!! HOLD THE LINE!! UPVOTE SO PEOPLE DON'T PANIC!

Posted by u/NeoJedi: Bob is about to get split open like a sorority sister . . . he don't even know . . . bitch about to get PLAAAAAYYYYED!! He gets the call now and he's already out $1 BILLION!! Buy, mother fuckers! BUY!!!!

Posted by u/FrogHater: Bob Jorgensen is the devil! Fuck him and the other elites!

Posted by u/POGballer: Can't believe razgo execs canceled @Burner_911! Free speech my ASS! THEY'RE FUCKING COMMUNISTS!!!

Posted by u/whiplashfargo: $CCFA at $35 bitches!!! We makin' tendies now! 🍗🐥🐥

Posted by u/pepper_psycho: HOLD THE LINE . . . DO. NOT. SELL!!!

Posted by u/BatttMan: Goldman analyst on Squawk Box RIGHT NOW saying price of $CCFA is IRRATIONAL! Damn right it's irrational! BURNOUTZ ARE IN CONTROL!!! 🤪

Posted by u/fittyflyfly: Institutional guys are losing their shit putting the squeeeeeeze on Nottingham to stop trading in $CCFA. If this is true, the Nottingham execs should all go to JAIL! THIS IS CLASS WARFARE!!! 💀

Posted by u/Netrat2020: Bought 35 shares at $37.08! Diamond hands, bitches! 💎🙌💎🙌

Posted by u/coketracks: Big hedge funds are buying $CCFA trying to ride the wave! 🏄 Expect lots of buy/sell activity from algorithms trying to figure out what's happening. VOLATILITY AHEAD!! DON'T PANIC!!! HOLD THE LINE!!!!

Posted by u/MI_BurnOutz: They just trying to chip away more and more retail investors. Ignore the noise. BUY! HOLD! I'M ALL IN!!! MY BALLS ARE DIAMONDS!!! 💎💎💎

Posted by u/whiplashfargo: $CCFA at $40!!! This is a rocketship!! 🚀🚀🚀

Posted by u/blackeyed_sheep: We are preparing a class action LAWSUIT against RAZGO for shutting down @Burner_911. DONATE HERE! SHARE!! UPVOTE!!

Posted by u/beachwall-e: Just got a tip the rats are fleeing the ship! Big boys are getting calls to cover their shorts! WE'RE BURNING JORGENSEN'S FUND TO THE GROUND!! 🔥

Posted by u/Netrat2020: Holy shit!! Share price just dropped 20% in two minutes!!

Posted by u/roosterjudo: WARNING! Retard alert!!! ITS STONKS YOU VAG! BUY THE DIPS!! I just added ten grand more! The big rally will happen soon! 💵💵💵 TRUST THE PLAN!

Posted by u/BurnerPlatoon: THIS IS IT BOYZ!!! I EMPTIED MY GIRLFRIENDS BANK ACCOUNT TO GO ALL IN ON $CCFA! FUCKING HOLD YOU PUSSIES!!!

Posted by u/bennietheburnout: Trust you @Burner_911. . . $20K into $CCFA! #yolo

Posted by u/TulsaApe: We're back! 🦍🦍🦍🦍🦍🦍 BurnOutz are driving $CCFA to the stratosphere! Never sell, cowards. HOLD THE LINE 💎 🙌

Posted by u/fittyflyfly: SEC and NASDAQ telling Nottingham to STOP TRADING $CCFA! BUY NOW BEFORE THEY SHUT US OUT TO PROTECT THEMSELVES!!!

Posted by u/whiplashfargo: $CCFA at $50!!!

Posted by Burner_911: $CCFA UP 100% AND IT'S NOT EVEN NOON!!! WAY TO GO BURNOUTZ!!! 🙌 KEEP BUYING!!! THIS IS FAR FROM OVER!!! HOLD THE LINE!!! 💎✊🚀

68

CHLOE

Perbacco, I type. The restaurant we went to on our first date.

Yes, comes the reply.

Where was I going when we first met in your Uber? I type.

Bloomberg, comes the reply.

Emotions flood through me—a burst of laughter, a surge of anger, overwhelming relief. Tears stream down my face.

I can't believe it's really you! I type, my knees tucked into my chest, perched on the white lawn chair, the boys encircled around the table, pretending to give me privacy.

Yup it's me! Shane types. *I can't believe it's you either!*

"What is it?" Nick asks, studying my expressions.

"It's him," I say, an uncontrolled smile settling on my face as I wipe a tear from my cheek. The others nod approvingly, like we just made contact with Earth from a distant planet.

"Give me the phone," Nick says, unmoved. He extends his hand toward me and claps his fingers expectantly against his empty palm.

"Give her a minute, *will ya*," Scooter says to Nick.

I don't have time for this. If Nick wants this phone, he'll have to rip it out of my hands. We have only five minutes.

The messages fly as fast as we can type:

> ME: It's so crazy. Everything that's
> happened.

HIM: I know . . . I'm SOOO sorry.

HIM: I never meant for any of this
to happen.

                                    ME: I know.

HIM: Are you OK? Safe?

                                    ME: Yes.

HIM: Are you *sure*??

HIM: Wayne said you have a
black eye!

                                    ME: I'm fine.

HIM: I can't tell you how sorry I
am. I wish I could undo all of this.

HIM: Where are you?

                                    ME: I don't really know. A house.
                                    ME: No idea where.

HIM: Did they really think this
would work?

HIM: Kidnapping you to get
me out?

                                    ME: Apparently.
                                    ME: But I can't really talk about
                                    that now.

HIM: I'm so fucking stupid.

HIM: You never should have been
with me.

HIM: Then you never would've
gotten mixed up in all this.

HIM: Will you ever forgive me?

                                    ME: I already do. I know what
                                    you were trying to do. You don't
                                    control these guys.

HIM: Yeah, but they're BurnOutz!

They're doing what they think *I*
want them to do! They kidnapped
you at gunpoint!

HIM: I thought they were going to
kill you!!

> ME: Shane. You can't blame your-
> self for that. I don't.

HIM: All the shit with your dad and
Kadabra. Not my best idea. I was
just so angry at him. I was so wrong
not to trust you.

> ME: I'm never speaking to my
> father again, after what he did.
> He betrayed you, and me!

HIM: Ego of a billionaire.

> ME: Exactly, and I'm sick of it.
> He's always just taken advantage
> of me. Propped me up to run his
> bullshit foundation, to shine up
> his image.

> ME: While at the same time
> always cutting me down. Telling
> me I'm not smart enough, or
> pretty enough, or skinny enough.
> I'm done.

HIM: I wish I could be with you.
I miss you so much. I LOVE YOU!

Another tear streaks across my face. This is what I've *always* loved
about him—his sincerity, his passion, his almost *naïve* idealism. He doesn't
think through consequences, he doesn't hedge, he doesn't curate everything perfectly. He says what he feels, and people *love* him for it. *I* love
him for it—that boldness, that brash, unfiltered, speaking truth to power
no matter what. The unadulterated commitment to effect change by any

means. To go to jail, to *die*, if he has to.

I may not agree with his tactics, but I do support his mission, because he *believes*. That's what's so unique. It's truly not about him, it's about the cause. That's what I found so endearing about him from the first time I met him. He was one of the only people I'd ever met who didn't want something from me. He wasn't glomming on to my celebrity or my wealth; that wasn't important to him. He had no interest in the persona I had created, just in the real me. I can always be myself when I'm with him. My *true* self. He brings that out of me. And now I may never be able to see him again. I need to say it.

Nick stands up, piercing my momentary reflection, and storms off, into the living room.

Scooter looks at the phone and says, "Keep going. You're running out of time."

ME: I love you too.

HIM: I can't stand the thought of
losing you.

ME: I know, me too! I'm so scared
about what's going to happen
though.

ME: Wayne says they are going for
the death penalty!

HIM: Yeah, they're trying to pin
everything that happened on me.

ME: Yeah. We don't have much
time. I have an idea for how we
can see each other again.

HIM: I know . . . I had the same
idea.

HIM: Burner_911 needs to post.

ME: EXACTLY! It will help prove
your innocence.

ME: Cast doubt that ur the person behind the account.

HIM: I agree.

HIM: But I need *you* to do it.

HIM: I can't do it from here. It's not safe.

HIM: I don't trust anyone else.

ME: Me??? Shane . . . I love you, but I can't do that.

ME: I wouldn't know what to say.

ME: Nobody would believe it.

HIM: Yes they will. You'll know what to say.

ME: Shane! I can't!

ME: I couldn't even log in. I don't know the password.

HIM: Yes, you do.

ME: What do you mean?

HIM: You already got your favorite restaurant.

HIM: But you also told me your favorite wine.

HIM: That + vintage = password.

ME: This is crazy. I can't do this.

HIM: Yes, you can! You *have* to. It's our only chance to see each other again.

HIM: You have to believe.

69

WAYNE

The way out through security is a hell of a lot less stressful than coming in was. No metal detector or pat-down this time. I almost did an about-face when I saw our guy Kryz with a different sidekick, but that guard must be on the take too because he gave me a nod and let me through with the phone no problem.

Now we're about to find out if the risk was worth it.

I walk up 7th Street to that same hipster coffee shop Valerie likes. I sent her back to the office to keep going through the mountain of discovery documents with the rest of the team. I don't need her guilt-tripping me about who I'm about to meet with.

Alex spots me right away when I walk in, like he's been staring at the door. He's sitting at a table with a pile of coffee cup fragments he's torn up, just across from an industrial-size coffee roaster that—along with thumping house music that gives me a headache—drowns out our conversation.

"Everything go as planned?" he asks, so quiet I can barely hear him over the racket.

"Easy as pie," I say, retrieving the burner phone from my convenient ankle holster. "One of the guards wasn't who we expected, but lucky for me he was a believer—either that or we've greased enough palms there that it wasn't an issue."

I hand the phone over to him. He flips it over in his hand a few times, like he's inspecting it for damage, then powers it up.

"Did he reach her?" he asks without looking up from the phone. I can see the glow of the screen in his beady eyes. Never liked this guy. Seriously inflated ego. Thinks running Razgo makes him some tech elite.

"Yeah, he did. At least that's what he told me."

"And did he give her the password?"

"Not sure. He wouldn't say. Isn't that what you're supposed to be able to find out?"

"It isn't that easy," he says.

"I still don't understand why you can't just get the password out of your database or whatever. Why we need to go to all this trouble."

"I already explained this to you, like, five times." He looks up from the screen, exasperated by my technological ignorance. "We don't store passwords. We don't store any personally identifiable information about our users at all—it's all tripcodes to verify account credentials. That's what allows Razgo to be totally anonymous. When a user logs in, we convert their password using the SHA-256 hash function into a 64-hexadecimal output that's impossible to crack, then we prepend that with a secure, randomly generated salt string. So even if hackers, or site admins like me, somehow accessed the password table, you're talking about a number of possible values roughly equivalent to all the atoms in the universe."

"Perfectly clear," I say. Luckily, his attention goes back to the device before he can see my eye-roll.

"That's why we need to go to 'all this trouble,'" he says with a dismissive head shake. He taps and swipes on the screen, eyes narrowed.

"So? Did we get it?" I ask after a minute or so.

He shakes his head. "He must have changed the auto-delete settings. All the messages are gone."

"So I risked my ass for nothing?"

"There's another way. I installed a keylogger. He wouldn't have had time to detect it. It's a little more brute force, but—*shit*."

"Let me guess, he detected it."

Alex drops the phone on the table like it just burned his fingers. He stares at in disgust for a second—the kind of look you use for a puppy who just took a shit on your carpet. Then he picks up his coffee, takes a sip, and looks toward me for the first time during this conversation, while still managing to avoid eye contact. As he does, I see a new thought bring a sense of relief to his expression.

"There's always the other phone."

70

SHANE

The banging has to stop before I lose my shit.

All night these motherfuckers have been at it. I can't even tell anymore which ones are banging to support me and which ones are banging 'cause they want to kill me. I don't even care. One of 'em's gotta have a steel pipe or some shit cause it's loud as hell.

"Shut the hell up!" one of the guards yells, but that just makes it worse. Catcalls echo through the dark.

It doesn't really matter. It's not like I would've been able to sleep anyway. I've been chewing on it all in my head, over and over again. It had to be her, *right?*

She got the answer, right away—Perbacco, our restaurant. I remember every detail of that night. I hope she does too. I know it was her. And I can't believe that she understood. That somehow she forgives me for all the shit I put her through. It just *sounded* like her. I could tell. There was too much that only she would know.

Unless . . .

Unless they were right there—threatening her, torturing her. They have to be getting desperate. The swap isn't happening. They have to know that by now. Maybe this was their game all along, to use her to take over the account. Worst case is they don't see *any* use for her anymore—then what will they do?

Another round of banging starts up. I guess it's supposed to intimidate me or something. Fuck these guys. Now I have a reason, a motivation to get out of this mess. She's the only person I trust. If Burner_911 posts again, it will show that I'm not the person, at least not the *only* person, behind that account, behind this movement. If I could log in from here, I would. But there's no chance. Encrypted messages on Telegram for three minutes every Sunday is the most I'm going to get. Even if Kryz got me a phone, I'd need my hash algorithm, I'd need a VPN, I'd need a Tor browser, and I'd need a network connection that can avoid detection. Never mind that if I did it from here and was caught, it would give the prosecution the definitive proof they need.

No. She can do it. She'll remember. She'll know what I was trying to tell her. And she'll know what to say, what to post. I trust her.

Speaking of trust—I've totally lost it with Wayne. Dude's dead to me. Just when I'm thinking maybe he's the only one on my side, he tries to fuck me over with that amateur bullshit? Unbelievable.

Everything I couldn't understand about him before now makes perfect sense. Turns out he's just another hack trying to take control. No way I let that slide.

71

COURT TRANSCRIPT

TRANSCRIPT OF TESTIMONY OF NICOLA EICHERT

DIRECT EXAMINATION BY MS. GIBSON:

MS. GIBSON: Thank you for testifying here today, Ms. Eichert. Would you please describe your occupation to the court?

MS. EICHERT: Yes, of course. I'm a senior special investigator at the US Securities and Exchange Commission. I've been at the SEC for over eighteen years and served the last ten years in the Trading and Markets Division investigating suspicious trading activity in the major securities markets, mostly stock exchanges.

MS. GIBSON: In your role at the SEC, what type of crimes are you responsible for investigating?

MS. EICHERT: The most common is insider trading, but my team investigates a wide range of securities schemes, such as attempts to manipulate share prices, accounting fraud, pump and dump schemes, even the occasional fraudulent securities offering.

MS. GIBSON: When did you first open your investigation into trading activity in CompassCard Finance & Affiliates, which trades under the ticker symbol CCFA?

MS. EICHERT: Actually, earlier than you might expect. As you know, that stock gained a high profile when speculative trading fueled by a Reddit discussion board drove up the price. But several months prior to that we had seen an unusually large volume of short positions on the stock.

MS. GIBSON: Short positions meaning investors who were betting the stock price would go down. What was strange about that activity?

MS. EICHERT: You usually see that volume of shorts on hyperinflated stocks with high volatility, but Compass-Card didn't seem particularly overpriced based on their fundamentals. The other suspicious dynamic was how concentrated that short position was. We identified several offshore holding companies that all turned out to be owned by the same individual, Robert Jorgensen.

MS. GIBSON: Did the SEC decide to open an investigation at that point?

MS. EICHERT: No, we were just monitoring the situation. There was nothing illegal about the trades *per se*, but we wanted to keep an eye on it in case there was more unusual activity. Another accredited investor, Kenneth Corbin, was buying up CCFA shares in small increments—three hundred to five hundred at a time—again through subsidiary companies to cloak his activity. At first, we thought this was just a billionaire showdown—one taking the short, the other taking the long, possibly vying to put the company into play or acquire a majority stake as part of a hostile takeover or something. Then one of our field agents identified this Reddit forum called Nottingham Justice where thousands of retail investors were suddenly talking up the stock. That's when things got interesting.

MS. GIBSON: Was that unusual, for stocks to be a topic of conversation in that subreddit?

MS. EICHERT: Not at all. That's what it was created for. Nottingham, you may know, is a retail stock trading app popular among Reddit users. But this particular forum was committed to stock schemes touted by the online persona Burner_911.

MS. GIBSON: And what did you know then about Burner_911?

MS. EICHERT: We knew that he—well, we assumed it was a "he"—had risen to notoriety on the far-right social network, Razgo. Whoever was behind that account would post long, sometimes rambling diatribes about billionaires and elites and how the whole financial system was rigged. A lot of the posts were somewhat unhinged conspiracy theories, but periodically the rants would focus on a particular security—a company stock, a cryptocurrency, a derivative option, whatever—that Burner_911 claimed would take money from a wealthy individual or company and redistribute it to his followers. He had a cult-like following, extremely zealous. It was like they would try to one-up each other in displays of sycophantic belief in the mission. A perfect combination of self-righteousness and greed.

MS. GIBSON: Had the SEC investigated Burner_911 or his followers at that point?

MS. EICHERT: Oh, they were definitely on our radar. There's a lot of this kind of stuff online—forums where retail investors talk a stock up or down. Most of the trades are small potatoes. Teenagers with a Nottingham account and a couple hundred bucks. Not worth our time. But this was different, a much more concerted effort. We found out the FBI was already looking into this same group for suspected wire fraud. The group had claimed credit for a range of website hacks, data breaches, denial of service attacks, and the like, engineered to manipulate stock prices. Burner_911 would rant about a "rigged system," but he and his group were the ones doing the most blatant rigging.

MS. GIBSON: So, did your investigators at the SEC start collaborating with the FBI at that point?

MS. EICHERT: Yes. We had just started comparing notes the week before shares of CompassCard Finance & Affiliates suddenly surged—more than doubling within the first hour of trading that morning. We automatically investigate trades on stocks where the trading volume and price are suddenly so far outside normal ranges. It's usually an early indicator of some type of insider trading.

MS. GIBSON: And was this a case of insider trading?

MS. EICHERT: It was pretty quickly evident this was something different. Insider trading means you're buying or selling the stock based on material nonpublic information about the company. This looked more like a coordinated effort by *outsiders* to push up the price of the stock. The motive users spoke about in the Nottingham Justice Reddit forum was to punish the wealthy individual I mentioned earlier, Robert Jorgensen, who had taken the large short position in CCFA shares.

MS. GIBSON: And what was motivating that coordinated activity?

MS. EICHERT: Retaliation. Mr. Jorgensen is the primary investor in Razgo, which had attempted to kick Burner_911 off the site. They felt if they drove the price of CCFA shares up high enough, it would financially ruin Mr. Jorgensen, and Burner_911 and his followers could take over the site.

MS. GIBSON: And did that strategy work?

MS. EICHERT: Spectacularly well, actually. The 100 percent increase in the first hour was just the beginning. The stock price went from about $24 at the opening bell to over $250 per share. By mid-morning, we had concluded the entire thing was a stock manipulation scheme, so we called on NASDAQ—and Nottingham, since that's where the bulk of the buy orders were originating—to halt trading on the stock. Eventually, around 1:00 p.m. eastern time, they complied. But the damage was done by then, and it was calamitous for Mr. Jorgensen. His short position was down over $6 billion. Even in their wildest imagination, I don't think the BurnOutz could have expected such an outcome.

MS. GIBSON: What did that mean for Mr. Jorgensen?

MS. EICHERT: He was financially ruined. He had margin calls from multiple banks coming due that amounted to twice his net worth. He was liquidating other assets as quickly as he could, but all he could do was negotiate payment terms. His hedge fund was forced to file for bankruptcy.

MS. GIBSON: In your estimation, did the actions of this mob and its inciter, Burner_911, constitute illegal market manipulation?

MS. EICHERT: Absolutely, yes. This was clearly a coordinated effort to orchestrate a short squeeze. All the evidence of that collusion is right there on the Nottingham Justice forum.

MS. GIBSON: Thank you, your Honor. No further questions.

CROSS EXAMINATION BY MR. YOUNG:

MR. YOUNG: Thank you, Your Honor. Ms. Eichert, you testified a moment ago that you believed the activity you described to be illegal.

COURT TRANSCRIPT

MS. EICHERT: Correct.

MR. YOUNG: I'd like to understand a little better the basis for that alleged crime. First, do you have any way of correlating posts on Reddit with individual trading activity? How do you know the people posting to that forum were even the ones buying the stock?

MS. EICHERT: Hundreds of them posted screenshots of purchase orders on their Nottingham accounts.

MR. YOUNG: During the course of that day there were 3,542 posts on the Reddit forum you mentioned that said their alleged purchase of CCFA shares was based on the strong fundamentals of the company and their loyalty to CompassCard Deluxe. Is that correct?

MS. EICHERT: I don't know the exact number, but, yes, several posts seemed to be legitimately valuing the stock.

MR. YOUNG: There were also 1,367 posts from users who appeared to be professional stock traders jumping on the bandwagon—just buying based on the upward momentum of the stock. Correct?

MS. EICHERT: Again, I don't know the precise number of posts, but I recall some that expressed that sentiment, yes.

MR. YOUNG: Is there anything illegal about buying a stock you believe will appreciate, Ms. Eichert?

MS. EICHERT: No, so long as you are not attempting to manipulate that stock price.

MR. YOUNG: Were any of the retail investors in this forum spreading deceptive or factually inaccurate information about the company in question?

MS. EICHERT: I don't recall.

MR. YOUNG: Did any of the individuals you assert were trying to manipulate the price buy enough shares to significantly influence the market?

MS. EICHERT: Individually, no. But, collectively, yes.

MR. YOUNG: Ms. Eichert, as you know, one needs both the *intention* and the *means* to be guilty of manipulating the stock market. How many individuals has the SEC identified who had both the intention and the means to manipulate CompassCard's share price?

MS. EICHERT: We are still in the process of definitively linking trade activity and online comments with suspected individuals.

MR. YOUNG: So what you're saying is that maybe, *possibly*, some of the people who posted in this forum, the majority of whom seemed to be investing tiny amounts for perfectly legitimate reasons, might have hoped the price of the stock would go up? Again, Ms. Eichert, is it unusual or illegal for a buyer of a stock to hope that stock appreciates?

MS. EICHERT: No, obviously not.

MR. YOUNG: And would you characterize the actions of this highly decentralized, uncoordinated group, even if they all wanted the stock to appreciate, to be any more unethical than the usual behavior of institutional investors?

MS. EICHERT: In recent years, we've witnessed the rising influence of indignant, vindictive, and economically irrational retail investors attempting to move markets in a coordinated fashion, increasing market volatility and distrust.

MR. YOUNG: Isn't what you're describing merely a shift in power away from the traditional Wall Street insiders toward less wealthy, less well-connected retail investors?

MS. EICHERT: I wouldn't characterize it that way. We prosecute market manipulation schemes regardless of whether they are perpetrated by large players or individuals.

MR. YOUNG: I see. So . . . have you brought charges against any individuals?

MS. EICHERT: Not as of this time.

MR. YOUNG: Speaking of individuals, you mentioned earlier that your team also investigated the trading activity of Ken Corbin around this time, correct?

MS. EICHERT: Yes, that's correct.

MR. YOUNG: You testified that he, under his affiliated companies, acquired a large amount of CCFA stock—by my calculations, almost $40 million, is that correct?

MS. EICHERT: Approximately, yes.

MR. YOUNG: After accumulating that many shares over the course of only a week, maybe you could explain to the jury what Mr. Corbin did with those shares?

MS. EICHERT: He sold them.

MR. YOUNG: All of them?

MS. EICHERT: Yes.

MR. YOUNG: And what effect did that have on CCFA's stock price?

MS. EICHERT: It dropped, precipitously. The share price was back down in the $20 range within two days.

MR. YOUNG: Given that Mr. Corbin purchased the bulk of those shares before the run-up and sold them at the peak of speculation, how much did Mr. Corbin make on the buying and selling of CompassCard's stock?

MS. EICHERT: By our estimates, about $416 million, before tax.

MR. YOUNG: And is it correct that the vast majority of retail investors whom you accuse of manipulating the CCFA share price were collectively responsible for about $25 million in purchases?

MS. EICHERT: We're still working on identifying who made all those purchases, but that's in the ballpark.

MR. YOUNG: So it is your testimony that hundreds of individual retail investors, many of whom bought in to CCFA stock at $100, $200, or more were part of an illegal scheme to manipulate the share price, but that Mr. Corbin, who, by your estimate, pocketed $416 million, has no culpability?

MS. EICHERT: I'm not maintaining that Mr. Corbin has no culpability. In fact, he is the subject of an active investigation, so I'm afraid I cannot comment further.

MR. YOUNG: With all due respect, Ms. Eichert, my client and every one of the individuals who followed his advice were financially decimated in the following days, while Mr. Corbin walked off with bags of money. If anyone is guilty of manipulating the markets, he is. No further questions, Your Honor.

72

TEXT MESSAGE FBI WIRETAP

TEXT MESSAGE EXCHANGE BETWEEN SHANE STOLLER AND CHLOE CORBIN
September 19, 2023

MR. STOLLER: WTF!?!?!?!?!?!?

MR. STOLLER: WHY IS KEN SELLING!?!?!?!?!?!?

> MS. CORBIN: what do you mean???

MR. STOLLER: YOU KNOW *EXACTLY* WHAT I MEAN!!!!

MR. STOLLER: HE'S SELLING HIS CCFA SHARES!!!!

MR. STOLLER: THE STOCK PRICE IS PLUNGING!!!!

MR. STOLLER: HE'S SUPPOSED TO HOLD, HOLD, HOLD LIKE THE REST OF US!!!!

> MS. CORBIN: 👻

MR. STOLLER: THAT'S ALL YOU CAN SAY?!?!?!?!?!

MR. STOLLER: A FUCKING SHRUG

EMOJI????

MR. STOLLER: HOLY SHIT CHLOE!
!!! HE'S FUCKING ME OVER!!!

MR. STOLLER: CORRECTION ...
YOU ARE FUCKING ME OVER!

> MS. CORBIN: what are you
> talking about?

> MS. CORBIN: I don't know
> anything about this

MR. STOLLER: THAT'S SUCH
BULLSHIT!!!

MR. STOLLER: YOU KNOW
EXACTLY WHAT YOU'RE DOING!!!

MR. STOLLER: IF YOU'RE SO
INNOCENT, TELL HIM TO STOP
SELLING ...

MR. STOLLER: NOW!!!!

> MS. CORBIN: I tried texting
> and calling him

> MS. CORBIN: he won't answer

MR. STOLLER: GO TO HIS FUCK-
ING OFFICE THEN!!!

MR. STOLLER: WE'RE GETTING
DESTROYED OUT HERE!!!

> MS. CORBIN: OMG! I don't
> control my dad!

MR. STOLLER: THAT'S RIGHT. HE
CONTROLS *YOU*!!!

> MS. CORBIN: fuck you

> MS. CORBIN: he did this
> because i asked him to

> MS. CORBIN: he did this to

help you

MR. STOLLER: HELP ME??? HELP
ME?!?!?!?!?!?!?!?!?!?!?!?

MR. STOLLER: HE'S SODOMIZING
ME WITH A BAZOOKA!!!!

MR. STOLLER: I'M GOING TO
BLEED OUT!!!! STOCK PRICE IS
ALREADY OFF 50%!!

MR. STOLLER: YOU SET ME UP!!!

MS. CORBIN: set you up????

MS. CORBIN: you're crazy!

MS. CORBIN: i did this for
YOU!

MR. STOLLER: BULLSHIT!!!
YOU SET ME UP!!!

MS. CORBIN: i had no idea my
dad would do this

MS. CORBIN: you have to
believe me

MR. STOLLER: YOURE SUCH
A LIAR!!!

MR. STOLLER: JUST LIKE ALL
THE OTHER BILLIONAIRE PRIMA-
DONNAS!!

MR. STOLLER: GO BACK TO YOUR
RICH FRIENDS!!!

MS. CORBIN: SHANE! You have
to believe me.

MR. STOLLER: I'M NOT SHANE.
I'M BURNER ...

73

SHANE

My whole life, I've never had someone I can trust.

Every time I got close to trusting someone, they'd let me down. Or they'd end up dead. All the times I've been betrayed, you'd think I would have had my guard up when I met Ken Corbin. It was a deal with the devil. I knew that going in. I just didn't expect him to fuck me over as hard and as ruthlessly as he did. Initially, the plan was a spectacular success—we absolutely destroyed Bob Jorgensen. The BurnOutz showed up big time. But when Ken dumped his position in CCFA, we were left holding the bag—big flaming bags of dog shit.

Once the sell-off started, it was chaos. Some guys got out before the stock dropped 98 percent, but the "hold the line" ethos was so strong that most of us went down with the ship—watching our Nottingham balance spiral down toward zero. I lost every dime I had, but that wasn't even the worst part. The worst part was that I'd screwed over thousands of followers who'd put their faith in me. Thanks to Ken, they wouldn't be able to pay for tuition or rent or food. They'd been fucked over by a billionaire, yet again.

When I realized what Ken was doing, I absolutely lost it. I threw my laptop against the wall, knowing I was helpless to stop it. All my frustration, helplessness, and desperation was distilled like a hyperconcentrated Molotov cocktail of anger. I was no longer in control. Burner had fully taken over. What *I* wanted didn't matter anymore. Only what *he* wanted mattered—and he wanted what *they* wanted . . . *revenge.*

Which is the same thing I want now against Wayne.

He's been babbling on for a while now, about evidence, about testimony. Our usual lawyerly conversation but with a new, nervous undertone—he knows I know. Valerie is diligently taking notes by his side, as always. Hours more of defense prep, but what's the point? They aren't my lawyers anymore. Besides, the Feds are gonna get me on *something*. Charges on top of charges on top of more charges. I wouldn't be surprised if they convicted me for marijuana possession in junior high. It's just me against the full force of the federal government, without even a defense attorney on my side. Worse than that, he's actively trying to screw me. I knew I never should have trusted this guy.

"Do you want to fuck Valerie?" I say, stopping Wayne midsentence.

His jaw slacks open and he stares at me for a beat. "I'm sorry?"

"You heard me. Do . . . you want . . . to *fuck* . . . Valerie?" I glare at him. "She's *hot*—that must be why you hired her. I see how you look at her. The short skirts, the perfect tits, the tight ass. Why *wouldn't* you want to tap that?"

Valerie blushes like a virginal sorority girl and turns away from the confrontation.

"Shane, that's totally inappropriate," Wayne says.

"Is it? Sorry. I've totally lost track of what is, and is *not*, appropriate." I lean across the table in this small briefing room. "Like, for example—just hypothetically speaking—do you think it's appropriate to put tracking software on your client's phone?"

Wayne stares at me for a few seconds, then gives the lamest of lame excuses: "I don't know what you're talking about."

"Oh, really? That phone just *happened* to come with keylogging pre-installed?"

Valerie glances at Wayne nervously.

"Don't fuck with me, Wayne. Everyone in my life has fucked with me. I thought you were different—that you were here to help me."

"I *am* here to help you." He tosses his pen onto the table. "I've been here for you from the beginning. Nobody else would have represented you. You're a pariah. You would have been stuck with some court-appointed public defender. I'm the best lawyer in the country at this type of case, and I'm doing it all *pro bono*."

"Out of the goodness of your heart, huh?" I say.

"*Yes*, as a matter of fact. I *told* you, I'm a believer in the cause." He frantically pushes up his sleeve to show off his tattoo again. "*See? Remember?*"

"That doesn't mean shit," I say. "It's probably temporary." I grab his hairy forearm and start rubbing against the tattoo like I'm trying to erase it.

He yanks his arm back.

"I've been with you since day one." He stabs his index finger into the table to emphasize his points. "Since before I even met you. I've done *everything* you've asked. I've assembled the best legal team. I've defended you in the media. I've been a hostage negotiator. What more do I have to do for you to trust me?"

"Simple. I want you to tell me *one* honest thing."

"What's that?"

"Do. You want. To fuck. Valerie?"

He exhales slowly. "Valerie is my colleague. I refuse to answer such a disrespectful and degrading question."

"That's what I thought," I say. "You can't even tell the truth about something so simple—and *obvious*, by the way."

"If you have any questions related to the case or our legal defense, I would be more than happy to answer honestly."

"Oh, yeah, in that case, I have a few: How'd you know to show up the morning I got arrested? Who's paying you? Why'd you tap my phone? Did you read my letters? Did you deliver my letters? Did you even see Chloe? And, most of all, why are you trying to take over my *fucking* account?"

"That's ridiculous. What reason would I have to take over the Burner_911 account? You're being paranoid."

"*Bullshit*. You thought I'd give Chloe the login credentials and just hand you the keys to this whole thing, didn't you?"

"I'm not going to sit here and listen to wild accusations." He stands up, shoves documents back into his briefcase, and pounds on the door to get the guard's attention.

Valerie stands, straightens her suit, and picks up her bag without even looking at me.

"If you don't trust me and my team, it's entirely your right to request different legal representation. Of course, new counsel will be less accommodating to your particular needs as a client, but it's your choice. Maybe communicating with Chloe again isn't important to you."

I glare at him, but he's not backing down an inch. He thinks he's got me—that I have no choice, that the connection to Chloe is too important, that nobody else will represent me. He finally blinks, and when his eyes flip back open there's a new look in them—a condescending sympathy, like he's looking at a caged animal in a zoo. I don't say anything.

"Let us know what you decide," he says as the door to the room swings open.

Without another word, they both turn and leave.

74

WAYNE

"Unbelievable," I say to Valerie as we exit the gauntlet of gates and doors out of the prison. "Who the hell does this kid think he is? After all I've done for him."

But she doesn't say anything and won't look at me. Her expression still slightly flustered. I should say something.

"Look, don't let any of that crap he said get to you. He's just trying to get under our skin. Don't let—"

"Is that why you hired me? Because of my looks?" she asks as we pass through the last gates and stand outside the metal detectors in the lobby.

"Of course not, I hired you cause you're a damn good lawyer," I say, pausing for the punch line, "who *happens* to be smokin' hot."

The joke lands, and she lets out a throttled laugh. So, I continue more sincerely.

"Look, I know I'm not taking home any woke-boss-of-the-year awards, but you're one of the best young attorneys I've ever worked with—I mean that."

"Thanks," she says. A smile takes over her face and tears gather in her eyelids that she dabs away with the tips of her fingernails.

"Now, I have a few more things I need to do here, so why don't you head on back to the office?" Those depositions aren't going to read themselves."

She nods, turns, and clicks across the marble floor. As soon as she's out the door, I turn back toward the whirring belt of the metal detector and see the person I'm expecting: Corrections Officer Kryzsiek.

He gave me the nod when I passed him inside a minute ago, then flicked his eyes toward the lobby. Now, he steps toward me, shoots a glance at the security camera in the corner of the ceiling, then asks me what he wants to ask me.

"So, for real, what's the deal with Stoller?"

"What do you mean?" I reply as innocently as I can, knowing full well what suspicions he has about Shane.

"Y'know . . . is he? Is he who they say he is?"

"Shane Stoller is my client. Anything he's said to me is attorney-client privilege and I—"

"C'mon, man—cut the lawyer bullshit. I know you're on the inside. Totally off the record. I need to know—we *all* deserve to know. Is he the guy?"

A plain-clothes detective walks in from outside, puts her badge, watch, and cell phone onto the conveyor belt, then hands her firearm to the guard on duty to place in a lockbox. After she's through security, I make a point of looking around like I'm checking for anyone within earshot. Then I give Kryz my best regretful look and simply shake my head.

"You *gotta* be kidding me." His shoulders droop in disappointment.

"Afraid not," I say. "At first, I thought he was too, but honestly, he's totally delusional."

"But he knows so much about the movement—insider stuff," Kryz says. "I thought for sure it was him. How else would someone know all that?"

"He's just a fan boy. My team and I have reviewed all the evidence. Some of it he made up, specifically to make people think he's Burner_911. And the Feds went along with it. They made up evidence too, just to pin it all on someone. They needed to make an arrest, but Stoller's a patsy, a *poser*. He might as well be dressing up as Burner_911 for Comic-Con."

"That little fucker. We stuck our necks out. Killian almost got put on administrative leave for protecting him. When I saw the latest drop last night, that was the last straw for me. It just didn't add up anymore, y'know?"

I nod sympathetically and think about Shane alone in his cell. It was his choice to play this game, so he better get on his big-boy pants. He's overplayed his hand. He doesn't realize how much this whole thing has unraveled. No idea that he's dangling by a thread. Most of all, what he doesn't know is that Burner_911 has posted again.

"That's what I'm saying. Shane didn't even *know* there was a new post. He can't be Burner_911." I wag my head mournfully. "It's okay. He fooled a lot of us. But these things have a way of working themselves out. Don't you think?"

75

TEXT MESSAGE FBI WIRETAP

TEXT MESSAGE EXCHANGE BETWEEN SHANE STOLLER AND CHLOE CORBIN
September 21, 2023

MR. STOLLER: hey

MS. CORBIN: who is this?

MR. STOLLER: it's me

MS. CORBIN: jesus, shane!

MS. CORBIN: every time you text me it's from a new number!

MR. STOLLER: I know. Sorry.

MR. STOLLER: Just being cautious.

MS. CORBIN: CAUTIOUS!?! 😭

MS. CORBIN: I'd hardly say you're being cautious.

MS. CORBIN: More like...
Irresponsible.
Immature. Petulant.

MR. STOLLER: Sorry, i was just upset.

BURNER

MR. STOLLER: Didn't mean to
take it out on you.

                    MS. CORBIN: Well you DID
take it out on me!

MS. CORBIN: And now your
FOLLOWERS are taking it out
on me!! 😾😾😾

MS. CORBIN: Have you SEEN
my Instagram???

MS. CORBIN: I might need to
shut down my account!

MS. CORBIN: They're THREAT-
ENING me, Shane! This is
serious!!!

MR. STOLLER: Don't use my
name.

MS. CORBIN: Do you hon-
estly think that makes a
difference?

MS. CORBIN: I'm not going
to get a new phone every
time I text you!

MS. CORBIN: I'm not going to
encrypt every message!

MS. CORBIN: I don't have
anything to hide!

MR. STOLLER: I need to talk
to you.

MS. CORBIN: I spent the
whole night reading hate
posts from your BurnOut buddies!

MS. CORBIN: I'm going to bed.

MR. STOLLER: I need to know if you knew your dad was going to do this.

MS. CORBIN: The fact you even need to ask me that question tells me every-thing 😔

MR. STOLLER: It's just very hard for me to believe you didn't know.

MS. CORBIN: Why would i do that?!?

MS. CORBIN: I can't believe you'd even SUSPECT that!

MR. STOLLER: I just wonder if maybe Ken put you up to this.

MR. STOLLER: As a way to take me out.

MR. STOLLER: He never liked me.

MS. CORBIN: HE DID IT AS A FAVOR TO ME!!

MS. CORBIN: Cause YOU asked me to ask him!!

MS. CORBIN: YOU started this! Are you suggest-ing you're in on your own conspiracy against your-self!?!?!?

MR. STOLLER: He's given me no choice now.

MS. CORBIN: No choice? What do you mean?

MR. STOLLER: I can't let him get away with this. I have to retaliate.

MR. STOLLER: Your dad stole $10 MILLION from me!

MR. STOLLER: Plus that's what the BurnOutz will expect.

MR. STOLLER: We can't let this go unpunished.

MS. CORBIN: you're talking about my DAD!

MS. CORBIN: He didn't do this to you on purpose!

MS. CORBIN: All he did was sell the stock

MR. STOLLER: Ur soooo naïve . . .

MR. STOLLER: OF COURSE he did this on purpose!

MR. STOLLER: If u don't think so, then he's taking advantage of you too

MS. CORBIN: I'm done with this, Shane.

MS. CORBIN: I just can't deal with your paranoia anymore.

MR. STOLLER: I'm just try-ing to open your eyes to what's really going on

MR. STOLLER: Who your dad really is.

MS. CORBIN: I don't want to

see you ever again.

MS. CORBIN: Don't text me.
Or call me. EVER!

MR. STOLLER: FINE!

MR. STOLLER: I don't want to
ever see you again EITHER!

MR. STOLLER: I thought u
were different, but ur just
like every other stuck up
princess!

MR. STOLLER: It would be a
shame if the BurnOutz
found out where you live . . .

MR. STOLLER: You can shut
down your instagram, but you
can't shut down life!

MS. CORBIN: goodbye,
shane ... ☹

76

BURNER_911

Three Weeks Ago

@Burner_911 post on Razgo.com

> *"It is impossible to suffer without making someone pay for it;*
> *every complaint already contains revenge."*
> −Friedrich Nietzsche

One billionaire destroyed. Another billionaire enriched.

FIRST, the one we destroyed . . .

BURNOUTZ!!!!! Your strength and valor exceeded my wildest expectations!!

Our mission to punish Bob Jorgensen succeeded spectacularly!!

THANKS TO YOUR BRAVERY AND DEDICATION TO OUR CAUSE, YOU RALLIED $CCFA UP TO $259!!!!!

That's just CRAZY!!! 🤪🤪🤪

I thought if we could get the stock to double, maybe triple, then we'd really put the squeeeeeeeeeeze on old Bob. BUT YOU ALL DROVE IT UP OVER 10X!!!!!

Bob was just barfing money at that point!!! 🤮🤮🤮🤮🤮

All his margin calls came due to the tune of $6 BILLION!!! 💰💰💰💰💰

HE. WAS. FUUUUUUCKED!!!

BOB JORGENSEN HAS DECLARED BANKRUPTCY!!!

But not everything went according to plan—another billionaire ENRICHED himself! Ken Corbin seemed to be siding with our cause at first, but he ended up BETRAYING US!!

He and his bitch daughter are just like every other billionaire family!!!

RIGGING THE GAME! STACKING THE DECK!! EXPLOITING THE LITTLE GUY! ALL JUST TO MAKE THEMSELVES EVEN MORE CRAZY RICH!

I know most of you lost big time on CCFA . . . some of you lost EVERYTHING you had in the name of this fight . . .

For all of you—faceless, nameless LOYALISTS who SACRIFICED everything—WHAT YOU HAVE DONE IN THE NAME OF THE CAUSE IS GLORIOUS!!!

Now is not the time to give up . . . NOW IS THE TIME FOR TRUE BELIEVERS TO STEP FORWARD!!!

THE DAY OF RECKONING IS COMING!!!

The sacrifices we've all already made are just steps in our journey. MERE SKIRMISHES IN THE LARGER WAR!!!

And you know what's coming???

OCTOBER!!! 🎃💀🎃💀🎃💀🎃💀🎃💀

As the calendar turns to the second week in October, the conditions will be PERFECT! The prophecy will come to fruition. The global financial system will begin to COLLAPSE!!!

FINANCIAL JUSTICE WILL BE OURS!!!

BELIEVE IN THE PLAN, BURNOUTZ!!!

BELIEVE. IN. THE. PLAN.

77

CHLOE

"You're a fucking *liar!*" Nick shouts, tiny projectiles of his saliva flying into my face.

I'm back in the living room now, again in my La-Z-Boy, again with my hands zip-tied, again defenseless—anticipating another blow at any moment.

"*C'mon*, Nick, if they were tracing the phone, they would have kicked down the door and busted your ass by now." Pete snickers at his own attempt to defuse the tension.

"Shut the hell up! You know how easy it is to track one of these things." Nick waves the burner phone Wayne delivered. The one he's just ripped from my hands. "You're probably helping her too! *Aren't you?*"

"We all gotta believe in The Plan, Nick," Scooter says. "This order came straight from Burner."

But Nick isn't listening. His attention returns to me. Leaning into my face, his hands on each armrest, he says in a rasping growl, "I'm only going to ask this one . . . more . . . time . . . *What are you up to?*"

"I already told you," I say, struggling to maintain eye contact. "He asked me to post as Burner_911."

"You think I'm a fucking idiot." He intones the words almost melodically, his face inches from mine. "As soon as we log in, they'll know it's us and hunt us down."

His paranoia is overshadowed only by his jealousy. My exchange with Shane was immediately flushed by the messaging app, vanishing in a digital vapor trail. He's infuriated at his inability to corroborate my story.

"I guess you'll just have to trust me," I say.

"*See?* She's a fucking liar!" Nick pivots toward the others as if what I just said affirmed his point. "She's manipulating us. Leading the Feds right to our door."

"Let's log in and find out," Pete says, rubbing his rough hands together in anticipation.

"What did he tell you to say?" Scooter asks me.

"He didn't," I say, trying to hide my lingering uncertainty, hoping they won't discover I already logged in to Shane's Razgo account before Nick took the phone. "He told me I'd know what to say."

"*Bullshit!*" Nick is triggered again, his anger escalating the more the situation threatens to escape his control. "It's a trap." His voice tapers off as he looks at the screen. He realizes now what he's seeing—the logged-in app, the keys to the kingdom.

"Well, I'm telling you, this is The Plan, Nick. I'm posting as Burner_911, so give me the phone." I extend my arms, my hands cupped together by my bound wrists. *I need to get that phone back.*

"No chance! He wouldn't leave that up to *you*. You're not even a BurnOut, for *Christ's sake*—you're the enemy!" Nick raises the phone. "If anyone's becoming Burner_911, it's me."

The boys shoot furtive glances at each other as Nick starts to type. Scooter looks at me with an expression that says, *What should we do?* And I return it with a shrug that says, *How the hell should I know? I'm the one zip-tied and duct-taped to the damn chair.*

I look back at Nick, his thumbs jabbing at the screen. In the past, he's recited his messages out loud, annunciating theatrically for all our benefit. His current concentration is disconcerting—like he's really doing this, like he's possessed, like he doesn't care anymore about being tracked because the power grab he's been waiting for is in his hands, like he knows no one can stop him.

Finally, it's Scooter who says, "Nick, *man* . . . I'm not sure that's a good idea."

Pete, his fervency suddenly tempered, concurs. "Yeah, Nick, this is a big deal. We should at least talk about what you're gonna say."

Nick doesn't respond, his eyes unblinking, his foreboding expression illuminated by the screen.

No one is going to stop him. I can't let this happen.

"You *can't* do this, Nick!" I shout, finally with enough urgency to break his trance.

"Watch me," he says.

"Shane asked *me* to post for him—*only* me!" I insist. "He would never trust that to someone like you."

Nick stares at me vacantly, as if lost in thought, the volatile reaction I expected at least momentarily delayed.

"This is what Burner wanted, Nick," Scooter says. "We can't go against The Plan."

"The *Plan?*" Nick asks in mock chagrin. "The *plan* was to bring down the financial markets. The *plan* was for her to be our negotiating chip. The *plan* was to get Burner out of jail. But all we got is this bitch and some loser I don't give a shit about. He's not Burner."

"*Yes, he is!*" Scooter insists. "He had the credentials for Burner_911. You're logged in to the account."

"That's right—I'm logged in to the account," Nick says, abruptly turning toward me. "So I don't see what good *you* are to us anymore." He reaches to the back of his pants, draws his gun, and points it at me, still holding the phone in his left hand, up in the air, angled toward him, toward me.

Of course. He's filming.

"*Nick!*" Scooter shouts, but the monologue has already started.

"Attention, BurnOutz!" Nick says for the camera. "This movement is about *sacrifice*, about taking back what's rightfully ours! Ken Corbin stole from us, now we're stealing his precious daughter from him!"

He stands over me now, arm extended, pressing the muzzle of the gun against my lips, pushing my jaw open. The cold metal scrapes against my teeth, a feeling that reverberates through my entire skull. I taste the gunpowder on my tongue. I close my eyes—the only defense I have against what will happen next.

Then, almost as if I'm imagining it, I flinch at the deafening blast of a gunshot . . . and the dull slap of a phone screen cracking against the floor.

PART III

78

PHONE CONVERSATION
FBI WIRETAP

**TRANSCRIPT OF FBI WIRETAP PHONE CALL BETWEEN
KEN CORBIN AND CHLOE CORBIN
August 22, 2023**

CHLOE CORBIN: What the *hell*, Dad!?

KEN CORBIN: Well, hello to you too, my dear. To what do I owe such a warm welcome?

CHLOE CORBIN: Don't act so smug. You know exactly why I'm pissed off. You didn't need to do that.

KEN CORBIN: Do what? You need to be more specific. I'm not as sharp in my old age.

CHLOE CORBIN: Sell the CompassCard stock! You cost Shane millions of dollars! He was totally exposed.

KEN CORBIN: He asked me to buy, sweetie. He never asked me to hold on to the stock. You were there. When the price broke $200, it just didn't make financial sense not to sell.

CHLOE CORBIN: Bullshit! You knew exactly what you were doing. I knew you never wanted me to date him. I just never imagined you'd pull something like this.

KEN CORBIN: I don't know what you're complaining about. I held up my end of the bargain by buying the shares, and Shane got what he wanted: Bob Jorgensen is bankrupt. But I didn't get what I wanted, did I? Burner_911 and Razgo are still online.

CHLOE CORBIN: You used Shane and the BurnOutz to make hundreds of millions of dollars!

KEN CORBIN: Please ... it was my investment that drove the initial bump in stock price. Then the retail and institutional guys saw it moving and jumped on to the bandwagon. I was just lucky enough to be in front of a bull run.

CHLOE CORBIN: It was the BurnOutz talking up the stock that drove the price increase.

KEN CORBIN: Hardly. That pack of misfits probably invested two million total.

CHLOE CORBIN: Shane invested *ten* himself! That's every dollar he has to his name! Don't you understand? You destroyed him—

KEN CORBIN: Destroyed Shane? Or destroyed Burner_911? Dear, you can't possibly be so naïve. You think I don't know who Shane is? You think I don't understand how he got $10 million in the first place? He's been manipulating you.

CHLOE CORBIN: What are you—

KEN CORBIN: I've never seen you like this, dear. Most boys you have wrapped around your finger. You act like this guy is the love of your life. But he's just a cyber punk who stumbled into a series of lucrative hustles. He's not good enough for you.

CHLOE CORBIN: You don't know what you're talking about. Shane's the most honest person I know. You're too old to understand. He's leading real change the only way—

KEN CORBIN: He's a common criminal. And he's played you for a fool.

CHLOE CORBIN: Then *you* were his accomplice!

KEN CORBIN: That's ridiculous. Now you're just talking nonsense. There's nothing illegal about buying and selling shares of a public company. I thought CompassCard could make a very interesting complement to Kadabra. But, ultimately, I changed my mind.

CHLOE CORBIN: You're unbelievable! Shane was right. You have no conscience. Is it all just about making more money for you?

KEN CORBIN: I have to admit, it did prove to be an outstanding investment. Almost a tenfold increase in twenty-four hours. Not even Kadabra stock ever did that.

CHLOE CORBIN: I'm done! As usual, you got everything you wanted. Jorgensen ruined, Shane and his followers broke, and millions in profit for yourself. I'm sure you'll be glad to know, we broke up too.

KEN CORBIN: That's the best news I've heard all day—and I made almost half a billion dollars this morning.

CHLOE CORBIN: You've ruined my life. You think you can just do whatever you want!

KEN CORBIN: Honey, you deserve someone better than him.

CHLOE CORBIN: You don't even know him!

KEN CORBIN: I know the type.

CHLOE CORBIN: Yeah, I know the type too. He reminds me of what you used to be: smart, ambitious, entrepreneurial. Before your ego took control. Do you know how much money Shane gave to charity in the last year? Almost $2 million! That's as much as the entire Corbin Foundation gave! And he did it out of his own pocket.

KEN CORBIN: He did it out of the pockets of people he ripped off.

CHLOE CORBIN: Ripped off? If you're talking about his stock trading, he's earned it from hedge fund managers who rip people off every day. And he gave it to people who need it.

KEN CORBIN: He only gave that money away to impress you.

CHLOE CORBIN: Well, I must be as gullible as you think I am then, because it worked. I don't care what you think about him. I love him. He's probably the first guy I've ever really loved. And now I'll probably never see him again, thanks to you.

KEN CORBIN: Honey . . .

CHLOE CORBIN: Goodbye, dad.

KEN CORBIN: Honey, wait! Honey?

79

BURNER_911

One Week Ago

@Burner_911 on Razgo.com

> *"Those who can make you believe absurdities*
> *can make you commit atrocities."*
> —Voltaire

IT. IS. TIME.

BurnOut Nation! The day of reckoning I have prophesized is UPON us!!!

THE SECOND WEEK OF THE TENTH MONTH IS COMING!!!

October 12th is almost here. The elites are finally going to pay for their crimes. Face punishment for a RIGGED system that has taken away money and opportunity and dignity from REGULAR, HARD-WORKING PEOPLE!!!

REMEMBER WHAT WE ARE FIGHTING FOR!!!

THE DAY OF RETRIBUTION IS ALMOST HERE!!!

Billionaires will lose everything.

Global elites will be imprisoned.

Corrupt politicians will be vanquished.

A financial SHITSTORM 🥀🥀🥀 unlike anything we've ever seen that will trigger the COLLAPSE OF THE FINANCIAL MARKETS!!

But UNLIKE in 2008, WE are the ones who will benefit from this collapse!!

That's why we BurnOutz are going to give it a nudge . . .

ON THURSDAY, OCTOBER 12TH, AT 8 AM, WE WILL GATHER AT THE CORNER

OF VAN NESS AND MARKET TO DEMONSTRATE, INITIATE, AND CELEBRATE THE INVERSION OF THE FINANCIAL WORLD!!!!!! 🌐💲🌐💲🌐💲🔥🔥🔥

For those of you in the know, that intersection just happens to be the WORLD HEADQUARTERS OF KEN CORBIN'S COMPANY KADABRA, INC!!!

Ken screwed us over, and now it's time for him and all the other billionaires to PAY!

But how will this happen? How will a ragtag bunch of DEPLORABLES bring down the ENTIRE FINANCIAL SYSTEM!?!?!?!?!

The amazing thing is they don't even know how perfectly lined up the dominoes are! 😂

DOMINO 1: Retailers are HIGHLY leveraged, with massive debt burdens. They also happen to be Kadabra's biggest customers. A coordinated hack of the leading retail websites and payment gateways will cause their operating revenue to seize up. That's the nudge. That's the flick of the first domino at 8 AM. Then we watch . . .

DOMINO 2: All that junk debt from retailers has been repackaged as CLOs, collateralized loan obligations. The same gimmick the banks did in 2008, warming over steaming piece-of-shit loans into bundles and giving them AAA ratings! This will make the 2008 crisis look like MOUSE NUTS! 🐭🐭🐭 Only a handful of retailers need to declare bankruptcy for these CLOs to start failing.

DOMINO 3: Guess who the biggest holder of CLOs is? Federal Pacific Bank has a CLO balance of $189 BILLION! It's a MASSIVE number. Particularly considering FPB's entire assets are only $118 billion. FPB claims to only own AAA-rated investments, but what they really own is tens of billions of dollars of worthless bonds that are about to DEFAULT! Nothing tilts the economy faster towards crisis than a bank failure, and FPB will be the first one, dragging others down with it.

DOMINO 4: The chain reaction continues as more big banks, who have been stashing their CLOs in so-called variable interest entities, begin to default. They will scramble to unwind these off-the-books positions. Desperately trying not to be the ones caught without a chair now that the music has stopped. Most will fail, running around like doped-up dealers trying to shove balloons full of heroin up their assholes before the police arrive.

DOMINO 5: With retailers and banks imploding, Kadabra will implode. Their payment reconciliation platform is extremely vulnerable to commerce slowdowns, and FPB just happens to be Kadabra's bank and primary lender, so no lifeline will be extended. Ken Corbin will either file for bankruptcy or start shoveling his own money into the inferno in a futile attempt to delay the inevitable.

DOMINO 6: As speculation runs rampant about which banks are near collapse, overnight lending, the backbone of the modern economy, will seize up. Trying to forestall a full-fledged panic, the Treasury Department will again be forced to come to the rescue of the global elites with a TRILLION-DOLLAR-PLUS BANK BAILOUT!

DOMINO 7: But THIS TIME the bailout will be OPPOSED BY THE PEOPLE!!! *Fool me once, shame on you. Fool me again, shame on me.* THE AMERICAN PEOPLE WILL REFUSE TO BAIL OUT THE BANKS AND BILLIONAIRES!! Both political parties will be *forced* to oppose the bailout. Without their governmental puppets to bail them out, hundreds more banks will become insolvent.

DOMINO 8: With no appropriation of TRILLIONS of dollars America NO LONGER HAS, the Fed will have no choice but to open up the Bureau of Engraving and start printing fat stacks of money to hand to their crony buddies at the banks to cover their asses. Of course, this will drive massive inflation and devaluation of the US dollar, but what other choice do we have? We need to keep the economy going, right?!?!?!?

DOMINO 9: That trick worked in the past, but it WON'T WORK THIS TIME! Cryptocurrency was designed with just this kind of calamity in mind—to avoid the consequences of central bankers and corrupt politicians who contort our economic machinery to protect the status quo. The private sector will recognize crypto as the ONLY safe harbor against the Fed's desperate pillaging. The price of crypto will skyrocket to the moon as the values of global currencies drop to the price of the paper they are printed on.

DOMINO 10: Oh, I almost forgot to mention the last domino, which makes this a full circle. We BurnOutz will already be 100% DIAMOND HANDS ALL IN ON CRYPTO!!! So we will finally be the ones who benefit, as the billionaires PERISH!!! Financial justice will be OURS!!!

This is the ULTIMATE vindication! The moment we've all been waiting for. And YOU are here for it!! You are unique. You are one of the CHOSEN ONES!!! You have the information, empowerment, and influence to create a BETTER LIFE. AND, BEST OF ALL . . . you'll gain your economic independence by taking it out of the pocket of the GLOBAL BILLIONAIRE ELITISTS!!!

Be ready, BurnOutz. Be ready for THE STORM! BELIEVE IN THE PLAN!!

80

COURT TRANSCRIPT

TRANSCRIPT OF TESTIMONY OF DR. MILES KOSTAS

DIRECT EXAMINATION BY MS. GIBSON:

MS. GIBSON: Mr. Kostas, would you please provide your background for the jury.

DR. KOSTAS: Yes, of course. I graduated from the FBI Academy in Quantico, Virginia, and have served as a criminal psychiatrist in the bureau's Behavioral Analysis Unit 1 focused on counterterrorism for seventeen years. I've analyzed hundreds of criminals over that time.

MS. GIBSON: And you were assigned to analyze the person, or persons, behind the profile Burner_911?

DR. KOSTAS: That's correct.

JUDGE MORENO: Dr. Kostas, did the FBI at this point have probable cause to believe Shane Stoller was, in fact, Burner_911?

DR. KOSTAS: Certainly enough to form the basis of an investigation, yes. We had accumulated quite a bit of evidence that Burner_911 was Shane Stoller and had warrants to tap his phones, monitor email and text messages, surveil his apartment. We were pretty convinced he was our guy.

COURT TRANSCRIPT

MS. GIBSON: And why did the FBI have an active investigation into Burner_911 and Mr. Stoller at that time?

DR. KOSTAS: The bureau has recognized for many years now, dating back to the Oklahoma City bombing, the threat posed by domestic terrorism.

MS. GIBSON: So you suspected Mr. Stoller might be behind a domestic terrorist plot?

DR. KOSTAS: That was identified as a possibility in our broader investigation, yes. But my specific role was to assess the psychological state of Burner_911, based on his online posts and messages.

MS. GIBSON: And what was your assessment?

DR. KOSTAS: First and foremost, the person behind these posts clearly had antisocial and narcissistic personality disorders. Traits that enabled him to amass and manipulate a large community of online followers and compel them to commit criminal acts. Burner_911 also had an elaborate worldview, including grandiose delusions of himself as a prophet and vigilante who was uniquely endowed with the power to bring about the end of the financial world.

MS. GIBSON: In your assessment, did you believe Burner_911 to be a single individual or an amalgam controlled by multiple people?

DR. KOSTAS: Oh, it was definitely a single individual. The tone, style, language, colloquialisms, and many other telltale attributes, consistent across dozens of posts, point quite definitively to this being the rhetoric of a single individual.

MS. GIBSON: How would you describe the personality and psychology of Burner_911?

DR. KOSTAS: He was self-directed, manipulative. The posts bore all the hallmarks of a rampant, virulent paranoia—convinced that someone or *something* was out to get him. Which he frequently redirected at perceived enemies he wished to confront and destroy. Much of his rhetoric was targeting elites, although what that meant, apart from wealthy individuals, was not entirely clear. While his rants bordered on incoherent at times, his pathology left him functional enough to plan effectively against his perceived adversaries. That was evident through the dozens of coordinated attacks he insti- gated, and his followers perpetrated. The message had strong appeal. His followers were obsessed with the notion that so-called elites had rigged the game against them, and that their lives would get better through some apocalyptic event.

MS. GIBSON: How would you characterize the ideology of Burner_911?

DR. KOSTAS: That's a great question. It's not really my area of expertise, but I'd say they sort of defy our conventional perceptions of left and right ideology. Certainly, it would be easy to classify Burner_911 and the BurnOutz as right-wing, and many of his adherents would probably self-identify as part of the so-called alt-right—railing against liberals, using misogynistic language, advocating libertarian ideals, and so forth. But you also see left-leaning rhetoric coming from both Burner_911 and his followers. In fact, many of their most closely held ideals, such as rectifying wealth inequal- ity, demanding higher taxes on the rich, and agitating for the downfall of the patriarchal financial system are extremely liberal. So I don't know how to classify them along the traditional political spectrum. Maybe populist?

MS. GIBSON: Since Mr. Stoller was taken into custody, you've had the chance to meet with him several times. What was your professional assessment of Mr. Stoller's personality and psychology?

DR. KOSTAS: He showed no evidence of being actively psychotic. Nothing in his speech or intonation suggested any cognitive disorder. His manner of speaking was perfectly normal, and he was able to maintain a thoughtful and coherent conversation. He responded directly to my questions. He did not appear to be distracted by hallucinations or other imaginary stimuli. And he did not exhibit any abnormal movements associated with psychosis. Overall, he struck me as a quiet, but intense and thoughtful, young man.

MS. GIBSON: What did you see as the drivers of Mr. Stoller's personality?

DR. KOSTAS: To start with, he's highly intelligent, likely in the superior IQ range. But his childhood developmental traumas, specifically growing up without either birth parent, suppressed that innate ability. In temperament, he is an introvert, and life in the foster care system only exacerbated his sense of isolation, even though he could be friendly and personable when needed. Despite those social skills, his life circumstances, including the dissolution of his foster family, the murder of a father figure close to him, and social isolation throughout his formative teenage years, caused him to not trust others or form close relationships easily.

MS. GIBSON: Is there any prior psychiatric documentation of Mr. Stoller's condition?

DR. KOSTAS: Some. When he was sixteen, he was seen by a psychiatrist with the state of California.

MS. GIBSON: This was after his arrest on juvenile charges related to automobile theft?

DR. KOSTAS: Yes, that's right. The behavioral psychiatrist noted that Mr. Stoller would often withdraw into video games, books, social media, and other diversions as a means of coping with a tremendously stressful and uncertain domestic situation. Several years later, the same psychiatrist evaluated Mr. Stoller after an outburst at his community college. At that point, he had witnessed the death of his foster brother's uncle as well as the disintegration of his foster family. The psychiatrist felt these life events had galvanized his sense of survivalism. That it was him against the world. Notably, this had severely dampened his interpersonal relationships with other people, particularly women. In fact, Mr. Stoller admitted he'd had no intimate relationship with a woman—or a man, for that matter—throughout his teenage years, which is highly unusual and often a precursor of antisocial behavior. Indeed, in his online personas, we see characteristics that are often associated with psychopaths—acting only in his self-interest, manipulating the behavior of others to achieve his desired outcomes, refusing to accept responsibility for his actions, and displaying paranoia, anger, aggression, and other impulsive emotions.

MS. GIBSON: How would you characterize the psychology of the BurnOutz as a group?

DR. KOSTAS: Like any group, they are hard to categorize. Each individual has his or her own psychological makeup, personal motivations, and differing degrees of involvement in this movement. But, in general, people are drawn to this type of leader and movement when their psychological needs are not being met in other social forums. Many harbor deep frustrations concerning economic instability, social isolation, absence of intimate relationships, and lack of agency. Rather than taking personal accountability, they look for scapegoats to blame for their feelings of resentment, indignation, and disenchantment about the world. That's why the narrative of corrupt elites working in secret to suppress them is so appealing.

MS. GIBSON: How did Mr. Stoller grow and mobilize these followers?

DR. KOSTAS: His narrative is all about good versus evil. The BurnOutz are "good," fighting for economic justice against globalist cabals. His targets—bankers, billionaires, business people, and others he wants to steal from—are "bad," which he reinforces by weaving elaborate stories about their secret diabolical plots. With those seeds planted, his followers extrapolate into ever-wilder, self-fulfilling conspiracy theories. Anyone who challenges the narrative or disputes the facts is attacked as a pawn of the elites and evidence of how crafty and ruthless they are in duping the public.

MS. GIBSON: And there was a strong financial incentive as well, correct?

DR. KOSTAS: Definitely. Burner_911's schemes and worldview gained more credence the more money his disciples made from them. Thousands of BurnOutz made money from the attacks he coordinated, and that was a powerful aphrodisiac—anointing him as a prophet, giving his adherents power and agency. They weren't just destroying the elites as some abstract cause, they were directly benefiting financially.

MS. GIBSON: In your assessment of this ideology, did you identify violent tendencies?

DR. KOSTAS: Not overtly, but the group's ethos is to achieve their goals by any means possible. Burner_911's posts never explicitly advocated violence, but when that sentiment creeps into a group's rhetoric, violence is no longer dismissed as an illegitimate tactic. Certainly, we have seen a subset of BurnOutz we would call "domestic violent extremists" or DVEs—people so thoroughly indoctrinated, dogmatic, and vitriolic that they become unpredictable. Many start to see the group's mission as their personal cause they are willing not only to fight for but potentially die or kill for. As those feelings are reinforced within the group's echo chamber, a strong impulse develops to damage or even destroy their enemies. They develop a sense of entitlement, a belief that they have the right to commit violence for the sake of the cause. That's when things can get dangerous.

MS. GIBSON: Dr. Kostas, the defense has claimed that Burner_911's posts, which we attribute to Mr. Stoller, are protected by free speech. That he never directly incited violence. That while he may have a personality disorder that caused his rhetoric to be more extreme, the violence that ensued was not his intent. What do you say to that?

DR. KOSTAS: I put near zero credibility in that claim. Mr. Stoller was not speaking in generalities or offering only high-level opinions. He was providing explicit, cogent direction. And he did it multiple times, with increasing levels of audacity and impact. As his converts issued increasingly violent threats and committed increasingly violent actions, he did nothing to discourage that escalation. I suspect Mr. Stoller became addicted, in a psychological sense, to the power and omnipotence he enjoyed as Burner_911—an exuberant, almost sexual high. And the significant personal financial reward he gained through his actions and organization point clearly to a man who knew exactly what he was doing and how to do it.

81

SHANE

Chloe,

> I have a bad feeling.

> I hate it when I get these, 'cause I'm usually right. I know when something bad is about to happen. I need to talk to you. Warn you.

> Three minutes of texting you wasn't enough. It was like taking a first hit of meth—it just made me want more. So I'm writing you another letter, but this time I have no one to deliver it. Wayne's not my lawyer anymore. Long story, but basically, he's a lying piece of shit. He isn't who he says he is. Don't believe anything he says.

> They played me a wiretap recording of you and Ken today, part of the investigation into your father. I wish I had heard that before October 12th. I would have called it all off.

> Maybe . . .

> Actually, probably not. It probably would have just stoked my hatred of your father even more. Not only did he betray me, he betrayed you. I needed to make him pay. Besides, I couldn't have stopped it even if I wanted to. The whole thing had just gained too much momentum at that point. The collective anger of thousands of BurnOutz was at its apex.

> But at least I would have warned you what was coming. I wouldn't have been so careless. It didn't even occur to me that you were an obvious target, that you could be collateral damage. I could have gone to you, reconciled with you. We could have gone somewhere, just the two of us. Left the bat-shit crazy

stuff I was doing. Nobody knew who I was. I could have just walked away. Unplugged Burner_911.

Why didn't I do that?

It seems so obvious now. The right choice was right there, waiting to be taken. Would you have done that? Would you have left with me? I was too insecure to even ask you. I felt like I never deserved you in the first place. I was a poser, a loser, a deplorable. An orphaned street thug who hustled, scammed, and stole my way through life, living in the digital shadows.

I always wanted to be good at something. Being Burner_911 was the first thing I've been good at, really good at—maybe the best at. I understood what motivated people like me. Everyone else's life seems so perfect, but our lives feel like shit. And that constant disconnect makes us angry.

You got that. Not only did you know what activated people, you believed in the mission as much as I did. At first, I couldn't get my head around that contradiction. Why would a billionaire's daughter want to eliminate wealth inequality? You were a product of wealth inequality! Perpetuating greed and envy every day through your Instagram feed. It seemed so hypocritical, so fake. Only now, with the hours upon hours I have had to reflect on everything from the confines of this cell, do I realize what really happened. You were trapped. Trapped all your life by the guilt over a father, and a family, and a lifestyle that you never chose—beholden to mind-boggling wealth, trying to do what you could to support the causes you believed in. But, at the time, I just couldn't reconcile the person I knew with the persona I saw on Instagram. I thought you had tricked me into believing you were something you weren't, or maybe it was me who was tricking you.

But now I finally understand: You didn't control your followers any more than I did mine. Like me, you had been conditioned to give them what they wanted. Whatever got the most likes, comments, views. We were no longer controlling the monsters we had created; they were controlling us. It was out of control, but I couldn't stop feeding it. Putting out a bonfire with gasoline. Strapped to the grill of a runaway freight train I was supposedly steering.

I knew I was making a terrible mistake. That my chance at a normal, happy life was going off the rails too. But I felt like there was nothing I could do to stop it.

SHANE

I always said I wanted to stick it to the elites, but really I just wanted to be an elite myself. I was jealous and envious and selfish and hypocritical. My real ideology was anger. If I couldn't have it, I just wanted to burn it all down. Get revenge on someone or something that made my life so fucked up, but I was never sure what to destroy or who to blame. So I just tried to get more, more, more. Just like the billionaires. Thinking that would somehow make me happy, make the pain go away. But, now I realize, the money, the prestige, the power—none of it really mattered. I still didn't have the one thing I really wanted. The only thing that mattered.

You were everything to me. And now I may never see you again.

—Shane

82

CHLOE

Blood runs down my forehead; chunks of flesh cling to my hair. Something is stuck to my lip—I try to flick it away and it's sharp against my tongue, a fragment of bone, of skull. My chest is spattered with clumps of hair entangled with yarn from the knit hat.

The gunshot rings in my ears; voices shout; everything is happening in suspended animation. My eyes drift downward, toward the floor, where Nick's body lies, propped up at a grotesque angle, planted in a pool of blood on what used to be his face, his arm contorted backward over my leg.

The breath has left my body. I try to catch it with short, hyperventilating gasps but cannot. Colors swirl in my eyes, my vision blurred from lack of oxygen. I look up and see Benny amid a charred halo of gun smoke, only now lowering his weapon. Scooter and Pete are imploring him to put down the gun, their hands raised defensively as if he might point it at them next, but Benny just stares down at the carnage.

Their words begin to transform from mere noise back into something decipherable. Fragments of language snagging in my consciousness—*"run," "neighbors," "no time," "leave her," "phone," "mountains," "fingerprints," "car keys," "gas can," "now"*—as they frantically devise a plan. I move to wipe off my face, forgetting my arms are still restrained.

Pete picks up the phone from the floor and then runs out the back door toward the garage; Scooter combs through piles of fast food wrappers and empty beer bottles, looking for something; Benny grabs a hunting knife from the dining table and strides deliberately toward me; Pete kicks open the back door carrying a red plastic gas canister; Benny points the knife at my wrists and slices off the zip ties; Scooter grabs keys, phones, and wallets, then leans down and pulls the gun from Nick's still clenched hand; Pete starts pouring gasoline everywhere, its acrid stench immediately assaulting my nostrils.

I hear the last strands of electrical tape fray as Benny saws through them. Free from the chair now, I stand, leaning at an angle, the room spinning. Benny rushes me toward the door as Pete shakes the last drops from the overturned gas can.

When I burst outside for the first time in twelve days, I discover we are not at all in the remote rural house I had imagined but in a nondescript suburban neighborhood, yards divided by chain link fences. Help might have been next door if I had screamed, fought, ran.

Scooter is already in the driver's seat of a pickup truck facing forward in the garage. The engine turns as a roar of flames ignites inside the house.

I freeze. This is my chance. To run, to escape.

Neighboring houses are less than a hundred feet away. *Can I make it? Would they chase me? Flee? Or just shoot me in the back of the head too?*

Before I can act on the impulse, Benny pushes me into the back of the cab. Pete sprints across the yard and jumps into the passenger seat, and the truck peels down the driveway, displaced gravel clattering in the wheel wells like silverware in a blender. Flames blow out one of the windows as we hurtle down the driveway. We screech onto the pavement, and I look back in time to see an orange fireball explode out of a window.

We aren't even a block away when I hear sirens. Pete turns, glares at me from the front seat, and thrusts the burner phone toward me.

"Start writing."

83

BURNER_911

October 25, 2023

@Burner_911 post on Razgo.com

> *"When rich people fight wars with one another,*
> *poor people are the ones to die."*
> —Jean-Paul Sartre

BURNOUTZ!!!!!!!

It's been a minute, but I'm *BACK*!!!!

I know the Feds want you to believe I'm in jail. That they have their man. Shane Stoller is detained tonight in solitary confinement in a maximum-security prison, completely cut off from the outside world, where he stands accused of being Burner_911!

And, yet . . .

Burner_911 posts. Freely. Defiantly!

HOW CAN THAT BE IF SHANE STOLLER IS BURNER_911?!?!?!?!

Maybe he isn't. Maybe Burner_911 is someone else. Maybe Burner_911 is many people. Maybe Burner_911 is all of us.

But REST ASSURED, Burner_911 is alive and well. It's going to take a lot more than that to stop me. So let me start by saying . . .

I'M SOOOOOO PROUD OF YOU GUYS!!!!

October 12th was everything I ever IMAGINED it could be!!! Of course, there are many things I regret. Collateral damage I wish hadn't happened. The loss of life is unfortunate. That's not what we're about. BUT . . . the DOMINOES are falling!

SO . . . BELIEVE. IN. THE. PLAN!!!!

Get as much crypto as you can, and HOLD, HOLD, HOLD WITH DIAMOND HANDS!!! 💎 🙌 💎 🙌 💎 🙌 💎 🙌

Your DISCIPLINE is your GAIN, and your GAIN is the BILLIONAIRE'S LOSS!!!

Don't let them distract you. Don't let them divide us. Don't let them confuse us about the real enemy, the real goal, the real purpose for us all!!!

And for those of you in BurnOut Nation who have any doubts about Chloe Corbin . . .

THAT BITCH CAN ROT IN HELL!!!!!

84

CHLOE

I can only hear the footsteps in front of me, am following nothing but intermittent shadows and the crunch of leaves and sticks. My vision is no longer impaired by a shroud, but instead by the near-total darkness engulfing us all. My ankle, still weak, buckles on the uneven ground; branches scrape my face as we ascend.

"*C'mon*, hurry up," Scooter says in an urgent whisper, momentarily giving me an auditory beacon to follow. He's the only one of the four of us who is supposedly familiar with this trail, if it can be called that—more a blind plunge into the frigid High Sierra wilderness.

"How much longer?" Pete asks, again illuminating the forest with the flashlight on his phone despite Scooter's repeated admonishments.

"Give me that fucking thing," Scooter says, crashing back downhill toward us through the undergrowth.

"Hey, man, I . . ." Pete stumbles backward but promptly relinquishes the device, casting us back into total darkness. "I turned off the signal."

"Doesn't matter. Give me yours too," Scooter says to Benny, who is behind us.

Benny hasn't said a word since he shot Nick, and his expression's still frozen in that same vacant stare. He's been following directions from Scooter and Pete like he's on autopilot. The faint glow of his screen floats past me into Scooter's hand, where it is extinguished.

"We can't risk these things," Scooter says. "We need to be totally off the grid."

"Fuck, man—this is crazy," Pete says. "We've been walking for hours."

"We didn't have any other choice . . . thanks to Benny," Scooter says.

It was a frantic effort to escape after leaving the house: driving for hours; rolling the pickup into a reservoir at the end of a forty-mile fire trail and watching until it sank; then proceeding by foot, already hours from roads, cell towers, civilization. Scooter is the only person who has any idea where we are, and he isn't about to let our position be compromised. The three of them are now wearing tactical gear they had stashed in the truck—vests, helmets, boots, and, disturbingly, assault rifles they wear strapped over their shoulders.

Now, after all that, I suddenly realize none of them forced me to come. I'm moving freely, with no constraints, no hands gripping me, no gun pointed at my head. With Nick gone, the constant threat of physical violence has disappeared. But it never even occurred to me that I'm now arguably here by choice. Less a hostage and more a member of this militia. I just didn't notice the moments when I could have made a different decision, simply started walking a different direction. And now it's too late. We're in total wilderness. I wouldn't even know which direction to walk. Just like that, I've shifted from captivity to dependence.

"You guys are lucky I'm prepared," Scooter says, his voice now rising from below us. He's kneeling on the ground, his hands searching through the leaves and pine needles. "We should have gone here in the first place." Suddenly, I see the shadow of his hand rising above his head, clutching a rock he's pulled from the brush, followed by the dull crunch of one of the phones being pulverized.

"*Scooter!* What the *fuck,* man! That was a new iPhone!" Pete shouts, his voice echoing through the woods. He gropes toward Scooter in the darkness, trying to stop him, but the sound of the second phone shattering comes before he can get to him. Pete groans. "I'm sick of all this survivalist bullshit."

"Oh, it's about to get a lot worse," Scooter says, still crouched on the forest floor. I can't see him, but I know he's speaking to me now. "C'mon, give me yours too."

My hand instinctively wraps around the rectangle of metal and glass in my pocket, briefly warming my frozen fingertips with the subtle heat of its battery discharge. My connection to Shane, my conduit to Burner_911. "But this is our only way to message Shane, to post to Razgo," I say. "Nobody knows this phone is ours. There's no reason it would be traced. We need *something*."

"Any device out here could be detected," Scooter says in a softer tone, trying to reason with me. "Besides, the battery will be dead soon, and you're not gonna get a signal where we're going anyway."

I pull the phone from my pocket and the screen flickers to life, like a digital mirage against the blackness. He's right—no bars, 5 percent battery. The lifeline I briefly regained, about to slip from my grasp again.

"How will we . . . "

"Don't worry, we'll find a way when the time's right," Scooter says, the reassurance in his voice indicating he knows the argument is already over.

Pete and Benny stand still, waiting in the darkness. I reluctantly extend the phone toward Scooter's voice. He pulls it gently away from my clenched hand. I flinch at the sound of the rock falling again, cutting us off completely from the outside world.

"Can you *please* tell me where we're going?" I ask Scooter again. The only answer to that question so far has been "the mountains," but I have no idea what that means, and I'm *freezing*—wearing nothing but this same thin pair of sweats, still splattered with Nick's blood, and my flimsy tennis shoes. We have no other gear to survive out here—no jackets, no backpacks, no tents or sleeping bags, no food or water. They're prepared for combat, but nothing else.

Scooter, still crouched on the ground, moving branches and bags and other objects I can't see in the darkness, doesn't respond. It's only when a large backpack lands near my feet that I realize we're at a hidden stash— supplies magically appearing out of a hole in the ground covered with brush. I can't imagine how Scooter found this place in the pitch dark, but his doomsday preparations are going to save us.

"Here, put this on," he says, pressing a bundle of clothes into my arms.

As my eyes adjust to the darkness, I am able to separate the items: sweatshirt, pants, socks, a jacket. All men's sizes and too big for me, but it's a relief to get out of the stained sweats and into something much warmer.

"And give me those." He takes my discarded clothes. I hear him gather a few other objects and the rustle of a plastic bag. Then the shadow of it all going back into the hole.

"This will be our last trace point," Scooter says, pulling out what sounds like plastic jugs of water. "From here on, don't touch anything without gloves, don't drop a cigarette butt or gum wrapper, don't spit on the ground, and definitely don't piss or shit, or our position could be compromised."

Pete grunts agreement, holding his rifle across his chest and scanning the woods.

"Okay, lift up your feet," Scooter says to Pete.

I hear the glug of liquid. Moments later, a powerful antiseptic smell hits me.

"Oh, my *God*," I say covering my nose and mouth. "What *is* that?"

"Bleach—to throw off the dogs," Scooter says. I hear the glugging again, and then he's next to me. "C'mon," he says, like it's for my own good.

I lift my feet and feel the icy chemicals soak through my shoes. He pours some on his own feet, then empties the jug over the items in the hole—including our phones, I'm guessing—and covers it all with the branches.

"Now, wipe this on yourself." Scooter picks up handfuls of dirt and leaves and starts rubbing them all over himself. We all do the same.

"Okay, let's go," he finally says. "Just a few more hours."

85

SHANE

"Yes, Your Honor, that's what I said. I want new counsel."

I'm standing at the defense table. Wayne is next to me and Valerie is next to him; both are looking down, pretending to be preoccupied with their papers. Judge Moreno has cleared the courtroom to hear my motion.

"Mr. Stoller . . . " the judge begins, exasperated before he even gets his sentence out. "I'm sure I don't need to remind you of the seriousness and complexity of the charges against you."

"No, you do not, Youro—Your Honor." I almost just called the judge "Yourora." I need to get my shit together—went a little heavy today on the self-medication. Slurring my words probably isn't the best way to make my argument. "I don't believe my current lawyer . . . is representing my best interests," I say after what I hope wasn't too long of a pause.

"Very well." The judge looks down at some sheet of paper. "The court will appoint a public defender to your case, but I—"

"No, Your Honor . . . excuse me . . . sorry, but I want to represent myself."

"Excuse me?"

"I want to represent myself. Is what I said. I say no to the public defender."

"Mr. Stoller, do you have a law degree, or any legal training or experience whatsoever?"

"No, I don't. But I understand my case." I hear Wayne audibly groan and shake his head, but I continue. "I know, better than anyone, how to defend myself."

"Okay . . ." The judge exhales, considering for a beat. "Let's do a trial run. Mr. Stoller, it has come to my attention that the Burner_911 profile has posted again. That is in direct violation of a court-ordered mandate not to discuss this case in any form of media. That includes anonymous postings, Mr. Stoller. What do you have to say for yourself? In your defense, as your own counsel."

"I . . ." *Fuck*, Chloe posted? At least, I *assume* it was her. It *must* have been her. I can't think straight. Why didn't I know? Everyone in this room knows except me. "I don't know what you're talking about," I finally say.

The judge pulls his glasses down to the tip of his nose and looks at me like I just took a shit on the defense table—which, honestly, I feel like I might have to do. "Mr. Stoller, the prosecution is calling for the death penalty in this case. And even in California, under federal guidelines, if you are found guilty, I have the power to grant it, and I am inclined to do so. So I suggest you think long and hard about the pros and cons of continuing with Mr. Young as your legal counsel. Mr. Young, are you willing to continue serving as defense counsel in this case?"

Wayne stands. "Yes, Your Honor, I am."

"Very well. I hereby adjourn our proceedings for today and suggest, Mr. Stoller, that you and Mr. Young sit down and hash out your differences. *Dismissed*."

I turn and stare at Wayne, giving him my best stink eye, but I probably just look shit-faced. I thought it would relax me, but four capsules was too much.

After what feels like a really long time, the bailiff reaches the table and leads me out of the courtroom. I didn't bother to change out of my orange jumpsuit today.

I feel like I might puke as I climb into the corrections van for the ride back to the county jail, as much from knowing Chloe posted as anything I took. I need to read it—to know what she said.

Out of the van, I'm taken back through the series of gates and into the solitary wing, where Kryz and Killian take over to lead me the last way to my cell.

Something's different. There's no eye contact. No meaningful glances. I notice it right away. Was it something she wrote? Something that wasn't credible? Or was it so convincing that now they don't believe me? I'm too dizzy to sort through the possible scenarios. I just need to read the thing.

"I need a phone," I say to Kryz.

He stares at me for a beat with an unreadable expression, like he did the first time I saw him. "There are no cell phones allowed," he says. All business.

"Obviously. But I need one. Right away. I know you can get one."

Killian hitches his pants under his gut and takes a step toward me. "I think you misheard. There are no cell phones allowed in this prison. If you are found with a cell phone, it will be confiscated."

My eyes bounce back and forth between them. "Guys, c'mon . . . seriously? It's me. I need your help. I've got to post again. It's urgent—for the movement. Even if it's detected, it's worth the risk."

The two of them look at each other for a minute. Like there's something they want to say but they're not sure who's going to say it. Then Kryz grabs his belt with both hands and shakes his head.

"We can't help you anymore."

86

COURT TRANSCRIPT

TRANSCRIPT OF TESTIMONY OF
FBI SPECIAL AGENT JOSHUA VANCE

DIRECT EXAMINATION BY MS. GIBSON:

MS. GIBSON: Thank you for testifying today, Agent Vance. You have spent a good amount of time on this case. Please explain to the jury how you first got involved.

MR. VANCE: Yes, happy to. I've been with the FBI for eighteen years, and for the last ten years I've specialized in investigating online extremist groups. We're looking for terrorist threats, assassination plots, bombing plans, anything that could result in physical violence. I first heard about the BurnOutz a little over a year ago. They mostly seemed to be focused on wire fraud, which wasn't really in my purview, so I referred the case to investigators at the SEC and coordinated with them on it. But when they pulled off the CompassCard short squeeze, the group got back on my radar fast. I was pretty focused on investigating them from that point forward.

MS. GIBSON: The CompassCard scheme was still just a stock scam though, nothing violent.

MR. VANCE: True, but there were two aspects about it that concerned me. First was an increasing aggression in the group's rhetoric. That's often a precursor to more violent actions. Second was the scope of the movement. Until that point, we assumed they had probably fewer than a hundred members, but thousands of people were involved in that scheme. So the threat level went way up. That led us to believe they might pull off something bigger, and that's exactly what they did.

MS. GIBSON: What did you know at that point about their leader, Burner_911?

MR. VANCE: We were starting to piece together a theory that it might be Shane Stoller. The first lead was purely circumstantial. One of our agents had come across another online profile on YouTube that went by the username of BurnerBro. We were able to affirmatively identify Mr. Stoller as the owner of that account based on facial recognition from about twelve seconds in which he was visible in one of the videos. We also had, through our contacts at the SEC, identified a substantial number of brokerage accounts opened by Mr. Stoller that participated in trades the BurnOutz organized. At that point, we combined with an existing investigation in our San Francisco Field Office that had obtained warrants to surveil Mr. Stoller's online activity, text messages, and phone communications. We also assigned agents to track his physical movement and pubic conversations, as well as undercover agents to infiltrate the group.

MS. GIBSON: One of those undercover agents was killed in the line of duty, correct?

MR. VANCE: That's correct. Special Agent John Stanley, an undercover agent who had successfully infiltrated the group was poisoned at the direction of one of Mr. Stoller's aliases, HappyCat18.

COURT TRANSCRIPT

MS. GIBSON: I'm very sorry about that loss. I should note for the jury that we will be presenting evidence in that portion of our case at a later date. So, Agent Vance, what was the result of your surveillance of Mr. Stoller?

MR. VANCE: Overall, he was quite skilled at covering his tracks. All his communication was encrypted. He used multiple devices, networks, and proxy services. Much of the illicit activity was committed by third parties, themselves operating through a complex web of proxies often originating in foreign countries where we couldn't easily subpoena network providers. Furthermore, many of the payments for these activities were made with cryptocurrencies, making them difficult to trace. The most promising thread we started to pull was actually his relationship with Chloe Corbin. Based on our surveillance of Mr. Stoller, we determined that Ms. Corbin was colluding in this criminal conspiracy, so we got a warrant to tap her phone, and that's when we got our first big break. She had several text and voice exchanges with him that were quite incriminating.

MS. GIBSON: Incriminating but still not definitive?

MR. VANCE: Correct. Before placing him under arrest, we wanted definitive proof. We wanted to catch him at his computer while logged in to the Burner_911 account. But that was incredibly hard to do since he only posted periodically. Finally, we got the help we needed—an inside informant within Razgo who could tell us the exact moment Burner_911 logged in. So we staked out his place for three days, waiting for the call. We finally got it early morning on October 12th. We couldn't wait any longer, so we went in full force. Unfortunately, in the time it took to gain entry, he was able to log out. But we still had our smoking gun. The FBI's Computer Analysis Recovery

Team confirmed that the laptop confiscated had accessed the Burner_911 account, and nobody else had access to that laptop in that timeframe besides him. There's no doubt in my mind Shane Stoller is Burner_911.

MS. GIBSON: Thank you for your service, Mr. Vance. And congratulations for solving this case.

87

PRESS CONFERENCE TRANSCRIPT

TRANSCRIPT OF PRESS BRIEFING:
KIANA BRYANT, FBI SPECIAL AGENT IN CHARGE
October 25, 2023

MS. BRYANT: Good morning. Thank you for gathering on such short notice. Today, we'll be providing an update on our Joint Task Force's ongoing investigation into the abduction of Chloe Corbin. Joining me today is James Rudiger, executive assistant director for the National Security Branch at the FBI, who will be briefing you on today's developments.

MR. RUDIGER: Thank you, SAC Bryant. And thank you to the San Francisco Police Department, the Sheriff's Departments of San Francisco, Solano, Butte, Yuba, and Plumas Counties, the US Marshals Service, and other members of law enforcement involved in this Joint Task Force investigation.

    Earlier today, authorities responded to a house fire in rural Solano County, just outside of Suisun City. A body coroners have tentatively identified as that of Nicholas Harper, one of the individuals wanted for the October 12th kidnapping of Ms. Corbin, was discovered at this location. In an autopsy, it was determined Mr. Harper was killed by a gunshot wound to the head, apparently inflicted prior to the fire. We believe this location was a safe house used to hold Ms. Corbin, and that the individuals detaining her have fled to another location. Late this afternoon, a submerged pickup truck was recovered at Sly Creek Reservoir in Butte

County, leading us to believe that these individuals are in Butte, Plumas, or Yuba Counties. I would remind the public that these individuals remain at large and are considered armed and extremely dangerous. I can assure you that the full resources of federal law enforcement are engaged in this search, and we will update you as we have new developments.

Are there any questions?

REPORTER 1: What do you know about the location of Chloe Corbin?

MR. RUDIGER: I'm afraid we cannot share specific details, as this is an active investigation. But we are focusing our search and rescue efforts on Butte, Plumas, and Yuba Counties, as I mentioned. Much of this area is extremely rugged and mountainous terrain, but we are confident we will find her. We have also set up a tip line for any information pertaining to her case, and there is a $1 million reward for direct information that results in her safe recovery and the capture of her abductors.

REPORTER 2: Are you confident of Chloe Corbin's safety? Her captors have vowed to kill her if Mr. Stoller is not released.

MR. RUDIGER: Despite the gruesome acts these savage criminals have posted online, we continue to believe Ms. Corbin is alive.

REPORTER 3: What about Ken Corbin? Is the FBI investigating him over the CompassCard scheme?

MR. RUDIGER: In consultation with the SEC and DOJ, we have decided that Mr. Corbin is no longer a subject of federal criminal investigation.

PR PERSON: No more questions. Thank you.

[REPORTERS SHOUTING QUESTIONS]

88

SHANE

We're back in the briefing booth with the glass divider—the same one I first met Wayne in, the day I got arrested. That was a long time ago. He asked for this meeting—said he had to tell me something before I get a new lawyer. I agreed, clearly, but I didn't know it would be in here, amplified voices talking through a protective shield. I'm not sure which one of us needs protection. Hopefully, I can hear okay.

"Hello, Shane," he says, his smoker's rasp generating a bassline of static over the speaker.

I don't say anything. I'm done with this guy.

"Look, I get why you're upset. I don't blame you. I would be too if I was in your shoes. But there's some things you oughta know before you make a final decision about your . . . legal representation."

"Yeah? What's that." I want to cut that dumb fucking mustache off his face with a steak knife.

"Well, for starters, you probably noticed our guys on the inside aren't quite as friendly anymore. You'll remain in solitary through the trial, but there won't be anyone to make sure what happened to your face won't be worse next time."

"Are you *threatening* me?"

"Not in the least. Just stating facts. So you can make an informed decision. See, they don't think you're Burner_911 anymore, especially since you didn't even know about the last drop. Here's another fact you might have missed: Ken Corbin is getting off scot-free. Barely a slap on

315

the wrist. So, all your little vendetta against him achieved was to get Chloe kidnapped."

"It doesn't matter. She has a phone now. I remember the number. I can message her once I get one too."

"How're you gonna get a phone, Shane? I'm not bringing you another one. You're in solitary, so you're not getting one from another prisoner. And Kryz and Killian think you're a lying son of a bitch. Plus, the prison has detectors and dogs that'll find that thing faster than you can say 'full cavity search.'"

I scratch my scar, which itches like hell. I know I don't have much of a plan, but I'm not letting him know that. "I'll find a way."

"I'm not sure you will," he says. "See, the house they were holding her in, the one I saw her at, burned down to the ground. They found the remains of one of the guys. The rest of 'em got the hell out of there. So something went seriously sideways. And the phone I gave her is off the grid. The FBI thinks maybe they escaped to the Sierras someplace, but they really have no idea where Chloe is, or even if she's still alive."

My stomach curls in on itself. That can't be. I just talked with her. Wayne could be lying again, but something tells me he's not.

"That's not good," I finally say, the words barely forming in my dry mouth.

"No, it's *not* good. And here's the thing: Chloe's phone had the same tracking software on it that you inconveniently discovered on yours. So, with that phone MIA, there's only one way to get what we want."

"What's that?"

"Give me the credentials to Burner_911."

"Why would I do that?"

"Because it's time, Shane. It's time to hand over the keys to the castle."

"What the fuck does that even mean?"

"It means you're *done*. You've taken this thing as far as you can. I give you credit, you built a passionate following. But did you really think you could turn this on Bob Jorgensen and get away with it? That he'd just sit there and take it?"

"Fuck that guy. He deserved it. And fuck you too—that's probably who's paying you."

"I gotta say, Shane, for someone as sharp as you, it's taken you a minute to figure this one out. Do you really still *not* understand how the world works? Why do you think you're here?"

"What do you mean? I got busted."

"You're here because Bob Jorgensen *wanted* you here. You cost him billions of dollars. You bankrupted his fund. He owns the majority stake in Razgo. All he had to do was have our buddy Alex tip off the Feds the second you logged in the morning of October 12th. Why do you think I got down here faster than the arresting officers? Cause they tipped me off too."

"Bullshit," I say, reeling him in just a little more. "I've been a step ahead of you guys the entire time."

"Oh, really—that's what you think, huh? You know what *I* think? I think you're a fucking punk. You're lucky Bob didn't just rub you out like he did with that undercover agent, ordering the hit from a hacked account of yours just to make sure your fingerprints were all over it. He wanted to, you know—to kill you. But I talked him out of it. Told him I thought you could still be useful. Now the only thing that's useful about you is that password in your head."

"No way. There's no way I'm giving it to you."

"Shane, this is what I like to call a 'Come to Jesus' moment. You have a simple decision to make. Path one is you give us the credentials to Burner_911. I continue to be your lawyer, and, although I can't make any promises, we've got a good shot at getting you off on the main charges. Maybe a twenty- or twenty-five-year sentence, and you're out on parole in your forties. Still a young man. Who knows? Maybe you even see your sweetheart again. Path two is you keep believing you actually matter. That this movement actually belongs to you. You fumble through your own defense or let some hack public defender represent you, only to be found guilty and sentenced to death by lethal injection—that is, assuming some guard or inmate doesn't whack you first."

I stare at him through the glass, trying to keep my poker face, knowing he's played right into my hand. "I'll take my chances," I finally say.

"It's totally your choice," he says. "But path one is the only way you live."

89

CHLOE

From my cot, I see the first glimmer of sunrise shining through the open porthole, giving me permission to forfeit my weak attempt at sleep after another restless night. Scooter must be up already. I stare at the curved ceiling of our underground bunker, recalling how I've started this day the last three years: the annual San Francisco Turkey Trot 10K—always one of my most popular Instagram posts. But not this year. Another day of silence for @RealChloeCorbin.

So many fans and followers. To them, I was the iconic ideal of the modern woman—glamorous, wealthy, philanthropic, social, popular at a global scale. They eagerly awaited my latest posts, liked and commented on them like we were best friends.

That was only a few weeks ago, but it feels like a different life now. Like the memories of a different person. One who never could have lived in an abandoned mineshaft in the mountains.

I swivel my legs off the cot, my raw, bare feet easing onto the cold, rocky floor, bits of dirt and stones clinging to my soles. I slide into my disintegrating sneakers and stand with my various blankets wrapped around me. Pete is still asleep; the sawing noise of his snore has been contributing to my insomnia. Benny's cot is empty. I don't hear any helicopters this morning.

I climb toward the opening, pulling myself up by rusted railroad spikes driven into the granite. Outside, the peak across from us is cast in a dazzling orange as the sun breaks the horizon.

I see Scooter where I expect him, brewing a pot of coffee over the camping stove. Drawn to its warmth like a moth to a candle, I sit next to him on a stump—reaching my frozen hands toward the flames, desperate for a source of heat. Scooter is unwilling to risk a proper fire, despite a dusting of snow last night and intensifying morning frosts. Even our body heat could be detected by infrared sensors, he claims.

Without speaking, he gives me a ceramic mug of scalding coffee, which I huddle over with my hands, legs, chest, face, trying to absorb every bit of warmth it has to offer into my body.

"How'd you sleep?" he eventually asks, adjusting his camouflage jacket with its Black Mountain Militia patch on the shoulder. His beard seems thicker and grayer every day. I've come to realize he's older than I thought. Maybe forty. Old enough to have a protective instinct—not paternalistic, more like an older brother. Like he's looking out for me.

"Not great," I say, burning my lips on the coffee, unable to wait for it to cool. "I don't know how you spend so much time here."

He shrugs and looks up at the glowing mountain peak above us, like the tip of a giant sun dial. "You get used to it. I never needed much. My dad and me found this place more than thirty years ago."

"What does your father do?"

"He passed. But he worked on a fracking rig, up in Bakken."

"Oh . . . I'm sorry." I look down. "Where's Benny?"

"He went down to the stream. See if he can catch some trout." Scooter sips from his mug.

"So, how much longer are we going to stay here?"

"Till things blow over."

"I don't think this thing is ever blowing over. Plus, pretty soon we'll be buried in ten feet of snow."

Scooter glances up at me and lets out an amused *tsk*.

"How'd you ever get involved in all this BurnOutz stuff, anyway? You don't really seem like the online type."

"I don't know . . ."

I wait for him to fill the silence.

"Me and Pete been buddies since high school. He got real into it a couple years ago, and I just followed along, I guess."

"Do you even believe in the cause?"

"*Which* cause?"

I peer at him through the steam rising from my mug, dubious. "You know . . . the whole mission of the BurnOutz. Punishing elites, solving wealth inequality, all that stuff."

"I guess I don't really think about what other people have that much. This is enough for me," he says, indicating our spartan camp with a nod of his head.

I turn to survey what he sees: rough wood beams holding open the mouth of the shaft; a camouflage tarpaulin covering a few canisters of propane, boxes of provisions, and clear plastic barrels of drinking water; a few logs around this patch of rock we use for the stove; and crates of ammunition stacked behind mud wall fortifications around the perimeter. As I turn back, he pours two scoops of instant oatmeal into a pot of boiling water.

"I know you guys are independent and everything, but you're part of a bigger movement . . . The BurnOutz are trying to make the world more equitable. Help people who have less. Doesn't that mean anything to you?"

"Last time I did something for the BurnOutz, what I got was a dead friend, my name on the FBI's most-wanted list, and a never-ending hostage situation. Honestly, I just want to be left alone. If I get through this, I'll go back to minding my own business. Other people can help themselves." I watch him stir the oatmeal, scraping a metal spoon across the bottom of the pot.

"No . . . no, then there would be no point to all this," I say. "Shane's in jail, people were killed, millions of believers are without a leader. This movement has meant too much to too many people for it to die on some hill in the middle of nowhere."

"The thing dyin' on this hill's gonna be us," Scooter says. "Don't you get it? They're gonna come. They'll find us, eventually—even here. They *always* come for guys like us. To take away the only thing we're supposed to *truly* have in this country: freedom." He turns off the burner, ladles some oatmeal into a bowl, and hands it to me.

The situation does seem helpless. From here, there's nothing we can do. We've retreated into the wilderness, as far as we can go. But it can't end here. I can't just go back to my old life like nothing happened. I have to *do* something. Have to make a difference. Have to help Shane.

And now, finally, I know what I have to do.

90

ANONYMOUS

The history of the world can be traced back to a few moments. A few decisions by a few people who had the courage to act. Small pivots or inflections that may have seemed insignificant at the time but turned out to change the course of humanity.

We are at one of those moments. I am one of those people.

The world has become too polarized. The difference between the haves and the have-nots is too extreme. It's simply not sustainable if eight billion people are going to live together on this planet. But the haves are never going to just voluntarily give away their fortunes. Redistribution of wealth doesn't just happen on its own. Those who have it always want to keep it, always want more. They will manipulate, contort, and outright rig the system to concentrate their wealth and power. Leaving regular people just further and further behind.

Things have gone on like this for decades. It usually requires something major—like the Great Depression or the World Wars or 9/11—to reset things. Systemic disruptions to reboot the system, but they came with a lot of collateral damage and massive loss of life. We need a better, more graceful way to disrupt the system now. A soft reboot, if you will, not a hard one. But you need to be ready to break the law. Laws are created by cronies to preserve and protect their wealthy overlords. Taking from them is breaking the law, by definition. So you need to break the law to create change. Sometimes you even need to kill. Small sacrifices to prevent more widespread loss of life. To keep things in control.

And that's what the BurnOutz are all about. Taking back control. Lever-aging technology to even the playing field. Exploiting the gaps, the glitches, the bugs, the blockchain to get what we want. It's the only way real progress will happen. We can't go back. Not after this. The potential for this movement is unlimited. So that's why things are about to change. Have *to change.*

Because this cause is bigger than me, bigger than all of us. And it can't end now. Not when we're so close. I know now how to restore trust. How to reinvigorate the faithful. How to push our mission forward. How to get every-one to BELIEVE IN THE PLAN again.

For us to move forward, Chloe Corbin must die.

91

CHLOE

Scooter thrusts the bowie knife downward, piercing through the clear plastic shell. The phone pops free from its encasement and lands softly on the carpet of pine needles. I eagerly scoop it up and power it on. Benny waits patiently for me to express my appreciation.

"Thanks for getting it," I say to him after confirming the device works and has enough battery for our needs.

He lowers his gaze but concedes a self-conscious grin under the brim of his baseball cap.

"Did anyone see you?" Scooter asks.

"Just the clerk," Benny says, shaking his head emphatically. "I waited till nobody else was in the store and wore a mask, like you said."

"You got everything else too?" I ask.

Benny nods and presents me with a plastic bag branded with the hardware store's logo.

I open it, take a quick inventory, then pull a case of shells out and hold them in front of his face. "You're 100 percent sure these are blanks?"

Benny opens the case and holds one up. "See how the tips are crimped?"

I drop the box back into the bag, set everything down on a stump, and return my attention to the phone. Composing a new email, I begin typing. My thumbs, suffering from reduced muscle memory and the numbing cold, are clumsy on the screen. But I try my best to type fast, knowing it's almost dark and wanting to conserve as much battery as possible.

"You know you won't get a signal," Pete says.

"I'm aware of that, Peter," I say, not looking up from the screen.

"I'm still not sure about this." Scooter this time. They all seem eager to tell me why my plan won't work.

"Look . . . as long as they think I'm out here, they're going to keep searching for us," I say. "This is the only way. Help me do this and everything will be over. You'll be able to go back to your normal lives."

"Except for the minor fact we'll be wanted for murder," Pete says.

"You're *already* wanted for murder," I say.

"That was his fault!" Pete says, pointing at Benny.

"Do you have a better plan? We need to put an end to this, and this way *I* won't be talking. Besides, without a witness, or a body, or a weapon, or any definitive forensic evidence, they won't be able to make a case, even if they do catch you. The only one of you who was ever positively identified was Nick, and he's dead. As long as you're not dragging me around, nobody will recognize the three of you. You can each go your separate ways and disappear."

Scooter scratches his beard pensively and exchanges looks with Pete. "She's right," he says. "We can't stay out here too much longer. We'll freeze to death."

"*Fuck!*" Pete shouts, like he's resigning himself to a least-shitty choice.

"This is a win all the way around," I insist. "I get liberated, the Burn-Outz get revenge, Shane gets reasonable doubt, and you all get to move on with your lives instead of living indefinitely in the wilderness. Or do you *want* to freeze to death?"

"I got a sister across the border, near Saskatoon. I can stay with her a while. Maybe she'll have room for one of you too," Scooter offers.

Pete rolls his eyes. Benny shuffles his feet in the dirt.

"It's settled then," I say, returning to my email. "I just need one of you to get back into cell range to send this and upload the video."

"I'm not fucking walking all the way down there," Pete says. "Besides, Benny's the only one they don't got pictures of." He snaps up the bag from the hardware store and marches past Scooter toward the encampment.

"I'll talk to him," Scooter says, darting me a look. Then he follows Pete into the shaft.

"So, Benny? Are you up for another hike?" I smile. "We'll shoot the video tonight and you can walk it down tomorrow. I'd really appreciate it."

"Yeah, no problem. I'll leave first thing," Benny says. "Oh, and . . . I got you something."

I cock my head, totally unsure what he's talking about or might say next. He reaches into his back pocket and pulls out a small, blue California license plate.

"They had your name," he says, kicking at the dirt again.

I can't help but laugh at the novelty when I see "CHLOE" printed in yellow block letters against the blue metal. It's just like one I got as a girl during a trip to Yosemite. But when I look back up at Benny, he's not laughing.

"Oh, Benny . . . thank you. This is perfect," I say, holding the plate aloft.

In the fading light, he gradually looks up from the ground. I see tears welling in his eyes. I know what he's going to say, and I know I don't want to hear it.

He wipes his cheek and then says it. "I . . . I think I love you."

92

INSTAGRAM

[CHLOE CORBIN SEATED IN CHAIR]

UNSEEN VOICE: We said this would happen. We have been patient. We could not have been more clear about the consequences of inaction. It was so simple. Why can't you people just follow basic directions? All you had to do was release Shane Stoller from prison and she would have been safe. Returned immediately. Nobody gets hurt.

But NO! Ken and the Feds had to be fucking assholes about it! Beat their chest and swing their dicks like a pack of fucking orangutans. *Why?* To prove to us what a well-hung stud you are, *Ken?* How you don't take shit from *nobody?*

The irony is Shane Stoller's not even Burner_911. You got the wrong guy! And even if you'd gotten the right one, this movement isn't going to die. But I'll tell you who *is* gonna die . . . Chloe Corbin.

CHLOE CORBIN: Please, no. Please don't!

UNSEEN VOICE: It's a shame too. So preventable. But, tragically, we've reached the end of the road and the end of her usefulness to our cause. Any last words, Princess?

CHLOE CORBIN: Please—*please!* I beg you! I had nothing to do with this!

UNSEEN VOICE: You had *everything* to do with this! You and your billionaire daddy and all the other rich elites!

CHLOE CORBIN: You don't have to do this! I'll give you anything! I—

BURNER

UNSEEN VOICE: Afraid it's too late for that, sweetheart.

[GUNSHOTS. CHLOE CORBIN SLUMPS TO GROUND.]

UNSEEN VOICE: That's what you get when you fuck with the BurnOutz. Believe in The Plan! We're close! Nothing can stop us now!

93

ANONYMOUS

I wish we didn't need to do that. It was so violent. That's not really what we're about. But it was necessary. It was the only way. Her death—"execution" is really the right word—is unfortunate but, in the grand scheme, just collateral damage in the larger war. Maybe Ken will learn a lesson for a change.

The world could really stand to have one less Instagram celebrity anyway. Do seventy-three million people really need to know the latest trivial details of Chloe Corbin's life? What did Chloe have for breakfast? What is Chloe wearing today? What type of toilet paper does Chloe use to wipe her ass? It's too much. Too many people give too many fucks about shit that shouldn't matter to them! Get a fucking life! @RealChloeCorbin had to go.

More importantly, this mends the rift that was starting to form in the movement. With her gone, there'll be no more dissension about what she means and whether @Burner_911's head is in the game or not. We can get rid of the distraction and focus our energy on moving forward. Because The Plan . . . it's a good plan.

The dominoes really are falling. The October Prophecy is coming true. I have to admit, that was some pretty incredible insight. To see those cracks in the entire financial system, how they could be exploited so elegantly. It's inspired. Visionary.

But like anything this complex, it's a marathon, not a sprint. The baton needs to be passed to a new leader with new energy, new ideas—someone who can get the next dominoes to fall. I see it. I see it now. How it will all come into place. How it was meant to be.

I believe in The Plan.

94

KTVU-TV

FOX 2 Eyewitness News Transcript, November 28, 2023

ANCHOR: Breaking news tonight in the Chloe Corbin case. Police say they have finally apprehended a suspect as part of their state-wide manhunt for those allegedly responsible for Corbin's abduction—a dramatic development in a story that began with this horrific scene, captured on video the day of the October 12th terrorist attacks. KTVU's Skylar Rossi joins us live from the Sierra Nevada Mountains with the latest. Skylar?

REPORTER: Thanks, Tom. I'm coming to you live outside the Plumas County Sheriff's Department in Quincy, California, where authorities announced this evening they have arrested a man believed to be involved in the October 12th kidnapping of billionaire heiress Chloe Corbin, as well as the arson and apparent murder of a man at a house in Suisun City, California, a few weeks ago. The suspect has been identified as Benjamin Tucker of Yolo County. I'm told the arrest occurred at 2:17 p.m. in the town of Meadow Valley, about ten miles west of here. Plumas County Sheriff Todd Jacobs described the intense scene just moments ago.

SHERIFF: Deputies positively identified the suspect outside the Meadow Valley Country Market. As they approached him, the suspect fled across a two-lane road and down a steep embankment to a creek. The officers followed and successfully apprehended him there. The man was unarmed, carrying only cash and a wireless phone. He was taken into custody at the Plumas County Sheriff's Office, where he's currently being held for questioning by federal agents.

REPORTER: Now, Tom, I'm told the arresting deputies were acting on a tip from a clerk at the Meadow Valley Country Market, who had seen the suspect yesterday. She said she had never seen the man in the store before and found his purchases suspicious, in particular a novelty license plate with the name "Chloe" printed on it. So, she called the tip line, and authorities staked out the store hoping he might return. It was just the lucky break they'd been hoping for.

ANCHOR: What an incredible development in this case that has gripped the nation. If you're just joining us, officers in Plumas County have arrested a man allegedly involved in the Chloe Corbin case tonight. Skylar, have authorities provided any more information about the other accomplices involved in this incident?

REPORTER: Yes, Tom, authorities say they are still on the hunt for Mr. Tucker's accomplices and, of course, Ms. Corbin herself. They are mobilizing a multi-departmental search-and-rescue effort to comb the area for any clues to Ms. Corbin's whereabouts and bring her abductors to justice.

Back to you, Tom.

95

ENCRYPTED MESSAGE

FROM: Chloe Corbin

TO: Shane Stoller

I did what you asked. It felt so personal. Pretending to be you. But I did my best to channel you. To compose a message that you would post. Except for one part, the ending—I added that line about the bitch rotting in hell. I'm not sure if you even saw it, but that was me. I know you don't think that. I just felt like @Burner_911 needed some distance from @RealChloeCorbin. I hope you agree.

I actually didn't need to pretend that much. See, what I didn't tell you before is that I'm starting to *believe*. It took a while, but I've come to realize that what you're searching for and what I'm searching for are really the same thing: *a more just and equal world*. We just had different approaches. Different camps, tribes, parties, methods.

But, with all this time to think about it, I see now that your approach may be the only way. We can't just wait for rich people like my dad to give their wealth away. That will take too long. Most likely it will never happen. We need to *take* it. What you did, what you said, inspired so many people. My followers just click "like" when I post something cute. Yours took to the streets by the thousands. That's real ability to affect change. Real power!

I love you. I've always loved you. And now I understand why. Because we're soul mates. Put on earth for this purpose. I want to help this cause, and what will help the most right now is if I'm out of the picture. No matter what I say or do, I'm the enemy. And our relationship is hurting your credibility.

So, now I have an idea . . . Just like you had the idea for me to post as Burner_911, I have the idea to stage my own execution. With Nick gone, I have been able to convince the guys to help me. All the billionaire drama will be done, I can be free, and the BurnOutz will have more street cred than ever before. Trust me, this is the only way we can be together again.

I wanted to make sure you knew this before you see the video. I'm sending this by the same Telegram connection Wayne set up for us before. We don't have coverage where we're hiding, but one of the guys will hike the two hours to get a signal and send this message. We don't have much time. By the time you see this, it will be up on Instagram.

I forgive you. I understand that you were motivated by a higher purpose. I know you feel terrible about what happened, but it's all going to work out. I can't wait to see you again.

Love, Chloe

[UNSENT MESSAGE ON DEVICE CONFISCATED FROM MR. BENJAMIN TUCKER BY FEDERAL MARSHALS.]

96

SHANE

I don't have words. They showed me the video—the video of Chloe's execution. How did they become so radicalized that they thought kidnapping and murdering the love of my life was what I wanted, what Burner_911 wanted? I just don't understand. Is that all this movement is now? Just a violent mob that kills without reason, mercy, or guilt?

What am I going to do? She was everything to me. I can't imagine my life without her. AND I HAD JUST WON HER BACK! Now she's gone. Not just out of my life but out of this *world*. There are so many things I wanted to say to her that I never did. All these words in my head that I've never had the courage to tell her. Now it's too late. I will never see her again.

This whole thing is my fault. If she had never met me, she'd still be alive today. It was just bad luck she happened to get me as her Uber driver. What did she even see in me? I'm just a hustler, a poser, a nobody—the Central Valley burnout I could never escape being. She had everything, until I took it all away.

I don't know how I can go on. What's the point? I've given up defending myself—Wayne can do it. I don't give a shit. Nothing else matters to me anymore without her. I have no purpose. No reason to continue. Believe in The Plan? I don't believe in *anything* anymore. I can't stand to live another day on this earth without her. I'm so sorry. So sorry for everything. I deserve the death sentence.

SHANE

In the end, we all go out of this world the way we came in: *alone*. If you're lucky, you find someone to share that time with, help overcome that burden of loneliness. Some of us never find that person. Some of us, like me, find them and then lose them. But in the end, it doesn't matter. Everyone we ever love dies. All we have is ourselves.

97

COURT TRANSCRIPT

TRANSCRIPT OF PROSECUTION CLOSING ARGUMENT

MS. GIBSON: Thank you, Your Honor. May it please the court ...

JUDGE MORENO: Counsel.

MS. GIBSON: Ladies and gentlemen of the jury. The acts of October 12th have ripped at the fabric of our nation. They were deliberately planned and perpetrated with the explicit intent of destabilizing our democracy, damaging our institutions, and harming our citizens. They were intended to sow unrest, uncertainty, and anarchy. In short, they were the very definition of an act of domestic terrorism.

The prosecution has demonstrated conclusively that Shane Stoller was the mastermind behind the October 12th terrorist attack. While he did so under an online identity that he thought was anonymous and he and his defense team have desperately tried to keep the true identity of Burner_911 concealed, digital forensic evidence, wiretapped calls, text messages, expert testimony, and firsthand witnesses all conclusively point to Shane Stoller as being the sole operator behind the Burner_911 profile and the massive online conspiracy of

so-called BurnOutz that his postings inspired. Although
he didn't personally commit the acts of terrorism on
our country that we are still reeling from to this day,
Mr. Stoller's aggressive, irresponsible, and inflammato-
ry rhetoric directly incited the mob. He organized it,
he directed the illegal actions, he arranged for cryptocurrency payments for a network of criminal computer
hackers, and he repeatedly posted and encouraged the rioters who mobbed the city of San Francisco.

The defense would lead you to believe that these
actions were somehow virtuous. That Mr. Stoller, as Burn-
er_911, was acting on behalf of the masses. That he was
rectifying wrongs in our financial system and that his
only victims were the billionaires he condemns so vehe-
mently. That argument is absurd.

We have demonstrated that Mr. Stoller spent most of
his life engaged in criminal activities. That he sold
drugs, fenced stolen goods, extorted, and blackmailed
for his own personal gain. Conspired with a network of
international cyber criminals to commit dozens of hacks,
data breaches, denial of service attacks, and other computer crimes. The defense would have you believe that
these actions were somehow charitable or altruistic.
That is ludicrous. His entire criminal enterprise was
engineered to benefit him and his most ardent followers
with massive, illicit financial gains.

The harm of Mr. Stoller's actions ranges far beyond the
wealthy elite, many of whom actually made money from his
schemes. The real harm was done to the regular people Mr.
Stoller claims to defend—small businesses that were vandalized, retail investors who lost everything on promises
that turned out to be Ponzi schemes, pensioners whose
retirement accounts have been decimated by the collapse
in the stock market, the murdered security guard at the
Federal Reserve Bank, the two slain San Francisco police

officers whose families will never see them again, and the five other people killed on October 12th—a construction worker, a veterinarian assistant, a food delivery person, a retail clerk, and a college student. Hardly the cast of global elites Mr. Stoller constantly vilifies. Dozens more like them are battling to recover from serious injuries. Make no mistake, it is real, regular people who have suffered as the result of Mr. Stoller's actions.

And now, with the horrifying, execution-style murder this week of Chloe Corbin by men aligned with the BurnOutz, we can see fully what this group really is all about—hate, anarchy, violence, and cold-blooded murder. With Ms. Corbin's death, the world witnessed just how depraved and dangerous this movement is. Like a snake, the only way to kill it is to cut off the head. And that is what Mr. Stoller, a.k.a. Burner_911, is: the head. The self-aggrandizing criminal mastermind of an organized, well-funded, violent, domestic terrorist organization.

Ladies and gentlemen, I ask, as you render a final verdict in this case you have graciously and patriotically served on the last several weeks, that you consider the victims. Not only the lives that were tragically lost in this vicious act of terrorism, but also the lives destroyed. Destroyed by physical injury, by financial destitution, by wanton recklessness. They are the people you are vindicating today with a guilty verdict. If Mr. Stoller is acquitted of these charges, it will only mean more destruction, devastation, and loss of life. I urge you, *implore* you, to convict Mr. Stoller of all counts against him. The healing of our nation begins today with you and your verdict.

Thank you, Your Honor.

TRANSCRIPT OF DEFENSE CLOSING ARGUMENT

JUDGE MORENO: Thank you, Ms. Gibson. Mr. Young, your turn for a closing argument.

MR. YOUNG: Thank you, Your Honor. Ladies and gentlemen of the jury, I'd like to start by thanking you for your service on this trial, and, by extension, your service to your country. Needless to say, this is not your typical trial. You have been sequestered and scrutinized. Spent time away from your family and friends. Cut off from the outside world. But that hasn't even been the most difficult part. No, the difficult part is that this isn't just a criminal trial of one individual. It's a trial of America and our values. You have been asked to answer some of the most fundamental and difficult questions of our time.

At its core, this is a trial about freedom of speech. A right so fundamental, so unassailable, so inseparable from the soul of American democracy that it was enshrined as the very first amendment to our Constitution—more important than any other. Allow me to read you the First Amendment of our Bill of Rights verbatim: *"Congress shall make no law respecting an establishment of religion, or prohibiting the free exercise thereof; or abridging the freedom of speech, or of the press, or the right of the people peaceably to assemble, and to petition the Government for a redress of grievances."* Beautiful in its simplicity—freedom of religion, freedom of speech, freedom of the press, and freedom to assemble in forty-five succinct words. Pretty fundamental to our government, society, and way of life.

But for two hundred years after the ratification of the Bill of Rights, those rights weren't fully exercised by every American. The wealthy controlled the levers of power. Their crony politicians wrote and enforced the law to their liking. Sure, there was freedom of speech, but it was the wealthy and powerful who spoke the loudest—whose words were amplified through the media, advertisements, and loudspeakers. Sure, there was freedom of the press, but it was the wealthy and powerful who owned the press. They controlled what the media said and manipulated it to their whims. Sure, there was freedom of assembly, but if you dared to do so the cops would show up with batons to break your picket line, bust your union, and forcibly disperse your numbers. The ability of an average citizen, a boy who grew up parentless and homeless and penniless, to actually exercise any of these freedoms was virtually impossible.

Then, after two hundred years of subjugation, of the game being rigged by the wealthy, of the deck being stacked by the elites to ensconce their permanent privileged status, something changed. With the advent of the internet and social media and smartphones, suddenly the average person had a voice. They finally had the power to exercise their freedom of speech and organize in ways they never could before. And guess who that threatened? The very elites who had stifled, controlled, manipulated, and thwarted the masses from having their seat at the table, having their voices be heard, having their constitutional rights realized.

So what have those wealthy elites done? Fight back with everything they have. Accuse the people fighting for their right to free speech of uprising, of sedition, of anarchy. Hire PR agencies and law firms and lobbyists to contort the truth. Harness the criminal justice system to crack down on anyone who would dare try to rectify the injustices they have wrought.

The prosecution portrays Mr. Stoller as a terrorist. But even if you believe he is Burner_911, even if you believe he wrote every word in those manifestoes, what more was he doing than merely exercising his constitutional right to free speech? Yes, many of the activities inspired by Burner_911 and executed by the BurnOutz broke the laws as written. They stole money, after all. But aren't *all* revolutions about money? About poor people rising up and saying they're sick of getting the short end of the stick, all the time? About the redistribution of wealth from the rich to the poor? Money is power, and the sharing of power among the people is the definition of democracy.

Just as our forefathers rejected the monarchy, we cannot be a nation of oligarchs who have unlimited wealth and power. If we tolerate that, then we have given up on democracy and returned to a monarchy, where fiefdoms preside over the peasants. I can't think of a more noble pursuit, a more just cause, a more righteous purpose than to restore the balance of power required for our democratic union to succeed. Further, I can't think of a more appropriate application of the rights enshrined in the First Amendment—a more obvious petition to the government for a redress of grievances. Wealth inequality is *the* grievance of modern American society. It is *the* grievance of every revolution, including the American Revolution and the founding of our nation.

So, ladies and gentlemen, as you consider this decision, as you ponder the fate of this man and the consequent fate of our country, I ask merely this: that you not view him through the tainted lens of the establishment but through the long view of history, and what this man and this movement may be two hundred years from now.

Thank you, Your Honor.

98

CHLOE

"Get up! We're going. C'mon, *get up!*"

It's Scooter's voice, pulling me out of a deep sleep—his words entangling themselves into the remnants of a terrifying dream, the memory of which slips out of my brain like frames falling to a cutting-room floor as I come to full consciousness.

He's waking Pete now. Shaking him until his snoring stops, replaced with grumbled expletives.

"Benny never came back." Scooter starts shoving items into a backpack. "We've got to get the hell out of here."

"He probably just got lost in the dark." Pete pulls up the corner of his sleeping bag.

"Nah, he fucked up—they got him," Scooter says, tossing Pete's boots onto his chest. "I can tell. There's a search party over on McRae Ridge. Another to the west near Table Rock, probably less than five miles from us. Way more than usual. I can see the flashlights."

I'm fully awake now, already dressed but pulling on my shoes and grabbing my few belongings. I squint toward the mountain range Scooter is pointing at but can't see anything.

"That fucking *idiot!*" Pete shouts, whipping open his sleeping bag.

"Shhh! Sound travels far at night," Scooter says. "And they'll be sweeping the area with acoustical monitoring devices to see if they can detect human activity."

"Wouldn't there be helicopters?" I've gotten used to the routine of concealing our campsite every time we hear search-and-rescue flights approaching, but I don't hear blades in the air.

"They don't want to scare us away." Scooter grabs several prefilled canteens, ready for this exact eventuality. "Helicopters would wake us up. They want to catch us."

"*Shit!* They couldn't have waited till morning?" Pete complains. He stands and wraps his chest with a holster, the butt of his firearm tucked under his armpit, then slings the AK-14 over his shoulder.

Scooter hands me a small pack. I put a canteen, map, and hat into it.

Within sixty seconds, we are all ready to leave. The scenario we've discussed and expected.

"Pete and I are headed east, over the top of Beartrap Mountain. We'll be fine." Scooter hoists his backpack onto his shoulders. "You're going east too, but down Hog Gulch till you catch the creek. Then just follow that to Poker Flat. Okay?" He looks around the bunker for anything else he needs, then pauses, facing me. "Well, I guess this is it."

I'm putting Benny's license plate into my pack. "Wait . . ." I say, petrified by the thought that has just blindsided me. "Do you think he sent the message? Uploaded the video? Do you think Benny . . . did those things . . . before he got arrested or killed or whatever happened to him?"

Scooter looks at Pete, as if looking for a cue. Pete just flicks his head sideways in a perturbed *we gotta get outta here* gesture.

"You can't worry about that now," Scooter says finally. "You'll know tomorrow, when you're back online. But I'm sure he did. As soon as he got a signal, the message would've gone through. So Shane should know what's up before he . . . sees the video."

"But what if—"

"You can't think about 'what if.'" Scooter places a hand on my shoulder. "You gotta focus on what we talked about. Focus on *surviving*. If you don't get out of here, nothing else matters."

I nod, pushing the spiraling scenarios out of my head.

"We gotta go, Scooter," Pete says. "Or this will turn into Ruby Ridge." He begins toward the trail without even looking at me.

Scooter watches him step out through the tarp, then turns back to me. Tears are rolling down his cheeks like mountain creeks into the thick bramble of his beard, but his voice is steady.

"There's most likely a police roadblock at Poker Flat. If you want to be found, that's your best bet. You can get there by morning. But if you want to stay missing, go the other way when you hit Canyon Creek till you make it to a campground about twenty miles upriver. It will take you a full day or more, but you'll be close enough to Sierra City that you can probably hitch a ride from there. Wear this and I doubt anyone'll recognize you." He places a musty baseball cap on my head as if my dingy hair, pasty complexion, and swollen face don't already make me look like a different person. "Remember, whatever you decide, you have your whole life in front of you."

I throw my arms around him, unable to suppress the tears of gratitude, fear, uncertainty.

He pulls me out of the embrace with a hand on each of my shoulders. "Now . . . *go.*"

99

PRESS CONFERENCE TRANSCRIPT

JULIE GIBSON, FEDERAL PROSECUTOR, UNITED STATES ATTORNEY'S OFFICE, NINTH DISTRICT

United States Northern District of California Courthouse, San Francisco, California

JULIE GIBSON, US FEDERAL PROSECUTOR: Thank you all for joining us today on short notice. I arranged this press conference with the expectation that we would be able to announce a guilty verdict in this trial in the case *US District Court for the Northern District of California in United States v. Shane Thomas Stoller*. Unfortunately, yesterday evening, prior to a verdict being rendered, the defendant, Mr. Stoller, was found dead in his prison cell.

[AUDIBLE GASPS, CROWD NOISE]

We are awaiting a full autopsy, but it is believed, at this time, that Mr. Stoller's death was self-inflicted. That said, there was no prior indication of self-harm and, as you all know, there was an attempted homicide committed against Mr. Stoller by another inmate. So we need to explore all possibilities.

Regardless, the initial toxicology report revealed a lethal level of pentobarbital in Mr. Stoller's system, which was most likely the cause of death. He was discovered unconscious in his cell and attempts to revive him were unsuccessful.

We will be conducting a complete and thorough investigation of how Mr. Stoller either obtained or was administered a potentially lethal barbiturate while in federal custody. Several corrections officers who had close contact with Mr. Stoller have been put on administrative leave.

While we feel confident that a guilty verdict would have been reached, and that, in that event, the judge would have given Mr. Stoller the death sentence, this is not an acceptable outcome to this trial. Nor do we believe this to be an admission of guilt or preemptive action ahead of his sentencing by Mr. Stoller. Based on handwritten notes found in his cell, we do know that Mr. Stoller was deeply disturbed by Ms. Corbin's abduction and apparent murder.

In addition to the notes, a voice-recording device was discovered in Mr. Stoller's cell. It appears to contain a conversation he had with his attorney, Wayne Young, in which Mr. Young admits to potential federal crimes. Mr. Young has been taken into custody, and a full criminal investigation into this matter has been opened.

Regardless of the circumstances, the fact is an inmate in federal custody and under federal protection is now dead before he received full due process under the law, and that is unacceptable. A full investigation will be conducted. We will not be taking any questions.

100

CHLOE

I have a confession to make. I'm not dead.

Not in the literal sense, anyway. Part of me did die though—@Real-ChloeCorbin is dead. That part of me was just so very tired. Tired of feeling like I have to be perfect all the time. Tired of living my life for the validation of others. Tired of pretending to be something I'm not. I refuse to continue feeling insecure, anxious, and depressed by what people say about me. I refuse to be tied to this static, inauthentic identity that has been forged by others, refuse to live my life beholden to my own followers and disconnected from what really matters.

What matters is love. And that part of me is dead now too. Shane, you were—*are*—the love of my life. I didn't know I needed you, didn't know how deep true love would change me. Despite your flaws, maybe *because* of your flaws, I love you so much. And now you're gone. I can't tell you how deeply, truly sorry I am for what I did. Maybe we were destined never to be—too different, too compelled to put each other at risk. In the end, my actions cost you your life, and I lost the most important person in the world to me. I can't imagine my life without you. You made me see the world differently. You changed me forever.

But without you, I would never be here now. I am finally free. Free to focus on what matters, orchestrating real change. I understand everything now. You were fighting to make the world a better place. You figured out the most powerful and effective way to confront economic injustice. And now I'm just as committed to the cause as you were. Through you, I have come to understand what my real mission, real *purpose* is.

It is for you, *because* of you, that I am finally able to liberate myself. For you that I muster the courage to do what I must. For you that I am now logged in to my Instagram account, deep in the settings, my fingertip hovering over the button they so desperately don't want you to find: "Delete Account."

Finally, I tap it, and, just like that, it's done.

"Goodbye."

101

BURNER_911

December 17, 2023

@Burner_911 post on Razgo.com

> *"Many of life's failures are people who did not realize*
> *how close they were to success when they gave up."*
> —Thomas Edison

BURNOUTZ!!! If there's one thing we NEVER do, it's GIVE UP!

Not when we're so close. They thought they could kill us! Kill ME! But their hatred and lies only make us stronger! 💪💪💪

Sure . . . we have had setbacks. We have had mistakes. We have had failures. BUT WE WILL NOT, EVER, NEVER EVER, GIVE UP!!!!

Especially when we are SO CLOSE!!! 👍👍👍👍

The stock market is DOWN 24% since October 12th! 📉 Four global banks have collapsed! Now CONGRESS IS SCHEDULED TO VOTE ON THE $1.8 TRILLION BAILOUT BILL!!!

We can't let that bill pass!

BURNOUTZ!!! WE'RE TAKING OUR SHOW TO WASHINGTON DC!! 🦍🦍🦍

We will march on the US Capitol on January 20 at 10AM to wreak havoc on the corridors of power!!

This time, we won't be taking anyone by surprise! The elites know what to expect! And they will do anything to stop us. So be PREPARED!! REMEMBER, we are NON VIOLENT! But we also will not tolerate violence inflicted upon us. So,

BURNER

DCPD and Capitol Police be warned, WE HAVE THE RIGHT TO PROTEST, AND WE WILL FIGHT BACK!

When it fails, when this bill is defeated, our final goal will be in sight! The hegemony of the US dollar will be under attack! 💵💵💵 A massive devaluation will cause the cash stockpiles of the billionaires to be depleted! The fiat paper they have used to manipulate the world and amass their wealth won't protect them anymore. Their precious dollars will go up in smoke 💸 as capital floods from the corrupt kleptocratic currencies of yesterday's failed governments to the free and open cryptocurrencies of tomorrow.

Only when we are free of the currencies of oppression will we be able to claim what's ours. Redistribute wealth fairly and equitably. So HOLD, HOLD, HOLD your crypto portfolios. Your DIAMOND HANDS, 💎 🙌 💎 🙌 more than ever, are the KEY TO YOUR SALVATION!!

See you in DC on January 20!!!

102

ANONYMOUS

It is done. The transition is complete.

Now the mission can move forward with renewed energy, a reinvigorated sense of purpose. More people are joining the movement every day. Making the BurnOutz stronger, more feared, more empowered. More inclusive.

See, the source of strength, the source of power, is BELIEF. That is all you need, is BELIEF. Nothing becomes something if you believe. Emptiness becomes fulfillment if you believe. A lie becomes the truth if you believe. Even hatred becomes love if you believe.

I believe. I believe in The Plan. And seeing my belief, others will believe too. The more ardently I believe, the more committed they will be. That's all they're all looking for anyway—something to believe in.

It took me a while to get over Shane's death. But losing him was what made me realize I had to let Chloe go. I could no longer be that spoiled rich girl preening over my latest cause of the week. I didn't really give a shit about all that stuff—sustainable fashion, horse rescue programs. How could I? I knew there was something more for me, and Shane helped me find it. Call it liberal guilt, call it what you want, but I feel like this is my mission, my purpose, my cause now.

It breaks my heart that it had to happen this way. But he's gone now, and the best way for me to honor his legacy is to carry it forward. I have the keys to the castle. I finally saw my path. How I was going to make the impact I always dreamed of. And all I had to do was log in.

I'm Burner . . .

ACKNOWLEDGMENTS

In hindsight, writing my debut novel, *Bit Flip*, now seems relatively easy. That book was based loosely on my own experiences as a founder and executive at various Silicon Valley tech companies. It was a familiar world, and I told the story through a third-person, past-tense, single-point-of-view narrative with thoughts and opinions not dissimilar to my own.

This book is nothing like that.

While this novel explores similar themes—specifically, the impact of technology on our lives, the challenges of growing wealth inequality, and the corrupting forces of our egocentric online culture—*Burner* borrows almost nothing from my personal life experiences. This book also really stretched me as an author, with three different first-person narrations, all present-tense, interspersed with found objects from court transcripts to media stories, delivered in a non-linear timeline. Putting it all together was like solving a Rubik's Cube, and I couldn't have done it without enormous help.

As with my first book, I worked with the incomparable Joshua Mohr on the early-stage developmental edit, and I couldn't have written this without his advice, candor, and creativity. Equally invaluable was my copyeditor, Krissa Lagos, who focused the manuscript and tracked down errors, inconsistencies, and superfluous content. I'm hugely grateful to the wonderful team at SparkPress, including Shannon Green, the senior editorial manager who kept me on schedule, Julie Metz, the designer who visually brought this book to life, and Brooke Warner, the publisher who has been so supportive of me and all her authors.

Beyond editorial help, I relied on many people for their domain expertise on a variety of subject matters key to the story. For depictions of the FBI and its investigative process, I am incredibly thankful to Frank Runles, FBI Supervisory Special Agent (Retired), Raymond Hall, Supervisory Special Agent in the FBI's Office of Public Affairs, and Jerri Williams, FBI Special Agent (Retired) and incredible podcaster and blogger. Having never been arrested or served time in prison, I relied heavily on fellow author James L'Etoile who patiently answered my questions and shared his expertise from two decades working in the criminal justice system. Finally, thanks to Lauren Glassberg, my good friend and an Emmy Award–winning journalist at WABC TV, for sanity-checking my depictions of media coverage. Any errors, omissions, or misrepresentations with respect to these or any other areas of domain expertise are mine or were deliberate in service to the story.

Getting candid feedback from real readers is always such a critical part of the process. I thank my friends Deborah Holstein, Mark Pastore, Mike Skov, Brian Hand, and Dave Beckwith for providing detailed feedback on early drafts, as well as my International Thriller Writers critique group and fellow authors Mysti Berry, Marilyn Escue, Kathleen Shumar, Cynthia Rice, and Bruce Johnson. I would also like to thank everyone who read and reviewed my first book. Your encouragement and enthusiasm truly inspired me to continue my career as a novelist.

Finally, thank you to my family—my incredible wife, Leslie, for always being my first reader, my trusted career advisor, and my biggest fan; and my two sons, Cole and Chase, for reading early drafts and always providing encouragement. I couldn't do any of this without your love and support.